A desert wind blew over the black sand. Blaise Omari saw no vegetation except a few scraggly thorn bushes. *The sun*, he thought. *Black . . . a black star*! Was it possible?

Then a shape blocked out the radioactive light. It was at least seven feet tall, a biped. A black, knee-length cloak hung from its shoulders and its face was masked—featureless except for two eye openings covered by wire mesh. Through the mesh, its eyes glowed like burning embers.

Blaise gripped the translator. "Peace to your way. I am Omari."

A gloved hand seized his throat. Light exploded in his head, blinding him as he fell, spiraling into cold oblivion . . .

THE CHILDREN OF ANTHI

JAY D. BLAKENEY

ACE SCIENCE FICTION BOOKS
NEW YORK

THE CHILDREN OF ANTHI

An Ace Science Fiction Book / published by arrangement with the author

PRINTING HISTORY
Ace Original / July 1985

Cover art by Griesbach & Martucci

For information address: The Berkley Publishing Group, 200 Madison Avenue, New York, New York 10016.

ISBN: 0-441-10399-5

Ace Science Fiction Books are published by
The Berkley Publishing Group,
200 Madison Avenue, New York, New York 10016.
PRINTED IN THE UNITED STATES OF AMERICA

Chapter 1

Blaise Omari sat tensed over his navigational controls, waiting. The needle-thin scoutship *Forerunner* swung smoothly into high orbit around Lambda Base, taking the controller's instructions to remain four thousand meters aft from a sleek liner. Beside him at helm Saunders muttered at the distance and glanced over her shoulder at the captain, who shrugged. Blaise did not relax. It seemed, as the low chatter of traffic control continued steadily over his communications line, that luck was with him this time. But Blaise did not believe in luck, never had, preferring instead to trust nothing but his own wits.

It was all a matter of time. Institute Security did not employ fools. He had been careless, rushing to send out the information over the last available seconds of reduced-rate communications, and Security's monitors had picked it up. In minutes they would break the code and know that the contents of that message were illegal. In minutes they would trace the sender, find that false, and trace further to one Major Blaise Omari, crewer on the *Forerunner*. Blaise's fingers beat out a rapid tattoo on the edge of his console. Demos, what a fool! If he hadn't been in such a rush to send out the goods for that final payment . . . With a grimace he cut off the thoughts and looked slowly around the narrow oblong confines of the bridge. His console stood in the front, practically in the nose, with the viewscreen and a row of storage compartments running underneath before him. On the right ranged the bank of highly complex sensors, along with engine monitoring. On the left hummed the ship's maintenance units, computers in charge of air, heat, light, and gravitational fields.

Staring ahead at the distant stars that were shimmering faintly through the liner's emissions, Blaise missed an order and pulled his thoughts together, angry at the lapse. The knot in his stomach tightened, and he flexed his fingers, which itched to send the ship flying. Blind running was not his way. He would wait until his mistake was confirmed. Security might possibly delay long enough to enable the *Forerunner* to leave orbit. And the farther away he got from Lambda Base, the better his chances of escaping without a trace for his hunters to follow.

"Relax, Omari," drawled Saunders as her freckled, beefy hands flipped down the switches that began warming the port and starboard reactors for implosion. "Routine stuff this time."

Blaise made no response, keeping his pale eyes locked on his tactical viewer, alert for any approaching patrol shuttles. For seven months he'd been harnessed to this console with her, this loud, hard-eyed woman, spawned in one of the mining belts. She had brawn to go with her bulk, which no amount of exercise would ever trim, and she wore her flaming hair cropped the regulation five centimeters short, making her square-jawed face look even plainer.

Now she snorted and leaned toward him, reeking of Drybath chemical. "Omari," she snapped, her eyes narrowed with suspicion, "if you're too strung for duty, report it to the captain at once!"

Her voice cut across the narrow bridge, momentarily silencing whatever Hassid was mumbling to the captain. Both looked Blaise's way, the captain's thin face narrowing even further in a frown. Blaise met his gaze, mentally cursing Saunders. But none of his anger showed as he answered her.

"I do not drink *saok* or lift zine," he said, his low voice as taut as the muscles across his cheekbones. Was she really stupid enough to think he would show for duty strung after seven months of perfect behavior, or did she suspect what had happened? But how could she know? He glared a warning at her. "You know that. Back off, Saunders."

She frowned and turned back to her own work, although he knew she was still keeping her eye on him. He tightened his lips and unleashed some of his mounting impatience by slowly clenching and unclenching one fist at his side. Just a few minutes more, and perhaps he would get away.

Ahead the liner gathered herself and shifted out of orbit with enviable ease. No g-lurch would upset her passengers.

The chatter on his line paused. Blaise's breath caught in his throat, and for the first time that day he allowed himself a flicker of hope.

"Clearance . . . SIS *Forerunner*," said the controller at last. "Departure course fifty-eight degrees mark four. Go light . . . in twelve minutes."

"Acknowledged," replied the captain.

Blaise nodded to the unspoken order and ran the coordinates into the navigational computer, which would transfer them to the helm. Beside him Saunders yawned, her broad jaws cracking. The sound grated, and he grimaced.

"Omari," said the captain. "We have ten-point-eight minutes to Go light. Plot course for Riban XII."

"Aye, sir." Blaise eased his tense back muscles a fraction. Time clicked over on the chronometer above his tactical screen.

"Crew, prepare for implosion drive," said the captain over the intercom. His voice held the flat tone he reserved for routine. "Implementation . . . now."

On reflex Blaise lifted up one hand overhead and grasped his harness, pulling it down until it clicked into place over his shoulders. Eyeing the computer readout, he punched in an acknowledgment sequence and was busy strapping himself into the webbing when the outside communications line buzzed.

The captain sighed. "*Forerunner* to base. If that cruiser crowding our tail wants prior clearance, forget it. We've a schedule to meet."

"Controller to *Forerunner*," replied the mechanical tones of the drone manning traffic. "Switching to Security call. Over."

A cold chill froze Blaise for an instant; then he blinked and calmly finished strapping himself into the suspended webbing. His fingers slipped in a special sequence code to the computer as he listened to the faint babble of noise while the base-to-ship message was relayed directly over the captain's line. It had come at last. Ignoring the twisting knot in his stomach, Blaise finished computing his coordinates, which had been selected as soon as he suspected what was to come. Behind him came the static-charged words of accusation and order.

"Acknowledged," snapped the captain. "Have your squad standing by. *Forerunner* out." There was a moment of silence on the bridge while Saunders and Hassid stared at Blaise and the captain's eyes seemed to bore through his back; then: "Helm!" barked the captain. "Lower us to close orbit."

"Aye, sir." Saunders spared one more narrowed glance at Omari and reached for the controls as the captain stepped to Blaise's side. He came around to the front of the console to face him, scowling, his eyes the color of lead.

"Omari," he said coldly, "consider yourself—"

Adrenaline surged through Blaise. His hands, deft with desperation, came down hard on the controls, and with a squawl of protesting metal the *Forerunner* heeled over and lunged into implosion drive. It was an insane thing to do, this close to a base with traffic orbiting heavily, but they missed collision in that helpless moment of changeover when everything blurred gray and a vast hand seemed to flatten Blaise until he nearly came through his webbing as pulp. Then his vision cleared and his hard body made the adjustment as the ship's inner gravitation field compensated for g-lurch. He rubbed his hand across his eyes and reached out to make a minor correction in their heading. At once the numbing vibration in the ship's hull ceased, and they plunged on fast and deep into interstellar space.

Only then did he notice the captain lying on the deck in a crumpled heap. Blood glistened in a red smear across that pale narrow face, but whether he lived was not at once apparent. On the opposite side of the small bridge Hassid dangled from his partially secured harness, his dark face twisted with pain. Slowly he tried to free a hanging arm, only to gasp and shut his eyes. Sweat beaded down his temple.

"Damn you, Omari!" Her broad face scarlet, Saunders began unstrapping herself in a frenzy. "Hijacking an Institute ship and killing the captain will see you ground to—"

"Shut up!" shouted Blaise, racing to free himself before her.

But despite her bulk and rage, she was quicker and had slapped open a bulkhead storage compartment and whirled around with a strifer in her hand just as he worked clear of his harness. He read death in her eyes and dropped flat to the deck behind the navigational console.

She held her fire, however, and he choked on a breath of relief, his fingers clutching at the steel-plated floor.

"I'm not that stupid, Omari," she said tensely. "We both

know I'm not going to destroy helm and navigation just for the pleasure of scrambling your neurons. But I shoot very accurately at close quarters, and if you don't want to be stunned and dropped through the jettison hatch to die eating space, then you'll stand up and re-mark our course back to Lambda Base."

Slowly, knowing she was one to back up her threats, Blaise stood up, keeping his hands visible. But he made no other move. His gray eyes were as hard as hers.

"Is the captain dead?" he asked.

Her mouth tightened with suspicion, but she let her gaze flicker down to the captain's body. "I don't . . . no," she said flatly, looking up quickly at Blaise. "He's still bleeding." She raised her weapon. "Turn us back."

Still Blaise made no move, and she frowned.

"Don't be a fool! By now the base has sent a ship in pursuit. And there'll be more called out. You can't outrun the Institute. Even *Forerunner* hasn't the speed of a patrol ship—"

"No one will follow where we're going," said Blaise. Recklessly he raised his head and dared smile at her. "Aren't you curious, Saunders? Don't you want to know what's up? What I've really done?" Holding his breath, he waited for her to take the bait as he silently counted off the remaining minutes at their current blast of speed.

She blinked at him, frowning. "I've never trusted you, Omari. Certain things about you never added up . . . until now. How you have stayed in the Institute long enough to get your present rank—"

"Simple." He shrugged, estimating his chances of getting the weapon away from her and deciding that the odds were not good. "I found an ident card on a skirmish field following one of your precious Institute's attempts to *reason* with colonists who didn't want Institute protection. I took the name and the codex number, changed a few personal facts, and made sure I was transferred to a sector far away from the late Omari's pals."

Her frown deepened as she considered this casual account of what was almost an impossible breach of Institute security clearance procedures. "You have been with us seven months. And on the *Priori* ship before that. Nearly two years of service *and* deception."

He shrugged.

"And who are you really?"

He laughed harshly, then stopped as her grip tightened on the strifer. "Demos, Saunders, but you're naive under all that grit and meat. Do you think I'll tell you anything besides a list of identities that mean nothing? Why bother?"

For a moment she said nothing, simply standing there with her strifer aimed steadily at his gut. Then almost reluctantly, she said, "What have you done?"

They were nearly close enough. The clock still hummed in his brain as the strain on the ship built up, hammering through bulkhead and deck into the bones of his cushioned feet. Involuntarily Blaise put out a hand to the console to steady himself, and as he did so he heard a sharp click. His blood froze. He knew that click. It was the sound of a straining safety. She had fired on him, but the strifer had not worked. Giving her no chance to recover from her split-second chagrin, Blaise threw himself at her in a long leap, his straining muscles giving him enough impetus to tip her off-balance despite her braced stance. She fell heavily to the deck, grunting, and kicked at him with a force that would have caved in bone had it landed. But with cat-quick reflexes he rolled and dived again, gaining hold of her wrist and applying pressure until the strifer fell from her fingers. It clattered on the deck, and she snarled an oath, getting in a blow with her free hand that numbed his shoulder.

Angrily he pushed clear and leveled the strifer at her as she rolled to her feet. He made sure she saw him disengage the safety, and her hard eyes might have been chips of the ore mined on her native world as she stood there, red-faced and panting.

"So you *can* make a mistake, Saunders," he said, watching her jaw muscles tighten. Equally deliberately he switched the setting from stun to kill and saw the answering flicker in her eyes. He drew in a breath. "Move over to Hassid and help get the pressure off that arm."

She glared at him but obeyed. Cautiously Blaise stepped around the captain's motionless body, but there was no trick waiting for him. The captain's breathing fluttered shallow and rapid; his ashen face glistened wet with blood and a faint film of sweat. Blaise frowned, then turned his attention to the weapons compartment. He aimed the strifer and fired, squinting against the answering spit and showering of frying circuits. The compartment would not open now for anyone.

A movement caught the corner of his eye, and he spun, aiming the strifer with a quickness that froze Saunders.

"Take your hand away from that communications panel," he said, making no effort to soften his voice.

She moved away, back to Hassid, who now sat huddled on the deck with his arm cradled in his lap. He looked at Blaise, then shut his eyes, his swarthy face pinching with agony. Blaise watched them both for a moment before going to the door that opened into the aft part of the ship. There had been no sign of life from the two crewers back there, but he was taking no chances. A careful burst from the strifer, and the door circuits fried with satisfying fury.

"Whoever you are," said Saunders angrily, "hijacking even a scoutship is a death offense—"

"Call me Omari," said Blaise absently as he returned to the helm. "I never go back to old identities." He eyed the controls and tightened his lips with satisfaction. With a flip of a fingertip he switched on the bridge viewscreen and rubbed his jaw thoughtfully as he considered the star systems ahead.

"My God," she said suddenly, and the fear in her voice made it sound wooden. Surprised, he glanced up at her, and as he did so her eyes widened. "You . . . you're a drone. An escaped . . . No one else could clear Security to assume a crewer's identity. But that's *impossible*."

"Is it?" he said flatly, seeing the revulsion in her eyes and feeling furious at the old, never-to-be-banished shame that swept over him. "A large sum of money removed the identity number off my jaw." He forced a smile, although it was merely a showing of teeth. "We don't always come out of the vats as morons. Some of us have brains and ambitions."

Fear flashed over her, shrinking the bulk and the loudness. She stared at him, her breathing audible. "We're going too fast to get anywhere," she said, as though reassuring herself. "In an hour we'll be stranded without fuel."

He met her eyes, his own gaze like steel. "In an hour fuel will not matter. There is only one place left for me to go, Saunders. One place where the Institute will not hunt me down."

"The Uncharted Zone," she whispered, glancing at the

viewscreen and back again. Then, with a visible effort, she regathered her self-confidence. "You're insane. There's nothing out there."

For the second time that day his laugh barked out, as bleak and harsh as space itself. "You forget we're both Institute, Saunders. I know what the zone contains and why S.I. ships won't enter it." He smiled at her, reading her thoughts. "Two years ago I had no choice left but to take on the most despicable identity in the world, that of an Institute crewer." She stiffened, and he tightened his grip on the strifer. "I knew," he continued, "what would happen to me once I was discovered. Now I have no choice but to do this. I always have an escape route."

An alert flashed across the viewscreen with insistent red blips. The ship shuddered and slowed. Swiftly Blaise overrode programmed course abortion and shot them past the demarcation buoy. Standing at the console with the strifer still trained on Saunders, Blaise called up a scantily plotted star chart on the astrogation screen, considered the remaining fuel in the reactors, and made his choice. Minutes later, with the course computed and laid in, he slowed the reckless speed that was gradually tearing the guts from the little scoutship.

Saunders watched him in silence, and when he had finished, she said in a low voice, "Where did you get that chart? It's not an Institute graph."

Eyes on the tactical screen, he did not reply.

She stepped toward him, stopping only when he raised the strifer. "Omari," she said, her voice loud over the steady hum of the instrumentation panel, "somehow I'll take you back. Murder, blackmarketing of Institute technology . . . whatever else you've done, will all be paid for. I promise you."

He met her gaze steadily. "If you try to carry out your promise, I'll kill you, Saunders, without hesitation." He paused a moment. "And without regret."

Seventy-four hours later Blaise opened one bleary, aching eye for a quick glance around the bridge. The captain had died more than a day ago without ever regaining consciousness. No sound had come over in-ship communications from the two crewers aft. Hassid lay huddled on the deck, still in agony and oblivious to the battle of wills between helmsman and navigator. Beside him Saunders lay stretched out, her face hidden but her breathing slow and regular. Blaise smiled slightly. She had tried to outlast him on the need for sleep, which was impossible. She was tough and well trained, but soon the lack of food and water would weaken her. He wasn't concerned about those needs for himself . . . yet. Cautiously, with one last glance at Saunders, Blaise closed his eyes again.

An insistent chime snapped him from his groggy state. His head jerked up, and he was on his feet and moving toward his console before his senses fully cleared. Behind him Saunders stirred.

"What is it?" she mumbled.

Blaise bent intently over his instruments, giving her no reply. With swift fingers he cleared memory of their present course heading and laid orbital coordinates for the fourth planet of the system they were entering.

"Prepare for normal space," he said. After a moment of hesitation he opened a line aft, his hail echoing through the sleeping quarters, the minuscule galley, and the engine room. "If you're still alive back there, prepare for normal space." He switched off before any reply could be made and gave the auto-helm its order to execute. A countdown light blinked on.

Although he half expected Saunders to jump him while he was bent over the astrogation computer, she remained standing by Hassid, her face and body tense. A panel near her lit in a rapid sequence of colored lights, but she made no move to receive the data coming in from the sensors. Now awake, Hassid sat up with a groan, his shadowed eyes fixed on the captain's body where it lay forgotten beneath the viewscreen.

When Saunders kept on staring at Blaise as though she were a carved figure, he reached up for his harness and scowled at her. "Ten seconds to slam, Saunders. Or do you want to hit orbit like the captain?"

That struck through her blankness. Her face did not change, but fury flickered in her eyes as she scooped a groaning Hassid to his feet and buckled him in before moving to her place beside Blaise. He kept his strifer trained on her, knowing the anger she was hiding would explode soon. Saunders was not the sort who accepted defeat.

She buckled her harness and accepted the instructions coming from Blaise's computer. The ship shuddered lightly as she punched in the sequence for taking manual control. Then she glanced at Blaise, her lips compressed tightly. "What are you going to do here, colonize?"

He smiled without amusement, then indicated the scanners still recording sensory data. "This planet is inhabited."

She stiffened. "No! Omari, you can't, not without Institute clearance—"

"Yes!" he snapped back angrily. "I can! I adapt everywhere. And I don't need your sacred Institute's permission to infiltrate an unclassified culture."

"You—"

But the slam of changeover blurred her words of protest. Thankful for it, Blaise squinted against the grayness of vision and fought to keep an eye on his board. A red light suddenly blinked.

"Damn!" she shouted. "We're . . ." The disorientation abruptly cleared, leaving her words hanging loud and harsh in the air. "Black star! It's blanking out the helm. I—"

She slammed one large hand down on the controls, and before Blaise could protest, she had wrenched them back into implosion.

"No!" Desperately Blaise flailed an arm, seeking to grab her and stop her. His harness bobbed and swayed him in the wrong direction as the ship lurched and tilted crazily. Furious, with fear clutching his lungs like an iron band, Blaise tore out of his harness and threw himself between her and her controls, ignoring her screams of rage as he strained against the crushing force of changeover. Readouts swirled before his eyes; he blinked fiercely and managed to keep things in focus long enough to give new instructions to the spinning helm directional. Damn her!

He didn't dare take time to check with the computer. As soon as the effect of implosion drive started to fade, he slammed them back into normal, wincing as the ship groaned at this tremendous stress on hull and bulkhead. Aft, he could hear the engines screaming; then grayness and an attack of vertigo overwhelmed him.

Coming to moments later, he found himself on the deck beneath Saunders' feet. Slowly, urgently trying to force his body to respond, he rose to hands and knees, spitting out a mouthful of salty blood, then got shakily to his feet. He clung to the console with both hands and shook his head experimentally, sagging with relief as he realized they were back safely in normal space.

"All right, bright boy," said Saunders grimly, her eyes locked on the tactical screen. "We're in atmosphere, and the controls are jamming from X rays off that blasted black star. Do you understand?" she shouted, glaring at him. "We're going to crash unless you can figure out some way to restore the helm! Omari!"

He nodded to shut her up, in no mood to let her work herself into hysterics. His brain went to work on the problem, ignoring the fear and pain pounding through the rest of him. "What's working?" he asked.

"Nothing!"

He frowned. "Take grip, Saunders! If we can fire the emergency braking pattern—"

"No," she snapped. "You can't land the *Forerunner*, dammit! She's not made to enter atmosphere. We don't have the shielding. . . ." With a catch in her voice Saunders wiped her dripping face with one sleeve. The temperature was already climbing past life support's capacity to regulate it.

Blaise grimaced and checked out the brakes anyway. Saunders was right; the instruments were fading in and out crazily. If only she'd kept out of his way! He'd had the compensation factors for the black star worked in. It would have gone smoothly, except for her—

Angrily he caught himself short. That was past. What he had to worry about now was getting them to the surface in one piece. Blinking fiercely as sweat ran into his eyes, he calculated the erratic shifts in instrumentation, trying to find a pattern.

"Fire reverse thrust one on my mark," he said grimly.

Saunders jerked around. For a moment she gaped at him in sheer disbelief, then grunted as the ship listed heavily.

"Fire!" said Blaise, and with an oath she obeyed. A shudder ran through the ship. Briefly he met her eyes, reading in them all the fury and puzzlement and fear at war there. The ship leveled slightly and bucked. "Demos, Saunders! Hang on to the helm!" he shouted. "You've got her now—"

"I've got nothing!" But with her jaw clenched till it was a ridge of muscle and bone, Saunders stayed with her controls, fighting them as they fought her. "All right, you did it once," she said more quietly, swallowing. "When do I fire the next brake?"

"On my mark," he said, concentrating on his panel.

"Seven thousand meters . . ." said Hassid weakly, startling both Blaise and Saunders. Blaise nodded toward him gratefully, and the engineer continued, ". . . six-five . . . five thousand—"

"Fire brake two," said Blaise.

Saunders obeyed, biting her lip in concentration. Again the ship bucked, more violently this time. Blaise barely kept his balance, concentrating fully upon the data line flashing steadily across the bottom of the tactical screen. In another five hundred meters he would fire brake three. That should enable Saunders to take sufficient control over their descent to level the ship out of her wild spiral. And he still had the fourth brake in reserve. He relaxed some of his pent-up fear. They could do it.

"Hassid," he said, not looking up. "Feed into Saunders's line. I need scanning data on terrain."

"My God," said Saunders beneath her breath. "You really think we can land her."

Blaise met her eyes steadily. After a moment she blinked and ducked her head. "Get into harness, you fool," she said.

He had just followed that advice when an explosion wrenched through the ship, which canted in a wild roll, slamming Blaise into Saunders. Desperately Blaise fought to get clear and dragged himself back into position, grabbing at the controls. But even as he gripped them, despair plunged through him. The fuel seams had burst, taking out what little helm management the black star had left them, as well as the remaining stabilizers. They were completely out of control, blowing fuel all over the atmosphere with a brilliant burst of purple and yellow flame that flared across the hull into range of the main viewscreen scanners. Blaise could smell the harsh odors of burning circuits, ozone, and urine. For a moment of sheer panic, he shut his eyes, his mind blanking out as the g-force and intense heat crushed him.

But some deep part of him tightened up and saved him from that cold panic. He opened his eyes, focusing them despite the wild spinning of the ship. As long as there was even one slight chance left, he would not give up.

"Saunders," he said urgently, shaking her arm. "I can't

reach your secondary controls from this angle. Fire the last brake."

She turned her head slowly to meet his insistent gaze with eyes that were blank with terror. "What?" she asked numbly.

"Saunders!" shouted Blaise. "Fire it! Number four! Saunders, damn you, *fire*!"

Groaning, Hassid began mumbling a prayer, his voice quivering so badly that he was unintelligible.

With an exclamation Blaise tugged violently at his harness release. They were at the zero point. If he didn't reach that brake, in a matter of seconds they would be so much pulp smeared in with the systems lubricant.

Grunting from the strain on his muscles, sweat dripping into his eyes, he held himself upright, then was thrown against the console as the ship rolled again. Somehow he hung on, his knuckles white with strain from the effort of keeping his grip. Saunders's bulk was in the way, but Blaise squeezed past her, timed himself, and with a gasp hit the final button of the braking sequence. The answering lurch and jolt flung him to the deck, pitching him under the lip of the console with enough force to knock the breath from him. He lay stunned, dimly feeling the ship lift and hang poised for an instant as though bringing herself to heel. *Get up*! screamed something within him. *Get up*!

Vaguely he threw out a hand, seeking to lever himself up. But there was no time. He heard the agonized twisting of tortured metal and Saunders's scream. Instinctively he shut his eyes, tensing as the ship crashed, lengthwise instead of nose first, her metal shrieking in death until at last all lay still and silent and broken.

Chapter 2

For a long while there was nothing but dark and numbness. Then cold crept in, a deep piercing cold that gnawed at his consciousness until it roused him. Blaise opened his eyes and blinked several times before he realized he was awake and alive. Disbelief washed over him. He shut his eyes again. Other sensations spread through him besides the cold. He became aware of the cloying smell of blood and a burst of pain in his chest each time he drew a breath. Frowning, Blaise opened his eyes once more and wriggled in an effort to throw off the weight crushing his torso. Nothing budged, however, and weakly he let his head fall back for a moment of rest.

He could see little in the shadowy darkness. The bridge lay in ruined silence, all instrument panels dead. With a chill Blaise thought of the implosion reactors, wondering whether their protective casings had remained intact. Even a hairline crack would be large enough to poison the area. Freeing a hand, he explored by fingertip the wreckage pinning him and decided it was the remnants of the helm and navigational consoles. His groping hand plunged into a tangle of circuitry, and he froze instinctively before realizing with a grunt of expelled air that he was not going to be electrocuted. Probably he was holding the astrogation computer's brains. Blaise gritted his teeth and shook his hand clear of the debris, nicking a finger in the process.

He brought up his hand to suck at the cut and realized with a start that he could see more clearly now. He wriggled his fingers before his eyes, then strained to look around at the rest of the bridge. The darkness seemed grayer; yes, he made out an outline of something through the shadows. Dawn must be breaking over the planet. Good!

Then he frowned. The ship must be broken open, or else

daylight would make no difference in here. He gazed upward, straining to see the hull overhead, hoping the split was here and not aft with the reactors.

"Saunders! Hassid!" he called, coughing as the words rasped in his throat, which was coated with the stale taste of dried blood. He grimaced and swallowed several times before calling out again. No one responded.

"Damn," he said softly, fighting down a spurt of panic. It did not matter if he was alone. He would find a way to get out.

The brightness grew quickly until a beam of sunlight spilled into the ship, stabbing downward. Dazzled, Blaise squinted and threw his free hand up to shield his face while the golden radiance streamed in with liquid intensity. Its warmth seeped into his skin, thawing him a degree or two. After a few moments, when his eyes had adjusted to the brilliant light, he lifted his head to look about.

The first thing he saw was a thick, freckled hand dangling several inches above his face. Startled, Blaise narrowed his pale eyes and stared up at Saunders. She hung tangled in her harness in such a way that he could not see her face. Glad he could not, he stared at her for a moment, then frowned and averted his eyes. There was no point in wondering why he, the only one not strapped in suspended safety webbing, had survived. It was a fluke for which he was damn thankful. He grimaced, able to see now the extent of wreckage lying across his body. Some of his self-confidence faded. Alone, he could never pull free of this mess, not unless he found some leverage.

"Hassid!" he called angrily, trying to battle down growing fear. "Damn you! Are you alive?"

His shout reverberated off the crumpled walls, then faded, leaving a deafening silence. And in that silence he heard a sound.

Blaise jerked up his head. Tensely he held his breath and listened, straining. The sound came again, faint and unidentifiable. Something scraped along the hull . . . *outside*! He held his breath, his heart thudding faster.

An unintelligible murmur of voices accompanied the scraping. Blaise's senses sharpened to full alert. The key data on the star chart had marked this planet as inhabited, but he had no knowledge of what kind of creatures lived here, or whether they possessed intelligence, or what their cultures were like . . . if they had any. And while he had not lied when he told

Saunders he could adapt anywhere, he still preferred to meet the unknown on his feet with a weapon close to hand, rather than pinned helplessly on his back. He drew in a deep breath of air scarcely warmed by the strengthening sunlight and kept his eyes on the split in the hull overhead, where the *Forerunner* lay open to the sky.

The voices ceased for a few minutes. Then, without warning, a shape blocked the opening, formless and dark against the light. The shadow of it fell across Blaise. Sharply honed caution kept him silent and motionless. He suspected curiosity rather than rescue had brought the creature, and he did not want to tempt it into further exploration.

Something was called out, and the creature above Blaise answered. Blaise frowned, striving to catch the speech pattern, but it was too rapid for him. He waited with held breath, willing the creature to lose interest and go away.

Saunders's hand dangling over him twitched, and she moaned.

"Quiet!" muttered Blaise beneath his breath. His momentary sympathy for her vanished.

She did not stir again, but the creature had heard. With alarming swiftness it dropped inside the ship like a swoop of great black shadow, landing soundlessly atop the edge of the sensors console in a feat of balance and agility that awoke Blaise's seldom-won admiration. For a moment he and the creature stared at each other. It was tall, surely at least seven feet, and a biped. A black knee-length cloak hung from its shoulders, and under the cloak it wore a black tunic, black trousers, and heavy black boots. The cloak possessed a hood, giving it a cowled appearance, and the creature's face was masked entirely with a hard, dull black substance—possibly metal—that was featureless except for the two eye openings covered by fine wire mesh.

Blaise swallowed hard, disconcerted by the silent appraisal from that masked face. After a moment the black figure stepped down off the console and picked its way over the wreckage with sure, crunching steps. Blaise stiffened, unable to stop himself from gripping the mass of twisted metal that trapped him, and wishing with all his might for his lost strifer. The creature knelt beside him with a swirl of black cloak that brushed Blaise's shoulder. He flinched and was immediately ashamed at betraying himself.

But he had no intention of letting fear get the best of him. He drew a deep breath of frosty air, winced as the pressure on his chest intensified, and said tersely, "Peace to your way. I am Omari."

He spoke in one of the standard dialects most used by both Institute-protected worlds and the Commonwealth of Planets, but the overture evoked no verbal response. Instead, the creature extended a gloved finger and prodded his shoulder and neck none too gently, awakening the soreness of dormant bruises and scrapes.

Blaise stared at him coldly. "Do not touch me."

The gloved hand seized his chin in a powerful grip and twisted Blaise's head to one side with a force that popped the vertebrae in Blaise's neck and sent pain plunging down into one shoulder blade. Compressing his lips, he brought up his free hand with a solid punch into the middle of the mask. It was like hitting a wall. Pain burst through his knuckles and shot up his forearm. With a stiffled cry Blaise glared fiercely at the creature, which had drawn back. It felt slowly along the edges of its mask as though to make sure nothing had loosened, then stood in one quick motion and turned its attention to Saunders.

A shadow blocked the light overhead once again, and Blaise looked up, startled. Another black-cloaked figure crouched by the split, cowled and masked like the first. This one spoke in a rapid, excited way, its voice a low rasp, and was answered by a sweep of a black-gloved hand extended palm up. The one outside vanished. With a grunt the creature beside Blaise began prodding Saunders, who moaned.

Annoyed, Blaise started to speak, then compressed his lips and remained silent. He was not her protector.

Taking advantage of the creature's preoccupation with Saunders, Blaise found a hold on the base of the smashed navigations console with his free hand. He was trying to pull himself loose when more figures appeared and began climbing inside. They moved with more care than the first had shown. All were tall, lean, and quick of movement. That they were excited was clear to Blaise, but he wished he could tell whether he and Saunders were about to be welcomed or dissected.

As if in answer, the first one drew a knife with a flash of green serrated blade and swung it down at Saunders.

"No!" cried Blaise.

But the blade struck only the tough cord of the harness webbing, parting the fabric as though it were paper. Saunders fell to the deck like a boulder, jolting the wreckage atop Blaise so that something ground a little deeper into his chest. He went cold, as though doused by icy water, and a tiny muscle in the side of his neck quivered in a brief spasm. The shattered chaos of the bridge blurred for a second, but he fought off the weakness, realizing with a spurt of alarm that they had lifted Saunders over their shoulders and were preparing to haul her out. And he was to be left behind, to die here in the wreckage either of exposure or of his injuries.

"No!" he shouted, startling one masked figure into glancing back at him. "No, by Demos." He panted as he struggled to regain his grip on the base of the console. "You will at least lift this muck off me. . . ." The muscles in his neck corded, and sweat broke out along his temples as he strained to drag himself free. Spots danced across his eyes, and the pain in his chest rippled out in a widening circle. Vaguely he saw them boost Saunders's heavy bulk out and over the side. They were leaving him; the last one was climbing out with a swing of his black cloak. *Give up*, pleaded something weak and exhausted within Blaise. But with a groan he strained his aching shoulder muscles once again, unwilling to accept defeat. Crimson stained his vision, and sweat poured into his eyes, stinging them; they were blinded now. He knew then that it was useless, but still he gave one last mighty jerk. Something seemed to snap in his chest, filling him with an agony so intense that he screamed. And the sound of that scream went on echoing as he spiraled down into a cold, frightening blackness.

The deepest, most elemental rhythm of the chanting first stirred him. But it was not until later, when he grew aware of the vibrant off-key tone of the noise, that irritation sparked him back to consciousness. With a glimmer of alertness he forced open his eyes and focused long enough to gain a confused impression of a bleak, dimly lit room. He lay covered on a shelf in the wall. That was all he noticed before he slipped back into the comfort of darkness. From then on it was no longer the deep black void but rather a gray shadowy realm of half consciousness and half sleep, where now and then he was aware of hands shifting his body and voices that faded in and out. Sometimes the harsh sound of his own struggling breaths disturbed him, and other times he cried out sharply in fear, only to have strong hands grip him and a voice repeat words he could not understand over and over until he slipped away again.

The chanting went on, a beating undercurrent of sound, disturbing him and gradually driving him up to the clarity of annoyance. Abruptly he opened his eyes, snarled an oath, and tried to bring up his hands to cover his ears.

"So you really are going to live," said Saunders's flat voice.

Blaise blinked for a moment, bringing the world into focus, and finally turned his head to look at her. He frowned. Her broad face was sunken under the flat cheekbones, and her torn, blackened coveralls hung loosely on her big frame. Even more startling was the sight of her flaming hair, which had grown out long enough to float, downy and fine, about her ears in wisps. His frown deepened, and he lifted his hand vaguely to his head.

"We've been here awhile," he said finally, not pleased to find his voice a rusty croak. He coughed and swallowed with difficulty. "How long—"

"Wait." Without gentleness she put her muscular arm under his shoulders to lift him and tilted the full contents of a metal cup ruthlessly down his throat. While he choked and sputtered and tried to regain his breath, grimacing over the cold greasy film left in his mouth, she set down the emptied cup with a bang and said, "We have been here approximately eleven standard days. This planet has a rapid rotation, and the normal sun rises and sets every nine hours."

She stopped speaking and gave him a flat, hard stare, her lips compressed in a rigid line. The off-key chanting rose and fell in a distant, steady cadence.

Blaise looked about the room, which was more a cell hacked from stone, containing only the stone niche in which he lay and the crude stool on which Saunders sat. He looked around, puzzled. "Where is that din coming from?"

A glimmer of a smile touched her colorless lips for an instant. She jerked a thumb over her shoulder at a barred cavity in the wall, through which came an occasional puff of warmed air. "It goes on day and night," she said. "You'll get used to it." After a pause she scowled and added viciously, "We're caged in this hole and treated far worse than labor drones on an unprotected planet. At least the Institute's detention center would have treated you humanely—"

"Demos, Saunders, if you believe that, you're a fool!"

Angrily he started to throw off the rough blanket and get up, but weakness sapped him. Wincing, he let himself fall back, striving to ease the catch in his chest by breathing shallowly.

"You've crushed something, probably your sternum," she said matter-of-factly. "I don't know why you haven't bled to death already, but getting up could ram splintered bone into one of your lungs and finish you off."

He gasped for breath, choosing not to tell her that this might have already occurred. If he'd lived this long without treatment, then he would survive, and that was all that mattered. But to taunt her he said with a crooked smile, "You'd like to see the end of me, eh, Saunders?"

"No!" She jumped to her feet, towering over him with a resentful glare. Then she looked away and muttered, "There are good rewards for bringing in renegade drones—"

"So that's all a life—my life—means to you, a promotion!" he broke in furiously, raising himself on one elbow. "Or maybe just a commendation. Well, thank you—"

"Stop twisting everything to fit your own false interpretations!" she shouted, whirling on him with clenched fists. "Drones aren't destroyed."

"No, just rehabilitated," he retorted sarcastically. "Drones aren't worth killing. Wipe clean their minds and retrain them. Dammit, Saunders, I'm not an android you can reprogram! I am a living being." He slammed his fist down beside him. "And I'll choose my own way of existence!"

"What gives you the right?" she snapped back, her face scarlet. "The Institute gave you life, gave you education and training, gave you—"

"Forget the Institute, Saunders," he broke in, having no intention of listening to the same stupidity he had heard so many times before. "Forget that damned code of regulations! We are on this planet *forever* . . . unless they have space technology." As he spoke he glanced around the bare stone cell again, noting the crude burning torch propped up at an angle in a bracket bolted to the floor. "And from appearances they do not have it. Listen to me!" He reached out and grabbed her muscular wrist, tightening his grip when she tried to wrench free. "Saunders," he said intently, "survival is what concerns us now. Not the Institute and not the past. If you want my help you'll cooperate. Understand?"

"Your help," she said harshly, her face twisted into something ugly and red. "Where do you get your arrogance,

Omari? Right now you couldn't lift a glass of *saok*. Do you really think I need *your* help?" She jerked free of his grasp, and he let her, watching her limp angrily to the opposite side of the cell. She shivered involuntarily and gave her arms a brisk rubbing, keeping her broad back turned to him.

He sighed, curbing his own temper. It did no good to wish himself unhurt and free of her. As long as he was in shaky shape, she could be useful. Slowly, moving cautiously, he levered himself into a sitting position and shivered as the draft through the grillwork brushed his bare shoulders. The room had the pervading chill only stone can give off, the kind that sinks deep into the bone. He realized that beneath his thin cover he was naked. When he was sure he'd caught his breath, he twisted the blanket around himself in a sort of makeshift sarong. His hands, now that he took time to look at them, were skeleton thin and blue with cold, the taut veins stretching like cords up arms that were sticks of bone and thin muscle with a bit of skin stretched over them. He flexed a bicep experimentally, frowning at how tired that small movement left him. His ribs stuck out around a shrunken stomach like bulkheads without a hull, and he could see a spectacular radius of black-and-green bruises across his chest. He fingered the spot, which was still puffy and sore, and rubbed the knob where bone had knitted improperly.

With a sigh he scratched irritably through his rough tangle of beard and glanced again at Saunders's rigid back. "Is there anything more to eat around here?"

She whirled as though stung and narrowed her eyes at the sight of him sitting on the niche with his legs dangling almost to the floor. She started to speak, then swallowed and shook her head. "Broth is all they bring for you."

Her voice was rough and unsteady, her eyes red-rimmed. He stared at her, boggled by the thought of Saunders in tears, but persisted: "What do they bring for you? And how often?"

She shrugged. "Twice a day. Some broth and something else of an odd consistency. Like dried rubber. I'm fed in my own cell."

"Then you're kept elsewhere? How far away? Is the cell like this?"

"Smaller," she said, her eyes betraying her resentment at answering questions—*any* questions—for him. "It's on a different level . . . higher in the citadel, which I think is partly carved out of a mountain's interior. The old part anyway, like here." She gestured. "My cell is not this old, and it's constructed of stone blocks. I have a window." Her eyes met his briefly. "It's perhaps the length of my arm and the width of my hand. Useless. It lets in bitter air and a thin crystalline substance like powder—"

"Snow," said Blaise absently, his thoughts busy twisting these facts about to find a use for them. He shivered again and thrust his hands under his thighs to warm them, knowing he could think better if he were not so ravenous. "What do these people look like? How do they behave?"

She walked across the room to the heavily armored door, then to the grilled air duct from which the chanting could still be heard, eerie and off-key. "They are soldiers," she said finally, placing one freckled hand on the bars.

He waited for a moment, then frowned, unsure if she was just being difficult or if her powers of observation were really this dull. "That's all?"

She turned to him, red faced. "They are soldiers. They bring food twice a day at regular intervals. Once a day they bring me here to tend you. Some of them keep up that damned chant constantly. That's all!"

He ignored her rising tone. "They all wear masks?"

"Yes!" she snapped. "I've never seen what they really look like."

"Have they tried to communicate with you? Have they shown curiosity about us?"

"Less in me once they thought you might live." Then she tightened her jaw, and her gray eyes glazed over with anger, and something else. "They meant to strip me as they did you. They would have . . . I did not permit them curiosity about me."

The wooden tone gave her away. Blaise looked at her, seeing through the fury and resentment. Beneath it all Saunders was very, very frightened, of him as much as of their captors. He could tell that by the way she kept looking at him indirectly like a cornered animal. He decided to ease up on her for the moment.

"Don't worry, Saunders," he said evenly. "We'll get out of this."

"Can that!" she snapped, kicking the stool. "I am an Institute officer. I do not need your false encouragement. I will not be patronized. My superior—"

"You are hysterical." His low voice cut through her bellow. And while she paused, furiously struggling for a retort, he went on, coldly. "Reciting your propaganda may work up your morale, Saunders, but all I want from you is a steady nerve when I make my move to get out of here. And if you can't supply it, then you're worth *flin,* Saunders, and nothing more, Institute trained or not."

Shaking, she clenched her big fists, drawing in an audible breath with ragged force. "You—"

Something drew his attention away from the quarrel. He raised his hand to silence her. "Listen!"

She frowned. "What?"

He gestured again. Yes, the chanting *had* stopped, and the last echoes of it were fading within the air duct.

"I thought you said it never stopped."

"It hasn't before."

Uneasy, he edged himself onto his feet and swayed slightly, cursing his weakness. He needed clothing, a weapon, and more food.

"We've got to get out of here," he said, walking slowly over to the air duct and bending to peer into it. The dry, dusty stench of old bones wafted into his nostrils. He pulled back, grimacing. "See if you can work any of those bars free," he said, grasping the edge of his blanket to keep it from slipping. "The duct is wide enough if we can just get into it."

She stood there, hands on hips, eyeing him with hostility. "And suppose we did crawl in? Suppose the duct narrows or brings us to a grillwork we can't open?"

"And suppose we rot here for the rest of our lives?" he retorted. "The bars are old, Saunders. Give them a try."

"While you do what?" she asked, lifting her square chin.

"Sit down," he replied with a gasp, as a sudden throbbing in his chest took him by surprise. He staggered across the room and dropped heavily onto the stool, which creaked beneath his weight. His head seemed suddenly light and cold.

"Omari!" She hurried over to him with steps that jarred his hearing.

Breathless and a bit dizzy, he said irritably, "I'm all right. I just need some food—" An odor stung his nose, and he raised his head. "What in Demos is that smell?"

Her big hand grasped his shoulder. "What are you talking about? Have you fever?"

The dizziness passed, and he looked up at her impatiently, his nostrils crinkling. "Don't you smell it? It's rank enough to topple a Rilgin."

She compressed her lips, looking oddly discomfited. "I don't have a sense of smell, Omari. But . . . probably it's me. They don't give out Drybath—"

"No, it's *not* you," he snapped, sneezing in a fruitless attempt to block off the odor, which intensified steadily. "It's like something dead. Damn!" He clamped his hand over his nose and mouth, rigid against the putrid assault.

Somewhere in the distance a hollow boom reverberated. He looked up abruptly, and Saunders's fingers dug painfully into his shoulder.

"They're coming," she whispered. "Early. *Why?*"

Blaise waited tensely, his heart thudding against sore ribs. There was nothing that could be used as a weapon. He cursed softly and viciously beneath his breath.

Saunders's hand tightened into an iron claw. He shifted in an attempt to work free and opened his mouth to tell her to ease up. A clank and rattle outside the door froze him. He glanced once at Saunders and could see only a quick rise and fall of her small breasts and the rigid set of her jaw. Then the door was flung wide with a shriek of rusted hinges. It slammed with a boom into the stone wall behind. A small trickle of dust and chipped stone clattered down onto the floor beside the torch, which guttered nearly to extinction in the draft of icy air now pouring in. Involuntarily Blaise shivered and hunched himself against that freezing blast, glaring defiance at the masked, black-cloaked figure standing in the doorway.

For a moment it stood there staring at Blaise as though stunned, then pointed at him. "*By'he, ah by'he n thul!*"

It sounded almost like an incantation, and something elemental in Blaise shivered in response. The stench suddenly intensified, wringing an exclamation of disgust from him, and the masked figure turned and fled, shouting.

Blaise grinned without amusement. "Help me to my feet, Saunders."

She did not budge. "Stay where you are. If you could see your face—"

"Help me up!" he said through his teeth, tired of having to argue over every order. "If that's the sort of reaction we're to expect, the stronger I look the better."

"That makes no sense," she said. "And if you think we can just stroll out, you—"

With a snarl of impatience he pushed himself up off the stool, gripping her arm and swaying until she sighed and gave him a steadying hand. "You do yourself no good with this pretense, Omari," she said insistently. "You're just squandering what strength you do have . . ."

Her voice trailed off as the soldiers reappeared in the doorway, eleven strong this time. They stared at Blaise for a moment in daunting silence, then abruptly entered the cell, parting ranks to stand on both sides of the door, at attention, black-cloaked, silent, menacing. Another figure came from the shadows beyond with such suddenness that it seemed almost to materialize from nothing. It was covered from broad shoulder to foot in a cloak of midnight blue, upon which the torchlight made liquid sparks of color shimmer. Immensely tall, perhaps eight feet in height, it towered over even the soldiers. Like the rest it was cowled in a hood and wore a mask, but the light caught markings like silver runes upon the mask's smooth surface, glinting there like little glimmers of life. Power and something more emanated from this figure. It lifted its gloved hand, long and supple, in a slight flick of a gesture, and the soldiers saluted by raising their fists into the air. Through the arch of these upflung arms the figure stepped forward with a gliding gracefulness.

Saunders, so rigid that she quivered, drew in a breath through her teeth. Blaise stood with his feet braced and his thin arms loose at his sides, conscious of his slipping blanket. He gave no outward sign of fear of the giant approaching him. Instinctively Saunders stepped half in front of Blaise and raised her hands, assuming the open posture of Institute kiamee fighting.

Infuriated, Blaise glared at her and said, "Stand away from me, Saunders, or by Demos I'll break your neck." The fury in his tone apparently penetrated, for she blinked and looked back at him in amazement.

Blaise flared. "Never step in front of me again. Do you hear? Back *off,* Saunders."

Slowly she obeyed, her scarlet face clashing with the orange flame of her hair. The soldiers stirred slightly, but did not lower their arms until the blue-cloaked figure halted before Blaise. Then one soldier detached himself from the rest and, drawing a short slim rod of an opaque crystalline substance from his wide belt, stood by Saunders with the rod pointed at her. Blaise eyed that weapon for a long moment in open speculation before turning his gaze coolly to the one before him.

The giant spoke in a deep, throbbing voice that reverberated in the crowded stone cell. When Blaise merely stared at him with an uplifted eyebrow, he thrust a gloved hand beneath the dark blue cloak and brought out a thick golden medallion, dangling it in the air by a silken-looking white cord.

"Does this speak in your way?" boomed a deep voice in an archaic form of High Standard.

Startled by so advanced a translator in the hands of this barbaric-looking figure, Blaise hid his reaction by inclining his head in a bow. He did not dare attempt a more formal show of respect lest he lose his already shaky balance.

"It does," he said, and listened to the medallion reflect his words in a rapid blur of inflected syllables. He frowned. Inflections were the most complicated aspect of languages to learn, especially since a mistake could so quickly prove fatal.

"You are . . . *n'ka* Ruantl." The silver-marked mask turned to regard Saunders, who was staring at him wide-eyed. "And you . . . *n'dl* Ruantl. Not of Ruantl at all, nor of Anthi."

It was said as a statement, but Blaise nodded. "This is correct. We come from a different planet."

For a long tense minute there was silence. Then the other said, "Speak to this question, *n'ka*: In your place of origin are there people who say Ruantl and talk of it? Is Ruantl a world known to you?"

Blaise shook his head. When this brought no reaction, he said firmly, "No. We know of this planet as only a number on a star chart, and no interest is taken in it."

That brought a stir among the soldiers, and the tall figure lowered the medallion for a moment as though discouraged. Then he silenced the soldiers with a gesture and lifted the translator once again.

"I have seen your ship. It is small but of an advanced design. Are you knowledgeable in the working of it?"

"Yes," said Blaise, ignoring Saunders's frantic head-shake. "I am the navigational officer and she is the helmsman."

"Understood. This is pleasing to us. We have waited long for *n'ka* such as you to come to Ruantl." There was a decided note of satisfaction in the creature's sonorous voice. He stepped nearer, towering over Blaise. "I am Picyt, First

Honored of the House of Kkanthor, and sworn to blood in the service of the goddess Anthi." As he spoke he brought the fingertips of his left hand to his mask in a quick gesture of respect. "She whom I serve has smiled upon you, *n'ka*, for the Bban'jen who summoned us to this citadel told us you walked to the hand of death."

Blaise had begun to feel as though he were still headed that way, but he managed a nod and a vestige of a smile that did not reach his wary eyes. "I am Blaise Omari," he said, conscious of a foolish urge to speak his true, original name. "And she is—"

"Major Ryhi Saunders, SIS *Forerunner*, codex number 997R412," she snapped.

Picyt curled one long finger around the curving edge of the translator. "There is a use for you, a thing we will ask of you . . . later," he said slowly, his voice so deep it almost seemed to awaken an answering vibration in Blaise's chest. "Will you be cooperative to our wishes?"

"No," snapped Saunders.

"We might be," said Blaise with a hard look at her. "What is it you want of us, Picyt?"

"Later," said Picyt, lowering the translator. Making an unidentifiable sound behind his mask, he whirled and strode out between the line of soldiers, raising his hand as he did so. "*An*," he snapped curtly, and vanished into the shadows beyond.

"Omari, you dirty—"

"Quiet," said Blaise, keeping his eyes warily on the soldiers. What had Picyt called them? The Bban'jen. He savored that name beneath his breath, his pale eyes narrowing as one stepped toward him, drawn rod in hand. Blaise moved in obedience to its sharp wave, keeping his hands visible and still as he walked unsteadily between the silent lines of Bban'jen. Behind him came the sound of a brief scuffle and a stifled cry from Saunders. Blaise, very conscious of the intent soldiers around him, did not so much as turn his head. He knew Saunders could take care of herself.

The Bban'jen closed ranks about him in dark silence, and they all moved with even steps down a dusty tunnel, unlit save by the dim glow of torchlight. Blaise stumbled over a stone, bruising his bare foot. He cursed, hopping slightly, and a gloved hand with the strength of a vise reached out of the shadows to grip his arm above the elbow. Blaise jerked involuntarily against the touch, but when it did not release him he was secretly grateful for the support.

He stumbled again and would have fallen but for the hand on his arm. Hauled to his freezing feet, Blaise merely stood in place, shivering.

"*An*," said the soldier, tugging on his arm.

Blaise shook his head, trying to get his breath, which the frosty air kept snatching from his sore lungs. The soldiers crowded about him in the cramped passageway, muttering among themselves, half seen and faceless in the gloom. Gasping for more air in this narrow, stuffy place, Blaise glanced up into the masked face of the man grasping his arm and stiffened as he glimpsed a glow of incandescent yellow light through the mesh eye guards. In the gloom all their eyes were glowing, some yellow, others red. A new, intense note entered their low, gruff voices.

"Omari?" asked Saunders, who'd been shoved out of the way against the stone side of the passageway. "What are you doing?"

"Quiet," he said, gripped by an inexplicable uneasiness. The moment of rest had helped; he had his breath back and was about to straighten up when a whiff of that putrid odor, hot and sickening, assailed his nostrils. Even as he reeled in disgust, the soldier grasping his arm jerked him close and drew a knife with a curved, serrated blade of wicked green metal.

"*Cha'hoi*," he hissed into Blaise's ear, and drove the blade hard.

Blaise reacted with reflexes honed sharp by years of the roughest in-fighting. Twisting his body, he felt the knife miss its mark by a hairbreadth. He slammed his weight into his attacker, setting his foot between the other's as he struck upward, hard, from beneath his man's knife arm. The soldier grunted but hung on to his weapon, preventing Blaise's swift grab for the rod in his belt. He tried to spin free of Blaise to gain space to attack again, but Blaise had already anticipated that move. Compensating for the other's size, Blaise ducked, parried with a swift hand chop, and took hold of his opponent, sending him sprawling in the dust. The knife clattered across the stone floor as a profound silence stretched over the passageway, broken only by the sound of Blaise's harsh panting.

The musk odor of the Bban nearly overpowered him now, and his half-healed chest threatened to collapse with every breath he dragged into his lungs. Dashing the sweat from his eyes, he eyed the motionless soldiers, all ten of them, then stepped toward the knife as its owner groggily started to pick himself up. His mask apparently had been loosened in the fall, for he paused on his knees to readjust its placement. Blaise bent for the knife in one swift motion. With a snarl the Bban let fall his mask in order to seize Blaise's wrist as his fingers came within an inch of the polished leather hilt.

For the space of a heartbeat they stared at each other. To Blaise it seemed an eternity. The first sight of an unmasked Bban branded itself upon his memory. Hammered plates of thick scarred skin formed the rough planes of that hairless oblong face. The eyes glowed yellow in twin lights of phosphorous above a nose that was but a slit of bone and cartilage. Double-hinged and powerful, the lower jaw was similar in design to an insect's mandible. This was clicking now, fast and furiously, as the Bban narrowed his burning eyes and gathered his long body to spring.

"*Cha'hoi*!"

One of the watching soldiers raised the cry, barking it out on a wild, keening note that sent a chill racing along Blaise's spine. But he kept his eyes on the unmasked Bban, dodging as the creature leaped. Blaise's straining fingers barely closed on the knife hilt, and as the Bban thudded a blow across the base of his neck that seemed to separate his head from his body, Blaise twisted with a jerk and rammed the blade into the Bban's breastbone. To his dismay, however, the point skidded across the Bban's chest, ripping the black tunic, but not penetrating. And he was losing strength. He could feel it ebbing away like water slipping down a drain. The Bban's hands closed around his throat to snap his neck. Gritting his teeth, Blaise struck with the knife again, aiming this time for those glowing eyes. The blade plunged deep with a sickening thud and scrape, sending hot fluid spurting over Blaise's hand. The Bban screamed horribly, arching back in a wild twist of agony, his hands clawing at his face. Then he fell, heavily, and moved no more.

Expecting the rest of the soldiers to jump him now, Blaise forced himself quickly to his knees. By sheer willpower he kept the dancing gray flecks from completely blurring his vision. Thus he faced them, the black-cloaked Bban'jen, who stood before him in a half ring, one holding a struggling Saunders pinned against the wall. Panting so hard that each breath rattled in his throat, awakening old pain, and conscious of the sweat dripping steadily into his eyes, Blaise looked around with a defiant hot-eyed glare and spat gritty dust from his mouth.

The cries of "*Cha'hoi*" had ceased abruptly with the death of his opponent. Now one tall lean soldier stepped forward, his booted feet raising tiny puffs of dust as they moved soundlessly across the stone floor.

Still kneeling, with his fists clenched white in an effort to contain the agony in his chest, Blaise watched him come with a sinking heart. By sheer grit and will he had won once. He knew he could not win a second time. Facing defeat, Blaise swallowed down the sour taste of it and managed somehow to get to his feet. His trembling legs braced to hide their weakness, he faced his approaching death with a bleak eye and a total lack of expression.

The soldier kept coming until he was scarcely inches from Blaise, close enough for him to hear the faint breaths from within the mask and to see a thin band of scarlet emblazoned upon the throat of the black tunic. He stood there for a moment, staring at Blaise, who felt consciousness slip. In anger he grabbed it back, refusing to take the easy way to death. Then, with that amazing quickness of movement that Blaise had noted was common among the Bban'jen, the soldier bent and jerked the knife from the body of his fallen comrade to hold it aloft, wet and glistening in the flicker of torchlight. Blaise held his breath, expecting this action to rouse all of them to fury. Even Saunders ceased her struggles against her captor and subsided, her face a white blur in the shadows.

But instead the soldier seized Blaise's left hand and forced open the fist Blaise had made of it. He wiped the blade clean upon Blaise's palm, smearing the flesh with the dark, sticky blood. As Blaise grimaced in revulsion, disgusted to find that his hand now stank with the putrid musk of the dead Bban, the soldier picked up the discarded mask and yanked free the cloak from his fallen comrade's shoulders. He thrust both at Blaise with such force that he had no choice but to accept them.

He frowned as the soldier stepped back and gave a preemptive order. When Blaise made no move, the soldier repeated his command with a fierce gesture.

"Do what he wants, Omari!" shouted Saunders. "Take the thing's clothes."

Blaise stared down at the dead Bban, his stomach crawling at the sight of that horrible face and the thought of yet a worse body inside the black uniform. Then he remembered that he was cold and naked and in no position to be squeamish. Steeling himself, he knelt by the man and stripped him with an efficiency born of frequent practice. When he was finished, dressed, and standing in the heavy black clothes that were too large for him, he gripped the mask in his hands, staring down at the skeletal white corpse at his booted feet in a final moment of revulsion. Then, at an impatient gesture from one of the Bban'jen, he fitted the mask into place beneath the heavy cowled hood, his fingers clumsy with the fastenings as his nostrils flared at the musk stench still lingering inside. But he got it on and stood waiting, his gloved hands at his sides.

The Bban'jen formed ranks around them again. This time Saunders was put beside him.

"*An*," said the leader bearing the torch, and with silent, booted feet they walked on through the tunnel, leaving the dead Bban in the dust and darkness without a second glance.

"Well!" said Saunders in a low voice, rubbing her wrists gingerly. Dirt streaked the side of her face, and her lip was cut at the corner. "I didn't think you had that much in you. At least you've got their respect now."

He glanced at her impatiently through the meshed eye guards of the mask. "I know it was a test of some kind, Saunders," he said wearily, not having much breath left for talking. "I'm not a fool."

She met his gaze quickly. "You think it was on Picyt's order? But why?"

He shrugged, his steps lagging a bit. "Either that, or they're animal enough to attack anything that shows signs of weakness. Think what you like. But, Saunders . . ."

"Yes?"

"If the chance comes, go for the rods they carry, not the knives. One way or another we're getting out of here." His jaw set with determination. "Be ready."

She nodded, for once giving no argument. "I will."

Chapter 3

Afterward Blaise recalled only a dim impression of that walk through long dark tunnels, some of which were so narrow that the sheer weight of stone all around seemed to be crushing down. Tiny passageways like crawl spaces fingered off from the main tunnel, and now and then some unseen thing rustled away into dusty shadows or panted behind tumbled stones as it watched them go by. Eventually the tunnel flared into a broad space with a square hole cut through the center of the stone floor. The torch was thrust at it, and the bluish-orange light flared bright as though caught by a rush of air, throwing illumination partway into the hole to reveal narrow, treacherous steps. Fighting off the feeling that he was descending into a yawning throat, Blaise balanced himself carefully, staying on his feet only by willpower strengthened with fear kindled in sharp bursts whenever he faltered and a masked face swung intently his way.

He had decided that Bban'jen intelligence was on a par with that of a clever pack of animals. He could not help but doubt that moment of respect paid him when he had defeated the soldier. And he grew certain that if he did not hold himself together somehow and keep moving, another would lose control and attack him. So, sliding his left sleeve along the rough surface of the wall, Blaise forced himself on quivering legs down the uneven steps, his sight hampered by the mask and the poor light. The reek of musk was fading, or else he was becoming used to it, for now and then he caught whiffs of other scents of warmth and age and the mustiness of rotting leather.

The descent was much shorter than he had expected, and it ended in a chamber that seemed to have been hewn out untold ages ago. Who had done it? he wondered, glancing at the polished places of stone where the touch of countless hands had worn away the roughness. It was damp here as well, making the chill more penetrating. Across the chamber rose another series of steps, these wider but equally as steep as the first. Longing just to be able to throw himself flat and never get up again, Blaise dragged in a deep breath and then another, dreading the climb before him.

"Can you make it?" asked Saunders in a whisper that echoed off the ancient stone.

"Yes," he said, gritting his teeth as the Bban'jen started up in double file. It was all he could do to bend his knees and drag up one leg and then the other. His muscles had softened to water, and his head spun every time he raised his eyes. For a moment he floated; then an impatient nudge from one of the guards behind brought him back to reality to struggle on to the next step.

"Saunders," he said in a voice that grated. "Put your hand against the small of my back. They won't notice in these shadows, and by Demos, don't let me lose consciousness."

With a grumble she placed her strong hand as he had asked, and the extra bit of support helped immeasurably.

"Why don't you forget your pride and let someone drag you up?" she asked.

"Because," he retorted, gulping for air and resenting the waste of breath required to answer her, "I'm not sure they wouldn't slit my throat and leave me here rather than go to the trouble. Damn!" He staggered off-balance, and only Saunders's steadying hand saved him from swaying over the edge of the steps to a long fall. "Thanks," he said, gasping.

"Save your thanks," she snapped, her face a blur in the shadows. "And stay against the wall. I may not hold you back the next time."

With a grimace Blaise struggled on, and after a while his entire attention focused down to nothing but his battle with the steps. The occasional throb in his chest became constant, and the mask stifled him as each breath grew more difficult.

When they finally reached the top, emerging through a hole in the floor into a wide hall of sorts with a tall vaulted ceiling held up by smoke-blackened beams, Blaise did not at first realize that the ordeal was over, and he would have stumbled blindly on had Saunders not held him beside her.

Soldiers were everywhere, some strolling through on their way elsewhere in the citadel, others gathered in small groups in the corners of the hall. At regular spaces along the wall, vast braziers filled with glowing yellow coals gave off a blaze of heat and light. Some of the Bban'jen stood near these, with their dark cloaks thrown back over their shoulders, talking among themselves somberly or with excitement. Other figures —female, perhaps—bundled in shapeless tattered garments with hooded cloaks shadowing their faces, moved about in silent industry, two shoving a crude bench against a wall, while the rest circulated among the groups of soldiers, baskets under their arms. The reek of fiery spices and cooking hung in the smoky air, overlaid by Bban musk and other unidentifiable odors. Along one wall a rack of barb-tipped spears—at least three meters in length—stood in a precise display surmounted by an enormous gold medallion of intricate design, in the center of which was a baleful stone of dark-blue crystal. Blaise stared thoughtfully at those spears, doubting if he could even heft one.

Barking an order, the guards moved Blaise and Saunders on through the hall, while around them conversations stilled and masked faces turned to follow their progress. They moved through a tall doorway whose two armored halves were standing wide, secured by stout metal hooks connected to rings bolted to the floor. The passageway narrowed past that point, but not to the extent of the old tunnels, and now that the going was easier Blaise noticed that the walls were constructed of small stone blocks not always well fitted together or smoothed.

Then at last the soldiers halted by a narrow door. One Bban stepped forward to unlock and slam it open. Blaise and Saunders were shoved through. They had barely stumbled over the threshold before the door was slammed shut and locked. Blaise swayed on his feet, barely able to believe he'd made it, then with an oath yanked off the stifling mask. Saunders glanced at him as she began prowling about the narrow room, examining the few objects lying on a triangular-shaped table. Blaise, however, had eyes only for the nearest of two niches cut into the wall, spread with one rough-woven blanket apiece. Dropping the hated mask on the floor, he stumbled to the left bunk and sprawled across it, uncaring about discomfort or cold or hunger as blessed nothingness washed over him.

When he awakened hours later he felt much better, despite the light-headedness of hunger and excruciating soreness in his back and legs. Groaning, he sat up and ran his fingers through his tousled hair, cocking an eye at Saunders who was standing beside the table, noisily chewing on something.

"Where's mine?" he said, coughing to clear the gravel from his throat.

She eyed him a moment, as unfriendly as ever, and with a swallow picked up a metal cup and held it out to him.

He took it reluctantly, knowing without having to look at the dark grease-spotted contents that it was the same ghastly cold broth as yesterday.

"I can't get my strength back on this," he said in disgust, setting down the cup untasted. "Come on, Saunders, share your portion."

She frowned as though she meant to refuse, then tossed him the second cube from the tray. He caught it, cupping his hands gingerly about it as a corner crumbled away into brown dust. After a cautious sniff, he bit into the side, expecting it to crumble to dry powder on his tongue. Instead he found it growing more chewy and substantial as it reacted with his saliva. He worried the tasteless stuff with his teeth until it suddenly fell apart in his mouth like coarse meal. He swallowed quickly, choking a bit, and resolutely broke off another chunk.

When it was all gone, his jaws ached from the tough chewing, and his throat was shriveled with thirst. He eyed the broth again, swirling the unappealing contents so that the film of grease on top sank momentarily, and out of fairness offered part of it to Saunders. She was still working on her cube and refused curtly. With a shrug he steeled himself and gulped down the broth, nearly gagging on the rancid taste.

She watched him without expression, her broad jaws making solid work of the remainder of her meal. Then with a final swallow she pushed her lengthening hair back from her face and said, "Do you still prefer this to detention?"

His brow furrowed as he lay back on his bunk, propping himself on one elbow. "Why is that so hard for you to understand?"

She laughed harshly and waved her freckled hand at the room. "The only way out is through that door. So what is your plan of escape? Picking the lock?"

He stared at her, pale gray eyes narrowed. He was annoyed, but he ignored it, refusing to let emotions get in his way. "Wait," he said calmly. "The moment will come."

She snorted, shoving the table aside with a scrape of the legs across the stone floor. "You have your share of *flin*, Omari, sitting there assuming I will follow your lead. As my prisoner—"

"No," said Blaise, a spark igniting in his eyes. He made sure that this time she saw his anger. "I am not your prisoner, Saunders. Get rid of that idea, because I am your only hope of freedom."

"Are you?" Her square chin jutted as she stood facing him, her big hands planted on her straight hips. "I am *not* helpless. And why should I trust you? You're a murderer and a thief and a—"

"Blackmarketeer and rebel," he finished for her, studying the tip of one finger.

"Damn you!" She gestured viciously. "I hold you responsible for the deaths of *Forerunner*'s crew. Four lives, Omari! And I intend to see you pay—"

He sprang off his bunk, seizing her arm and pinning it so roughly behind her that she broke off with a cry.

"Now," he said through his teeth, threading his fingers through her short red hair to yank back her head. She struggled, the powerful muscles in her broad shoulders bunching beneath the tattered fabric of her coveralls, and swung her free hand back in a blow to his ribs.

He dodged most of it, but it hurt enough to make his slight hold on his temper slip. Snarling, he hurt her just enough to make her cease struggling.

"Have I your attention, Saunders?" he asked, tightening his grip in her hair.

She kicked backward at him, only to scream as he twisted her arm to a point just short of breaking.

"Have I your attention?" he repeated through his teeth as she sank to her knees with a gasp and a stifled moan. "Well?"

"Yes!" she shouted, her eyes flashing with murder behind the tears.

"Then listen," he said, releasing her head but not her arm. Warily he kept himself balanced lightly on the balls of his feet, ready for whatever her fury might force her to try next. "I brought us here, yes. And I'll take the blame for what happened to the captain. But look at your own actions, Saunders, if you want to blame the crash on someone."

"*No!*"

"*You* threw the *Forerunner* at the black star!"

She jerked in his hold. "I won't take the blame, Omari! Not for you, not for anyone. I'm getting out of here and—"

Again he put pressure on her arm, making her gasp. "The Institute trained you to handle a starship and to defend yourself. It did not teach you how to break jail. Nor did it show you how to blend in with another culture to survive. I can do both, and much more. I *can* get us out of this citadel, but only if I have your cooperation."

She made a harsh sound of contempt. "And if I withhold it? If I decide to act on my own? It would be better—"

"Then I'll have to kill you," he said, his voice hard. Inside he winced as he spoke, for taking lives gave him no pleasure, and he did not want to kill her, troublesome as she was. But he would do whatever was necessary to survive, just as he always had. And as long as she planned revenge for her dead crewmates, she was a definite danger to him.

He waited for a moment, and when she said nothing, he said, "It will be the only means of keeping you out of my way, unless you decide to be smart, Saunders, and follow my orders with no more trouble and no more argument. Understood? The arm of the Institute does not reach here. You will never take me back to that travesty you call justice." He snorted. "Institute justice. It is nothing, Saunders! So what is your answer?"

She did not reply. He could feel her rigid, unyielding muscles, and knew, with a stir of mingled contempt and regret, that she was a fool. With a sigh he raised his hand behind her head, but without warning the bolts slammed back and the door crashed open. He turned around quickly and nearly lost his grip on her as she heaved to break free.

"No, you don't!" he said grimly, bracing himself harder against her powerful struggles.

With a shout two Bban guards ran inside. Rough hands seized Blaise, dragging him away from Saunders, who lashed out with her fist, sending a lance of agony through his chest. He gasped, doubling over, and by the time he had recovered his breath he was hard held in a Bban's grip, as was Saunders.

The guard snapped something unintelligible at him and jerked him along, forcing him toward the door.

Blaise glanced over his shoulder at her scowling face. "Don't worry, Saunders," he said lightly, masking his alarm. "It looks like you won't have to team up with me after all. Institute pride is salvaged." He grinned at her. "And I always do get away, even from the Institute."

With an answering oath she tried to hurl herself at him, only to be knocked sprawling to the floor by the second guard. He snarled something at her, drawing his knife.

She rose to her feet, pressing her hand to the bleeding corner of her mouth, and lifted her head high. "To quote you," she said coldly, the anger undimmed in her eyes as Blaise was shoved through the doorway, "just wait. You will pay for their lives, Omari, and whether these Bban'jen take care of you now or I have to do it with my own hands, you *will* pay."

In emphasis the door boomed shut and was bolted with a hard twist of a square metal key. Then, flanked by both guards, Blaise was dragged away down another dark, dusty tunnel.

Not eager to face whatever lay ahead of him, he tried stiffening his knees to slow their rapid pace, and received a sharp cuff on the side of the head that almost stunned him. After that he cooperated, keeping himself alert for the first chance to break free.

But only a few hundred yards away from his cell the guards halted before another armored door, grimly black and encrusted with age. The guard on his left rapped sharply on it with his knife hilt, and when it swung open from within, Blaise was thrust inside roughly enough to send him stumbling to his knees. For a moment, as he gasped from the jolt of that fall and sought to right himself, he wondered if he had not simply been transferred to a separate confinement. But when he caught his breath and lifted his head, it was to find the tall creature in the blue cloak standing before him once again.

A sharp command sent all the guards outside. The door slammed and Blaise was left alone on his knees before the masked stranger. His eyes narrowed, and he considered seizing the smoking torch from its bracket near him and using it for a weapon. But there was no escape from the dark, cavelike room save through the door and the guards waiting beyond. Regretfully Blaise abandoned the urge for action and struggled to his feet, wincing.

The creature in blue pulled out the translator as he had before and said in a deep, stilted voice, "It pleases me to speak with you, not to harm you. Attempt nothing foolish, *n'ka*."

Blaise braced his feet slightly apart, settling his wiry body into an easy, deceptive stance. "I'm listening," he said, his gray eyes cold with wariness.

"You are distrustful. Please . . ." The creature's hands swept out, gloved in gauntlets with wide embroidered tops. "Take no alarm."

Blaise raised an eyebrow. "If you don't intend to harm us, why are we kept prisoner, Picyt?"

The creature withdrew one hand into the generous fold of his sleeve and inclined his head slightly so that the torchlight glinted off his mask with its decorative tracings of silver. "You recall my name. Splendid. You are kept here within the citadel as a precaution for your safety. Now, *n'ka.*" Picyt stepped forward eagerly. "I have a proposal to lay before you . . . a request."

"Yes?" said Blaise, his attention caught. The situation began to look more advantageous.

"Your spaceship will never function again," said Picyt slowly, choosing his words with care. "And although once we had the ability to go from one world to another, this ability is no longer ours. You can never leave Ruantl. You have no choice but to make your life here."

Thinking of the crimes sprinkled through his past and of the vindictive search for him now being conducted through every corner of Institute-controlled territory, Blaisc kept his satisfaction at this refuge he'd found from his voice as he coolly replied, "I understand. What is it you want from me?"

"First, stand quietly for a moment and allow me to look upon you. If you are indeed the one sought . . ."

A light finger, something alien and cold, brushed Blaise's mind. Well aware of the techniques of telepathy in its many forms, and hostile to all of them, Blaise stiffened and promptly raised the mental barriers he had learned to erect with much difficulty over the years of thwarting reformations and other rehabilitation procedures.

Picyt withdrew at once with a slight gesture. "Forgive me," he said after a pause. "I had not suspected you were of caste. But you are also of—" He broke off at Blaise's frown and came a step nearer. "I realize you do not trust me, *n'ka*, yet there is not time to gain trust in the proper way. Ruantl—this planet—was colonized long ago by the Tlar race. The Bban'n are native. They possess no political power, no rights, and are dependent upon us for food and other . . . things." Picyt lifted his hand, turning the palm over. "The Tlar are few. Less than a hundred families of pure lineage exist. Our ruler is a young tyrant, incapable of seeing past his own pleasure. I wish to free this planet from its stagnation and technological decay. The Bban'n are intelligent and full of potential, but they must have the chance to grow."

Blaise rubbed his stubbled jaw, swiftly considering options. A planet under civil war offered many opportunities, provided he attached himself to the winning side. "Does this revolt involve the whole planet or—"

"No, only this continent has been settled by the Tlar," said Picyt quickly. "Elsewhere the native populations are primitive. No contact has been made with them for years. Now tell me, *n'ka*," he continued eagerly. "Will you help us? Will you share your skills with my technicians and train them in the knowledge that has been forgotten?"

"Perhaps," said Blaise. Confidence rose in him; there was always a way out when one looked for it. "And what would I gain from this association?"

Picyt gestured broadly. "Your mind tells me you are an outlaw, a hunted man. I can grant you a new identity."

Blaise laughed at such naiveté. "Sorry, but I can always—"

"No, you misunderstand!" broke in Picyt. "What I offer is more than a change of name! Guarded within the caverns of M'thra are the forms of Ruantl's four greatest rulers, preserved perfectly in the cold heart of Anthi. Were you to take on the body of Leiil Asan and raise the Bban tribes against Hihuan, he would have no—"

"Wait a minute!" said Blaise sharply, a chill spreading through him as he realized he was facing not just a conspirator but a fanatic. "What do you mean, take on his body?"

"Precisely that," said Picyt in a calm, reassuring way that did not reassure Blaise at all. The translator dangled and spun on its cord. "We have used the regeneration process many times in order to keep valued slaves or—"

"And how long would I be in this body?" Blaise asked with rising revulsion.

Picyt spread out his hand. "The exchange is permanent."

"No deal." Blaise backed up a step. "No."

"You decide too quickly," said Picyt, his voice softening to a more persuasive tone. "Consider. You would have all the honor of the Tlar leiil without the responsibility of that office. You would have ample food and—"

"*No.*" Blaise shook his head, imagining himself as a stinking Bban with corroded skin and a jaw like a . . . He shuddered and turned away from Picyt. "Forget it! I won't—"

Deep, melodious laughter interrupted him, as soft and gentle as the fingertips that brushed his mind.

Blaise jerked around, his fists clenched. No one played around with his mind and . . . His eyes widened with alarm as he saw Picyt raise both hands to the fastenings of his mask. Blaise's breath came a little shorter. He did not want to look behind that mask and see the living horror of another Bban face!

"So this is what you fear, *n'ka*?" asked Picyt, and pulled mask and hood away in a swift movement.

Blaise flinched, then blinked in surprise. Whatever Picyt might be, he was *not* Bban. Chagrined, Blaise stared at the golden-skinned face that regarded him with a smile. He took in the details of slanted dark-brown eyes with no whites, sharply ridged cheekbones padded over by the fleshy jowls of middle age, and a sensitive humanoid mouth. Picyt's dark hair, catching red glints from the torchlight, grew to a low point on his forehead and lay back in sleek, well-groomed waves to the base of his neck. It was an elegant face, a face of civilization and advanced culture, and in this cavelike room lit poorly by fire it looked distinctly out of place. Curbing his first swell of relief, however, Blaise glanced down at his clenched fist, then up at Picyt once again. This time he saw the lines of fatigue and worry carved around eyes and mouth, saw a slight droop in one of the cheek muscles, saw when the gleam of torchlight struck those dark eyes a suggestion of a dull bluish haze over them. He frowned.

"You see?" said Picyt quietly while the shadows brooded about them. "Far, *far* different from the unfortunate Bban'n. Perhaps on your world it is a source of pride to be small of stature and dark of skin, but if it is not, then think on having a height like mine with the thews and strength of a warrior and a face to rival the sun in glory—"

Wanting no poetry, Blaise cut him off with a skeptical "Why me? Why not anyone on this planet? Why not you, since you obviously want to rule here?"

The maskless Picyt narrowed his eyes, then smiled faintly. "You have the technological advancement we have lost. And you have no interest in our politics. Take the position, *n'ka*."

Blaise considered the proposal without much interest. "No, Picyt," he said, shaking his head. "No deal. I'll give your people a few lessons on engine repair, but I won't trade off this." He tapped his chest. He was what he was. His pride would not let him accept Picyt's offer and deny himself.

Picyt looked displeased, but he said, "Another arrangement can be made to replace this disappointment. Very well, *n'ka*, but we will talk again." With a swift movement he pocketed the translator, replaced his mask, and strode to the door, where he snapped out an order. At once the door opened and the Bban guards gestured for Blaise to come out. In minutes he found himself deposited back in the cell with Saunders.

She sat up on her bunk, glaring at him. "I see you didn't get away."

He shrugged, moving over to his bunk with his thoughts still on Picyt. He did not trust the priest's quick acceptance of his refusal. Absently he said, "Ready to call a truce yet, Saunders?"

She reddened. "Never!"

"Oh, don't be stupid!" He frowned at her. "Demos, Saunders, if you'd meant to slit my throat, you'd have done it days ago."

"Killing you is not—"

"Institute regulations. Yes, I know." He shook his head, wondering why she couldn't thrust aside Institute brainwashing and think for herself.

"If you weren't a drone, Omari," she said icily, "if you hadn't been born in a *vat*, you would realize that justice is best dealt by trial, not by strifer. What did they want with you?"

"Why should I tell you?" he retorted.

She jumped to her feet, her eyes flashing with accusation. "You have sold us out! Omari, you filthy piece of—"

"Shut up!" He snarled at her so viciously, she fell silent, her face draining of color. He took two steps toward her, his fists clenched and his pale eyes cold. "Anything that is to my advantage, I take, Saunders. And if you want to survive on this planet, you had better learn the same lesson quickly." His shouts echoed around the narrow room. A tense silence followed. Finally he eased out a harsh breath and uncurled his fists. "As a matter of fact," he said, looking away from her white, strained face, "I refused." He coughed. "We may never get out of here."

"We will," she said in a low, almost inaudible voice.

He looked at her in surprise.

She met his gaze, her eyes hardened, and she drew her shoulders erect once more. "I *will* take you back. For now we work together. But don't expect more than that. I never give up, Omari."

That was it; he could never trust her. Accepting the fact, he smiled mockingly. "Saunders," he said, "neither do I."

Three days later his patience had worn considerably. Twice a day a bottom section of the heavy door was wrenched open and a tray of unappetizing, unvarying food was shoved through. They had seen no one but each other in that time, neither was inclined to talk to the other, and both were growing heartily tired of such proximity. The cell might be similar in size to the *Forerunner*'s bridge, where they had rubbed shoulders daily for seven months, but then they had had duties to occupy them and shared no open hostility. Now there was only confinement and hatred.

Saunders paced up and down the length of the room incessantly. Her reason was exercise. Blaise, knowing better, lay on his bunk and contemplated the ceiling, his mind working idly on the question of what made the square of pale illumination there. Like Picyt's translator, it was an incongruous note of technology in a culture that had thus far appeared to be completely barbaric and backward. Blaise considered. Obviously Picyt had spoken the truth. But why hadn't he returned to try to persuade Blaise again? And if he had accepted Blaise's refusal, what was intended for them next?

Saunders abruptly stopped her pacing, glanced at the ceiling, and then glanced at him. "We're under surveillance, aren't we?"

He was startled. That thought had not occurred to him.

"Up there, where the light is," she said with a shrug. "I feel someone watching. Don't you? You look at it enough."

"Feel?" he said sarcastically. "I thought you were trained to rely on Institute training, not hunches."

Her eyes flashed. "Look, Omari, just because you didn't think of it . . ."

"All right." He gestured to cut her off.

"Yes. And here's something else for you to chew on." She pointed at the ceiling. "Suppose they've bugged this room with one of their translators?"

Blaise sat up, even more irritated by that idea. He was annoyed with himself. Clearly he was being an idiot in underestimating the Bban'jen and their masters. There were too many unknowns around him for him to dare relax or judge yet. "I take it back, Saunders," he said slowly. "You are not useless. But I wonder—"

He never finished his sentence. A sudden clatter outside the door brought him to his feet. He waited, eyes on the door, as the heavy locks ground back. It slammed open with customary force, scarring the wall behind it. A squad of black-cloaked soldiers leaped inside to fan out, half crouched, rods drawn and aimed. Outside, a pair of torchbearers stood with tall flaming brands in their hands. Slight of build and scarcely taller than Saunders, whose height topped Blaise's by three inches, they wore ragged, rough-spun cloaks of a grayish-brown color rather than the uniforms of the Bban'jen. Nor were they masked. Without obstruction their eyes glowed red and feral through the deep shadows beneath their hoods. Bban musk wafted thick and nauseating through the stale air, and from the shadows came low, excited clicking muffled by masks and restless stirs.

Swallowing down a surge of revulsion, Blaise exchanged glances with Saunders, whose lips were thinned and colorless. She questioned him with her eyes, but he hesitated and gave his head a slight shake, conscious of prickling dampness in his palms and a tightening line of tension stretching out between his shoulders. Counting the torchbearers, it was eight against two. He did not like the odds.

Rather than just stand there and quake, Blaise took an assured step forward, smiling slightly to conceal the knot in his stomach. "What—"

A bolt of blue fire crackled across the room, frying ozone in the air and blasting into the stone floor close enough to Blaise for him to feel the heat of its passage. Recoiling with an oath, he dropped flat, rolling against his bunk in anticipation of a second, more accurate blast. None came. After a second his heart ceased pounding madly, and warily he rose to his feet, wincing a bit at the pull of a sore muscle. Saunders also picked herself up off the floor and stared bleakly at the blackened mark smoking between them.

The Bban'jen stood impassively in their black masks.

"Don't make any more stupid moves, Omari," snapped Saunders, her voice croaking unsteadily.

He was annoyed, but he took the advice.

Just then a tall Bban with a scarlet band of rank at his collar—possibly the same officer who had given Blaise the dead soldier's clothes—strode in at a furious pace and barked out something that set the guards snapping to rigid attention. The officer glared at each of them, clicking his jaw behind his mask, then swung to Blaise and spoke with an impatient gesture.

Blaise looked at him blankly and shrugged.

With a snarl of impatience the officer reached beneath his cloak and pulled out a translator, which he tossed to Blaise. Catching it deftly, Blaise turned the metal disk over in his hand, hefting the weight and noting that it was smaller than Picyt's translator and tarnished. But it worked.

". . . is your mask?" the officer was saying. "Quickly. Wear it and come."

Blaise obediently walked over to his bunk and picked up the mask, which he'd been using as an unsatisfactory pillow. But he did not fit it into place.

"Why?" he asked, staring at the officer. "What is the mask's purpose?"

"What difference does it make?" put in Saunders nervously as the officer set a hand on his knife hilt. "Quit stalling, Omari, before someone decides to shoot at us again."

The officer drew himself more erect. "The mask," he said sternly, "is of need. Wear it and come. *An!*" Gesturing, he spun on his heel and strode out.

With a grimace Blaise motioned Saunders to precede him and fitted the mask under the hood of his cloak, gasping at the stuffy restriction of air. It took a moment to adjust to the reek of musk, which had not completely faded. Every sense on the alert, he walked out of the cell, the Bban'jen moving into formation behind him. Scarcely had he stepped out into the passageway when he was seized by the arm, pulled to one side into deep shadow, and shoved forcibly through a narrow split in the wall.

Stumbling in an effort to keep his balance as he plunged suddenly into a dark, damp place as cold as the pit of hell, Blaise whirled in alarm and tried to return to the passageway. But before he could do so a faint humming sang through his ears, and accute nausea and dizziness gripped him. No! he thought in anger, clinging to the damp stone wall with numbed fingers. He wasn't weak anymore. This was no time to—

The darkness smothered him like a living thing, robbing him of breath. He gasped, suddenly flattened by an unseen force that seemed to crush him to nothingness. Then he blinked and cringed at the unexpected blaze of light that struck him like a blow. Equally abruptly the cold, damp, and dizziness were gone. Bewildered, he lowered his hand and turned slowly around, blinking behind his mask at the bright sunlight flooding in through the wide mouth of an immense cave.

"So this is the intruder," said a rich, petulant voice out of nowhere. "It does not wear the jen uniform well, does it, Aabrm?"

Blaise whirled and stood half crouched, his heart thudding as his dazzled eyes strove to see through the inner gloom of the cave. His fingers clutched harder around the hard metallic surface of the medallion as it translated the sneering voice that echoed and boomed at him from a point he could not find.

"A puny type of creature, this *n'ka*," agreed a second voice, its rough, accented tone smoothed by oily obsequiousness. "It does not even realize that the seizert has brought it here to us, noble leiil. Obviously Picyt tries to play an intrigue of trickery, seeking to make us think this *n'ka* a creature of superior intelligence. We need not fear."

"Chi'ka!" snapped the rich voice, deepening with anger and filling the cave.

Silence, abashed and total, followed.

Blaise stood where he was, just short of the sunlight penetrating partway into the cave. Outside, a dry desert wind blew a desolate sigh across the stony slope stretching down from the cave's lip. He kept his back turned to the unfamiliar landscape of ridge and dune of black coarse sand, featureless save for an occasional jut of gray tor lifted against a sky of pale amethyst. Realizing that he had been brought here by some sort of teleportation device, the sophistication of which was incompatible with the rough stone dwellings and crude ways of the Bban'-jen, Blaise gripped the translator tightly in his hand and spoke to the interior of the cave, which lay wrapped in dark mystery.

"My name is Omari," he said evenly, his voice coming back at him from inside the stuffy confines of the mask. For an instant he was tempted to tug it off, but he did not, choosing to accept the officer's word that wearing it was somehow necessary. "My spaceship crashed here due to a malfunction caused by the black sun. I mean you no harm and do not understand why I am held prisoner."

Mocking laughter was the response to this diplomatic overture.

"Prisoner?" said the rich voice. "But you are not. You are

dead, *n'ka.*" The voice grew louder, and Blaise stiffened as a tall slender form appeared from the depths of the cave. For a moment Blaise stared at the speaker, dazzled by such magnificence. He was covered from shoulder to foot in a bronze cloak that shimmered from a thousand metallic threads woven into the cloth. Every glimmer of sunlight that penetrated the shadows enough to touch it woke it to molten life. It glistened and rippled with each movement of its owner. At the neck it flared into a tall, stiff collar behind the speaker's head, which was covered by a mask of bronze mesh so fine that Blaise could almost see the outline of his features behind it. To one side appeared another figure, the voice called Aabrm, no doubt, cloaked in lesser brown and wearing a dull mask marked with a pattern of gold tracings. This one held a rod of opaque blue crystal aimed at Blaise.

"No," continued the figure in bronze. "No prisoner now of the Bban'jen or of any jen. Our guard is not with us . . ." He spread out his gloved hand in an eloquent gesture. ". . . save for Aabrm, who is ever faithful to our service." Aabrm bowed, and the rich voice went on. "I brought you here, *n'ka*, to show Picyt that his secrets are not as close-kept as he believes."

"Who are you?" demanded Blaise, impatient with the man's self-importance. He wanted answers, not speeches.

But it was Aabrm who answered sharply, "Mind your tongue, *n'ka*! It is the Tlar leiil before you."

Blaise chose his next words with care. "Picyt has told me nothing of what he wants . . . Leiil," he said, adopting the stilted formality of the others. "How can I matter so much to Ruantl?"

Ignoring his question, the Tlar leiil said in a voice of silken menace, "A pity this creature did not crash in the south, eh, Aabrm? Then we should have had his knowledge of the ways of Beyond before that cursed Picyt."

Aabrm flicked his palm over. "It is still possible to interrogate him, noble Leiil. He—"

"I have told Picyt nothing," broke in Blaise, quick as always to spot an opening. "But I'm willing to talk if it's to my advantage."

"No!" A bronze gauntlet was swept out, palm down. "We shall not come after Kkanthor, to take its leavings!" The Tlar leiil turned away with an angry swirl of his cloak. "Our way is best. There shall be no change, *no* birth. Picyt's vision is insane." The Tlar leiil shook his fist, his other hand clamped hard on the jeweled knife hilt at his wide belt of woven leather. "By this jen-knife I swear that blood shall spread deep across the sand if Picyt dares raise the Outerlands against our glory."

"The Bban tribes are not tame, good Leiil," soothed Aabrm. "If he raises them, they will turn on him before Altian is ever reached."

"Not if he has this *n'ka*!" screamed the Tlar leiil, drawing his jen-knife to point the wicked green blade Blaise's way.

Blaise edged back by slow, imperceptible degrees toward the lip of the cave, trying to judge the drop, his peripheral vision hampered by his mask. His fingers flexed longingly at his sides. If only he could get that rod from Aabrm! But a highly developed regard for his own skin held him back from trying to jump the man as the argument raged on.

"My Leiil, consider!" Aabrm was saying, his voice thickened with urgency. "Even Picyt would not dare raise the Jewels of M'thra. If he intended this blasphemy against all that is sacred, then surely he would have placed his own life into the attempt. Thee need not fear this thing, Leiil."

"Fear?" The Tlar leiil rounded on his companion so fiercely that Aabrm cringed, and Blaise dared a full step backward. "*Lea'dl*, do you think I *fear*? I am Tlar! I am leiil! The city holds firm in my hand, no matter how much Picyt shakes the Bban'n to his bidding. He does not rule the Tlar'jen. *I* rule! And I shall continue to rule as long as the Jewels remain untouched."

Abruptly he strode toward Blaise, who froze in alarm. "You . . . *n'ka*," he said, breathless after his outburst. "Before you die, answer this. What meant your people by sending you to Ruantl? Do others follow? Is invasion planned? Did Picyt, Lli curse his blood, summon your kind?"

Blaise shook his head. "No. I came here because I am an outlaw among my own—"

The Tlar leiil shot out his long arm with unexpected quickness and ripped off Blaise's mask.

"So," said the Tlar leiil, tossing the mask out over the ledge and backing away so that he was clear of the aim of Aabrm's rod. "This is not much for Picyt to send against us." He laughed, a mocking, hollow sound through the bronze mask, which glittered brightly in the sunlight. "Hear me, you of the striped eyes. I have taken your mask and exposed you to the bite of the Outerlands. Thus you stand dishonored and thus I send you to the shadow land of Merdarai, where your soul may rot unclaimed for all time. Pray to Anthi, or to whatever god you serve, *n'ka*, for this minute is your last." He lowered his knife and turned away. "Kill the *n'ka*, Aabrm," he said coldly, "and let us go. I weary of this game."

Aabrm aimed the rod, and Blaise tensed, gathering himself to dodge. He had only a split second; he'd better make it count. Then from the corner of his eye he saw the Tlar leiil's arm blur, hurling the jeweled knife straight at him. With an oath Blaise dived to the ground. The knife missed him, ripping through his cloak, but it forced him to throw himself into Aabrm's fire. The blue bolt crackled across the cave, frying the air, and slammed into his thigh like a hammer blow, knocking him out over the ledge.

He fell in terror, flailing his arms uselessly. Blinded by the white haze of agony and certain that his leg had been blasted off, he landed on the rocky slope below the cave with a jolt that knocked the breath from him and tumbled him down faster and faster in a whirl of dust, tangled limbs, and pain until he came up hard against the base of a boulder. Nearly suffocated with dust, he lay there facedown, half dead, his cloak tangled about his head, while dislodged pebbles continued to rain down on him in a shower of pelting blows. Exposed, helpless, he waited for Aabrm to finish him off, certain that this time was indeed the end of him. But no further attack came. He heard nothing but the rasping sigh of desert wind.

After a few minutes Blaise managed to lift himself out of the dust enough to cough with a violence that seemed to finish collapsing his tortured chest. Slowly he moved a shaking hand down to his thigh to feel for the stump.

Instead his trembling fingers touched solid flesh. He lifted his head and twisted around to look back at his leg. Yes, it was there, mangled, blackened, but *there*. He stared, reluctant to believe. Then, with a faint sob of relief, he shut his eyes and fell back into the dirt.

•

Chapter 4

The rings of the day had been shattered, permitting avenues for rage and frustration. Picyt n'Kkanthor dl'Mura-an, noble servant to the goddess Anthi, strode rapidly along the lower corridors, his cloak billowing out behind him. With an effort he kept his expression set in rigid lines of serenity, striving to refocus his rings of order. But it was impossible, even for his degree of attainment. His mind kept slipping ahead to anger and the consuming worry of bringing the *n'dl* here. It was dangerous, especially in his own personal transport, for should the Tlar'jen capture the vessel and find her within . . .

The rings shattered again, so violently this time that he was forced to pause in mid-step and shut his eyes to regain personal control. After building the first ring of inner awareness, he opened his eyes and hastened on. Time had run out on his carefully laid plans, nurtured all these years only to be extingushed at the verge of success. He clenched a fist hidden within the wide sweep of his sleeve as he hurried down a spiral of steps and on through a door opened for him by bowing Henan slaves clad in belted tabards of brown leather. Halting breathless on the balcony overlooking the cavernous transport bay, he placed that clenched fist on the railing, waiting alone, eyes slitted and bleak as he watched the bay doors creak open to admit the dull, squat craft that served as his personal vehicle. It came in on pulsing jets of air, cut to landing jets with a lurch that made Picyt wince, and rested its armored belly on the blackened bay floor with a final echoing whine.

At once technicians ran out in a blur of activity, swarming the transport with cloths to whisk away all traces of the corrosive black sand. The hatch swung open and up like an unfurled wing. After a pause two figures in the masked, black uniforms of the Bban'jen came down the steps. Picyt released a pent-up sigh, obliged to once more shut his eyes in order to reestablish inner control. A desire for *yde* stirred within him, but he shoved it away impatiently. Tuult has come, he thought with relief that beat close upon the third level of intensity. And Tuult had brought the *n'dl*. All was not entirely lost.

Opening his eyes, Picyt leaned forward slightly and watched the tall Bban bring her along. Burning disappointment rose within him like a sickness of the stomach. It should have been the *n'ka*. Lea's blight upon Hihuan! Had the fool not meddled . . .

"Noble Picyt, I have come." Tuult's rough-edged voice rang out. He stiffened to attention at the head of the steps leading to the balcony and lifted one fist in salute. His other hand remained clamped on the arm of the prisoner, and Picyt detected the faint scent of Bban musk.

But despite his bitterness Picyt could not help looking upon Tuult with a surge of pride. He had come so far, this Bban. He was one of the few who gave Picyt hope even in the bleakest hours. The fact that he had crossed the Outerlands in a transport, rather than astride the unwilling back of a chaka, and had brought the *n'dl* unharmed and protected, in a jen uniform, which no female was permitted to wear, spoke of great progress. Looking upon the Bban with truth, Picyt saw that Tuult's pride was deeply wounded by the loss of the *n'ka*. Picyt expelled a breath. Good; for when a Bban warrior lost pride he lost honor, and for that he would fight to the blood against Hihuan.

Picyt raised his head high. "You have come, Pon Tuult dar J'agan."

"The *n'dl* is brought, revered noble."

"Yes," replied Picyt, glancing from the masked glow of Tuult's scarlet eyes to her motionless figure. The mask and cloak hid none of her hostility. Picyt's gaze narrowed as he gently extended his senses over her. Ah, she feared, but with the fear of a cornered animal. She could prove dangerous.

"Noble?" Tuult hesitated, his mask glinting as the light over the balcony glanced off a worn place on its surface. "The *n'ka* is not found. The citadel has been searched and beyond. On my blood, I—"

"No." Picyt lifted his hand in placation. "Do not make the oath, Tuult. If Leiil Hihuan has stolen the *n'ka* by means of the seizert, then he could be anywhere." Picyt allowed a sigh to escape him. "And we may be certain that his life has been spared."

Tuult bowed, raising his free hand to his mask. "I am shamed, revered noble."

"But we have the *n'dl*," said Picyt, resolutely shoving aside disappointment. "She will serve us."

"A woman of no caste!" Tuult swung out his hand in a gesture of contempt, only to drop it abruptly as Picyt's unmasked gaze hardened. The Bban bowed. "As my noble commands."

"Yes, and I command that she be not despised, pon!" snapped Picyt. He turned away, ready to leave the balcony. "Bring her to my chamber of council. And tell your men to continue the search across the wastes for the *n'ka*."

"But if his blood is spread upon the sands—" Tuult questioned.

"Search," said Picyt, setting aside his own doubts. "The *n'ka* is no common man. Perhaps Anthi has granted him favor of life." He started for the private steps. "Search."

"As my noble wishes," said Tuult's gruff voice as the door shut behind Picyt.

He moved quickly, and reached his private apartments minutes later. Drawing in a deep breath of warmed air, Picyt tossed off his long cloak with its stiff high collar of rank. The walls of his bedchamber circled around him, lined with the colorful woven litanies of the goddess. Footed braziers of glowing coals gave off heat, and he warmed his hands at one, wriggling his long fingers to shake off the chill. How he dreaded the coming season. A faint, melodious chime sounded, and he summoned a smile for his servant Jutuu, who entered softly on his old crippled feet with a goblet of scented wine.

"Noble," he intoned quietly, kneeling before Picyt, the goblet tendered forth reverently in his knobbed hands. "May this please you."

"I am well pleased," said Picyt, and took the cup to sip its contents appreciatively, letting them soothe his weary soul. It had been a long day since he had risen at dawn for worship, and the meeting Basai had insisted upon to discuss the increasing difficulties in collecting taxes in sector five had prevented Picyt's noonday meal from being served. Once again he put aside his anger over the theft of the *n'ka*. He must not hope for the man's recovery. He must not depend upon it. Another catalyst would somehow be found.

For a moment Picyt luxuriated in the comfort of his surroundings and the small pleasures he cherished. How good it was to sit by a glowing fire, soothed by wine steeped in spices and the gleam of firelight upon the gilded scroll covers of his private library. Anthi's benevolent eye watched over him from one curved wall, and here was Jutuu to fit his feet into warm fur-lined slippers. Picyt sighed and closed his eyes, letting the rings slip away.

But no. Time shortened. He could not give way to pleasure now when Hihuan's hand might reach forth to smash the remainder of his plans.

Finishing off the wine, Picyt stood up and handed the empty goblet back to Jutuu. "I have audience. Prepare me."

The old servant scurried away in silence to throw open a golden chest and draw forth Picyt's stole of office, the rich blue fabric rippling in his gnarled hands as the firelight brought it to life. He laid the folds across Picyt's white-robed shoulders, his twisted fingers arranging the pleats with great exactitude over Picyt's left arm so that they draped correctly. A corner of Picyt's mind moved away from the gnawing problems caused by a lifetime of secretly arranging revolt against the Tlar leiil of Ruantl to consider the worn flesh stretched so tautly over Jutuu's ribs and hip bones. The leather, knee-length tabard of servitude that he wore was fastened at the throat by the blue collar of Picyt's ownership and belted at the middle, leaving the sides bare from shoulder downward. It was a useful garment, worn by all servants of third caste, because it allowed complete freedom of movement. But it also permitted any critical eye to see the pallid thinness and deterioration of age. Picyt frowned. It did his station dishonor to keep a slave of such condition.

"You must eat more, Jutuu," he said a bit sharply. "Tell the garners I wish your rations increased. From my private store if necessary."

Jutuu bowed deeply, his cold dry fingers falling away from

Picyt's arm. "Whatever pleases you, noble, shall be done."

Regretting his sharpness, Picyt nodded and adjusted his inner rings to circles of wholeness and patience. He left his apartments, this time choosing one of the middle corridors. His young secretary, Uble, appeared almost at once at his side, following him one pace back in courtesy.

"Revered noble, a delegation from the merchants of Spandeen—"

Picyt lifted his hand to silence him and strode on. The middle corridors were very long, and busy at this hour with the comings and goings of priests and shaven neophytes. Conscious of his rank as First Honored of Anthi and most noble *ka* of the House of Kkanthor, he walked erect, giving serene response to acknowledgments of respect, with his blue stole of office brushing gently against the hem of his long white robe. Within, impatience and ever-mounting anger battled against the rings he had formed to contain them, rings of calmness and clear thought and purpose. The catharsis of emotion could be performed later. Now he must permit nothing to interfere with questioning of the *n'dl*. If she indeed possessed knowledge of the working of the old technology, he must gain it swiftly before Hihuan chose to strike in earnest.

Reaching the chamber of council, he motioned for Uble to await him at the door.

Uble's handsome young face creased at the dismissal. "But, revered noble, this matter—"

"It will wait, Priest Uble," said Picyt with a wearied look of censure. He watched dark copper stain Uble's cheeks and added firmly, "The Spandeen will wait."

"Then, revered noble," said Uble with a stubbornness that displeased Picyt, "have I permission to conduct them to an audience with Noble Basai?"

Picyt's lips thinned, and only long-mastered emotional discipline enabled him to keep his temper. "It does not please me to award you permission."

"But—"

"Chi'ka!" snapped Picyt, shocking Uble to silence with his use of the fierce Bban term. With a stern look at the chastened priest, Picyt placed his fingertips on the door panel and stepped forward as it slid silently aside.

Tuult stood beside the doorway, booted feet braced and

arms crossed over his chest in the patient stance of the Bban warrior on guard. He raised his fist in a salute as Picyt passed him, then returned to grim immobility once more. Picyt came partway into the room and paused to watch the *n'dl*, who paced restlessly along the opposite side of the room. For a moment Picyt wondered if he should send Tuult out. No, he decided with a deep intake of breath. She could not be trusted. Tuult must stay, and hear, and learn the weight of new responsibilities of knowledge.

Drawing out the medallion of tongues, Picyt held it up, letting it spin from its silken-looking white cord. The movement caught her eye, and at once she halted. Abruptly she tugged off her mask and flung it down on the council table, scratching the surface of the rare orad wood. Such disregard for property caused Picyt's great displeasure. The *n'dl*'s square face, with its odd flat cheekbones and prominent nose, blazed scarlet with defiance. He met her hostile gaze levelly and found himself repulsed by her peculiar eyes, which were colored only in the center and ringed with the opaque white of blindness.

For a long moment of tense silence he permitted her to stare boldly at him in return, accepting this assault to his personal honor as a noble, in exchange for the chance to look upon her with truth. But he was unable to clear away the cloudiness of hostility, anger, and fear raging within her for a deeper sight before her gaze flickered uneasily and she made a restless gesture of repudiation.

Startled by her ability—however undeveloped—to sense a look of truth, Picyt withdrew it.

She glared at him. "Who are you?" she demanded loudly, shattering the stillness of the room. "And why have I been brought here? Where is Major Omari?"

Tuult growled softly behind his mask, clicking his jaw.

Picyt frowned. "Anger does not serve you," he replied, fascinated as always by the chance to observe the working of his medallion. They had become objects of great scarcity, and even as he spoke he knew a pang over the loss of the one given to the *n'ka*.

"My questions are valid," she snapped, gloved hands on her hips in a manner highly unbecoming to a *dl*, noncaste or not. "Answer them if you expect me to answer yours."

Her show of spirit pleased him. He moved to the nearest of the four council chairs and sat down, draping his stole gracefully over the arm.

"Very well," he said, laying the medallion on the table between them and allowing the silken cord to dangle off the edge. "I am Picyt, most noble of the House of Kkanthor." Her eyes widened with remembrance, and he smiled. "Yes, we have met once before. You have been brought here because the citadel is no longer a safe holding for you. Here, chances of detection are less."

The hardness of her expression did not waver. "And where is Omari? What has happened to him?"

He read not concern but frustration within her. Puzzled by this, he said slowly, "He has been abducted by agents of Leiil Hihuan. The Tlar leiil is desperate to maintain his throne, even at the cost of mental and cultural stagnation for an entire people!" His rings shattered, and he slammed a hand down on the chair arm. "Once, *n'dl*, we had all things. In the far past Ruantl was a colony planet, ruled by a leiil who was indeed *Tlar*. Under the dynasties of Asan, Rim, and Vauzier, the upper continent of Ruantl was settled, Altian built, and the Bban'n tamed. But the heirs of Vauzier died of the bite of the black sun, as did many others. No more of the golden race came to live here, and we were left, dwindling under the lesser rule of lesser men. And knowledge of the ways of machines—"

"Yes, your problem is quite apparent," she said arrogantly, breaking in on his careful blend of lie and truth without compunction. "I have studied the histories of declining civilizations. They are usually marked by lax standards, a decrease in the birthrate of the upper class, and a decay of all technological ability. Judging by the faulty performance of that engine that flew me here today, you shouldn't use it again until it's been thoroughly overhauled. Now, Picyt—"

There came the hiss of blade upon leather and the rising stench of Bban musk. Picyt corrected her swiftly. "Address me as Noble Picyt, *n'dl*, and with suitable respect in your tone, or Tuult will enforce my honor."

She frowned, looking toward the Bban crouching with drawn jen-knife.

Picyt saw her rising protest and added quickly, "It is a thing that is done. I do not control it."

"Then Omari was correct," she said half to herself, her gaze narrowing. "The guard *did* attack him just because he was weak." She moved her gaze to Picyt and blinked. "You said the Bban were *tamed*? Aren't they—"

"Your questions waste time," broke in Picyt sharply, too well aware of Tuult's presence. Were his level of *yde* higher, he could control the Bban without difficulty, but he had taken none since that morning. He sighed. "Heed me now, *n'dl*—"

"My name is Saunders," she said sharply. Tuult took a quick step forward and raised the knife. "Noble Picyt," she conceded, inclining her head slightly. "The term *n'dl* is not translated to me."

"It means you are not a daughter of Ruantl," said Picyt, watching Tuult straighten. He sighed faintly. "It means also that you are apart from caste."

"I do not wish to be called by it," she said, head high. "Now, Noble Picyt, where is Omari?"

His lips tightened. Annoyance swept through his rings of inner wholeness. Sternly he said, "You will go to the lower levels, to work there among my technicians and to train them. You will also explain the functions of what we have salvaged from your space transport."

Undaunted by him or his position, she replied, "And if I do not . . . noble?"

He snorted, displeased now with her boldness as much as by the way she measured him in a warrior's way of challenge. *Lea'dl*, what sort of females were raised on other worlds? This one was of neither type he knew.

He said curtly, "It is not desired to make you a prisoner, Saunders. But if you do not serve willingly, then it is always possible that you may fall into the hands of the Tlar leiil's agents. They will find no use for you, and on Ruantl what is without use is discarded."

There was a pause. Then Saunders lifted her striped eyes to his. "Understood, Noble Picyt," she said, but not submissively.

It was enough. With an outward serenity he did not feel, Picyt rose from his chair, already directing his mind toward other matters. The merchants of the Spandeen would not be happy at this delay; but then, they were always difficult. And he should have eaten. Food would have held off the need for *yde*.

But she was not done. "Noble Picyt," she said, "just how valuable are we, Omari and I, to you?"

Startled, he evaded the question, his gaze going to the eye of Anthi watching from the wall. "The *n'ka* is dead."

"I don't believe that," she said, shifting her weight from one foot to the other. "If this Hihuan you spoke of intended only to kill Omari, then he would not have gone to the trouble of having him abducted from the citadel. A knife in the back would have served the purpose much more efficiently."

Silence hung over the room while Picyt considered the shame of being matched in mind by this female.

At last he said, "It is possible, yes. Jen cohorts continue to search the wastes in hopes that it pleased the Tlar leiil to strand him there. And if that is so," he added grimly, "then the *n'ka* Omari will not live long. Death comes swiftly in the Outerlands."

"Why?" she persisted. "What are the specific dangers? Physical ones? Omari can handle those. Or do you refer to the X rays emitted by your black sun? Are they strong enough to cause radiation poisoning? That *is* partly why these heavy cloaks and masks are worn, isn't it? And why there is so much lead content in your metal alloys?"

In spite of knowing her to be a *n'dl*, and one of technological advancement, Picyt was astonished by the casual manner in which she spoke of the great blight of Ruantl. No one could have told her these things, for the Bban'n cared nothing for science or machinery. Indeed, her mind was far more clever than he had at first thought. She must be watched with great care.

But for the sake of curiosity he chose to counter her sharp questions with one of his own, even as an inward stirring of restlessness threatened the order of his rings. He gazed fully into her peculiar eyes and asked, "How have you determined the composition of our metals without instruments?"

She smiled and raised her head proudly. Fine wisps of red hair floated back from her face. "I was born and bred in the mining colonies. I could grade mineral deposits even before I learned to read computer codings. Now, back to my question concerning Omari's chances of survival out there. What are they?"

Picyt swept out his hand, frowning slightly as the need for

yde twisted within his veins, becoming impatience, craving, *hunger*. He could not remain here much longer. "I . . . he may not be in the Outerlands. He may be here, somewhere within the city."

She was plainly irritated by his response. "I see you do not intend to give me a straight answer. Very well. At least, if he is out in the desert, he has a jen uniform for protection."

"Why . . ." With effort Picyt wrenched his straying gaze away from the eye of Anthi. "Yours is not concern for his life, but . . ." Conscious that he must never appear hesitant or uncertain, Picyt fought back the desire for *yde* now skittering through his veins, mentally cursing it with loathing, and tried to look upon her with truth, only to clench his fist hard within his sleeve as truth did not form. *Yde*-hunger blinded him, and again he cursed it. Had the measure lasted but a few minutes longer . . .

"I'll be plain," she said while he looked grimly at her through a haze of impatience. "I'll cooperate with what you want in exchange for Omari, if he's found alive, and also I want a spaceship when we're through."

The hunger abruptly died, driven down by surprise. He stared at her, seeking to reform his rings of wholeness, not certain he had heard correctly.

"And you needn't deny you have old ships, noble," she continued before he could gather himself enough to speak. "I saw them along the edge of the bay we landed in. With repair and some parts salvaged from what's left of the *Forerunner*," she said grimly, "I think we could get off-world." She raised her chin as his eyes widened. "Major Omari is accused of serious crimes. It is my duty to return him for trial and imprisonment. If I help you and a ship can be overhauled sufficiently to withstand the stress of leaving this system, then I intend to carry out my duty." Her striped eyes held his. "Do we have a deal, Noble Picyt?"

He blinked, marveling fuzzily at how she spoke of spaceflight as the Tlar-spoke of going to another street within Altian. For a moment he knew a longing to go with her, to see the wonders of the rest of the universe, to see those things once again of which the neophytes chanted in the litanies of history. He opened his mouth, giddy with temptation. But the sight of Anthi's baleful eye upon the wall sobered him. *Yde*, he thought, clutching at his faculties. He must have *yde* before he lost all wholeness and was left in shame.

"Yes . . ." By supreme effort he managed to form one tiny ring as fragile as his own ebbing control. But it gave him enough strength to face her with a semblance of outward calm. "It pleases me to agree to your words, *n'dl*." He caught himself as her eyes narrowed. "Saunders. But if we do not find the *n'ka*? I warn you the chances are small."

She nodded her head in a gesture he did not comprehend. "Understood," she said, something of a smile playing upon her thin, colorless lips now. The odd white-striped eyes gleamed. "But I think you'll find him, noble. He's equally as skilled and trained as I. And two of us would help your cause tremendously."

Clutching at the last of his strength, Picyt gestured to Tuult, who strode forward at once to seize the arm of the *n'dl*. She stiffened, then with a glare grabbed up her mask and allowed the Bban to lead her out. As soon as the door closed behind them, Picyt staggered across the room, knocking a chair out of place, nearly falling over it. With a grunt he caught himself, heedless of the stole of office that slipped from his shoulders. He stumbled on, forcing each step, and barely caught himself on the wall. The light chill of the room intensified as his veins contracted. Nearly blind, and unable to focus his rings, which swirled about in dizzying fragments, he slid partway down the wall and groped with fumbling wooden fingers until he touched the edge of the huge silver medallion that represented the eye of Anthi. Running his fingertips rapidly over the intricate design, he found the place at last and pressed it. With a faint click the metal warmed beneath his touch until his arm tensed to draw his fingers back from the heat. But by then his flesh was melded with metal. Energy, blue and raw, shot through his shriveled veins, and with a roar that sang through his throbbing head, Anthi spoke to him with words too terrible for anything but the spirit to hear. The room spun and darkened. Then the blue fire spread to his brain, burning away all other things until only the vision of the stark grandeur of the Outerlands remained within him. He saw the black banners of the Bban'jen lift over the desert ridges, and wave after wave of the Bban tribe poured forth. He saw Altian aglitter like a vast carved gem in the darkness. And at last he saw the sacred Jewels of M'thra, sworn to his safekeeping as they lay glowing with faint golden radiance in the black depths of their cavern.

He trembled, the blue fire bursting through his veins and the vision unbearably clear in his head. The words of prayer quavered out from his soul.

He lifted forth his question to the goddess, weakening beneath the sweep of her power yet desperate to have his answer. *Did the* n'ka *live? Would he be found*? So much might rest upon this stranger from another world. So much. . . . Anthi! he cried from his heart, anguished by fear as terrible blackness struck away the vision. For an instant he was left in a horrible void, abandoned and lost. Then the fire blazed through him again like a swordthrust. Once again a vision came to him, and it was the dark, guarded caverns of M'thra, where the long slim capsules of crystal lay glowing faintly in the silence of age and dust.

"Asan," said Anthi.

Frightened of the insistence of that vision, Picyt shrank from Anthi's command, knowing he could never raise the mighty Asan himself. Someone else, perhaps . . . The *n'ka*? he asked with hope, and again blackness buffeted him.

Abruptly the fire cooled, and thc blackness faded, releasing him. The eye of Anthi stared cold and silent once more. With an unsteady hand Picyt fumbled within a pocket in his sleeve and drew out a small vial of fine blue powder. He struggled for a moment with the stopper, but at last unsealed it and with both shaking hands lifted it to his lips.

The *yde* left a slightly acrid aftertaste in his parched mouth. He coughed, rubbing his lips with the back of his hand as he put away the emptied vial. Strength returned with a surge to his trembling limbs, and almost on their own the rings began forming. He opened his eyes, seeking to focus them upon the overturned chair, and finally succeeded.

But the rings of composure were false, bolstered by the strength of *yde*. Deep within the shrinking corners of his soul lurked the horror of Anthi's answer. This was not the first time the vision of the Jewels of M'thra had been thrust on him when he questioned Anthi for guidance. And he could not face the prospect of raising the Jewels himself. No, in all else he served the goddess. But not in this.

With a sigh he stood, his fingertips pressed together to enlarge the ring of composure, smoothing his rebellion away to a hidden place within his mind. The flush of *yde* still swelled his veins. Concerned with the violence of this attack, he knew it would be necessary very soon to purge himself of the drug so that he might again sustain himself on only a few grains. He dared not encourage worse attacks. Drawing himself erect, Picyt set up the chair and replaced the stole of office across his shoulders. Yes, he must purge soon, but not—and he brushed away that tiny glimmer of fear at the chance he took—*not* as long as he had Saunders here and Leiil Hihuan knew of it. Losing her as he had lost the *n'ka* Omari could not be permitted, not if Ruantl was to survive and the Bban to fit themselves to the true purpose. Risk to his own survival must be taken. He dared do nothing less.

Perhaps it was the *yde*, perhaps the curiosity about how well the *n'dl* would work with his technicians, perhaps the lingering uneasiness over the communication with Anthi, or perhaps all of them combined to distract him during the lengthy meeting with the representatives of the Spandeen merchants, so that in the end they went away dissatisfied, and Noble Basai dared frown at him in rebuke.

"We dare not offend them, revered noble," he said, his thin, shrill voice piercing over the faint sounds of neophyte chanting coming from the hall of worship. "They have power within Altian, and it is to our profit to ally ourselves with them. Revered noble—"

Lifting his hand impatiently, Picyt stood up. "You sound like one of the merchants, Basai," he said, gesturing at Basai's quick gobble of protest. "No, do not offend yourself. I understand the need of their use."

"I think you do not, my noble," said Basai quickly. "They have *come*—"

Picyt quelled him with a sharp glance. "Yes, they came, Basai, but only to make petty judgments as to how much they dare play us against the palace. I do not intend to make Kkanthor their toy." Basai sniffed and began tapping his pudgy fingers on the council table. Picyt continued: "When they are indeed ready to cooperate with us, then be assured my attention will be upon them. Until then—"

"Forgive me, revered noble, but I think your attention is too much upon these strange intruders." Basai swept out his hand, his slitted green eyes hard upon Picyt. "What can one female do to change our world? *Merdarai*, all know that the

Bban'n are far from ready for what you would thrust them into! More time—"

"No!" Picyt turned on him furiously, his inner rings breaking into spears of anger. "The Bban tribes are in ferment. Are you content to wait until Anthi's hand can hold them no longer? For with our guidance or in their own violence they will soon come down upon Altian. The season is upon us, and we all know that a starving, freezing Bban is the most dangerous of all creatures. I know what I do, Noble Basai! Grant me that." With a curt gesture Picyt strode out, leaving Basai fuming behind him.

Fool, Picyt thought, belatedly composing his features into a less harsh expression after meeting several startled priests in the public corridors. *Complacent, stupid fool*!

The next day saw him in no better humor. No word had yet come from Pon Tuult, and Picyt's last glimmers of hope died. Nor did he trust Hihuan, expecting the Tlar leiil to do more against him than merely steal away the *n'ka*. Hihuan's spies lurked not only among the Bban'n, but even in the House of Kkanthor itself, necessitating a constant monitoring of all within. What next would he do?

Frowning, Picyt ceased these worried thoughts, listening to his voice glide on, instructing his class of neophytes in the advanced *sonthi* methods of inner control. These boys were nearly ready for induction into full priesthood. He paused in speaking to study every face as they sat in still obedience, their eyes shut, breathing in trained unison. Their hearts almost beat as one. Ever sensitive, ever in control, Picyt placed his fingertips together, but held back from looking upon each with truth, as was his custom at this hour. One heart, one set of lungs was *not* in unison.

He became instantly suspicious. In the younger classes such a thing was commonplace, but it should not occur here. He extended his sensitivity, *yde* enhanced and powerful, over the room, probing gently. No, the ring was not complete. One had not joined it. With a sharp intake of breath, Picyt withdrew into himself and stood before them in the midst of the circular pale-walled chamber, a brazier of coals at his back and the eye of Anthi over them all.

The sense of danger, now confirmed, heightened within him, locking his own rings into iron bands of defense. But still, although no Kkanthor-ka was ever wholly free of the threat of assassination, the nearness of this trap shook him. He drew in a slow, deep breath, his hands tensed within his sleeves, and considered how, in his distraction over so many problems, he had come close to entering the thoughts of the one who waited now with intent of murder rather than of submission. His gaze moved slowly across each somnolent face as the neophytes knelt, calmed for his touch. Who was it? Which expressionless face hid Hihuan's hireling?

Now that the first start of fear was fading, anger rose unchecked in its stead. Picyt studied them, these boys who served him so eagerly by struggling to discipline their youth and vigor to Anthi's stern rule. He loved them as his own sons. But one was a traitor.

Which?

The question seared him like a brand. He knew Hihuan's other spies within his domain. Carefully he had them monitored, giving them sufficient leeway to betray themselves. But no one of this class had been suspected. To discover such a betrayal now was like a stab to the heart.

Was it Braal? Aar? Riidul? Was it . . . and his breath faltered in anguish at the thought . . . was it Oliir, the only Bban of his students, his special protégé for whom he had such hopes? He frowned at the boy, barely able to hold back his desire to strike out as he studied those repulsive skeletal features so shyly revealed in the maskless confines of the House. Then Aar stirred restlessly, and Picyt turned his gaze to the slim, high-caste youth.

He must decide now, before the dark one suspected discovery.

Quickly Picyt extended his senses into a ring surrounding the boys, concealing his horror and fury from them behind a haze of false serenity. Once they took their first *yde*, tonight, this deception would no longer succeed with them. He must act now.

Calmness . . . submission . . . oneness. . . . His presence encircled them, soothing them back into perfect unison as if he were unaware of the one upon the fringes of the circle. Regulating his breathing to theirs, taking control of even that part of them, Picyt stepped silently back to the curving wall, where the eye of Anthi watched. He shut his eyes and looked upon Aar with truth, feeling the boy jerk with that brief spurt of rebellion he had not yet learned to tame. Relaxing, Picyt shared himself with the boy for a moment, smiling within as Aar clung to him. Then he withdrew and looked upon gentle Braal, who was not the dark one either.

That left Riidul and Oliir. Picyt hesitated, the grief twisting through his anger. Oliir, being Bban, was the perfect target of Aabrm's briberies. And it was certain no one of the palace wished any Bban to rise beyond the place of warrior and slave. But Oliir had not released his musk. Either he had learned more of the *sonthi* teachings than even Picyt suspected, or else he was innocent.

Slowly, barely able to keep his emotions from the serenity of the rings, Picyt steeled himself and reached out a hand to place his fingertips lightly upon the edge of the medallion. Then with extreme care he faced the risk and looked upon Oliir, opening himself to the sharing. Now the attack would come. But Oliir met him gladly, with the shyness that had become so endearing, and in his relief Picyt nearly overwhelmed the young Bban with his feelings. He withdrew abruptly, leaving Oliir to sway at the violence of that departure. With a sudden blast of fury Picyt shattered the rings holding all the boys.

With a hoarse cry Riidul jumped to his feet and rushed forward, his hand at his belt. Picyt's fingers pressed the eye of Anthi, flesh melding with fiery metal as the blue fire smoked forth through him, blazing from his eyes, until his entire form was consumed. His mouth opened and he uttered two words—Riidul's name and another so terrible that it shook the room. Riidul screamed, clapping his hands to his ears, then stiffened as the blue fire crackled out from Picyt's pointing finger to engulf him. For an instant the room hung frozen, the other boys glazed with fear as they stared, cringing from Riidul's writhing body held in the awesome blue fire.

Black things, like shaped, monstrous obscenitites, rushed at Picyt's mind, but the fire of Anthi consumed them all.

Then with a final horrible scream Riidul crumpled to the floor, his outflung hand spilling an inkpot that spread out a slow purple stain across the woven mats. Picyt dropped his hand, and the fire ceased, leaving him standing tall and fierce, a blue haze still clouding his sight. Inside, his soul curled, sickened by the sight before him. The room would have to be cleaned of the taint.

The room was silent save for the panicked gasps of the three remaining students. Slowly they turned away from Riidul's smoking corpse to stare up at Picyt. Aar clutched his chest as though it hurt him, but his eyes remained fixed on Picyt. As the fear and shock faded from his gaze, awe replaced it, stirring with the gleam of worship.

Pleased, Picyt looked away, staring at the others, who huddled, stricken. For a minute longer the power of Anthi sang through his veins; then it faded sufficiently for him to be able to see normally again and to speak. He heard the sound of running footsteps in the corridor outside and Uble's voice lifted in anxious query.

"Riidul was a traitor to the House," said Picyt, and Anthi still thundered sufficiently in his voice to make the boys bow hurriedly. "Go. Purify yourselves, and think on this shame until you have mastered it. The ceremony will still be at the last hour." He lifted two fingers in dismissal, and as one Aar and Braal fled, flinging open the door to dart out past the alarmed Uble. Oliir lingered, his jaw clicking nervously as though he wished to question Picyt. Then he lowered his hairless head and scurried out after the others.

Uble, his youthful self-assurance for once shaken, clutched his blue robes and stared aghast at the body. "My noble!" he exclaimed. "We all heard the great voice of Anthi! What—"

Others were coming in a babble of disorder, Basai's shrill voice above the rest.

Great weariness struck Picyt, and he swayed, frowning as he felt within his sleeve pocket for a vial of *yde*. "Cover him," he said shortly, stepping heavily down from the dais. "He was an assassin and will be disposed of without honor or word to his family. Let the matter be ended." At the door Picyt paused, anger still raging beneath his heart. That Hihuan would dare strike at *him* . . .

"What has happened?" demanded Basai, panting at the door with his robes drawn up in one hand. A crowd was forming behind him. "Revered noble . . ." His voice trailed off with a squeak as he looked past Picyt to a white-faced Uble, who was spreading his cloak over the body. "Great Anthi!"

Picyt looked at him bleakly, in no mood to master himself for further questions. "Basai, inform the palace that it pleases me to seek audience at once with the Tlar leiil."

Collecting himself, Basai opened his mouth, then hastily bowed low at the expression in Picyt's eyes. "At—at once, Noble Picyt!"

With a gesture Picyt summoned his strength and pushed himself out into the corridor, moving through the crowd of curious and alarmed priests without a glance at anyone. He heard their murmurs, but he gave no notice to any; therefore, none could dare question him. It had been many seasons indeed since he had been forced to use the power of Anthi so violently. But let them look. Let them learn; let them fear.

Reaching his private apartments at last, Picyt drew out the vial with shaking fingers and swallowed its bitter, powdery contents with a grimace before striking the chime that summoned Jutuu. By the time the elderly servant appeared, bowing reverently, the *yde* had permitted Picyt to compose himself enough to look no more than mildly distressed. Letting the stole of office slip to the floor, he seated himself unsteadily near a warm brazier and closed his eyes, giving way to exhaustion and grief and all the other pent-up emotions of the past few days.

"*Yde*, Jutuu," he said quietly, bringing up his hand to cover his aching eyes. When he closed them, he could still see a faint blue glare. "Bring it in a goblet, much spiced."

A pause followed his command. Then Jutuu's soft voice said worriedly, "It has great potency in the liquid, my noble. Let me bring you a small dish of the pow—"

"I have said what pleases me!" said Picyt sharply. He glared at the old man. "Riidul is dead. One of my most promising students, lost on the eve of service, to that . . ." He twisted his lips, but he held back the word. He sighed as his gaze darkened. "A goblet of *yde*, Jutuu. This once will not overwhelm me."

"I obey, my noble." Jutuu hobbled away, and not until he was out of the room did Picyt draw out the empty vial to smash the thin glass between his fingers and sprinkle the tiny shards over the singing coals in the brazier, where with a faint burst of thin blue flame they melted away.

Chapter 5

Three days passed before the Tlar leiil permitted Picyt an audience, impatient days that saw the annual rising of the four full moons and subsequent nights of violence and riot within Altian. Henan brigands roamed the streets, falling on victims with a boldness increased by the advent of season. Tension hung in the air as clouds gathered in rolling purple masses overhead, struck now and then by a piercing ray of sunlight that stained them bloody. Omens of such evil were counted. Business in the marketplace rose to a frenzy, with theft and chaos rampant. Food vendors were set upon and robbed of their precious wares. Jen patrols, in a grim determination to keep order, blocked off streets leading into the avenues of the high-castes. Few ranking citizens dared venture forth from the walled protection of their villas, save to join heavily guarded processions to the temples of Lea, taker of men's souls, and Anthi, who was the guardian of life.

Even within the House of Kkanthor, where the evil days of season were understood as natural disturbances caused by the shifting orbit of the black sun around the powerful yellow one, order was not easily held, and serenity seemed lost forever.

Wrapped in a long blue mantle, Picyt stood atop the tower of his domain, buffeted by the harsh wind that plucked at his clothes and threatened to rip away his mask. Within the protection his face was carved in grim lines as he looked out over the city below him, watching the Henan beggars clinging piteously to the barred gates of Kkanthor as other citizens struggled along the streets with their bodies bent nearly double against the wind. Picyt lifted his eyes to the ugly purple clouds spreading across the sky. The wind screamed about him, splattering a handful of raindrops across the tower with savage force. Picyt winced beneath the sting as it pelted against his back, and behind him he heard faint gasps from Uble. Still he lingered out in the elements, his burning gaze always returning to the north, where at the end of a broad avenue of graceful villas sprawled the vast palace of the Tlar leiil. Few lights shone there despite the deepening darkness beneath the storm. Picyt smiled slightly to himself. How Hihuan and his pompous court must be cursing Kkanthor now for this delay in raising the extra shields!

Let him curse! The city would not be sealed yet.

Lightning crackled across the turbulent sky in a veined network of blue-white energy, and almost simultaneously thunder boomed after it with volume enough to shake the tower beneath Picyt's feet. Involuntarily he ducked, and a hand seized his arm out of the damp-stung twilight.

"Come away, revered noble!" shouted Uble against the wind. "We must raise the shields."

Freeing his arm, Picyt turned in scorn. "Not yet!" he shouted back, and strode inside with a swirl of his mantle.

Within the confines of the tower he unfastened his mask and tugged it free. The warmth struck his face like a gentle blow. Sighing, he sniffed gratefully the incensed air wafting up the stairwell from the lower levels. Overhead the door to the tower roof closed with a bang that was echoed by a crash of thunder. Picyt turned in irritation, then calmed himself, willing away the impatience he felt rising like a canker. Or was it yet another hungering for *yde*?

"But Noble Basai says we dare not antagonize the palace at this time. The riots—"

"We must conserve our resources," Picyt said with purposeful sharpness, lifting his hand to silence Uble's protests. "As for what Basai says . . ." Picyt swallowed and formed an inner ring to contain his anger. "You would do better, young Uble, to listen to what *I* say."

Uble, his mask held stiffly under his left elbow, paled. "Revered noble, I assure you—"

"The shields will not be raised for one early storm," said Picyt. "Regather yourself lest others be infected with your fear and know shame."

Uble frowned for a moment before docility glazed his face. He bowed low.

But this show of submission did not please Picyt. He was weary of the intrigues running between factions within the House, intrigues that too often extended outward to the palace and beyond. He looked up as thunder continued to roll overhead. Soon season would be upon them in full spate, with black devis raging across the desert wastes of the Outerlands. Storms a dozen times fiercer than this one tonight would lash out with killing rains of ice needles, destroying the crops in the fields on the fringes of the wastes, and again the people of Altian would know hunger. But their riots would mean nothing to their tyrant, Hihuan, who cared not for their plight as long as his palace lay safe beneath the protective bubble.

Picyt's eyes blazed as anger flared within him, shattering his rings of control. He turned on Uble, startling the young priest. "Do you know, *ka'n*, that for the blessing of Anthi alone I would lower all shields and shatter the bubble of safety forever!"

Uble faltered behind him on the stairs and gripped the banister hard with one gauntleted hand. "Revered Picyt!" he breathed, his eyes enormous. "Such words of treason are not safe even within our walls. Have care, I beg you. Surely," he asked querulously, "the hour of confrontation has not yet come—?"

Picyt snorted in derision. If only he had the *n'ka*, he would strike, and Merdar take the consequences. But his outburst had been sufficient loss of control for one evening. Swallowing his bitterness, he contented himself by glancing over his shoulder and replying, "It will take more than Hihuan's evil to bring down the House of Kkanthor, just as we cannot alone bring down Hihuan. Be at rest, Uble."

Gathering his mantle closer, he started down the steep spiral of stairs, the echo of their footsteps reverberating through the well. On he went past the landings with corridors leading to the chancery halls and dormitories, ignoring a faint stir of hunger. Not until he reached the lower levels did he step off the stairs, startling the brown-robed technicians in the transport bay with his unannounced appearance. Teecht came hastening forth, wiping his blackened hands with care before kneeling and lifting fingertips to his lips and forehead in a quick salute to Anthi.

"Revered noble," he said, lifting his eyes trustingly to Picyt's face, an act that was permitted to all within the House. "Do we raise the shields?"

Picyt stared at him for a moment, then said in an undertone, "Is there power?"

The man lowered his eyes as he swept out his hand palm down. "No, revered noble. But by dawn, we can—"

Picyt lifted his finger. "Not yet. The age of the machinery . . . We dare not strain it in our eagerness to avoid discomfort."

"But the palace! Leiil Hihuan and—"

Picyt turned away, his restless gaze sweeping over the cavernous expanse of the bay. It was not as well lighted as in the past. He had no intention of sharing with anyone his real purpose in holding down the shields. "Where is the *n'dl*?" he asked softly. "Does she work well?"

Teecht rose stiffly to his feet, a frown on his jowled face. "Ah, yes, revered noble. Harder than we can—"

"Revered noble!"

Startled by the interruption, Picyt turned sharply, his heart thudding in sudden expectancy. He extended his hand in permission for the tabard-clad slave to approach him.

"Your pardon, revered noble," gasped the shaven man, Henan by the look of him. Several of those standing near Picyt drew back with small gestures of disgust that normally were forbidden within the confines of the House, but Picyt was too intent upon the message to rebuke them. "A messenger from the palace awaits by the gates. The Tlar leiil has summoned your presence this hour."

Picyt's dark eyes shone, but he gave no other outward sign of satisfaction. "I come," he said, dismissing the slave, and turned to his technicians. "Has word come from the Pon Tuult?"

"None, revered noble," said Teecht.

Picyt curbed the pang of disappointment and raised one finger. "It pleases me to have full jen guard as escort. And set Oliir to watch the *n'dl*." Seeing Teecht's craggy face cloud with doubt, Picyt added, "The boy is Bban. He will not fail his honor." Tucking his mask more securely beneath his arm, Picyt left the transport bay with a faint, unreadable smile on his lips.

• • •

The storm rendered seizert foolhardy and the violence in the streets made use of a litter unsafe. Thus Picyt crossed the city in the comfort of his transport, closing his conscience to the display of ostentation at such an ill-judged time. At the protected sector of the city no one delayed his admittance, for no pon of the Tlar'jen had sufficient arrogance to dare annoy the First Honored of Anthi. Once beneath the protective bubble, the transport jetted smoothly along broad avenues, no longer buffeted by the force of high winds. Overhead the storm clawed at the bubble with jagged blue-white forks of lightning, thunder booming ominously as the darkness continuously split wide in blinding flashes of stark light.

The curtains hung back from the view window, but Picyt sat motionless, his gaze focused inward, heedless of the glimpses of villas and ornamental gardens slipping by in the darkness. No traitor stood in the guard escort tonight; the Bban'n did not shed their sworn loyalty readily, and all with him were blood-bonded to his service. Still, because Tuult was not with him this night and because the memory of Riidul's death continued to sear his heart, Picyt looked hard on them with truth until they stirred restlessly. But he found no darkness concealed in their midst. He sighed. It was one small assurance to count on as the transport paused once again, giving a slight dip as the air jets cut to landing support. Before them rose the black palace walls. The pass was presented, and still they were not admitted through the towering gates. Picyt frowned, his long fingers flexing impatiently. In the narrow aisle behind his seat the jen escort stirred with faint clickings of their long jaws.

The transport's steward, a slender ty-boy who had retained his soft mannerisms and pale gracefulness despite being retrained from the ways of the brothels, which the priests had cleared away from the temple avenue, now glided back to where Picyt sat waiting impatiently. He bowed, his sensitive lips curving in a sweet smile that less pure-minded citizens would have found provocative.

"Your pardon is craved, revered noble," he said in his low musical voice. "The pon on duty insists on inspection."

Bban murmuring rose heatedly, causing a flicker of fear to cross the steward's face, but with an uplifted finger Picyt checked his guards. He fitted his mask carefully into place, drawing up the hood of his cloak, and turned his palm up. "It pleases me to allow this," he said without tone, curbing the angry pulse that hammered within him.

The hatch lifted up and outward, letting in the shadows of the night with a slight hiss of air. Out of those shadows stepped a black-cloaked officer, the tracings on his mask vividly marking his personal caste and house, the band of scarlet at his throat giving his rank. Every Bban hand moved to the hilt of a jen-knife as the Tlar ducked his head to enter. He saw Picyt and saluted stiffly.

"Your pardon, Noble Picyt!" he said brusquely.

At the sound of his voice Picyt made a small sound of recognition. "Pon Fflir!" he said with an edge in his voice. "I thought you above gate duty."

The pon lowered his saluting fist. "A small indiscretion displeased the Tlsa leiis. The assignment is not of long duration, however. Now, noble. Why have the shields remained lowered?"

Picyt made a gesture of scorn. "Do you also fear the first storm of season?"

"This is no minor blow!" Fflir gestured vehemently, and with an expulsion of pungent musk the Bban nearest Picyt sprang to a crouch of readiness, whipping out his jen-knife. *"Merdarai!"* said Fflir harshly. "Is this an example of the Bban tribes you would have us give place to? Call off your brutes, noble."

Lips compressed behind his mask, Picyt lifted his finger, and at once the Bban moved back and returned the jen-knife to its sheath with a soft *snick*.

"Now, noble!" continued Fflir, setting one gloved hand on his hip in a manner that reminded Picyt of the *n'dl*. "The shields must come up. Vector six has been struck, and fire is raging through the Henan shacks."

Picyt raised his eyebrows. "The entire outer city will be swept into panic."

"*Lea'dl!* What care we about that?" snapped Fflir. "It is the inner city and the palace that matter." He pointed impatiently at the communicator set into the bulkhead facing Picyt. "Call your technicians, noble, and give the order."

Picyt's long fingers touched the vial of *yde* pocketed within his sleeve. "I did not come here for that purpose, Pon Fflir."

He paused. "Or did *you* summon me in the name of the Tlar leiil? I thought it was the Tlsa leiis you served."

The insult of his words was not greatly veiled. Fflir stepped back in anger. "Take care with your words, noble," he ground out. "Such accusations challenge many honors, all of which I am sworn to defend."

Picyt gathered the forces of his inner rings and focused them tightly as he leaned forward in his seat and swept out his hand. "I have business with the Tlar leiil," he snapped, weary of this pon, who was as an insect in the major intrigues of power. "Delay me further if you dare."

The cabin grew very still save for the low hiss of ventilated air. Picyt sat motionless, his masked stare unwavering as he waited to see if Fflir was stupid enough to risk carrying this further.

Fflir stood so rigidly that his ribs stretched tautly against the sleek expanse of his tunic. Picyt, alert in ways this hotheaded young officer knew nothing of, sensed Fflir's retreat even as the five Bban'jen tensed expectantly, their eyes glowing through the mesh eye guards of their masks. Smiling slightly, Picyt lifted his finger to quiet them.

With a growl Fflir raised his fist in a vicious salute, turned on his heel, and exited the transport with his cloak whipping out behind him. A low barking chorus of amusement circled through the Bban'jen as the steward bolted down the hatch. After a moment the air jets boosted the transport forward through the tall bronze gates, which had swung wide.

Not until the transport halted before the palace and the Bban escorts leapt out to split into their guard formation did Picyt have an opportunity to tilt up his mask and swallow the vial of *yde* unseen save by the furtive, discreet eyes of the steward. Then he refitted his mask and formed his rings with a surge of renewed potency. With his gloved hand resting lightly on the gleaming hilt of his jen-knife, he ducked out the hatchway and descended the three steps to the stone-paved courtyard with the serene demeanor of his position. Certain that many unseen eyes were upon him, he paused assuredly for a moment in the light of flambeaux held aloft by a contingent of slaves emerging from the entrance portico. With lights blazing boldly like Bban eyes stabbing into the night, the palace sprawled before him in two arched wings, vast, columned, powerful. Placing his fingertips together, Picyt lifted his head to an angle befitting the First Honored of Anthi and went forward past the crouched stone griflings, whose extended claws were tipped with gold. He climbed the broad steps that stretched to the flared columns of the portico. There the majordomo waited, bowing in his long, gilded tabard, a jeweled collar of servitude winking about his plump throat.

"Welcome, noble," he said smoothly, looking quickly at Picyt and then away again as he bowed a second time. "The Tlar leiil awaits."

Overhead a broad spear of lightning stabbed from the sky, seeming to skim the protective bubble that reflected blue light. Thunder boomed with a vehemence that made the slaves cringe. Even Picyt flinched.

Nervously the majordomo raised his fingertips to his brow in quick supplication to Anthi before gesturing with yet a third bow. "Come, noble," he said, preceding Picyt courteously through the wide doors, his back carefully turned from Picyt and his eyes averted so that he had to scuttle sideways with awkward little bobs of his plump body.

Picyt strode after him at a contained pace, seething behind his mask. *Lea'dl!* To squander food on fattening slaves while the Henan, starved in the squalor of Altian's slums and the Bban'n scavenged the Outerlands in desperate hordes was one too many of Hihuan's galling string of injustices! Anger swept aside the inner rings of caution, and Picyt's pace quickened, leaving his Bban escort out of step. On they went through magnificent archways of smoked crystal and jate stone, and along corridors that widened into galleries hung with woven tapestries. Soft-footed servants—the men clad in tabards of scarlet leather and the maidens in green silk—moved aside with startled grace, the jewels set in their collars and ankle-bands winking in the soft clear light. No smelly torches blazed on the walls. No braziers stood in corners with singing coals. They were unneeded, for in the palace of Leiil Hihuan heat and light were plentiful, provided from deep in the mysterious power base that hummed below the city. Indeed, an open flame was a mark of poverty and shame . . . or religious abstinence.

They approached a guarded door and halted there while the masked sentinels relieved Picyt of both his jen-knife and his escort.

"On your blood, start no incident this night," murmured

Picyt to the Bban'jen, knowing too well how easily the storm and Tlar'jen taunts could rouse unstable Bban natures to folly. "On your blood," he repeated sternly, enlarging the ring of his authority around the five.

They saluted with a clash of heavy gauntlets upon knife hilts. "It is sworn."

Satisfied, he pulled his dark-blue cloak more closely about his tall frame and followed the majordomo again. He had come this way many times before, too many times to be awed by the wealth of beauty surrounding him. Thick carpets now covered the polished jate stone floor, and mosaics fashioned from brightly hued enamels and precious metals adorned the walls. The glitter of light off such magnificence hurt Picyt's eyes, even through his mask. The warmth in these chambers grew oppressive. He longed to throw back his heavy cloak and divest himself of mask and gloves, but he made no attempt to do anything so casual. They passed many doors. Now and then one stood open, permitting glimpses into opulent chambers where members of the court relaxed on low couches, banqueting with low witty laughter or accepting the trained caresses of ty-boys.

Picyt's gaze remained sternly ahead, and within him the rings of caution and alertness drew taut, protecting him from the distraction of revulsion. They approached a spacious foyer whose vaulted ceiling swept high on the support of fluted columns. Here many corridors converged, including the guarded one that led to the private gardens and the court of women beyond. Picyt looked down at his guide. Much of how this meeting would go depended on whether he was received in the halls of state or in Hihuan's private apartments. The fact that he had been separated from his armed escort suggested a private meeting. Picyt's muscles tensed uneasily, and he groped within his wide sleeve for the comforting feel of the *yde* vial. The unwary too often found assassins in the dark corners of Hihuan's private court. He could not depend upon Hihuan's sense of prudence to hold a check on their rivalry for Ruantl.

Other courtiers stood in the foyer before him, talking to one another in low, excited voices, now and then laughing rapidly. One saw him and, with a gesture of respect, came forward.

"A fiendish night for late audiences, eh, Noble Picyt?" he

said, tugging off his mask as he spoke to reveal a hawkish face, the high sharp features now blurred beneath dissolute flesh. His dark reddish-brown hair swept, straight and coarse, back from his brow above slanted weary eyes ringed in green and amber flecks, which stared out with level directness at Picyt. The priest started at the sight of that face he knew so well.

"Noble Stregth," he said, unable to keep surprise from his voice. "How many seasons have raged since last I saw you?" Careful as always of protocol and watching eyes, he did not remove his mask, but as he spoke he made a discreet signal of warm welcome.

"They are too many," replied Stregth, tucking his mask under his left elbow in the jen way. He glanced briefly at the tall doors that led to the halls of state, thus turning his profile to Picyt, who smiled within his mask at the sight of the scarlet brand burned into one cheek. "But as you see, I stand here once again."

"And reclaimed to honor by your house," said Picyt, his eyes still upon the burn, which was recent.

"Ah? Yes." With a self-conscious smile Stregth tapped the mark of his high birth. "Reburned by Damc Agatc's own hand."

"Impressive. The Soot'dla so rarely forgive," murmured Picyt, withdrawing slightly as the doors to the halls of state opened to allow a man to emerge. He dragged along a cloaked, hooded figure who was weeping with ugly wrenching sobs. Picyt frowned. If Hihuan had chosen a new concubine tonight to add to his court of women, he would be puffed with arrogance and hard to frighten.

"No markings," muttered Stregth as he watched the departing pair. "I wonder which house has bought favors this night with the innocence of a daughter?"

The majordomo caught Picyt's eye and beckoned. Drawing himself erect, Picyt gestured to still his friend's ill-judged words and said formally, "It pleases me to welcome thc rcturn of your honor to the House of Soot'dla. May it also please the Tlar leiil to remove the shame of exile from your name."

Stregth bowed, but as Picyt moved away, he laid his hand briefly upon Picyt's wrist. "It has pleased me well to see you this night," he said, his green eyes serious.

Startled by the unexpectedness of that touch, Picyt halted, staring, unable to shake off the certainty that blackness had brushed between them. His senses heightened by the *yde*, he frowned and dared look upon Stregth with truth. At once Stregth stiffened and denied him sight, but it was enough. A cold chill passed through him. Picyt extended his hand and said urgently, "Even the honor of the Soot'dla is not worth what lies in your heart. Do it not, Stregth." He paused, troubled by the defiance in Stregth's green eyes. "I need your stance with mine—"

A gleam flickered in Stregth's gaze. "You have found one worthy?"

The raw bitterness that lingered in Picyt like a shard of poisoned crystal twisted more deeply. He looked away. "One was found," he said in a low voice, clenching his fist. "He has been lost."

"By the Tlar leiil?" Stregth raised his head. "By the four moons of Lea's court, I shall—"

"Noble Picyt!" called an impatient voice.

Cursing this meeting ground, Picyt dared linger for a moment longer. "Will you not have patience? I have not exhausted my—"

"Patience? *Merdarai!*" Stregth snorted, no longer taking care to school his unmasked features. "How much longer can we wait, Picyt? As of today he controls the merchants' fields; even the private lands of Dame Agate are no longer sufficient to hold the Soot'dla beyond his grasp. Will you have patience while our starving bellies betray us?"

"Noble Picyt!" called the majordomo again, more loudly this time.

Picyt whirled away from Stregth, too shaken by the news of the Spandeen conciliation to be able to react. A cloud of guilt smothered him. Had he listened to Basai and been more attentive to the merchants . . . *no*. He withdrew from such thoughts. His judgment of their motives had been correct, and groveling to please them would have perhaps only delayed this blow. But the fields! *Merdarai*, even Kkanthor could starve now if Hihuan chose for that to happen. His eyes sparked with anger as he strode forward, shedding mask, cloak, and gloves in response to a signal from hovering minions. He must put a stop to Hihuan. Stregth was right; this could not continue.

Bowing his head as he crossed the threshold into the first hall of state, he asked Anthi to preserve him and swiftly put all from his mind save Leiil Hihuan.

The enormous hall was triangular in shape, with the apex opposite the door. It was also empty. Picyt paused, in no mood for Hihuan's games. Folding his hands within his wide sleeves, Picyt stood in the center of the vast room and went no farther. Cautiously he extended his senses, well aware of mental traps that could be laid here for him. Finding Hihuan in an alcove, he withdrew his senses as softly as he had extended them and waited, holding his rings firmly about himself.

After a moment Hihuan strode into sight as Picyt had expected. The leiil was young, with a tall, well-knit frame softened by an abundance of food and dissolute living. He came forward, his handsome head held high so that his straight black hair just touched his shoulders. His were the pure features of the old line: the straight nose, sharply ridged cheekbones, glinting black eyes full of boredom and conceit, sensual lips curving above a petulant chin. Only a certain narrowness of skull betrayed the inbreeding that had become so rampant as the diminishing Tlar'n strove to keep their lines pure. He wore tonight a short wide-sleeved robe of rich purple brocade handwoven by skilled Henan women in the merchant district of the sixth vector, and soft scarlet thigh-tall boots. Rings adorned his fingers, and jewels glittered vividly from the hilt of the jen-knife at his belt.

Picyt watched him come and, at a moment just short of actual discourtesy, bowed.

The Tlar leiil's eyes narrowed. He jerked to a halt. "We have just communicated with Pon Fflir at the outer gates," he said, his rich voice sharp with anger. "You purposefully refuse to raise the shields, leaving us exposed to danger. It might almost be considered a deliberate act against us, Noble Picyt. Why do you toy with treason this night?"

Picyt thought of Riidul, and his eyes grew cold. "I come regarding a different matter, Noble Leiil."

"You come because we summoned you to explain this disobedience!" shouted Hihuan, turning away with a violent gesture. "You must learn your place, noble. You are not as irreplacable as you think."

Picyt met this outburst with a voice like ice. "Is that why my leiil sends men to bribe neophytes into becoming assassins?"

The coppery hue of Hihuan's cheeks darkened. But when he faced Picyt, he appeared unashamed.

"We have sent no assassin *yet*," he snapped.

Picyt stiffened and said softly, "Perhaps my good leiil blinds himself to the actions of his servants."

"You go too far!" His face twisted by fury, Hihuan whipped out his knife and sprang forward before a startled Picyt had time to build a natural force field. The knife point pricked against Picyt's chest. "Now, by Lea herself," snarled Hihuan, "we shall have no more of this! Raise the shields, priest, or I swear on this blade you'll not leave my hall living."

Picyt sighed with unconcealed impatience, leaving his defenses down and curbing the urge to slap away Hihuan's toy. "It is only the first storm, Leiil. Not enough—"

"The city has been struck three times in the outer vectors!" said Hihuan, digging in the knife as Picyt started to speak. "It takes only one strike of lightning to shatter the protective bubble, and if that is lost, we are *all* lost, priest." He jabbed again with the knife, and this time Picyt felt the skin break.

Fury surged through him at this insult. His blood rose, but his Kkanthor training superseded the hotter reflexes of his Tlar breeding, and he held himself in control.

"Yes, Picyt, you had better hold back," said Hihuan, his black eyes boring insolently into Picyt's. "You had better remember that I am Tlar leiil. You had *better* see that you protect the city, the palace, and the Jewels of M'thra for *me*."

An involuntary shiver moved up Picyt's spine at that mention of the Jewels. And at the same time his veins shrank in the first stirring of need for *yde*. Not so soon! he thought in despair as he stepped back, answering with as much scorn as he dared.

"My leiil knows I am sworn past blood to protect the Jewels," he said, raising rings of control over a surge of hatred for this stupid hedonist. For a moment he was tempted to bring Hihuan's greatest fear to life and put himself into the sacred body of Leiil Asan, but even as he savored the idea the leaden coldness of cowardice sank in. He did not dare, and Hihuan must have read the lack of courage in his eyes, for with a short laugh the leiil sheathed his knife.

"So you are sworn, Noble Picyt." The amusement in his

young face darkened to anger. "Then keep your oath! Raise the shields now!"

There was nothing to do but accede. But the resentment built up through the years since Hihuan had come to power could not be completely submerged. He was not the rightful leiil; this palace had not been built to honor his glory. Taking savage comfort in that, Picyt lifted his left wrist, but instead of activating his communicator he glared at Hihuan, his look as cold as the ice needles raining down outside.

"The power generators are old, Noble Leiil," he said bluntly, making no effort now to maintain the pretense of serenity. "If the shields are raised too swiftly, they may fail. That is why I hold back."

Hihuan's black eyes widened with rage. "Fail!" he shouted, panic tinging his voice. "*Merdarai,* Picyt, you dare too much—"

"Kkanthor has kept the repairs for centuries," broke in Picyt. "But even we have our limitations. No doubt had the *n'ka* not *vanished,*" he said tightly, daring at last to bring the matter into the open, "he could have solved the problem. But—"

"Silence!" screamed the Tlar leiil. "No more of this is permitted! Guards!"

Perhaps he *had* gone too far. Tensing as the doors were flung open behind him, Picyt raised his wrist and summoned Teecht by communicator. Mind-touch was swifter, but he dared not open himself here, especially not in Hihuan's presence. "Picyt speaks," he said hurriedly into the communicator, turning to one side so that he could watch the guards closing in on him with purposeful strides. "Raise shields. *Now!*"

Rough hands seized him, pinioning his arms even as Teecht began a startled query. Breaking communications, Picyt curbed the instinctive urge to raise his force field, knowing that to do so was an open confession of guilt, and stood erect and motionless in the cruel grip of the masked guards.

"Too late, priest," spat Hihuan. "Tonight you shall learn a lesson of obedience."

"I am no underling for thy pleasure," snapped Picyt, unable to hold back his defiance further. "Will thou raise the Bban'jen and my house to retaliation?"

Hihuan's face darkened with fury and he slitted his black

eyes. "Treason has been spoken here," he said. "Take him out!"

Picyt was jerked around so roughly that he nearly lost his footing on the polished floor. Within him fear battled self-recrimination. After all his prudent warnings to Stregth, *he* had been the fool this night. At least Stregth would have plunged a knife into the heart of the Tlar leiil and not merely stood mouthing defiance.

But before Picyt could be dragged out, an enormous explosion deafened him, and the entire palace shook violently enough to fling him and his captors to the floor. Chunks of rubble and dust rained down from the ceiling. Abruptly the lights cut out, plunging them into total darkness.

Stunned, Picyt rose unsteadily to his hands and knees, faltering as he tripped on his robe, and struggled to drag air back into his lungs. His rings had left him; he might as well be blind for the moment. Through the darkness he could hear Hihuan coughing and someone else swearing. The smell of dust hung thick in his nostrils. Somehow he staggered to his feet, desperation driving him as his hand fumbled inside his sleeve. He heard grunts and the scrape of boots over stone and knew the guards would seize him at any moment. *Lea'dl!* Where was that last vial of *yde*? Tensely hunting, he found what he searched for and threw the powder down his throat in one rapid gulp, his heart pounding.

"Lli take you, Picyt!" shouted Hihuan through the darkness. "You have brought destruction on us. Let it fall upon you as well!"

Picyt's rings formed, and at that moment only the extension of his senses saved him. He heard the hiss of metal through air as the jen-knife hurtled toward him. He twisted to one side, his unsteady powers deflecting the blade. It clattered harmlessly on the stone floor. As it missed, Hihuan responded with an oath.

"Guards!" he shouted. "Spread his blood!"

Picyt started to run, but he knew escape from the palace was hopeless. Suddenly the lights flickered on, blinding him, then winked out again. The power was coming back, and once it did, he would have no chance at all. Desperately he collected himself, sending all his strength into his inner forces as he closed his mind to the fear of such recklessness. To seizert during a storm was madness. He could easily lose control and end up inside a wall or scattered as widely as the wind. But it was too late for prudence; they were coming at him fast.

He gathered himself and leapt. Vertigo gripped him, spinning him through a gray void. Then he blinked an instant later. He was safely in the transport bay, which had emergency torchlight blazing against the darkness. The bitter reek of fire and smoke hung in the air.

"Revered noble!" cried an astonished priest, and at once a babble of thankful, panicked voices surrounded him.

He staggered out of sheer surprise at his success. He glanced only briefly at the destruction around him, then regathered his wits. He drew himself erect as the smell of burning ozone and shorted circuitry stung his nostrils, and he flung out his hand to ward them off.

"Gather yourselves!" he shouted hoarsely, cutting silent the uproar. "Ammal, Raan, Mliit! Seal the House. Raise all guardian systems. Now!"

Their white faces gaped at him out of the shadows. "All?" faltered Ammal as Uble stumbled into sight beside him. "Even the—"

"My noble," broke in Uble wearily, "it is too late. The tem ple has been struck by light—"

"It is not the weather we need fear," snapped Picyt. "I have commanded you. Go!"

As one they fled, gathering up their robes and seizing torches from other hands to light their way.

A quivering slave, burned and gibbering, crawled across the floor to clutch at Picyt's feet. Impatiently Picyt kicked him away as he caught the hot scent of fire.

"Teecht!" he called in alarm, glancing again at the chaos. Part of the upper balcony that ran the full length of the transport bay had fallen, leaving torn and twisted strips of metal and wire hanging through the shadows. One transport lay on its side, its hull caved in by a mass of stone and wreckage fallen from above. The control centers were nothing but blackened holes belching smoke. Someone had made an effort to organize, for wailing grime-streaked slaves were hauling in containers of the precious food stores and piling them along a wall in haphazard stacks beside the injured, who lay moaning and unattended. Picyt looked up to a door above the balcony and saw that it was open, swinging on ruined hinges, and beyond in the stairwell orange flames licked out hungry tongues.

"Teecht!" he shouted, angrily this time. He saw priests scurrying about, stumbling over technicians, who swore at them. Ah, there came the head technician, unhurt and erect as he strode grimly through the confusion. He picked his way around a mess of rubble and twisted metal and came up to Picyt, towing the *n'dl* firmly by one arm. Her clothes were torn, and as they stopped Picyt saw that one side of her face was burned. But both were safe. In relief he stepped foward to meet them.

"What damage?" he asked curtly.

Teecht's craggy face, streaked by dirt and smoke, looked weary and old. "Lightning struck the temple. We had no shielding to raise over it. Damage is heavy through the entire complex save for the lowest levels." He pointed about them. "And fire . . . there is much of it."

Involuntarily Picyt looked again toward the stairwell door, where the orange flames were brighter, as though raised in anger at the black shadow of a man valiantly beating them back. The tension within Picyt tightened, constricting his lungs until for one desperate second he knew only the overwhelming need for *yde*. How tempting it was to give way to despair and drown himself in the drug until he could crawl into a safe corner and sit locked in visions. Angrily he forced his weakness back, clearing his mind to deal with the problems before him. There was not much time. As soon as Hihuan could gather his forces, he would come.

"The damage does not matter," he said, quelling Teecht's start of surprise with a frown. "I have sent Ammal and Raan to activate the guardian systems. Help them. They must have all power available to protect what is left of the House." He paused, staring at the *n'dl* without really seeing her. "Was the bubble struck?"

Teecht swept out his thick hand palm down. "No, revered noble. But the storm has worsened, and it is raining ice needles. They could damage the bubble beyond repair."

"Understood." Picyt's gaze flickered back to the *n'dl*, who stood taut and silent, her broad face drawn beneath the angry red mark across her cheek. But if she suffered pain or fear she did not show it. And despite the emergency of the moment he was impressed by her calm nerve. Involuntarily he smiled at her, then turned back to Teecht. "The palace will come against us as soon as this storm abates. We must hold our position here until we can evacuate to the northern Bban citadels and the Tchsco Mountains beyond."

Teecht caught his breath and raised his shaggy head. "Then the uprising—"

"It has begun," said Picyt grimly. He considered the inadequacy of their present position. Little preparation, the Bban'-jen scattered, season raging, and this, their most important stronghold, destroyed so totally. "Send word to the tribes, and I must know what casualties and how much food we have. We must begin strict rationing at once. There will be no more food available, especially if Leiil Hihuan confiscates our fields."

Teecht's eyes narrowed, but without question he bowed. "Yes, my noble. And the *n'dl*? I cannot work and guard her too."

Picyt frowned, distracted, as his mind began to work on strategy and future moves. "Leave her with me. Go."

Picyt's presence alone went far toward reestablishing order, and under his direction the House gathered itself and descended to the lowest level beneath the city, where the hum of sealed machinery could be felt faintly through the stone tunnels. The priests no longer knew the location of the access point to that power source that supported the bubble and all devices providing heat and light within the palace and villas. Even Picyt was not certain how to reach it, although for a moment he was greatly tempted to destroy such comforts as another goad in Hihuan's side. But destruction was not his purpose, and he directed his concern to the more important transfer of the sacred scrolls away from the hands of the looting Henan'n who would come as soon as the storm ceased. Picyt permitted himself no regrets for the ruined splendor of the temple. There was not time. Sustaining himself on *yde* and refusing to consider the danger of the diminishing supply of the drug, he toiled through the night, overlooking no detail, making sure nothing of use to his enemies was left behind. And when all was done, he donned his stole of office over a fresh robe of white and stood before the assembled group of filthy, exhausted adults, boys, and slaves.

Saunders, who had worked as hard as anyone, stood in a

corner once again under Oliir's eyes, her bewildered gaze not wavering from Picyt.

He eyed her for a moment, remembering her momentary excitement over the vast power sources hidden down here and how she had quieted and grown thoughtful when no one had spared time to find a medallion of tongues to answer her questions. He was tempted to send forth a bit of reassurance to clear away her frown of exhaustion, but he had not the strength left to touch her mind with his. Almost all of his inner resources were depleted by *yde* and fatigue. His rings swirled and disintegrated in ragged splinters, leaving his nerves raw. But still he stood erect and summoned a serene expression for the sake of his priests.

He lifted his hand, and the low murmuring swelling through the assembly hall hushed and died away into a weary quiet. The room held the tainted smell of rot, and the damp walls and floor were uneven and broken from the pushing of settling earth. Dust webbed the corners in sodden piles of filth. Here and there he saw men shake themselves as tiny unnamed insects dropped from the cracked beams overhead. But all eyes, glazed with weariness and despair, were upon him. And he, First Honored of Anthi, accepted that responsibility, holding himself together for their sakes despite his grief and heartache and guilt at not having lifted the shields. In his pride he had taunted Hihuan, but it was Kkanthor that had suffered.

The *yde* hunger tightened his veins, leaving him lightheaded and momentarily witless. To sleep, to purge, to be done with it . . . But it was just beginning. Ruthlessly he pushed away the weakness and focused his gaze.

"We suffer this night, my *kai*," he said in a low, gentle voice, drawing upon old methods to put reassurance and comfort into his tone. "We despair. We grieve for what is lost. But our war has begun, and we must win it. We shall win it. That we must throw forth blood in challenge to our own brethern, our own Tlar kind, does not matter. Of all the Tlar, only we remember the purpose that Anthi gave us. The true birth shall be brought about, no matter what price we must pay." He saw an answering in some of the weary faces and let his own gaze flash. "This dawn shall see the Kkanthor-kai gone from Altian, to walk its streets with authority no more—for a time. Let them seek us. Let them wonder. Let them fear! Divine Anthi's departure from their city is sufficient omen." He lifted one long-fingered hand. "Now we go to cross the Outerlands. But when we are victorious, Anthi shall return to Altian to raise a new temple over a shining city. On my blood I swear it!"

And as one they raised the laud chant to Anthi, voices husky and cracking.

Moved, Picyt blinked fiercely and left the room, suddenly able to bear no more. At least no one had raised questions; at least no one had demanded to know why they must flee Altian at such an ill-timed moment. He hoped no one thought to wonder how Hihuan's wrath had been incurred. Outside in the corridor he stopped, bracing himself upon the wall with his hand to his eyes. The chant rose up more strongly in the other room. He sighed, his body sagging. To rest . . . Dear Anthi, to rest . . .

"Revered noble," said a soft, concerned voice.

He had heard no one follow him out. Wishing only to be left alone, Picyt raised his head, which suddenly seemed to weigh tons, and saw Oliir, Uble, and Teecht ringed around him, anxious. Where Basai had gone, he did not know. Behind them stood the *n'dl*, thinner than when she had first come to Ruantl. Somehow she looked, at this moment, particularly short, alien, and very much alone. He wondered how much of this she comprehended or cared about. Yet she had worked hard this night, giving no trouble. He would continue to find a use for her.

He sighed. "Teecht, go and seal the middle levels behind us. Hihuan cannot reach us now. Not for a time."

"It shall be done," said the technician, but he lingered, his grimy face creased in a frown.

"Please, revered noble," said Oliir in his shy, harsh voice, which no amount of training could ever soften. His young, skeletal face showed little expression in the wavering light of the torch Uble held, but Picyt knew how to read Bban eyes. He held his breath as those glowing golden orbs, now lightly tinted with a blue haze, stared into his. "How can we fight?" asked Oliir. "Who is to lead the Bban'jen? Is it not too soon? Have the elders been consulted? Can the tribes be made ready? Will they trust . . . us?"

Weariness and a great sense of inadequacy stabbed deep into Picyt's soul. It would have to be done, no matter how much he quailed inside from the thought. Asan must come forth from the caverns of M'thra. He would have to enter Asan, thus sacrificing his *yde*-riddled soul to raise the greatest of the Jewels. But he did not want to die just to bring Asan forth. The fear and sense of rebellion that never left him struck anew. Why should he die and give the full glory of the purpose to Asan?

"Oliir's questions are wise ones," he said at last, goaded by their respectful silence. "But I know not when—" He faltered, hesitant to admit his own doubts when courage was so desperately needed. "If only—"

"Revered noble!" A familiar, unexpected voice rang out from the length of the corridor, a gruff, firm voice filled with triumph.

Disbelieving, Picyt saw a masked, cloaked Bban striding forth from the musty shadows, dust streaking his uniform and the black sand of the Outerlands still clinging to his boots. The eyes of the figure glowed a fierce scarlet through the mesh guards of his mask. For an instant Picyt clung to the wall, certain *yde* deprivation had raised a hallucination before him. But no! The others saw the Bban too.

"Pon Tuult!" said Picyt hoarsely, stepping forward.

"My noble." Tuult came to an abrupt halt and knelt. As he did so, he took an object from beneath his cloak and sent it spinning across the stone floor to Picyt's feet.

Unsteadily Picyt bent to pick it up and for a moment stared uncomprehendingly at the unmarked mask in his hands. Then hope gripped him. "Tuult," he said, his voice failing him. "You have—"

Tuult rose to his feet with a proud gesture. "The *n'ka* is found!" he said, his voice ringing out over the chanting beyond. "And he lives! The Bban'n stand in honor once again!"

Chapter 6

Blaise came back to consciousness slowly with the sun beating down on his back. Around him the sigh of the desert wind blew over the black sand, eddying it in tiny waves. Cold bit under the breath of the wind with a chill that undermined the sun's warmth. Blaise stirred slightly, dragging one hand through the coarse sand. The cloak tangled up about his neck and head was stifling him. With a groan he stirred again, his mind slowly clearing. The sun, he thought dully. The sun was cooking him in this black gear. Black . . . black sun . . . black star . . . X rays . . . *mask*! Understanding dawned. Of course they wore protective clothing and lead-lined masks. Otherwise they'd die of radiation poisoning. As he would, if he did not find his mask.

With a grimace Blaise lifted his head, scraping his cheek on the gritty sand. This gave him a bleary glimpse of rock-strewn slope, but nothing else. Drawing in a deep breath, he levered himself onto his hands and knees, only to fall again with a sharp cry as agony from his leg washed over him in a crimson wave. Not for several minutes after the pain finally eased to a bearable degree could he bring himself to try again. This time he managed to balance himself upright on his left knee and to cling, gasping, to the gray boulder beside him until the throbbing eased in his head and his vision cleared. Sweat dampened his back, making him shiver as the wind fingered him. Squinting against the glare of the sun, he scanned the slope reaching up to the cave mouth. Ah, there it was.

Bleakly he stared at the mask, lying half buried in the black sand at least thirty meters away. He wasn't sure, as he glanced down at the seared, bloody mess of his right leg, that he could even drag himself half that distance. And yet he had to try. Unsure of how many hours he'd lain unconscious, he dared risk no more exposure. Blaise licked at his dust-coated lips. Water was something else he'd better find, although this terrain did not promise much chance of that.

But the mask was of primary importance. Digging his fingers into the boulder's pitted surface, Blaise gritted his teeth and pushed himself forward in a slow crawl, dragging his right leg and forcing himself to keep a steady, deliberate pace despite the fire that flamed through bone and flesh. It was like no pain he had ever experienced before. Even a strifer burn did not torture like this. It was as though the blue fire contained a chemical designed to linger in the wound and go on lacerating the tissue.

Demos! he thought, dragging his quivering body forward inch by inch. Sweat poured into his eyes and his temples pounded. Blaise was not, by profession, a scrupulous man, but he had his own code of honor, and part of his ethics was to make a quick, clean business of killing. But to deliberately maim . . . He scowled, his lungs rattling harshly as each breath grew more difficult. Whether Hihuan knew it or not, he had made a mistake in leaving Blaise alive, for as he pulled himself along through the choking dust he vowed he would see the Tlar leiil pay for this.

But as the going grew harder and slower and the mask seemed as far from reach as ever, thoughts of revenge faded, and a fog settled over him. He sagged lower and lower to the ground until he was crawling along on his belly with all his weight pulled by the flagging strength of his shoulders. Dust and sand ground into the raw flesh of his wound. His hands grew leaden. When he paused to wipe the sweat from his stinging eyes, he saw in horror that his hands were bleeding, shredded by the coarse sand that clung to the blood in thick clumps of black granules.

For a moment Blaise could only lie still with his hot, sweating face buried against his arm. Gloves, he thought desperately, once his fevered mind finally realized that his jen uniform was impervious to the sand's abrasion.

Several days ago, in the idleness of captivity, he had stuffed the heavy gauntlets into the toes of his boots to make them fit better. Now they seemed as far beyond reach as the mask. But he would not give up.

Coughing with a violence that pained his chest, he rolled over onto his back. For a minute or two he rested, his eyes shut against the sun as he counted his uneven breaths. When they had slowed, he clenched his hands and levered himself into a sitting position. Removing the left boot was relatively easy, once his head stopped spinning. Removing the right one was a nightmare that left him sick with pain. And when it was over and the immediate torture faded once more, he could still feel the fire grinding along the bone in his thigh as though it were gnawing it away. Fear touched him then. Angrily he pushed it away.

He wiped his swelling hands on the edge of his cloak, leaving red stains that soaked into the black fabric, and grimly fitted on the heavy black gloves. He refused to wonder if he'd ever get them off again. Survival was his field of expertise, an expertise honed to a fine craft since those first terrifying days of escape to a nonprotected planet. And while most of his experience lay with devious city streets filled with the shadow of the sophisticated dangers that lurked inside the deadly circles of the black market, he would not let this desert and its barbaric despot defeat him.

With renewed determination he rolled back onto his stomach and resumed crawling toward the mask. Either his nerves were giving way to exhaustion or the pain was fading. He did not care which as long as hc could kccp going inch by slow, straining inch up the slope toward the mask.

And then, incredibly, his outflung fingers grasped it. With a hoarse cry of triumph he pulled it down to him and lay exhausted with it held against his chest. Perhaps he was in time. Depending on the length and degree of exposure, he might get by without damage. Coughing, he snatched a deeper breath, wincing at the soreness in his chest, and opened his eyes. He noticed that that the grains of sand were crystalline, some the color of smoke, others slightly bluish in tint, and others dark purple. Beautiful, but of no importance.

Focusing his attention on the task at hand, he forced himself up on one elbow and awkwardly drew up his hood, fastening the mask into place. At once the chill bite of wind and the glare of sunlight were cut off. He sighed, his confidence unconsciously renewed. Then he sat up by slow degrees, carefully stretching out his leg, brushing away the clinging sand from the edges of the thigh-long wound before leaning back to prop his shoulders against the hard surface of a boulder. Idly he brought out the translator from his cloak pocket and stared at it. Round and intricate, the medallion was of no design he recognized. Too weary to be deeply curious, he shrugged and tucked it away, letting his gaze wander out over the vast and lonely landscape around him.

Beyond the hillside on which he sat the ground descended in a series of short, rocky ridges like the spines of old skeletons bleached gray against the black sand. The sun hung lower now, its large bronze orb staining the lavender-tinted sky a bloody purple as it neared the horizon. He saw no vegetation other than a few scraggly thornbushes that grew no higher than his knee, and no animals or insects. It was a daunting emptiness, but he sternly forced himself to remember that there was life here. He just had to figure out how to find it.

As though in answer, a distant howl, shrill and eerie, lifted through the cold air. The cloudless sky turned ocher as twilight deepened with startling swiftness. For a moment the wind lay stilled from its restless questing. Blaise sat tensely, beginning to shiver as the temperature dropped, with the sun now beneath a far, black horizon. He watched a trio of tiny moons ascend one by one, followed by a vast one, whole and ghostly white, that appeared to fill the night sky. It seemed to crush him with its nearness, and its light stretched over the silent desert with cold barren fingers, casting Blaise's hunched shadow into line with the straighter one of the rock. The wind rose up more strongly and cut him through with cold at the first touch. Shivering, he pressed his palm against the edge of his throbbing wound and flinched as the distant howl rose again. It sounded closer this time, but how he hoped to the mercy of Demos that it was only a trick of his imagination.

To distract himself from the eerie howls and the night cries that answered, Blaise attended to his pangs of hunger and dug through his pockets for chunks saved from several ration cubes. Storing up had not been easy, for the Bban'jen clearly did not believe in fattening themselves or their prisoners. Now his fumbling, eager fingers found only crumbled powder. Disheartened, he shook some out into his gloved palm and licked up the dry stuff, choking a bit as his parched mouth and throat failed to produce sufficient saliva to start the chemical process. The taste was awful, and he wondered how much dirt had mixed itself with the food. After a while he gave up.

Chance, or perhaps some extra sense, made him look out across the rock-strewn ridges to his right. Lean, furtive shapes ran over the crest of one, dropping out of sight only to reappear moments later in quick silent leaps from the shadow of one stone to another. Blaise's breath caught in his throat. He turned to the left. Yes, there was a flick of movement from that direction too: vague lean shapes keeping out of the bright moonlight as much as possible. He swallowed hard, his parched throat sore. They were hunting him.

Fear swept through him. Sitting out here in the moonlight, he was a far too visible target. But where could he go? Where could he hide?

In silent, deadly determination the hunters closed in, surrounding him on three sides. And at his back rose the steep cliff and the cave above. He drew his good leg beneath him with a grimace, his heart thudding with a sudden urge to run. But running was out of the question. Could he make the cave? Even as he considered it, he felt despair. The climb was steep, and even with two good legs he'd have a hard time getting up there.

Then, on a sudden crosscurrent of wind, the scent of Bban musk reached his nostrils. He panicked, shoving himself up on his good leg and trying to hobble up the slope. But with one step the wound on his leg opened and half his blood seemed to spew out, plunging him into agony so great that he screamed aloud. An outcry went up behind him. Trying to ignore the pain, the feeling of renewed fire burning away bone and muscle, he kept going, only to lose his balance and stagger to his knees. A javelin whistled over his shoulder, missing by centimeters, and thunked into the earth ahead of him. Blaise crouched where he was, panting, trying to drive back the pain as he glanced quickly over his shoulder.

"*Choi-hana! Chi! Chi!*" screamed a fierce wild voice.

They were on their feet, running swiftly up the slope toward him. He counted eight, all swathed in ragged cloaks and masked with strips of cloth wrapped across their faces. Their eyes glowed brightly, intent and triumphant as they howled, leaping from rock to rock with quick surefootedness. Another javelin hurtled toward him, catching his cloak and pinning it to the ground.

Blaise broke loose from his numbed terror. With a wild cry of his own, he seized the javelin in both hands, jerking it from the ground so violently that sand flew, and hurled it back at them as hard as he could. It hit no one, but it checked the impetus of their rush. For a moment they stood still, eyes glowing incandescently as they huddled together and growled at each other in swift conference. Blaise seized his chance to crawl up the slope to the other javelin. Then he faced them with it, his face grim and hot behind his mask. Why didn't they come on and finish it? He no longer held hope of escape or survival, but he wanted to go out fighting. Blood still oozed down his leg; he waited, furious at them for toying with him, feeling weaker by the second. His vision blurred, and their lean figures shimmered in the wan light as they picked their way up toward him at a steady pace, jen-knives glinting in their hands.

Anger at them and at his own helplessness coursed through him, and with a last burst of defiance he raised the javelin in one hand, aiming it at the nearest figure, while with the other hand he pulled the translator from his pocket.

"I know Picyt," he said, desperately seizing the first words that occurred to him. "If you honor him, leave me to my own way."

They stopped, but merely stared at him without response. He gripped the translator harder.

"I am not from this world. I have no quarrel with you."

Finally one stepped forward a pace. "This is territory of the J'agan-dar. No jen may come here unbidden. You are our meat."

Bban-meat, he thought with a sudden wild urge to laugh. Fire seemed to engulf him, blurring his vision, further and leaving him cold in its wake, but he shook off the feeling, driving the point of the javelin into the ground and using it for support as he levered himself to his feet.

"I am no one's meat!" he shouted back, his voice as hoarse as theirs. It echoed across the desolation surrounding them before the wind blew it away. "And I am here not by choice, but because some damned *flin* named Hihuan brought me out here and shot me. Now you—"

"You are sworn enemy against Leiil Hihuan?" asked the Bban with sudden interest. "To the blood?"

Blaise set his jaw. "Dammit, yes."

"He is a jen spy," said another suddenly.

The scent of Bban musk, raw and horrible, filled the air. Blaise choked on it, felt his grasp on the javelin slip, and suddenly fell to one knee. Immense weariness rolled over him, pressing him down.

"Any enemy of the Tlar leiil has place," said the first Bban. "But a friend of the Noble Picyt must be considered with suspicion. We shall put it before the elders to be weighed." He walked toward Blaise, extending a bony hand. With hesitation

Blaise held out his own, only to gasp as he realized too late the creature's intention. The Bban struck, snapping Blaise's head back violently enough to make his neck crack. Light exploded within his brain, blinding him so that he was only dimly aware of his dislodged mask slipping down as he fell. . . .

He awakened to the intriguing scent of something cooking. Blaise blinked at the shadows overhead, bemused by the ruddy flicker of firelight on the rough stone ceiling. For an instant he thought himself back in the Bban citadel. Then a noise caused him to turn his head, and he stiffened at the sight of a woman nearby tapping her long horn spoon on the metal edge of a cooking pot that was suspended over the hissing yellow flames of a small fire. Aromatic steam rose from the bubbling contents of the pot. Hunger gnawed through him, but he did not so much as breathe until she turned slightly to lay her spoon down on a curiously hollowed stone. His breath eased out at the sight of her smooth, high-cheeked profile, firm, slightly rounded chin, slim straight nose, and clear brow. She was tall, like the people of this planet, and moved with supple grace as her slender form cast a shadow on the opposite wall. Her clothing was simple, consisting only of a thin, untanned leather garment fastened at the throat with a jeweled brooch, falling in a straight sheath to her knees. The slit up one side gave him tantalizing glimpses of a slimly curved thigh. Her hair hung straight and thick down her back like a veil, glittering gold in the firelight.

Where, he wondered in a daze, had she come from? Was she an off-worlder stranded here too?

He lifted his head slightly, and at once she turned with a sweep of her unbound hair to regard him with silver eyes that glowed in the way of the Bban. Jolted, he frowned, staring at her delicate, golden-skinned features. She was not Bban, and yet . . .

Quickly she reached into the pouch tied to the braided thong around her waist and held out the translator. "Lie quietly," she said in a husky voice, her silver eyes regarding him from under knit brows. "You must not reawaken the blue fire."

Obedient to that suggestion, Blaise nodded and let his head drop back. At least the Bban had not killed him . . . yet. "My name is Blaise Om—" He broke off, suddenly tired of an identity that no longer served him. "Just Blaise," he said, his voice weak. "Am I—"

She gestured with a graceful lift of her hand. "You are within the *dara* of the Bban tribe J'agan-dar. Scouts found you while hunting a chaka escaped from the herd." She cocked her head to one side. "You wear the cloak of the jen, but you are weaponless. Why? Have you been stripped of honor and left to spread your blood upon the sand in shame? And you are neither Bban nor Henan nor Tlar. The warriors know great bewilderment."

Blaise felt rather bewildered himself. "*You* are not Bban," he said finally, refusing to answer questions. The steam from the cooking pot again drifted his way, and his mouth watered longingly. "May I have some of that?"

Her cheeks had darkened at his first statement, but now she glanced at the cooking pot. "It is not yet time," she said, then looked at him hesitantly. "No, I am not Bban, but Henan. Do you think anyone of caste or honor would tend a stranger with striped eyes and no weapon?"

The scorn stung. Blaise said tersely, "I come from another world—"

"Blaspheme not the powers of Anthi!" she broke in with a swift gesture. Her silver eyes narrowed at him. "You are a spy of the evil Tlar—"

"Hihuan and his scumy friend Aabrm?" said Blaise with a snort, and she gasped, looking at him in shock. He eyed her, wondering how much of a rebel she really was. "They are responsible for this leg." As he spoke he reached down beneath the heavy fur robe covering him, only to stiffen in alarm as his probing fingers awakened no feeling in his thigh. "Demos!" He heaved himself up on one elbow, then gasped as the cave spun before his eyes.

She moved swiftly to his side and pushed him flat. "Fool," she said, checking the bandages swathing his leg. "It has taken me many hours to deaden the fire. Will you awaken it? Lie still!"

Obedient to her sudden fierceness as well as the weakness causing his heart to flutter oddly and his lungs to struggle, he lay still save for the bandaged hand he reached out to grip hers.

"The leg," he said through his teeth. "What can you do for it?"

She drew back, her silver eyes growing as chilly as ice as he defied pain to hold her fast. "Release me," she said coldly. "Perhaps we shall cut off your leg, striped-eyes, and eat it."

Her spirit roused a weak laugh from him. Lacking the strength to argue, he slackened his hold. She snatched free her hand.

"What is your name?" he asked.

Her delicate nostrils flared as she rubbed her wrist. For a moment he thought she would walk out. Then her set mouth softened, and she brushed back a straying strand of golden hair. "I am Giaa," she said, "and your leg has had all the care due to a stranger of no honor. More, perhaps."

"Giaa," he said, liking the sound of it. "You must believe that I am no spy for Leiil Hihuan. Picyt asked me to help him when—"

"The revered noble!" She widened her silver eyes, their glow suddenly intense. Swiftly she raised her fingertips to her lips and forehead. "You serve the First Honored of Anthi?"

"I serve no one!" flared Blaise without thinking. Then, seeing her expression, he realized the rashness of his outburst. Demos, where were his wits? "But," he amended hastily, "you might say Picyt and I have worked out a deal—"

"The elders must be told!" Even as she spoke she turned, hastening toward a shaggy leather curtain.

"But wait!" he called desperately, not trusting her sudden eagerness. "Giaa—"

She halted, making no attempt to hide her impatience. "The legends tell of you, striped-eyes." Again she touched her brow in a swift gesture of respect. "You are the harbinger of the rising, when our true leiil shall return to lead us. Oh, I must tell the elders!"

He tried to sit up. "No, Giaa! Wait!"

But she was gone.

"Demos," he said in disgust, and dropped down on one elbow. He frowned. A thousand credits said Picyt had set up this legend to suit his own grisly purposes. Blaise lay further down with a grunt, fretting at his weakness. Perhaps escaping to Ruantl had not been such a bright move after all. The Institute would not pursue him here, but still, he'd not been free of injury since the crash. Lying on his back at the mercy of these people was not the way to get ahead. It was time he took the offensive.

His frown deepened. By now he should have had some idea of this planet's resources, government, and police control. Instead all he knew were confusing bits of superstition, a native population that set his teeth on edge despite years of xenobiological exposure, and hints of a conquering race no longer in control. Well, then, why had the Tlar come to Ruantl at all? Surely any scouting party would have reported the X rays and other hazardous conditions of this rock. Yet they had come here anyway and settled. Why? Had their own world been dying? Was it overpopulation that drove them here? Or greed?

He sat upright again, ignoring the tilt of the room as he stared at that tantalizing cooking pot. It was fashioned of a peculiar bright-green metal. A memory tickled the corner of his mind. Yes, the jen-knives were made of it, too, but he had seen it somewhere before, very long ago. Unconsciously he brought up one of his bandaged hands to rub his jaw, where faint tracings of the old identity number remained despite the skills of a very expensive eraser. Realizing what he was about to do, he stiffened and slowly lowered his hand. Of course!

The memories came back in a sudden flood of unwanted venom, filling his veins with the strength of old hate and rebellion. It happened when he was a threeling—one-third grown—and assigned to work at simple tasks in Laboratory 80. They had brought in an unusual alien specimen for analysis and dissection. Blaise, sickened and shaking, had done the cleaning up, and he had held for a moment a finely wrought armband of strange green metal, silky smooth and oddly warm to the touch.

Then a hand, supple, white, and smelling of disinfectant, plucked it from his grasp.

"Corybdium bracelets are too costly for vat boys."

Even now the words burned through his brain like a white brand, and the shame boiled through him again. But the past was over, said a cold part of his mind as it pulled him back to the cavelike room where animal skins covered his bed and hot coals sang from the fire. He narrowed his gray eyes. Corybdium was so rare that he had never seen it again until coming here. And by her own words, Giaa was of small importance to her tribe, yet she wore gold and jewels and carried a knife with a blade that would bring thousands of credits on the black market.

Excitement leaped within Blaise, driving away all thoughts of pain, hunger, and weakness. Ruantl must be a treasure trove of costly minerals! And this Picyt was waiting and anxious to hand the whole planet over to Blaise in exchange for . . .

He winced with revulsion. True, he was a vat boy, created in the Institute laboratories for the labor supply, and therefore, logically, his body should mean little enough. To be vat grown was to be the lowest and most despised of all creatures in the Institute's hierarchy. To be vat grown was a shame overcome only by conforming to the Institute's ways more rigidly than everyone else, to fight not for advancement but for acceptance that seldom came, to attain humanity by becoming less than human, in short, to be the perfect little drone. Blaise gritted his teeth. He had refused to conform. He had fought to be different, rebelling until he had been forced to escape to survive. And he *had* survived, as renegade, robber, and spy. He was proud to be a miscalculation, to have won the small victory of individualism. Vat born or not, committee designed or not, numbered BLZ-80-4163 or not, he was his own man and not just one more number owned by the Institute.

Was that achievement worth exchanging for an alien body? He looked again at the green cooking pot and grew thoughtful. Wealth enough to stagger the galaxy could lie beneath the barren surface of this planet. He considered the gamble with a quickening heartbeat, his eyes beginning to gleam even as a throb of pain through his thigh made him grimace. He lowered himself flat again, drawing a shaky breath.

The hide curtain moved aside and Giaa ducked through. Her silver eyes shone at him through the shadows like pools of mercury. For an instant he heard the faint melodic strumming of an instrument set on a key that vibrated through him with every twang. She let the curtain fall behind her, and the music was cut off.

"Giaa," he said, motioning for her to produce the translator. "Do you know Picyt? Can word be sent to him? I must—" He broke off with a wince as the pain intensified, sawing through his leg with a viciousness that left him white.

She hastened forward, and her golden hair brushed his scraped cheek as she bent over him. "Later," she said, laying a slim hand on his forehead as though to check for fever. "You must rest . . . sleep. The dara-elders are in conference with the council of warriors." Her gentle mouth twisted with bitterness, and for a moment she stared into the distance, her eyes opaque and flat with a hard sort of anger that seemed out of place there. "For once a Henan was heard."

He caught a faint whiff of her scent, which was nothing like the sour sweetness of Bban musk. Instead it was a fragrant mixture of smoke and wind and warmth. With her unbound mane of hair and lithe slenderness, she was like a creature of the wild, both shy and bold. Slowly he raised one of his clumsy, bandaged hands to caress her throat and the full curve of her breast as she bent to straighten the fur robe covering him.

At once her gaze sharpened, and she moved abruptly away. "All Henan women are not seducers from the marketplace of Ty!" she snapped. "I am sworn follower of Anthi and the purpose. Touch me not again in violation of my vows." She walked over to the cooking pot and filled a cup from its contents then returned to thrust it to his lips. "Drink and sleep."

Pungent-smelling steam rose from the cup. Puzzled by so angry a rejection, Blaise sniffed at the drink, his mouth watering for anything, even a concoction of medication. He noticed the cup was made of green metal, warm and vibrant in color against the palm of her slim, golden hand.

He raised his eyes to her glowing, angry ones. "Picyt must be told where I am. Do you understand?"

"Have I not said I am sworn to the purpose?" She replied sharply. "But the revered noble is not for us to command. Still . . ." She sighed and lifted her fingertips swiftly to her brow as though warding off misfortune. Her eyes were suddenly troubled. "You are the one he told us would come. The tales are old and hard to believe . . . or were." Her gaze shifted uneasily away, and she again held the cup to his lips. "Drink, striped-eyes."

He refused, and asked again. "Will Picyt be sent for?"

Her eyelids, so delicate that he could see the faint tracery of veins across them, dropped to veil her silver eyes. And when at last she spoke, her husky voice was lower than usual: "The dara-elders are old men, fearful of the Tlar leiil and his blue fire, and fearful of the supreme elders of the greater council." As she spoke her hand gently touched Blaise's thigh, making him shiver. "They may decide to make you Bban meat, *n'ka*. But though I be Henan, I am not ignorant. I will send the message to the jen of Kkanthor *if* you are he whom we seek." Her eyes blazed with sudden fervor, compelling an honest answer. "Is your coming a herald for the return of the Great Ones? Or are you a lie?"

For a moment Blaise's nerve failed him. Perhaps he could get off this planet. Perhaps there would be other worlds, other opportunities; he wasn't sure he dared risk joining himself to a band of superstitious fanatics who needed a mystical figure to rally around. But he stared at the jeweled brooch, blazing in the firelight, where it held the fastening of her thin leather garment and heard himself say, "No lie, Giaa. The Great Ones will return."

She lifted her head swiftly, and he saw her suspicion. Then her face quivered, and he knew she believed him in spite of her distrust.

"And there will again be justice for Henan and Bban as well as Tlar?" she asked, staring at him. "There will be no more empty bellies to make proud warriors slaves?"

"On my word," he said gravely, well aware that his word meant nothing. But at that moment as he faced this slim proud creature through the fire-lightened shadows and felt the hum of fever in his blood, he wished it did.

"Drink," she said, and this time he let her tilt the warm, bitter stuff down his throat.

In moments the pain had subsided, and a warm drowsiness washed over him in its stead. Veiled in her hair, she seemed to grow very far away, her eyes glowing brighter and brighter until she burned through the deepening shadows like a candle flame.

Disjointedly he wondered about Saunders and whether she, too, had been abducted. With her mining background she was necessary to the success of his plans. He blinked, and it was as though a thousand years had passed. With sudden clarity he saw Picyt again, standing before him as he had that day in the Bban citadel, wrapped in a shimmering blue cloak. There was no return from an exchange of bodies.

Demos! thought Blaise. *What have I done?*

"Need . . ." he said, trying to lift a hand to attract Giaa's attention. "*Need* . . ." But the candle flame dimmed and finally snuffed out in blackness. He slept, with the chain of the potion holding him deep beneath the nightmarish tossings of his fever.

Chapter 7

The caverns of M'thra ran deep below the snow-encrusted peaks of the Tchsco Mountains. "Teeth of the Sleeping Giant" was their name in the Bban tongue. They lay far to the north of the savage desert wastes, beyond the last Bban citadel, brooding dark under an angry season sky of black and purple clouds, the highest peak ringed by cold white fog. Below the mountain ran several narrow valleys, with one wide one cutting deep through the land. It was bottomed by a long, still-surfaced lake that reminded Blaise of Giaa's eyes. Sitting propped up by the viewing port in the tall-backed, thickly cushioned seat as Picyt's personal transport jetted him, Giaa, and his Bban guards northward, Blaise rested his forehead against the cold gray metal of the inner hull and watched as the pilot carefully skirted the edges of the lake, bringing them dangerously near ice-coated rocks and skeletal botanical growths as though he had some superstition against flying over water. Their low progress startled a vast, shaggy animal with a bulbous, snouted head. Angered rather than frightened, it reared its massive bulk up on a single, enormously broad hind flipper and extended long claws in a futile swipe as they passed over.

Giaa touched Blaise's arm. "Borlorl," she said, pointing to the heavy fur robe tucked around him. "They are dangerous to hunt but well worth it."

It was an effort to lift his head and look at her, but he managed it, trying not to betray how frightened he was, as his leg worsened daily. A fast recovery rate had been bred into him by the Institute; he had never known an illness that he could not quickly shake off. But now he feared that he might not make it to Picyt.

Giaa sat on the edge of her seat in barely contained excitement, now and then leaning over him to see out through the viewport. "Look!" she cried, her golden face lighting up much as the lightning sparked life from the mountains ahead. "Zantza . . . an entire herd. Look!" Her finger stabbed at the glass until he reluctantly turned once again to the window.

Below on the slope lifting away from the valley, the deep white snow rippled and burst with sudden sprays in a complex, rapid pattern of movement. Blaise frowned, unable to see any animals.

"They are quicker than thought," said Giaa, her sweet, smoky scent releasing to fill the stale air of the cabin with fragrance. "The flying of snow is when they surface for scenting direction, but you must not strike there, for they are always beyond. To hunt the zantza you must guess ahead of where they will go."

Blaise sighed as the transport wheeled and rose above the valley, leaving its animal life behind. He had no interest in hunting game and wondered with a qualm if any part of Ruantl's population knew how to mine. Of course, labor could be trained in manual excavation, but for his plans he needed the enormous mechanized shovelers of Saunders's people, great automated machincs that could gnaw out the inside of a mountain within hours. He furrowed his brow, and Giaa's excited description of the slim, white-furred zantza abruptly faltered.

"You grow tired," she said, lifting her slim golden hand in swift summons to the steward.

"No!" said Blaise sharply, disliking the small, cat-footed boy with his watchful eyes and slow, teasing smile. Realizing as he saw Giaa frown that he'd been too vehement, he lowered his voice. "No," he repeated, glaring at the approaching steward in a way that sent the boy retreating with a grave bow. Rather than answer her look of puzzlement, he tried to shift his position on the seat, winced, and asked rather fretfully, "How much longer?"

"Soon." Her silver eyes clouded and shifted to the masked, silent Bban'jen. One gestured curtly at her, and she lowered her eyes at once. A dull copper flush stained her cheeks. "Soon," she repeated, her fingers clutched tightly together in her lap. She collected herself, hiding the anger from long habit, and lifted her head. "The sacred caverns of M'thra are worth waiting for. Only because of you, Noble Blaise, am I to see them."

He frowned, shifting again, and did not answer. Nervousness was making her chatter far more than her usual reserve permitted, but he thought also that she was a little afraid.

The hum of the engines altered, and his pilot's instincts told him the air jets were being reversed to slow them. The transport came to a gradual halt, hovering before the central peak of Tchsco. Now that they were closer, Blaise could see a gigantic steel wall set into the side of the mountain beneath a jutting overhang of rock. As he watched, it slowly slid open.

"*Bh'ya tel awn ra mere*," whispered Giaa, lifting her fingertips to her forehead with her eyes fixed on the sight. On the right the Bban guards stirred with clicks and guttural comments. "It is the eye of Anthi," said Giaa, noticing Blaise's puzzled look. "She opens unto us. Do not fear." But her hands clenched in her lap until the knuckles whitened, and her fragrant smoky scent warred with the reek of Bban musk, making Blaise cough.

Slowly the transport jetted forward with short spurts of propulsion that betrayed its pilot's trepidation and made Blaise long to run forward and jerk the controls from his hands. But at last they were inside the black, moist mouth of the mountain, with the steel door closing behind them so that they were shut in total darkness. Beside him Giaa gasped, her hand gripping his arm hard. Then the cabin lights blinked on, and the steward in his scarlet tunic glided forward to begin opening the hatch.

Commands were snapped out, some too low and rapid for the translator hanging around Blaise's neck to catch. The potion Giaa had given him had begun to wear off; he could feel himself fraying at the edges. Soon the pain would be back, pain more excruciating than he could now bear without medication. He must do all that Picyt wanted, he told himself, refusing to worry, or doubt, or think about alternatives. It was either go through with this, or lose his leg and maybe his life. From what he had seen of Bban culture thus far, the thought of amputation at their unskilled hands chilled his very soul.

Grumbling, the guards surrounded him, picked him up awkwardly in the narrow space between the seats, and none too gently carried him out the hatch and down the short series of steps. Squashing his fierce desire to protest being handled like a crate of merchandise, Blaise let them place him on a litter. Four muscular bearers, half clad in queer garments that covered only the front and back of their bodies waited to bear it. For a moment his surroundings seemed taken from a hellish nightmare. Bban faces, uncovered and skull-like, hung disembodied around him in the deep shadows masking the interior of the transport bay. Curiosity flickered in their glowing eyes, and he heard snatches of conversation spoken in guttural, clacking voices as torchlight glinted off bony angles of temple and jaw. The stench of the place was horrible, with the scent of dusty rock overlaid by Bban musk, unwashed bodies, animal dung, burning torches, and transport exhaust. Blaise coughed, his muscles drawing up against the intense leaden cold, and at once Giaa pushed her way through the small crowd to throw the fur robe over him. It immediately protected him from the icy drafts blowing about, and he smiled gratefully at her. A small frown creased her brow, and she stared for a moment, ignoring the jostling about them, as though she might never see him again. Her fingers moved gently to his forehead to smooth back his hair.

"Hu't!" snarled one of the guards, shoving her roughly aside so that she nearly fell.

"Hey!" said Blaise in anger, but a command cracked out, and the bearers were already carrying him away before he could finish his protest. Propping himself up on one elbow, he looked back at her where she stood alone and vulnerable among the masked, cloaked cadre of Bban'jen.

"Let her come with us," he said, but his guards ignored him, and the bearers never slacked pace as they carried him down a steep tunnel bored through solid rock. The orange flame of the torch ahead turned his half-naked bearers into enormous black shadows, grunting in rhythm with the booted strides of the guards. Then the tunnel opened abruptly onto a tall cavern as narrow and long as a gallery. Great iron braziers, their feet cast as the brassy heads of monsters, supported flames of white fire that shot incandescent light up toward the ceiling where crystalline stalactites hung like multiple fangs. Small, glowing incense burners stood beside the braziers, sending forth fingers of scarlet smoke that writhed about the white flames like sensual caresses. Through the center of the cave lay a long ribbon of water, no wider than a man's stride, but so still and black that Blaise suspected it was bottomless. He gripped the side of his litter as the bearers wove along the narrow trail that alternately bordered the water or hugged the wall.

Beyond this cavern lay a tiny chamber filled with formations of translucent stone descending from the ceiling in wide folds as delicate as a woman's draperies. The torchlight flared in the hands of their guide, tinting the stone with the hue of pink flesh. It was difficult to maneuver the litter through, and Blaise was jostled roughly enough to send him skidding near the raw chasm of reawakened agony. He gritted his teeth, on the verge of an oath, only to choke back an exclamation of wonder as they ducked through another narrow tunnel that wound up and around sharply before opening onto a vast, seemingly endless cavern of crystal, glittering in a blinding myriad of colors by the light of a thousand burning torches. Blinking, Blaise dragged himself up and stared. It was as though jewels had been scattered by a more than generous hand. Were these fantastic crystal shapes, Blaise wondered, the fabled Jewels of M'thra?

But his bearers did not pause, although the jen guards muttered and lifted furtive hands to their masks in quick gestures of obeisance. The aroma of incense thickened, becoming increasingly pungent. Weakly Blaise lay back on the swaying litter, shutting his eyes for an instant's rest. He must have dozed, for when he awakened with a start it was to find himself lying on something that alarmingly resembled a bier. The darkness around him was warm, almost alive in its blackness.

Then, as though something had been activated by his return to consciousness, a faint white glow appeared at his feet, emanating from a small cube no larger than his fist. He blinked at it, brought to alertness by yet another reminder of an advanced culture, one akin to his own, and one no longer dominant here.

Why had they left Ruantl? Why had they abandoned the colonists? What had gone wrong? Suddenly it seemed important to know these answers. He shivered despite the warmth, unable to overcome a formless sense of unease and dread. What if he were wrong and Ruantl was nothing, *had* nothing? Like a spoken answer, words formed in his brain. *I want this planet*, he thought savagely, clenching his fists. *I want to have the control of it in my hand*. Power, he thought, feeling the intensity of that longing that throbbed through him almost as sharply as the misery in his leg. Absolute power over his own world was the only way to burn away forever the shame of being vat born. He might still be full of doubts and, yes, fear, but he was willing to pay the price of ambition and freedom, willing to enter whatever game of power plays and rebellion Picyt was staging here.

Now he was tired of waiting and tired of pain. With a grunt he levered himself up, his ears straining for a sound, any sound, to break the oppressive silence. Drafts of warm air crisscrossed him like the breath of an animal hovering over its prey. He shivered and lifted an unsteady hand to wipe away the beads of sweat breaking out along his temples. It was a mistake to sit up; even in the gloom the world seemed to tilt. Gritting his teeth, he hung on.

"All right, Picyt," he said loudly into the darkness, his words reverberating off stone and silence. "I'm here. I'm willing to reconsider your proposal. Where are you? *Picyt!*"

The light intensified, driving back the shadows slowly. With a start Blaise saw that he was sitting in the center of four oblong boxes fashioned, apparently, of crystal. They should have been clear, but within them an opaque milky gas swirled about, concealing their exact contents. He swallowed hard, turning his head to look at each one. Instead of seeing their intrinsic beauty of workmanship he was drawn by memory to grimmer, less free days when he had walked through a storage warehouse of laborers frozen away in narrow steel compartments, held until surplus left the markets and full production could begin again in the companies that employed them.

Frowning, he wrenched himself back into the present and eyed the boxes critically. One of them, he assumed, held the body he was to inhabit. Despite the control he held on himself, he could not relax the tight knot in his stomach.

Something light, almost imperceptible, brushed his mind. Stiffening in protest, Blaise swung his head around to glare at the far end of the cave, where a tall, masked figure in a blue cloak had appeared.

"Picyt," he murmured.

The priest came toward him, gesturing for those following to remain where they were. Only two black-uniformed escorts continued with Picyt. One was tall and assured despite the frayed edges of his black cloak and the scuffed places on his mask. A scarlet band at his throat marked his rank. The other figure was short, almost squarish in shape, and walked with a belligerent stride Blaise immediately recognized.

"Omari!" Her loud voice reverberated through the cave, shattering the silence. She would have rushed forward had the

Bban not seized her arm and brought her up short. He barked a curt order at her, and she said nothing more.

Picyt glided on as though he had not noticed the disturbance and came to a halt with one of the crystal coffins between him and Blaise. For a moment he stood still, silently regarding Blaise while the light glinted off the silver tracings on his mask.

Fever twisted through Blaise, making him shift impatiently under Picyt's gaze. "Well?" he demanded. "I am here!"

Picyt lifted his hand gracefully revealing the same silver markings embroidered upon the wide cuffs of his gauntlets. "You are dying, *n'ka*. There is no recovery from the touch of blue fire."

That knowledge had lain within Blaise for a long time now, but the finality of those quiet words knotted his stomach even tighter. *No*! he wanted to scream. But he held off the urge as he had held off fear, driving it away, refusing to think of anything except the way out Picyt offered.

He said, "Draw your knife, Picyt."

The priest dropped his hand in startlement. "I . . . do not understand. To spread your own blood is forbidden."

Saunders came up to stand nearby, the Bban close beside her. But she said nothing.

Blaise glanced at her, then back at Picyt. "I'm not going to kill myself," he said impatiently. "Please. Just do as I ask."

Slowly Picyt drew the jen-knife from his belt and held it forth so that the soft clear light shone along the green blade.

Blaise made no move to take it. "Saunders," he said, struggling to keep his voice steady, "is that corybdium?"

She gasped and snatched the weapon from Picyt's hand. The soldier beside her growled and moved to interfere, but Picyt swept out his hand palm down.

"No, Tuult!" he said sharply. "Leave her untouched."

For a moment it seemed as though Tuult would protest. Then with a salute he stepped away to stand with legs braced apart, his arms crossed over his chest in disapproving silence.

"Well?" demanded Blaise, fighting off the growing desire to lie down and let things slip away for a while. Now was not the time to rest. There might not be any more time. "Saunders!"

She looked up with the blade cradled in her hands. "It's very like," she said excitedly, her voice muffled by her mask.

"Of course I would have to make an exact test, but . . ." Her voice trailed off. Abruptly she squared her broad shoulders, her gloved hand closing on the hilt, which was wrapped in gold wire.

He tensed, knowing her intention as surely as though she had spoken it, but to conceal his alarm he returned his attention to Picyt.

"The metal of this blade," he said sharply, conscious of a growing sense of urgency around him. "Is it plentiful?"

"Yes," answered Picyt in puzzlement. "Do you value it? Many metals are found on Ruantl, with lead the most . . . useful." He swept out his hands. "You delay the matter to no purpose, *n'ka*. We must—"

"I agree to your terms," said Blaise quickly, raising his head, his heart thundering. "The original ones. Everything."

Picyt took a half step forward. "That is known," he said impatiently, unable to keep sharp triumph from his voice. "But why? Because you fear death?"

"I have found other reasons for changing my mind," Blaise replied.

"Corybdium!" cried Saunders, jerking up the knife. Swiftly Tuult snatched it from her, and she swung her fist at him, cursing as he dodged with twice her quickness. "Damn you, Omari!" she said, whirling to throw herself against the coffin separating them. "You're after the wealth in minerals here, with no thought of—"

"Chi'ka nun dl!" snapped Picyt with sudden, unexpected fierceness. "You have not leave, *n'dl*, to interrupt this!"

With a growl Tuult seized her arms and shook her into momentary submissiveness.

"Now," continued the priest, with a ragged edge to his voice as though he, like Blaise, stood at the limits of his physical endurance. "Reasons no longer matter. The moment we raise the Jewels and reactivate the purpose, Hihuan will know of it and send forth an attack to stop us. There will be no opportunity for doubts."

"I'm ready," said Blaise, swallowing.

"No!" cried Saunders, despite Tuult's attempts to silence her. "You lied to me! Noble Picyt, I had your word that I could return him as a prisoner—"

Picyt gently placed his fingertips on her mask. "A second oath does not bind the first," he said with a harshness that belied his quiet gestures. "I serve Anthi and her will above my own and above yours. Now be silent and look upon the wonders that are here."

Turning away from her, he pressed his fingertips together for a moment, gathering himself, then stripped off his gloves and lay his left palm upon the top of the nearest crystal box, holding it there as a faint hum slowly filled the air.

"Anthi," he chanted, his deep voice swelling with volume. "*M'thra en t'blis al ty i rantaun*. We seek our fathers. We beg you for their return."

Narrowing his eyes, Blaise watched as the milky gas within the crystal container stirred and blazed with a sudden blinding white light. Blaise covered his face, cringing back. The pressure on his leg caused it to throb viciously. He gasped, clutching his thigh with both hands in an unsuccessful effort to ease the torture. When he looked up again, the brilliant light was gone and the inside of the container clear.

Blaise's heart seemed to stop as he stared at the woman lying inside, covered only by the thick wealth of her coppery bronze hair. She looked as though she were sleeping, her mouth curved in a faint smile. No garment concealed the golden, clean-limbed perfection of her beauty. Not even Giaa could begin to match her in sheer loveliness. To gaze upon her like this seemed almost a sacrilege.

Saunders wrenched free of Tuult's slackened grip and drew nearer the container, ripping off her mask so that she might have a better view. A look of awe and wonder grew on her broad, scarred face. Then she frowned and turned away, one fist clenching on the crystal surface.

"Who is she?" Saunders whispered.

Picyt lifted his head, and as he did Blaise glimpsed a queer blue glow shining through the mesh eye guards of the priest's mask.

"Aural," said Picyt, his deep voice reverberating through the cavern with a power and resonance not his own. "Leiis."

It was enough to break the spell holding Blaise. "I'll not take a woman's form!" he snapped, his voice nearly failing him as the pain grew worse, robbing him of strength. Limply he sagged onto the bier. "Picyt, *no*! I—"

But the priest removed his palm from the top of the woman's container and with a solemn step moved to the next, placing his hand upon it and repeating the same incantation. The white light blazed forth more quickly this time.

"Vauzier," said Picyt, his voice rumbling like thunder.

Relief flooded Blaise, and he lay still, keeping back the lapping waves of unconsciousness but making no further attempts to move or to watch as Picyt moved to the third and activated it.

"Rim," he announced, and swayed before moving to the fourth. Tuult hastened to his side as Picyt hesitated, and put out a hand to steady the priest's elbow, but he did not touch Picyt. After a second the priest placed his palm upon the last box. He was directly behind Blaise now and out of sight.

For a moment there was only silence. Puzzled by the delay, Blaise lifted his head slightly but still could not see the priest. The crowd, which had ranged itself in the shadows along the cave walls, now drifted forward, moving close together in a tight huddle.

Blaise's head fell back with a thud. He blinked, fighting off the heaviness clouding him. He had not yet heard the name Picyt had once said he could become. This had to be it. Why was Picyt so slow? Blaise knew he couldn't hold out much longer, not with the fever crawling through him again. His vision blurred as shivers wracked him, and as he opened his mouth to call for Giaa he heard, as though from a long distance, Picyt's voice, ragged now with exhaustion, calling forth the final incantation. The light flashed brightly enough to make Saunders and Tuult flinch.

"Asan," said Picyt, his voice like the rushing waters of the ocean. "Father of our fathers. First of the great. In death we serve him as in life."

Hypnotic in their intensity, the words swelled through Blaise. They forced back the fever and left him suspended between two forces. Has it begun? he wondered dully.

A hand, the fingers so icy they shocked him, gently touched his brow, brushing his eyelids closed. "Sleep," whispered Picyt's normal voice, hollow with exhaustion. "In an hour you shall be beyond pain."

He thought he shut his eyes for only a few minutes, but when he next awakened—disturbed by urgent, almost angry voices and the muffled sounds of machinery being set up—it was to find that he was lying strapped on his back, a glass dome fitted over him. The air, what there was of it, smelled stuffy and old. Alarmed, he tried to move and found he could not. He had been stripped. Even his bandages were gone, leaving the black corrupted mess of his leg exposed. The stench of it, freed from Giaa's salves, overwhelmed him. He twitched, testing the bonds again, and panted under the bright cube of light focused over him, feeling exposed and trapped like a specimen fixed to a microscope slide. His lungs heaved for air, and the fever throbbed through his brain, blurring his vision as he strained to see what was going on around him. What was Picyt doing?

Intent Bban'n, maskless and brown-robed, moved in and out among the four glass cases surrounding his. He shrank now from calling them coffins, as his eyes focused desperately on the arc of glass only inches above his face. Fear, nameless and cold, crawled through him, refusing to be beaten back any longer by the promise of wealth or new life. Precious metals meant nothing. He knew instinctively that this was a mistake. Even if Picyt, with his odd mixing of superstition and knowledge, could do what he attempted here, something was still wrong. An error had been built in and was compounding as time trickled out. Sweat beaded along Blaise's spine, sticking his flesh to the surface of the bier beneath him.

A man with the elongated head and plated skin of a Bban, yet with Tlar eyes and jaw, paused, his vivid green eyes intent on the square metal pole he was erecting near Blaise's head. Panting with the sensation of being cooked alive under the bright lights, Blaise spread his fingers, curling them as he strained to break the cuff of mesh-woven metal binding his wrists. If he could just get a hand free to pound on the glass . . . Why wouldn't the man look at him?

"You!" he shouted, knowing that if he could hear them they could hear him. "Hey! I want to talk to Picyt! Let me—" He broke off, exasperated as the worker hurried away.

". . . but you told me this machine would heal his leg!" said a strident, familiar voice over the din of the workers. "Not transfer him into another body. You can't—"

"The process works," said Picyt's deep voice, still strained with weariness. "You have done well in assisting Teecht with his tasks, Saunders. But do not seek to interfere now."

Blaise twisted his head to the side and saw Picyt's blue-cloaked back. Above the collar the priest's thick dark hair waved sleekly in the brilliant lights. He lifted his golden, tapering fingers in a gesture. But Saunders, whom Blaise could not see, did not back down.

"We made a deal, noble," she snapped, and Blaise could

imagine her broad face reddening. "You gave me your word that we could go, that he would be returned to me as my prisoner. And now you're trying to use him as a symbol in some insane kind of holy war. You lied!"

Again Picyt lifted his hand, but this time it was to quell the black-masked Bban who stepped forward to intervene. Tuult, Blaise guessed, seeing the narrow band of scarlet at the soldier's throat. The glass wavered over him. Cursing, Blaise forced himself to regain a hold on consciousness and heard Picyt's low, impassioned answer: "You know nothing of the purpose, *n'dl*, nothing!" he said in a tone as glacial as the snow-covered slopes outside. "Every lie spoken in the cause of the purpose is justified. Do *not* interfere. We must make this transfer!"

"But you cannot!" Now at last she stepped into Blaise's line of vision, unmasked like Picyt and flushed with anger. The new scar on her cheek stood out white and drawn as she stared unflinchingly at the priest. "Don't you understand? He's not . . . he wasn't . . ." She waved her hand in exasperation, searching for words, as the tendons in her neck spread and corded. "He was vat made! Grown in a laboratory for a cheap labor drone. He wasn't *born* . . . he wasn't created naturally."

Picyt turned to signal at someone. "Raise power levels. It is time to activate direct linkage with Anthi."

"Why won't you listen to me?" she shouted, while a sudden hum of vibration started up around Blaise, setting his teeth on edge. He smelled a peculiar pungent odor, not unpleasant, and a milky-white gas, as cold as death itself, began to fog over the glass covering him. "This is all so futile—"

"If you comprehended what we are doing—" began Picyt impatiently.

"I do!" she retorted as the fog obscured her. But he went on straining to listen, as if their voices were his last link with life. "Picyt, listen to me. You will destroy him, and possibly your king as well. Blaise Omari's psyche is artificial. He was built in a lab. There is *nothing* in him that can be put into another body, no matter how advanced your equipment. . . ."

The fog wrapped icy tendrils around Blaise's body, searing him with cold. He could no longer hear Saunders's voice, nor Picyt's answer, if any was given. Anger spread through him. How did she know he had no soul? Had she created the universe? Damn her!

But anger could not overcome this fresh fear. *No soul* . . .

The words pounded through him, shredding what scant courage he had left so that all that remained was growing fear, overwhelming and raw.

No soul! An artificial psyche! No transfer!

That was the error in Picyt's calculations, the one factor neither of them had considered. Saunders was right. He *did* lack what real men possessed. The scientists of the Institute were not God; there were limits to their abilities of creation. That was the real point of shame, being half a man.

Demos, he thought as panic throttled him beneath the white fog's groping touch. He drew a hasty breath and it was like inhaling cotton. Choking, he strained to free a hand, to scream, to do anything to make Picyt stop.

But there was no stopping. The vibrations ran straight into his veins, and he felt a rhythm of incantations spoken over him in slow candence as the fog froze him. Something infinitely colder began to suck the very essence from him.

"No!" he screamed, struggling.

But there was no way to fight or to hold back. He was slipping away, faster and faster as the greed of the other intensified. It was as though something fed upon him, and what had been Blaise shrank smaller and smaller, becoming a speck of quivering terrified flesh in vast darkness. His brain seemed to explode, and then for a split second of stability everything stopped. Shaken, he dared try to comprehend, only to cringe as he suddenly confronted his own mind. Every compartment was flung open, spilling out all that had always been carefully held. Memories, thoughts, fears, and hopes jumbled around him in myriad forms and colors, overwhelming, incomprehensible . . . terrifying. The pull resumed, dragging him screaming through his own mind as though he were being inverted through a thousand nightmares of knowledge. No one was meant to encounter himself in this way! He sensed, with a fresh spurt of panic, that he was being pulled down to the very center of his being . . . to the soul, the thing he did not have. He wondered how many creatures had faced their own souls and lived, and he knew he could not survive facing the emptiness that awaited him.

Something snapped, and suddenly he was warm, resting thankfully in a soft, dark, fluid place, protected and safe and surrounded by . . .

Her.

Only for an instant was he given that sensation, but it

locked itself vise-hard about him and would not let go. No vat boy had fetal memories of womb and . . . and of *mother*! He had not been created out of chemicals and bacteria. He was not a drone inexplicably more intelligent and rebellious than the average product. What he had valued as independence was *life*. He was real! He had been *born*. Damn the Institute! Whether they had stolen him to put him in the lab as an "improved" model or punished a nonsanctioned pregnancy by raising him as a drone—the lowest, most degraded form of life among the upper species—did not matter. What was important was the reality.

Triumphant, he forgot to fear the pull and threw himself at its source, wanting to be free. The void rushed upon him, black and endless and horrible, but he hurtled onward through its spinning cortex, stretching farther and farther. There must come an end to how far he could go.

He reached it with an unexpected, excruciating wrench of pain. For a moment he remained poised, suspended motionless. Then, just at the instant of rebound, a blue beam of light, as incisive as a laser-scalpel, sliced behind him, and he flew onward, faster and yet *faster*, bridging a place that had not even a void to fill it. Then blackness—alien and unreceptive—engulfed him again. And with a shock he encountered another where there was space for only one.

For a moment they faced each other, he having no choice but to go forward, the other blocking him.

Go back.

Fear struck Blaise, dimming his confidence. He could not. The way had been severed. Picyt had said there was no return, and Picyt had made sure of it.

Go back. You are not the one.

The darkness faced him. Blue force raged behind him. Blaise felt himself part, and in sudden fury fought the division, knowing now that Picyt had deceived him too. He was not meant to take on Asan's body but instead Asan was to take him. Well, he was not a tool—not of the Institute's and not of Picyt's. With all the stubbornness lying at his core, Blaise hurled himself at the other, who held firm for a terrifying moment before crumbling away as though brittle with age.

Now the pull was gone, replaced by a push from behind, as everything rushed forward to fill the vacuum. Again Blaise knew a swift, incredibly harsh lance of pain. Then light flooded the darkness, driving it out with a vengeance, and its brilliance was so great he blinked against the pain in his eyes.

That physical movement, slight as it was, roused him to consciousness. Once again he was lying in the midst of the white cold fog, half frozen, aching, and weak. He groaned, turning his head to one side in the bitterness of disappointment. After all that pain, terror, and struggle, it had not worked.

The fog thinned. Blaise lay motionless, too tired to react or even think as he heard muffled unintelligible voices and dimly saw shapes hover over him as the fog dissipated. The shapes were blurred and wavering. He blinked, frowning, but they did not clear. What was wrong? The blurring increased; their shouting voices faded. His lungs caught, strove for another breath, and caught again.

"Picyt!" he tried to call as vision failed him, but no sound came from his throat. Death faced him, not as he had imagined it, not as he had minutes before fought it, but strangely like some . . .

With an ear-splitting screech the crystal dome lifted. Blaise opened his eyes to glimpse Picyt's ashen face, lined with fatigue, bending over him.

"My life to thee," he whispered hoarsely, placing his cold fingertips upon Blaise's cheeks. "Anthi speaks. Take her calling unto thee and *live*!"

His dark burning eyes suddenly glowed with a blue flame. Energy crackled into Blaise's veins. He felt them expand fully as though they had been shriveled for an eternity. His heart began to beat with new vigor. His lungs filled, exhaled, and filled again. The awful, final coldness faded, driven back by Picyt's stength. Relaxing, Blaise basked in it, letting it wash over him entirely. For a moment he seemed surrounded by rings of wholeness, strength, and *life*. He grasped them gratefully, then felt the support recede, bit by slow bit, giving him time to steady himself.

A strong hand slid under his shoulder, lifting him to a sitting position. Blaise shut his eyes and drew in several more breaths, amazed by his new sensitivity to every powerful expansion of his lungs, to every heartbeat. He seemed to be able to feel the blood surging through his heart. And smells . . . never, even with his keen senses, had he noticed so many. They bombarded him almost overwhelmingly, yet he could sort through them all, identifying the perspiration-soaked scent of Saunders; a fainter, acrid, almost chemical odor hanging upon Picyt; a hundred variations of the Bban musks, Henans, and . . .

Suddenly Blaise opened his eyes, only to be stunned by vision suddenly clearer and far sharper than ever before. He could see across the cavern, even through the shadows beyond the hot lights, to observe the jagged stalagmite formations piled along a curve of the wall. He frowned and raised his hand to stare at it. It was lean and supple, the fingers long and tapering. There was a large black-stoned ring encircling his right forefinger.

No . . . He gave his head a slight shake. It was not *his* hand. His fingers were thin and dark, his hands small and scarred. Blaise narrowed his eyes, seeing the long, muscular arm attached to the hand that was not his. On the inside of the sleek, golden forearm a lengthy white scar marred the skin. It was not *his* scar. It was not *his* body.

Faced with it, expecting it, prepared for it, still Blaise could not believe it had actually been done. Wildly he sat forward, despite the many steadying hands, and noticed the shriveled, unrecognizable thing lying on the central bier before him. A craggy-faced priest, shaven-headed and garbed in a stained brown robe, threw a cloak over the carcass and gestured for two slaves to bear it away. Something twisted within Blaise. They bore *him* away.

No! He must get a grip on himself. The body was gone, but *he* existed. That was all. He grew aware of the total silence surrounding him, and for the first time turned his head to gaze into a face.

Less than a hundred individuals formed the watching, awestruck crowd. At once he picked out Giaa. She had crouched upon the dusty floor, her hair hanging over her face and her shoulders shaking. He stared at her, and as he did so she raised her head, her hair swinging back to reveal her tear-streaked face. Then her eyes met his and widened, shocked into enormous silver pools of light. She lifted a trembling hand, and slowly the light of astonishment filled her face, brightening to worship. Others around her began to sway and bend and kneel, Bban and priest alike. A few feet apart from them Saunders stood rigidly, held by shock. Or was it disbelief?

Then a young priest lifted his hands into the air and in a clear, trembling voice began a chant that was taken up by the others. Blaise frowned, turning his head away as the adulation began to pour forth. It was wrong. They should not look at him like that. He *wasn't* Asan; he was . . .

A flicker of excitement reached through his shock. He had survived, and now he was their leader. The first step to getting what he wanted had been successfully taken.

He turned around abruptly, startling those who steadied him, to stare at Picyt. The priest stood pressed against the edge of the bier. His face had lost color, and the straight, serene features had shrunk in as though the firmness had been drawn from his flesh. Deep lines of exhaustion carved down from his dark slanted eyes to the drooping corners of his mouth. But he lifted his blank, blue-filmed gaze to Blaise's own questing one, and his eyes gradually sharpened their focus as he drew forth one last bit of strength long held in reserve. He blinked, and his own questions trembled on his sagging countenance with a naked eagerness that shocked Blaise.

Picyt had not believed the transfer could really happen! All of his assurance and monumental serenity had been false! Realizing that he had let himself be a guinea pig, Blaise sat more erect, pulling away from the hands upon him. Anger swept him with sudden violence.

Damn you, Picyt! He tried to speak and found he still had no voice. The anger swelled, frustrated by having no outlet. Then suddenly the words crystallized in his mind and burst forth like an explosion.

He saw Picyt flinch and reel back. The dark eyes widened, and with a mental force that rammed steel splinters through Blaise's skull, he said: *My . . . leiil?*

No! retorted Blaise, fury enabling him to adapt swiftly to this new telepathic ability. *I am not your leiil* or *your Asan! Damn you! You lied, Picyt! You* knew *I was not supposed to survive transfer. You deceived me into being your experiment, when all the time what you really wanted was the original Asan back.* Blaise gritted his teeth, his eyes hot as he glared at the priest. *Forget that, priest. Asan's body is all you have. The rest is me, and now you're going to accept my plans and my—*

He did not survive? Picyt's thoughts jumbled around Blaise in distorted sequences. *The time span was too great. Ah . . .* A spasm of grief twisted Picyt's features, and he lifted his fingertips to his brow, a gesture hurriedly copied by all those surrounding them. But when Picyt's eyes met Blaise's again, they had lost their eagerness and their fear. *You survived against Asan, the most powerful of all wills. Anthi was right; I . . .* He swallowed with obvious difficulty. *I could have survived.* I *could have been the one. . . .* Hatred blazed from his eyes, darkening them to a black fire. *Your plans*? he said with a mocking laugh. He swept his hand out angrily. *Never! You are mine to command. You shall obey* me, n'ka!

Here is my enemy, thought Blaise, his own anger overwhelmed by the degree of hate unleashed against him.

Then, without warning, the priest's eyes flickered, and he crumpled soundlessly into a limp heap on the floor.

"Revered noble!" The priests surrounding Blaise hastened to their fallen leader, only to be shoved aside by Tuult, who knelt to gather Picyt up tenderly in his arms. He stood, half turning to Blaise so that Blaise had a clear, unpleasant look at Picyt's hanging head.

"*Leiil*," said Tuult's guttural voice, gruff yet pleading.

Blaise drew back involuntarily. They were all staring at him, looking to him to take charge just as moments before they had looked to Picyt. Nervousness rippled through Blaise. Suddenly his stomach hurt and his eyes burned from the lights. A wry sense of disgust twisted within him. This was his chance, and he could not take it. He did not know what to do.

He started to speak, then hesitated, unsure of his voice and realizing that without a translator he could not communicate at all. Even if he lifted a hand, it might convey the wrong gesture.

Taking a deep breath, he reached out and drew the cloak from the shoulders of one of the priests beside him. At once the man guessed what he wanted and helped wrap the cloak about Blaise. The heavy weight of the long folds of cloth were oddly comforting. Carefully, none too certain his legs would support him, he edged himself off the bier. Again quick, reverent hands steadied him.

"Leiil. The Tlar leiil. Great One. *Asan*." The words lifted high and low through the chanting, and the worship came at him like a wave.

Blaise lifted his head, drawing himself erect to stand poised with one foot braced slightly ahead of the other. Suddenly it seemed natural to stand thus, like a king. He gazed out at them all, savoring this new feeling of power that began to reach through his sense of disbelief.

With a quick look at Tuult, who still waited with the unconscious Picyt in his arms, Blaise swept out his hand palm up, imitating a gesture he had seen countless times.

"*An*," he said, and to his astonishment a voice of tremendous strength and resonance vibrated forth from his throat.

A collective sigh gushed out from the crowd. Tuult inclined his head, and even that simple gesture held a mixture of reverence and impatience that caused Blaise to pause.

He took an uncertain step and then another, his muscles stiff. Tuult fell into step beside him, carrying Picyt effortlessly. The Bban warrior emitted an even stronger arrogance, almost as though he had won a victory. Around them a phalanx of brown-robed priests and black-cloaked jen gathered, and the small, tattered crowd parted for their passage with whispers and many bows.

What have I done? Blaise wondered, beginning to be awed himself. The quivery soreness in his legs faded as each step grew stronger and lengthened into strides that amazed him with their rapid ease. His head lifted, his nostrils flared at each crossed and blending scent emanating from the crowd. A queer, restive excitement stirred within him. He frowned at the sensation, not understanding it, then suddenly he whirled around. His eyes blazed, questing over the crowd swiftly as he sought the woman whose scent, Bban sweet and heavy, rose above the rest. Ah, there she knelt, a huddled figure in a tattered robe and cowl. He halted, his nostrils quivering as his blood heated in a compulsion to approach her.

"Leiil!" said Tuult's gruff voice, breaking the spell. As Blaise turned to the warrior, he blinked at the fierce scarlet glow shining through the eye guards of Tuult's mask. *"Ny rol'an tu r!"*

The rapid string of words blurred through Blaise like a language known long ago and forgotten. Understanding tickled along the corners of his brain, but he could not grasp it. Annoyed at this inability to communicate, he turned away from the woman and drew his borrowed cloak more closely about him. The rough cloth scratched his skin, and his blood cooled abruptly, leaving his flesh chilled.

Tuult strode on, and after a moment of hesitation Blaise followed, with a final glance at the woman. She lifted her bowed head as he passed by her, and the cowl slipped back to reveal a hideous Bban face, the eyes glowing with a horribly fascinating allure. Blaise averted his face and strode on, appalled by his desire for her. For an instant, as they left the cavern to enter a passageway formed by one gigantic slab of rock leaning against another, he thought he would be sick.

Then, with a desperate wrench of will, he forced himself to forget what had happened. Obviously the Tlar had no compunctions against mingling with Bban, or there would not be creatures like Giaa—disturbingly lovely yet cursed with those strange silver eyes. Something deeper than his own revulsion stabbed through him, and by instinct he realized that his new body had lived under firm discipline once and must again be brought under control.

The passageway narrowed ahead, forcing them all to stop and squeeze through one at a time. The torchbearer went through first; plunging them into deep shadow. The weight of rock pressed heavily overhead, and as he watched Tuult struggle to maneuver Picyt's limp body through, grunting in the effort, a tickle of unease stiffened Blaise. The Bban'jen pressed closer about him in the darkness, the second torchbearer lowering his torch to his side so that the flame flickered almost to extinction. It was a good place for an ambush, Blaise thought, his instincts honed by years of danger. Faint pricklings rose up and down his arms, and, feeling half foolish at his own suspicions, he moved to place his back against solid rock.

That shift of weight was all that saved him from a quick stab of a knife blade. It scraped his ribs and tangled in his cloak, missing him by so narrow a margin that his stomach froze in disbelief that he was untouched. Furious, he sought to clamp the wrist of his attacker, who moved in swiftly, blocking the dim light from Blaise's vision as he pinned Blaise against the wall.

"Tuult—"

Blaise's cry was cut off as powerful hands gripped his throat, the fingers digging in, trying to rip it apart. His air choked off, Blaise tore at those immovable forearms, unable to free himself even with the greater strength of his new body. Dimly, as his brain spun and his lungs heaved desperately, he was aware of other Bban'jen shuffling about, masking the silent, deadly struggle between him and his attacker.

Blaise shut his eyes, gasping for the air that could not reach past those viselike hands. A tremor ran through him; he felt his consciousness slip.

But then, as his own failing faculties permitted others to come to the fore, he dropped his hands and ceased struggling.

"Ah!" His attacker shifted one hand to grip Blaise's hair and jerk his head back in an effort to snap his neck.

Even as pain flashed through Blaise's spine, a deep anger focused within him, rising up to explode and burst forth.

With a high-pitched scream the attacker fell back, dropping his ruthless grasp on Blaise as he staggered into another Bban.

"*Ny! Ny!*" he screamed, collapsing to writhe on the floor.

Blaise glared at him with burning, merciless eyes, aware of nothing save the rage that consumed him. Then the Bban gave a final choked cry and moved no more. Blaise lifted his head and swept his gaze at the remaining Bban'jen, who threw their knives on the floor and fled. A bolt of blue fire crackled through the passageway, cutting them down. Screaming, they fell twitching in the dust as the stench of burning flesh rolled back across the air. The flame in Blaise's eyes faded as his anger abruptly died. He blinked, dazed, and lifted a hand to his throat. His eyes ached fiercely, as dry as if the moisture had been scorched from them. With another blink he squinted down at the attacker before frowning at Tuult, who was tucking his fire-rod back into his belt.

The Bban paused to look up at Blaise, his mask a formless blur in the shadows. Blaise caught a sense of growing respect in the man, overlaid by urgency.

"Thou *art* the Tlar leiil," Tuult whispered, his voice rough with grudging belief. Then he gave himself a shake and swept out a hand. "Great One, come! The revered noble has need of thee."

But Blaise did not move. He slid his hands behind his back to press against the damp, gritty surface of stone. Once before he'd been attacked while in Tuult's care. And the fact that the officer had just killed two of his own men did not make Blaise any more willing to trust him. Death meant nothing to the Bban'jen. They killed their own kind as readily as they killed anyone else. Blaise had no intention of stepping into another trap.

He suspected that the fact that he could now understand Tuult was related to the mental force that had shot from him and killed his attacker. His eyes narrowed.

"Who were these men?" he asked, his words those of Ruantl. He gestured at the dead Bban'n lying sprawled in the passageway, trying to deny the tremor going through him. If his thoughts alone could kill, how could he ever learn to control his powers?

Tuult's gloved hand tightened on the hilt of his jen-knife. He coughed with a queer barking sound. "Leiil, the time is not for questions. Come. I beg it. I did doubt thee, but thou hast the true power of Anthi." As he spoke he lifted his hand quickly to touch his mask, but it was a perfunctory motion, lacking the respect it was supposed to signify. "Thou art the Leiil Asan. Have mercy and do not let the revered noble die."

The pleading in that rough, proud voice pulled at Blaise. But he held off sentiment, tired of being constantly on the defensive, never quite understanding all the moves made by those who sought to use him.

"I will have my answers first," he said, resisting Tuult's growing impatience, which was strong enough now to be felt as one of his own emotions. He could also smell Tuult's musk beginning to intensify. Blaise's senses went on alert, and he shifted his feet, poised, wary. "Why was I attacked? Who were they?"

Tuult clicked his jaw rapidly behind his mask, a sign of nervousness he seldom displayed. "Leiil Hihuan knows of thee now, Great One. All Bban'n are not loyal to the revered noble." He extended his hand. "*An*, Great One. Please. As a pon of the first cadre, possessing full honor, I give my blood to thee in this request."

Blaise stared at him, surprised by such a vow.

"He dies, Great One. Time is small."

Blaise frowned and reluctantly stepped forward one pace. "What is wrong with him?"

Tuult sighed. "To serve Anthi is hard, my Leiil. Thou knows it. He gave all of himself to bring thee forth. Save him now in return."

"But I don't—" Blaise's frown deepened, and he broke off as something queer brushed his mind. A small part of him seemed to ebb away.

Tuult whirled as though struck, his hand flying instinctively to his knife hilt. "*Lea'dl*, the circles of all wholeness are breaking. We lose him!"

He ducked through the low place, already running, and Blaise followed in spite of an urge to go the other way. He had to crouch lower and lower as the passageway narrowed, and he cursed as he failed to keep pace with the Bban. Abruptly Tuult pulled to a halt and darted beneath a low overhang, from which spilled golden light. Panting, Blaise bent down and scrambled after him into a small, overheated chamber filled with light and argument.

Picyt lay on the stone floor with his blue cloak spread

beneath him. Ashen-faced, with the flesh shrunken below his sharply ridged cheekbones, he seemed scarcely to draw breath. Beside him knelt a young Bban, unmasked, with the cowl of his brown robe thrown back, grieving in an anguish clear in every line of his rocking body. Two men—one old and pudgy with lines of discontent and arrogance carved into his sallow face, the other young with thin, sharp features—stood over their leader, arguing heatedly.

"You must, Uble," the old one was saying as Blaise ducked inside. He held out a goblet, its gold-encrusted sides winking brightly in the intense light flaming forth from the braziers in each corner. "I am too old to withstand the effects. If you do not seek to enter his mind and reform the rings of union, all will be lost. *All!* Contact with Anthi must not be broken." He glared at young Uble, his jowls quivering with vehemence.

Uble drew back with a gesture of distaste. "Basai, you know I am not sufficiently trained—"

"I know you dare defy the will of Anthi!" shouted Basai. Again he thrust the goblet at Uble, this time with such violence that part of the dark contents sloshed over the rim and ran dripping down his hand onto the floor. "Drink the *yde*, coward. You—"

Tuult strode forward with a swing of his black cloak, and his growl sliced off the argument, leaving a ragged silence in the air. "Leiil Asan is with us, priests. There is no need for this." Contemptuously he dashed the goblet from Basai's hand, the clatter of metal upon stone ringing out over the priest's exclamation as the *yde* spread across the floor in a thick dark stain. Tuult turned and extended his hand to Blaise, who stood there trapped by their gazes, once again uncomprehending. "Anthi lies within him in the true way," said Tuult, his harsh voice strident. "He can destroy. He can give life. Truth is in him, not *yde*."

Uble shut his eyes, drooping in relief. Basai, however, flicked a hard, angry look at Blaise before bowing deeply.

"So be it," he said, lifting his eyes to glare at Blaise. "If thou *art* leiil, and not an image of Anthi to soothe us yet again into false belief." He drew his cloak tightly about himself. "I must go back to the main cavern and see the litanies do not falter." He inclined his balding head. "By thy leave."

Blaise stood aside and he went out, grunting as he bent under the low overhang of rock. The room seemed to shimmer before Blaise. He blinked, frowning as his sense of uneasiness deepened.

"Ah'hi!" wailed the boy kneeling beside Picyt. He lifted his ugly, scarred face to them, the features contorted even more by grief. "He dies. He *dies*!"

Uble turned toward Blaise, reaching out a hand, then hesitated, uncertain how to approach him. "Leiil," he whispered, his thin face intense with anxiety. "Forgive my unbelief, and act now, I beg thee! Anthi must not withdraw from him."

"The rings must be reformed. *An*." Tuult took Blaise by the arm and led him over to Picyt.

Bewildered, Blaise knelt as he was instructed by the impatient Bban and started to place his fingertips on Picyt's temples, only to draw back with his hands curling into fists. He pulled in an unsteady breath, his heart pounding.

"I can't do this!" he said savagely. "I don't know how!"

Uble groaned and turned away, but Tuult clamped an iron hand upon Blaise's shoulder.

"Thou art he," he said sternly. "I saw. I *believe*. The blue fire of Anthi is thine. Give way to her, Leiil, and she will be thy guide to what thou has forgotten."

Blaise's bare flesh crawled at the words, but he bent his head, no longer able to escape comprehension. Unwillingly, aware of Tuult's nervous hand grasping his knife hilt, Blaise placed his fingertips upon Picyt's temples. The skin was clammy cold under his touch. Blaise's face tightened as he waited. Nothing happened.

He looked up in frustration, conscious of their stares. "What do you—"

Fire suddenly flamed to life in his veins, making him start and cry out. Gasping at the intensity of that agony, he tried to pull his hands away and could not. He was trapped, unable to move, while the flames shot through him, burning up his brain and dulling his vision behind a fiery blue haze. Dimly he was aware that the others had cowered away, swiftly donning their masks, and huddled as far from him as possible. But they no longer mattered. Even consciousness of his own pain faded as a part of his mind crossed a threshold into a place of vastness where all seemed tiny and indistinct. Unnameable things bumped into him and swirled about. Then an icy clarity gripped him. He saw the entire molecular structure of all that made up Ruantl—the planet, the atmosphere, the system, the dimension in space and time. It was all there around him, in him, and in its perfect logical order. And he saw a twisting, a shifting, as he found Picyt the focal point of a growing distortion. It was like looking at a black hole on tactical graphics, yet far beyond that. For an instant he knew a temptation to let himself surge forward and be pulled down into that vortex. But to enter the depths of Picyt's soul was not his desire.

He knew now what to do and stretched forth his center of calmness, expanding the source of the blue fire within him until sheets of flame swept over the hole of distortion to seal it off. A faint cry came to him, but he ignored it. Then the fire retracted through his veins, leaving him cleansed and exhilarated.

He blinked, dropped his hands from Picyt's head. Lifting his eyes to meet the masked faces of the other three, he said, "The rings are restored." And his deep voice thundered with the awesome power he had just experienced.

Uble and the Bban boy dropped to their knees, bending in prostration upon the floor. "We give thee the thanks of our blood and our life," said Uble, the boy soundlessly echoing his words.

But Tuult, although he knelt, did not bow. "Leiil," he said, his masked gaze upon Picyt. "The revered noble still suffers. Will thee not take mercy on he who guided thee to life again?"

Blaise stared at him, robbed momentarily of breath. Didn't they realize who he was? Surely they could not believe the original Asan had returned. And yet, why should he expect them to deny the evidence they had seen? He wore Asan's body and had the ability, however limited, to use Asan's powers; only Picyt knew his secret, and if the priest remained ill and unable to denounce him . . .

Blaise stared down at Picyt's unconscious face. "The Noble Picyt," he said slowly, revolted by the drug-riddled body before him, "must make his own recovery."

Suddenly consumed by hunger, Blaise rose to his feet, but with a leap Tuult blocked his path.

"Where is Tlar justice?" he cried hoarsely. "Thou must—"

Blaise threw up his hand to cut him off. "Why? Why do you want more? Picyt will not die. In time he will overcome what the drug has done to his body. But justice lies in allowing him to pay for self-abuse." He frowned. "Step aside, Tuult. I must have food and clothing and time to—" He broke off, unwilling to admit how shaky his mental balance still was. To be Asan, *not* Blaise or even BLZ-80-4163, was going to take some adjustment. "Let Giaa tend him, and come with me. I'm not going anywhere after this without trustworthy protection."

From the sudden tension in the room, he suspected he had perhaps gone too far. What constituted insult here? he wondered, watching Tuult's hand clench. Tlar leiil or not, and whatever else he might now be, he was not safe. Tonight's attack had shown him that.

"Leiil, please—" began Uble, his green eyes clouded. "We accord the truth of thy words and bow to their wisdom, but time—"

"There is no time!" cut in Tuult with a savage gesture. "Soon the horde of the Tlar'jen will rise. Picyt must be restored now."

Anger flared once again in Blaise, lifting more than adrenaline through his blood as challenge-readiness stirred.

Perhaps Tuult read that in his eyes, for he stiffened. But this time his gloved hand did not reach for his knife.

Conscious that he was tempting that forbearance possibly further than it could stand, Blaise did not let his eyes waver from the Bban's mask.

"Why," he repeated angrily, "must Picyt be restored now? Can *you* not prepare the army, Pon Tuult?"

The boy gasped, and even Uble lost color.

Tuult's chest expanded, and when he spoke it was with an explosive clicking: "I think my Leiil would test me too far! But, *Lea'dl*, is the answer forgotten in the mists of eternity that have held thee, Great One? The Bban'jen must have Picyt to father us. We can wait no longer." With those words, he reached up both hands to pull off his mask, revealing a narrow bony face puckered by crossing scars. His glowing scarlet eyes, deep-set beneath a jutting ridge of browbone, bored into Blaise with inescapable intensity. His voice dropped to a husky, broken whisper: "If thou wilt not permit the revered noble to father us, wilt thou then take the act unto thyself?" He knelt as if removing his mask had removed the last measure of his fierce pride. "Father us, Great One, into Tlar. We have served thee long for this promised reward. Give us now the hand of Anthi, who rules us so harshly, that we may know freedom from the oppression that crushes us."

"Yes, good Leiil!" said Uble eagerly as Blaise gaped at

Tuult. "Tuult speaks well. The Bban tribes must be summoned at once for their transference. The purpose must be accomplished."

Blaise furrowed his brow. A buzzing seemed to impair his hearing. He gave his head an impatient shake, certain he was not hearing this correctly. "Explain the purpose," he said.

Uble opened his mouth, but Tuult rose swiftly to his feet, his scarlet eyes blazing.

"Deny not Anthi's will!" he shouted. His hand clamped hard upon his knife hilt. "Even the Tlar leiil may not refuse Anthi. Father us, or restore Noble Picyt. That is the choice laid before thee."

Chapter 8

Hihuan pushed aside his ty-boy in sudden boredom and left the silken cushions. Throwing on a crimson robe, he crossed the room to lean against a fluted column and stare at the leisured courtiers strolling by the fountains that splashed on the colonade below his balcony. Their muted conversations and laughter floated gently up to him, accompanied by strains of bailanke music, as mournful and delicate as a sisen's call across the wild lakes. He frowned, pain rippling through him at the remembered beauty of . . . home. His fingers dug into the tracery carved in the stone of the column. What had dredged up that old memory?

"Leiil?" The ty-boy's voice called, throaty softness mingled with pleading.

Hihuan turned his head, but even as he glanced at the slim Henan youth, golden-skinned and perfect as he lay upon the purple silk of the cushions, crimson and turquoise smoke curling over him with caresses of costly incense, his heart hardened. He was bored with desire and too restless for passion. Almost absently he cooled the practiced emotions stirring his blood and averted his cold eyes from the boy's smoking gaze. It did not matter that he had raised the boy to the fifth level, which if unfulfilled would soon plunge his hireling into agony. Even the most costly pleasures meant nothing as long as Picyt coursed the Outerlands like a mad chaka.

Hihuan's supple hand clenched and abruptly he whirled away from the balcony to gesture at the boy.

"Wine would please me," he snapped. "Rise and fill my goblet."

"My Leiil." With a gasp at this unexpected show of temper, the ty-boy slid off the cushions with sinuous grace and moved to a small, triangular table where a silver ewer and jewel-encrusted goblets waited. His slim hands trembled slightly as he poured, making the tiny silver bells tied to a silken cord about his wrist tinkle in tremors of sound. Several times his glowing scarlet eyes shifted to Hihuan, who stood again upon the balcony in a brooding stance.

"Hurry!" said Hihuan with a snap of his fingers, and with a bow the boy glided to him.

Taking the proffered goblet, Hihuan glared at him, contemptuous of the mingled expressions of fear and longing on that delicate mixed-blood face and pleased with the headiness of holding absolute power over this small creature of pleasure. That was as it should be, absolute control over every being that inhabited Ruantl. Hihuan lifted the goblet to his lips and tipped back his head, drinking down the heavy rich wine thirstily. But his power was challenged as long as Picyt ran unchecked, spreading his disease of rebellion and revolt throughout the Outerlands. Hihuan's eyes blazed, and he threw the emptied goblet at the boy, who caught it and stood quivering and pale, his naked body drawing up as if he expected to be struck.

"Please, my Leiil," he said, his trained voice still soft and persuasive despite the distress that had drained his face until the bones stood out sharply under his skin. "If thou would permit a tye-maid to join me, I am certain we could please thee greatly."

Distracted from his thoughts of the priests, Hihuan looked on the boy in fresh anger. "Miserable Henan dung," he said contemptuously enough to make the boy flinch, "do you expect me to pay your master double for doubly wretched goods? If I desire a maid, I have a court full!"

The ty-boy hid his ashen face and dropped to the floor in a low crouch. "I crave pardon," he whispered, his voice without breath. A tremor shook his slim body. "Please, leiil. Allow me to finish—"

"Silence," snapped Hihuan, tired of his sniveling. It would have taken only a flick of thought to release the boy from the fifth level, but instead Hihuan stepped around the wretch and struck the chime of summons with a small gold-encrusted mallet.

In less than a minute the Pon Fflir stood saluting before him, the bronze badge of the Tlar leiil's personal cadre gleaming upon the black tunic of his jen uniform.

"Service to my Leiil!" he snapped out smartly.

Hihuan eyed him with petulance, wishing to see what smug expression lay behind that black mask. He knew well that the Tsla leiis had preference for this piece of arrogance, and even the thought of Zaula's soft, musky flesh given to any save his own boiled his blood to the point of challenge. But he curbed himself, for he had need of the pon just now. Later, when Picyt and his uprising were dust ground before the boiling force of a black devi, he would see that Fflir received exactly what his insolence deserved.

None of these thoughts betrayed itself in his voice, however, as he faced the pon with his crimson robe slipping negligently from one broad, fleshy shoulder. He even managed a slight smile, although his eyes remained as cold and black as the blood coursing through his veins.

"I would have news of your progress," he said over the faint strains of bailanke music still being played below the balcony.

Fflir hesitated, casting a pointed look at the ty-boy, who still huddled on the floor of polished, red-veined jate stone. "Hirelings can carry tales beyond the palace walls, Leiil."

The ty-boy had begun to weep, silently, of course, but Hihuan was aware of his misery. He lifted his head proudly, shaking back his hair so that it brushed his shoulders. Some faint stir in the air shifted the colored smoke his way, and for a moment incense stung his nostrils.

"The boy does not matter," he said, impatience rising again within him. "He will not leave us before the morrow. Now, pon. What news? Or do you offer us yet more failures?"

Fflir stiffened, his gauntleted hand flying to the jeweled jen-knife at his belt. "Good Leiil, we have captured two lesser houses of the Kkanthor-kai along the Ddreui plains and destroyed them. The prisoners will be brought here as soon as season abates."

Hihuan's black eyes brooded upon Fflir's jen-knife, knowing the perfumed hand of the Tsla leiis had given it to him. Again the Tlar leiil's blood burned within his veins.

Through his teeth he said, "And what will we do with these few priests you have captured, Fflir? They will not share their knowledge of the heart of Anthi. And their deaths will bore us, no matter what clever device you invent to bring it about." With the back of his hand he struck Fflir's chest, rocking him slightly off-balance. "Do you think these petty efforts appease us?" he shouted. "What of that *merdar* Picyt? Has he been found? What of the caverns of M'thra? Have your forces been stationed at the valley pass to guard it? What do you, Fflir, on these things?" He stepped back with a snort and gestured, sending the ty-boy scurrying to the table to pour more wine and bring it to him. Hihuan snatched the heavy goblet from the boy's shaking hand and shot Fflir a glare. "You do not answer our questions, pon," he said coldly, filling his rich voice with menace. Fflir would never tremble and quake before him, but there were other ways of impaling the officer on his will.

Fflir stood now at attention, breathing rapidly, the symbols of family, house, and caste glittering on his mask. He raised his head. "Good Leiil, I do not fail in my duties. We cannot transport jen to the northern peaks now, with the black devis tearing up the desert in between—"

"Excuses," snarled Hihuan, gulping down his wine. It settled heavily in his stomach, swelling it to the point of discomfort. The taste cloyed his tongue with sticky sweetness. He frowned and set the goblet down, half emptied. "You—"

A chiming for admittance made him whirl around, further angered by the intrusion as three courtiers entered in the wake of a cringing servant. Infuriated, he opened his mouth to scream dismissal at them, then swiftly controlled his temper as the foremost removed his brown mask.

"Aabrm," said Hihuan, raising his brows. Despite the wine and the presence of the ty-boy, his senses were not so distracted that they could not catch the secret signal from his counselor. Something was very amiss. Aabrm's lined, pouchy face was carefully devoid of all expression, which in itself said much. "Speak." Hihuan extended his hand palm up, and at once Fflir sheathed his drawn jen-knife and stepped back. "We give you leave."

Aabrm inclined his head, expelling a faint sigh. He had doubted his leiil's temper would stand the strain of an unrequested audience. But he did not delay matters with his usual habit of portentious preamble. "Leiil," he said, still somewhat out of breath from his brisk entry. "The spies in the House of Soot'dla report that Dame Agate has sensed the opening of the mysteries of Anthi—"

"No!"

That cry of protest wrenched itself from Hihuan. For a moment he stood frozen, locked in the grip of horror. That Picyt could be such an insane, reckless fool stunned him past thought. And yet . . . in his inner self he had known Picyt would dare this blasphemy to the rings of life from the moment he had escaped the palace. *Lea'dl*, but the very thought of this shook the blood. Clenching his fists, Hihuan raised his head. He must know more.

"Let there be silence," he said, sweeping out his hands as Aabrm opened his mouth to continue. Slowly, reluctantly, Hihuan brought his fingertips together and shut his eyes, concentrating on his inner being and the rings that formed his circle. When they were grasped, he focused harder, bringing them into a clarity almost painful to consider, and extended the rings, brushing them past the others, who flinched, and on, farther and farther past Altian, past the forbidding cliff holdings of the Soot'dla overlooking the Sultzah River, which bordered the wastes, past the Bban citadels, and still farther to the Tchsco Mountains at the northernmost rim of the world. Strained and shaking, with the sweat running down his back beneath his robe, as he forced himself to the discipline of holding his senses spread fully, Hihuan paused for an unsteady breath. He hesitated, wary of the danger that could meet him so swiftly there among the priests who lived constantly on this plane. But he also knew they did not suspect he possessed so complete a grasp of his powers. They thought him undeveloped in the ways of Anthi, and those who underestimated him would find that mistake costly.

He concentrated, tensing so hard that his muscles ached, then forced himself to relax physically as he moved forward into the caverns of M'thra. The vision wavered, cleared, then grew murky again. Annoyed, he started to exert more of himself, but suddenly forbore. Danger lay near . . . danger that smelled of Picyt. Cautious, he froze where he was, unable to see clearly from the shadowy fringes of the deep inner cavern. The unformed rings of Bban'n, dampened and held in the control of Anthi's greater power, jostled him to the point of anger. But despite their distractions, he knew where he was, for the white vibrant light of the Jewels of M'thra could not be mistaken. Picyt had activated them! The fool must be stopped!

But even as he gathered himself to sweep forward, he realized the deed had been done. He was far too late to stop it. Small wonder he had been so plagued with unease and restlessness these past few hours. The heart of Anthi had opened, disturbing the natural order of the rings that had encircled

Ruantl since the coming of the Great Ones. Why? he wondered furiously. Why had Picyt insisted upon completing the purpose when all was already arranged so advantageously? As long as the Great Ones slept, he ruled unchallenged. Picyt was a fool.

The disturbance lingered on, however. Alarmed by it, Hihuan brushed aside his anger. More was wrong here than the rising of a Jewel.

Cautiously he crossed the cavern, seeking answers, and found only the despised priests leading a rabble of Bban'n and a few Henan outcasts in chants of praise to Anthi. Of the four glowing Jewels, one lay open and empty . . . Asan's. This time fear clutched Hihuan, nearly destroying his extension altogether. Picyt's presence lay everywhere, overshadowing the rings lapping and overlapping, and yet Picyt was not here. Hihuan withdrew sharply, his mind questing so rapidly that again he nearly lost control of his senses. If Picyt had *dared* transfer himself into Asan . . .

Desperately, unwilling to consider the overwhelming implications of the threat now before him, Hihuan swept through the rest of the caves swiftly, hardly bothering to protect himself against detection.

Ah . . . there!

He paused, caution reasserting itself as he watched a tall Bban carry Picyt through narrow, twisting passageways of ancient rock. In Picyt lay a widening rift; Hihuan knew at once that his enemy approached death. That was good. The joy of relief swelled strength into Hihuan, clearing the vision yet more. Picyt had failed, coward that he was, to obey his destiny and raise Asan.

Yet . . . *Asan walked.*

Galled to his core, Hihuan stared at the tall man striding easily behind the Bban who bore Picyt's limp form. Memory sharp as ice needles flashed through Hihuan, cutting away forgetfulness, and he saw Asan as Asan had been centuries ago, and as he was still. Hatred burned in him, a hatred seared through with envy, as he watched the man move through the passageways with his escort of Bban'jen. The broad shoulders, muscular and powerful, were draped by a long-sweeping cloak of rough cloth ill-suited to cover that golden, magnificent body. Asan bent to duck beneath a long-hanging stalactite, and Hihuan saw his face, noting again the sharp flare of ridged cheekbones and the long curved nose with its thin sweep of nostril. The jaw was clenched hard as though with annoyance, and from beneath black, flared brows intensely blue eyes flecked with amber, jade, and silver swept here and there impatiently. His black hair, thick and vital, sprang back from his high brow and reached almost to his broad shoulders.

But who had raised him? *Who?*

Hihuan gathered himself and leaped, brushing that haughty mind with lightning speed. Had the total Asan walked, he would have caught Hihuan and crushed him. But it was a stranger, one bewildered and unsure, who barely sensed Hihuan's mind touch. Then Hihuan recognized the mental pattern, and fury leaped through him like a flame. So the *n'ka* had not died! Merdar take him!

For a moment Hihuan could do nothing but seethe, his rings trembling from the force of his emotions. Picyt was a fool, an imbecile twisted to utter madness by his obsession with duty and obedience to something that no longer existed. To turn the great Asan and all that awesome power over to a blundering *n'ka*, who had no conception of the ways of Anthi, was more than folly. The *n'ka* could destroy all order. He must be eliminated.

Not stopping to consider the ramifications of what he now dared, Hihuan swept into the loathesome minds of the Bban escort, overwhelming them with more force than skill. Bban'n were so easy to manipulate into attacking. The first one struck, and in his heart Hihuan laughed, no longer afraid as he watched Asan struggle and falter, helpless in the Bban's deadly grasp. Clearly he had no idea how to employ his personal protections. Hihuan laughed again. So this was what came of all Picyt's conspiracies. A swift twist of a golden neck, and the mighty Asan would crumble back into dust, never to rise again, never to make Hihuan kneel to him again.

A sudden flame of blue-white fire lanced through the rings of existence, trapping Hihuan in its agonizing brilliance. For an instant pain cut him so intensely that he could only writhe in its grasp, his screams piercing nothing but his own mind. Then it faded, and he was left gasping and mercifully whole, with one final glimpse of Asan standing unharmed, the dead Bban'jen at his feet, his eyes still glowing blue flame in the darkness of the cave.

Hihuan fled, withdrawing his rings rapidly in an ever-tightening concentric circle until at last he was back in the private rooms of his palace. Jolted, he blinked, realizing with displeasure that his robe was soaked with perspiration. Angrily he threw it off and summoned a servant to fetch him a fresh garment as Aabrm and the rest stood staring at him foolishly.

He glared at them, reached for the ewer of wine, and this time poured it himself with hands that shook. His chagrin deepening, he shut his eyes for a moment, then gulped down the wine, seeking to ease the ache still parching his veins. Lli grace them, but Asan had wielded whole power with terrifying strength. Whatever the *n'ka* was, he obviously had sufficient grasp of principles to be a tremendous threat. The *n'ka* owed nothing to Picyt's dead purpose, or to Anthi, or to the present regime so carefully crafted in Altian; what if this new Asan chose to take all of Ruantl for himself?

Hihuan poured more wine, nearly choking on it this time as his dazed brain staggered under the thoughts crowding it.

"My Leiil, what have you seen?" demanded Aabrm, his voice shriller than usual.

Hihuan winced and slammed down the goblet, whirling on them as purpose and determination entered his heart. He was no coward to quake here until disaster fell on him! Asan was not in full control as yet, and Picyt walked toward the hand of death. The time to strike was now.

His black eyes glittered at them. Tensely he addressed Fflir. "How soon can the Tlar'jen be gathered?"

The pon drew himself erect, gesturing in puzzlement. "Ten cohorts are assembled now, my Leiil, and along with the urban cadres and palace guard—"

"Anthi take your tongue!" shouted Hihuan, snatching an emerald robe edged in white borlorl fur from the hands of a cringing slave. He shrugged on the garment, making no attempt to control his rage as he savagely knotted the silken cord around his middle. "Will you prate to us of numbers? We desire the entire jen. Do you understand? How long?"

Fflir stood frozen while beside him Aabrm frowned and exchanged quick glances with the other two courtiers.

"Some . . . time, Leiil," said Fflir, sweeping out his hand. "With the storms, it will take at least two weeks for the outer patrols to come in. And at this time of year the Bban'jen are not reliable—"

"We do not request Bban," snapped Hihuan, in barely controlled desperation. "Use the Henan cohort as front shock troops; they do not matter. But no Bban'n. Drive them out, even the servants in the palace."

Aabrm stepped forward, his pouchy face more crumpled than ever by alarm. "Is it the uprising?" Hihuan threw him a contemptuous look, and Aabrm rubbed at his mouth. "The slaves in all the villas must go as well. . . ."

"A project for you to oversee," said Hihuan. He looked back to Fflir, wishing he could see through the protection of that mask. "The Tlar'jen will march in one hour. Give the orders. We must be in the valley of the Tchsco Mountains within three dawns."

"But, Leiil!" Fflir spread out both his hands, palms down in protest. "There can be no marches across the wastes *now*! The black devis alone will cut us to pieces—"

"A dust storm defeats you!" said Hihuan, mocking him. "Is this Tlar honor mewling before us? Transport them if you must."

Fflir jerked, stunned.

"Or seizert them. I care not," continued Hihuan with a snap. "Haste is essential. We must have that valley!"

His words rang out over the silent room. They all stared at him, afraid of his temper, distrustful of what their brains could not comprehend. Breathing hard, Hihuan knew a sudden temptation to leave them to their own fates and be done with the fools for all time. But even as the thought crossed his mind, he dismissed it. To remain as Tlar leiil meant power, sweet and absolute; to return to the former circle meant to stand as a speck of insignificance in the shadows of the Great Ones. His powers and Picyt's were as grains of black sand in comparison to Asan's, or Aural's, or Vauzier's, or even Rim's. He would not go back to the old ways, bowing to *them*. He would not!

Furiously he faced Aabrm, his jaw clenched as hard as the fists held at his sides. "Do you not understand? Asan is risen!" Heedless of whether his words carried to members of the court below his balcony, he swept out his hand. "And if you do not know what that means, then you should. Anthi sleeps no more. She walks, and Asan is her arm. Send the word, Fflir. The Tlar'jen moves north within the hour. Even the guards of the fields."

On his way out Fflir came to a halt and turned back in protest. Aabrm, whose face had shrunk upon mention of Asan, now took an unsteady step forward.

"My Leiil, consider!" he cried, his shrill voice grating on

Hihuan's hearing. "The fields must be protected at all costs. Our food—"

"Will mean nothing if Asan is not prevented from raising the Bban'jen and their tribes against us!" A vein began to throb in Hihuan's temple. He glared at Aabrm, so angry that he could barely control the urge to lash out his rings and crush the old fool. "Or if the eight thousand are brought forth," he said more softly, watching Aabrm flinch, "will it please you to give place to their pleasure?" He clenched a fist. "Do not tax us further!"

Saluting, Fflir strode out, and Aabrm hastened to bow.

"I beg my Leiil's mercy for the slowness of my mind," he said, grunting as he straightened from his bow. "Shall I go to prepare thy transport, Leiil?"

Hihuan drew a ragged breath, his temper fading at last as the fear steadied beneath a return of self-confidence. He had the advantage. His army would be swift despite the storms raging between Altian and the northern mountains. Asan could never call enough Bban'n from the wastes in time . . . providing he even knew how to call them at all.

Smiling faintly, Hihuan gestured assent. Then he glimpsed the ty-boy huddled in a far corner, and a malevolent glitter entered his black eyes.

"Stay a moment, Aabrm," he said, lifting his finger as the courtiers started out. "Let the others go. We must talk."

Aabrm puffed, an eager expression lighting his face as he came near Hihuan, entering the close distance reserved for matters of strict confidence or intimacy. "Yes, my Leiil?"

Hihuan hesitated. "Not here. The Tsla leiis has her spies too near this chamber."

"Ah?" Aabrm's small eyes widened knowingly. He lifted a finger.

Hihuan caught his meaning and turned over a palm. As soon as this was over, Fflir must be removed.

Aabrm bowed. "I await thy instructions on how it shall be done." His smirk left no doubt that he knew exactly what the Tlar leiil intended.

Hihuan frowned, disliking that his secrets were so well-known, even by his closest adviser. Perhaps Asan, Picyt, Fflir, and *others* would learn not to underestimate their leiil. They had better all learn it.

"One moment, Aabrm," he said, deliberately smoothing his voice to a registry of tones that made the shivering ty-boy look up. "I have a small matter to finish first." He lifted his finger. "Come, boy."

The hireling came at once, his slim, nervous body pathetically eager, his glowing Henan eyes glazed with misery. His hands twisted together in an urgent, frightened gesture as he bowed, and the silver bells chimed prettily.

"I see," said Aabrm, seeking to withdraw. "Shall I await my Leiil outside—"

"No." Hihuan's eyes flicked to him, hard and cold, although his voice grew even warmer. "This will be brief. Stay, Aabrm, and increase your education."

He noted Aabrm's distaste and laughed as he stepped forward to the boy. He knew very well that many of his dissolute habits shocked even the mind of his counselor. But he cared not.

"Approach me," he said to the ty-boy, watching in amusement as the hireling's eyes widened as he attempted to throw off fear in order to resume his trained skills. "Gently," said Hihuan, his voice deepening to a low, vibrant pitch. He extended one hand and placed his fingertips against the bare, shivering flesh of the boy's chest. He pushed away the boy's responding hand. "By ring, not flesh. I shall lead this. Obey." His blood stirred on command, but only enough to communicate itself to the boy, who moaned, unaware of the deception as Hihuan took control of his nerve centers. The boy shut his eyes as Hihuan gave his commands, standing well away as the boy began to sway, his responsiveness heightened to an extreme degree by his fearful desire to please.

Hihuan put him once again on level five, listening with boredom to the shift in the boy's breathing. Then suddenly he raised the boy to six. And, *Lea'dl*, was it possible the boy could be brought to attain level seven, this scrawny Henan? Hihuan hesitated, his own blood beginning to truly stir as he considered the temptation of a new experience. Women reached the sixth and seventh levels of arousal frequently enough under the guidance of his skill to make the sensations for him in return rewarding but no longer special. But never before had he put a ty-boy above a five. He had not even realized such a thing was possible. Curiosity excited him, and he wondered, as he watched the boy stand trembling, poised, and joyous beneath his light touch, if his brush with Asan had heightened his powers. But the thought of Asan darkened his mind, clouding the swirl of passion. Hatred blackened his soul into something twisted and cold. With a swift, utterly ruthless violence, he extended his senses over the boy, forcing the trembling creature past the thresholds of the hireling's abilities into level seven, where despite his cold detachment he could feel the boy's thundering heart and follow the dizzying spin of reeling, impossible passion.

"My Leiil! My Leiil!" gasped the boy, writhing back in a rush of ecstatic anticipation.

And at that precise moment when the boy could be brought no further, Hihuan dropped his hand from warm pulsing flesh and walked away, cutting off the contact of his rings and not even turning his head for a last glance as the ty-boy collapsed, screaming in such piercing agony that Aabrm whirled to stare at him with a gasp.

"By the grace of Anthi," he whispered, white-faced and horrified, raising his fingertips unconsciously to his lips and forehead as the ty-boy convulsed on the floor, his glowing eyes the color of blood and his young features twisted into contortions of unspeakable torture. Then the wild screaming stopped as though a knife had ended it, and for an instant there came no breath of sound through that section of the palace save the faint bubble and splash of the fountains.

Hihuan laughed, his voice rich and deep as he threw a scornful glance at the servants crowding to the door, their ugly faces frozen with shock as they stared past him at the ty-boy, lying still now in his final contortion, teeth clenched and open eyes colorless in death.

"Clean it away," he commanded with a careless gesture. "And double the ty-master's payment to replace his loss of investment." Hihuan glanced at Aabrm, who still stood rooted, and lifted his finger impatiently. "It does not please us to await you, Aabrm."

The counselor stirred at that petulant snap and came along hastily, but as they left the chamber and strode down a carpeted gallery of narrow windows and soft hangings washed in gentle artificial light, Aabrm cleared his throat.

"I know he displeased thee, Leiil, but surely such harshness against a mere ty-boy of no worth—"

Hihuan stopped abruptly and met the revulsion in Aabrm's eyes full on. "He was a spy, noble." Hihuan's black eyes narrowed, daring Aabrm to call his statement a lie. "Do not accuse us further." And he strode on, his thoughts already flying ahead to war, with a subdued Aabrm at his side.

• • •

Dawn brought a lightening of the black sky to a leaden purple, and for a time it seemed as though the storm would clear in good omen. But the true sun remained lost, sullenly hidden behind the dark masses of clouds that hung over Altian with such heaviness that they seemed almost to brush the protective bubble. It seemed that the world held its breath. In the districts of the seventh vector, where the court of merchants guarded its own walls, shrewd Bban eyes watched the city.

"The slaves are being released. Why?"

The question came up again and again in the low-ceilinged room of council, its earthern walls smoke-blackened from the torches blazing fitfully in each corner. In the center of the room, three elders sat around the fire pit—honored thus by being closest to its warmth—and were encircled by the rest. All five merchant guilds stood represented, and the orange torchlight in that windowless room flickered off scarred Bban features and the rich colors of green, russet, gold, crimson, and purple cloaks shining somberly from the shadows. Eyes glowed fiercely at the elders, one of whom sat erect with a silver cloak spread out from his shoulders, his legs folded under him, both palms held flat upon a small glass viewscreen that flickered a dim picture of the black palace walls and the activity surrounding them. A grim cadre of battle-shielded Tlar'jen was herding wailing slaves forth from the crescent of villas, pushing them out into the unprotected vectors of the city, where their starving cousins or the savage Henans fell upon them fiercely, stripping away garments, gold anklets, and sometimes even the collars of slavery as loot, no doubt to barter in exchange for food.

"Has *yde* rotted their minds at last, that they do this?" said someone with a growl worthy of his desert cousins. "They cannot live without slaves."

The tallest elder lifted his silver gaze from the viewscreen, and said in a deep voice that filled the room: "Kuubral, it is my thought that these slaves should be brought within our walls."

The elder on his right, a Bban so old that his scant scarred flesh had blackened and dried to the texture of a mummy's, nodded once. "This is wise, Ggil. They will die in the unprotected sectors."

"And," said the third elder with a bob of his head, which he covered to hide the deep cleaving scar across his eye, "they have knowledge of the Tlar that would be useful."

"They are spies for the Tlar, their masters!" spat a member of the council. "They would betray us!"

An angry murmur arose, not silenced until Ggil lifted his thin, long-fingered hand, smooth-skinned for a Bban, from the viewscreen. The picture at once scrambled with static that did not clear until he replaced his palm upon it.

"It is they who have been betrayed," he said quietly, his deep low voice once more filling the room. "They are Bban'n; they will not forget this treatment."

"What say you, Ookri?" asked Kuubral.

The scarred elder inclined his head. "I say that the Tlar mean to depart Altian and do not trust Bban'n in their holdings while they are away."

"Depart? Where? Where?" asked several of the council.

A harsh voice jeered, "They fear those puny slaves will find the courage to make use of their hoarded food and perhaps their smooth-skinned wives."

"Enough!" said Ookri sharply, as Ggil and Kuubral exchanged glances. "We know the House of Soot'dla does not stand with their brethern. We know that Dame Agate has seen the heart of Anthi open."

"Then the Tlar legends are true," said Kuubral, widening his eyes.

"True indeed," said Ggil, thinking of his daughter so far away in the frozen north. She had forgotten his teachings; she had allowed herself to be seduced by lies. But guilt rather than anger pained him at the thought of her, for he had let the seduction take place. She believed in Anthi and the lies of Picyt because he had not protected her. And now . . . Beneath his hands the viewscreen flickered, no longer showing the palace but instead the forbidding peaks of the Tchsco Mountains. The others crowded around.

"By the moons, what do they do?" asked a breathless voice in awe.

A cold anger filled Ggil. Abruptly he removed his hands from the screen, letting it go black as Kuubral said, "Picyt, deceiver of the Outerlands, has called the Bban'jen to his hand. He is the betrayer of all Bban'n, for he would have us become what is not to be. And now, by the warning of Dame Agate, we know he has raised things from the beyond, ancient things not to be brought forth again. Evil taints our land, my *kai*, great evil."

Ggil raised his head high, his silver eyes burning with a deep anger. "So do I now declare unto you that Leiil Hihuan has raised the Tlar'jen and sent it north to destroy the deceiver."

Ookri's one yellow eye glowed fiercely as the murmurs rose up again. "Rejoice not, for the Tlar leiil will destroy the Bban tribes who gather to Picyt's call. It must not be allowed!"

A furor ensued, and angry voices argued for several minutes until sentinels from outside ran in with warnings to be quieter.

Kuubral raised his hand, and gradually the noise subsided. He said mildly, his ancient bones seeming almost to rattle as he drew breath, "The training of Anthi is strong within the tribes. But as we of the true way have taken on the guise of merchants to the Tlar in order to keep our power hidden, so are we yet stronger than all suspect, for our strength is unknown to the followers of Anthi. Let us raise our own call across the wastes, that the tribes do not go north."

"This is wise," said Ggil, but Ookri shook a fist at the murmur of agreement.

"Wise, yes, but not sufficient!" he said angrily. "What are the tribes if the jen is lost? Already it bows to Picyt's hand. And the Tlar'jen will spread the blood of our warriors upon the sand. Jen-knives and lances are no match for the fire-rods."

"You speak of physical war," said Ggil, clicking his jaw with impatience. "With the Tlar, battle will be with the circles of their true power. With the mind they will slay, not with the hand."

"Even more reason why we must act in many directions," snapped Ookri. "We must journey to the Outerlands."

Kuubral poked at the fire, stirring the singing coals to fresh flames. "If we act on the mental plane, we are lost. All is lost. We have forgotten too much of the old ways. Let us go to the Outerlands, yes. But let us also find one who will betray Picyt. And," he added swiftly as Ookri started to interrupt, "let us act against Leiil Hihuan in the same way."

"How?" asked Ookri as Ggil narrowed his eyes in thought, concealing dismay. "He is Tlar. He cannot be touched."

"He can be if he is kept on the physical plane," said Kuubral dryly.

Ookri drew in a sharp breath, but it was Ggil who spoke

with a rising flare of excitement: "Dame Zaula!"

"Yes!" Kuubral leaned his thin body forward, his scarlet eyes ablaze. "Was not your daughter once her slave, Ggil? Did Giaa not tell you of the Tsla leiis's empty womb? Unlike the leiil, she does not use her mind, and there has been no union between them."

"By Lli herself, Kuubral, we all know the Tlar can mate either way," snapped Ookri, shifting himself closer to the fire and sending Ggil a sharp glance. "What use is court gossip—"

"Of much use," said Ggil slowly, refusing to let his musk release as he fought down anger. Long ago in the fierce vigor of his days as a warrior of the dara he had been a member of a raiding party that fell on one of the fields of the Mura-an. There he had taken a Tlar woman as his booty, mating with her in the savage wilds of the Outerlands. Defying the laws of his tribe, he had kept her, and when she had born a Henan child, dying in the birth of it, he had kept Giaa, refusing to break her neck as commanded. Eventually, to save his honor he had been forced to sell the child to a villa in the city, but Bban'n memories ran long, and although he now stood as one of the supreme elders, there were those who still looked hard upon him for what he had done. Now he sat erectly, refusing to betray his thoughts as he considered what plan Kuubral was proposing. He knew—they all knew—who would have to carry it out. "If the leiil could be distracted physically," he said reluctantly, clicking his jaw, "he would lose considerable mental force."

"Yes!" said Kuubral eagerly. "And since he must be the focal point for full Tlar power—"

"Understood," said Ookri's voice, rasping with impatience. "But we cannot guide his actions. We learned that when we tried to influence him to accept the Soot'dla assassin back within his court. We cannot force him to approach his wife. Especially not now, with his thoughts on war."

Kuubral's eager scarlet eyes gazed steadily into Ggil's silver ones. Distaste flooded Ggil, but he knew what must be done. And the fact that of all the elders he was the only one who had joined completeness with a Tlar made him the one to do it.

"She will approach him," said Ggil softly, staring into the fire.

Ookri's hand tapped his arm, and he flinched, startled. "You are willing to do this?" he asked gruffly, his single eye unwavering.

Ggil looked at him. "We are agreed that it must be done," he said harshly. He lifted his head in pride. "I shall do it."

"And the danger?" persisted Ookri, cocking his head to one side so that the firelight glinted off his empty eye. "Should the Tsla leiis turn on you, Ggil—"

"I do not fear the risk!" began Ggil hotly, but Kuubral lifted his hand.

"Gently, gently," he said, clicking his jaw in reproof at both of them. "Who shall be Picyt's betrayer? Surely the priest is doubly guarded now, both by that *chielt* Tuult and the ancient one that has been raised to life."

"Asan," said Ggil, narrowing his eyes as the old blood in him stirred. "He has no right to walk the sands of our world. Let us destroy him first."

"In what way?" demanded Kuubral.

But Ookri was slapping his hand on the packed earth in comprehension. "Giaa!" he said, hunching his shoulders forward. "She is there. She shall be made to do it. Yes. That is just." As he spoke his single eye burned at Ggil.

"Then we are agreed," said Kuubral. "Let us first seek the Tsla lciis."

Slowly he stretched out his fist toward Ggil, as did Ookri. Intense silence fell over the room of council, broken by not so much as a stir, click, or uncertain breath. Ggil's extended fist touched the others', and he closed his silver eyes and focused inward, unsettled for a moment as the forceful rings of Tlar psionic power made themselves felt upon his awareness. Then he grew steady and intent and sure. Building a picture of the palace in his mind, and harnessing the strength of Ookri and Kuubral into his own focus, he went there seeking the court of women.

"The direction of the black devi is being tracked closely, Leiil," said Pon Fflir in a stiff tone. Masked, cloaked, and battle shielded, he stood at attention before Hihuan, who paced about the vast triangular chamber of state with ill-concealed impatience. "It caught only one transport, and although damage was severe, more than half the troops aboard are still functional."

Magnificently arrayed in bronze cloak and tunic with intricately hammered battle shielding fitted upon his torso, Hihuan ground his teeth together.

"And they were only Henans, Leiil."

Hihuan whirled to glare at Fflir. "Fool!" he snapped. "They are expendable in battle, not elsewhere. We need every possible Henan to attack the Bban'jen. Without that distraction, the Bban'n will never permit themselves to drop guard against the rings—" He broke off, hearing a footfall behind him, and turned haughtily to frown at this courtier who dared interrupt him.

The man bowed, obviously not relishing taking on a task reserved normally for slaves. "Forgive this intrusion, my Leiil, but the Noble Aabrm desires me to inform your greatness that the Tsla leiis requests audience."

Startled, Hihuan lifted his eyebrows. "Now?"

"Indeed, now, my Leiil. She is reported most anxious to speak with thee before thy departure."

Hihuan sneered. He had not slept, spending the remainder of the last night giving orders and planning strategy. Now it was dawn, and half his forces cowered stranded in the wastes of the Outerlands, seeking to avoid the vast devi that could cut the transports to ribbons with its lashing force. The rest of his army had yet to set out at all. He had no time or patience to deal with an unfaithful wife.

"Inform the leiis it is not our wish to grant her audience," he said, unable to resist a glare at the unmoving Fflir standing by the crystal mapboard. Malice darkened Hihuan's eyes. "Perhaps you would care to comfort her fears, pon?" he said softly.

Fflir swung out his hand in surprise. "My leiil, I—" He collected himself. "Yes, I shall obey thy wish." He stepped toward the courtier. "Conduct me to the Tsla leiis."

Jealousy blazed in Hihuan's heart, blackening it to a shriveled knot. What did she see in this stripling, to make her look on her leiil with less favor? He clenched his fists.

"No!" he shouted as Fflir reached the doorway.

Startled, both men turned to look back at him. Catching up his mask from a low-slung chair, Hihuan strode forward, his bronze cloak billowing out behind him.

"See to our transport, Pon Fflir," he said, shouldering past the officer. "Well?" he said to the hesitant courtier. "Where is she?"

The man bowed, his eyes shifting furtively to Fflir, then away. "This way, my Leiil."

They had scarcely turned down the corridor when a figure in

a plain cloak and mask stepped from an alcove to block their way.

Infuriated by this audacity, Hihuan drew a sharp breath, and his escort said fiercely, "Fool! Stand aside for the leiil's passage."

"Please, my Leiil," said the man, not moving. His thick muscular body was taut with urgency. "I beg word with thee." Quickly he pulled off his mask, shoving back the cowled hood of his cloak to reveal a craggy, middle-aged face. It was firm of jaw, with hard ocher-green eyes set deep beneath heavy brows. A peculiar but well-known burn marked one cheek. He stood there, his eyes never wavering from Hihuan, who frowned in sudden understanding.

"Yes, Leiil, I am Stregth n'Dubrk dl-Soot'dla, banished once by thy hand to the Outerlands, but reclaimed to honor by my house." He turned his branded cheek so that Hihuan could see the mark more clearly. "I beg thee, Leiil, show mercy and reverse thy displeasure that I may once again bear weapons for thee."

"More likely you would bear weapons for our betrayal," snapped Hihuan, looking at him with such open contempt that Stregth flinched. "We know well of your words against us and of your blooded friendship with the traitor Picyt. Do not approach us again, *merdar*, or your blood shall spread across these stones!"

With a sneer Hihuan strode on, the courtier hastening to keep step beside him. Stregth was left white-faced and trembling with a terrible fury in his eyes. For a moment he stood still in the center of the corridor. Then, flinging his cloak over one arm, he turned and hastened away in the direction opposite to Hihuan's.

Aware of all this, for he had no liking to put his back to an enemy, Hihuan relaxed and slowed his pace a fraction, permitting the gasping courtier to catch up. Stregth was a coward as well as a fool. Whatever prompted his desire for reinstatement to the court after years of open rebellion could not be trusted. Hihuan inclined his head.

"While I speak to the Tsla leiis, you will inform the guards that Stregth is to be denied all future admittance to the palace."

"It shall be done, my Leiil," said the man with a vehement gesture. "With pleasure. Rabble of that kind have no place here."

Zaula had chosen neutral ground for their meeting, the chamber a private one located neither in her court nor in his. Dismissing his guide, Hihuan entered with an assured, arrogant step and stopped, his black eyes appraising her as she rose from her chair, laying aside her bailanke to kneel and bow low to the floor. As she did so her shining jet hair swept forward, then swung back as she rose, giving him a clear glimpse of the curve of her full breasts and the golden flesh between them. She was not tall by the standards of their race, coming barely to his shoulder, but it hardly seemed a defect in view of the rest of her attributes. Her gown, fashioned of handwoven pria cloth and so fine that the least careless touch could tear it, swathed her in shimmering amethyst, the gleaming threads taking fire in the light so that with every movement—whether the swell of her breasts as she drew breath or the shift of a leanly curved thigh as she stood up—she flashed with color and brilliance like a faceted jewel held up to the sun. Her skin was dark, tawny gold, softened with scented ointments, her lips full and ripe, her eyes liquid brown with a fiery hint of russet in their depths.

As always, the very sight of her aroused him. He swept out his rings, seeking hers, and found them held flat about her, lifeless, as usual. Furious, he drew back and turned away from his wife and leiis, the only woman he could not excite.

"Hihuan," she said quietly, her voice a curious husky mixture of music and fire. "I beg you to hear my words."

He caught the urgency in her then and turned back, reluctant and impatient. "What would you say, Zaula, except no?"

"You go to war!" she said as though her throat ached. Her eyes, widened and anxious, stared up at him, and the ruddy glints seemed to swirl in their depths.

But he held himself cold against her charms. "Yes. Perhaps soon you will be free of me." He clenched a fist. "Free to claim openly the one you claim now in secret!"

She came forward to lay her fingers upon his fist, her touch cool, light, and electric. "Please, Hihuan. Do not let this rage eat at you. I am your wife."

He snatched his hand away from hers, fearing the weakness her very touch put in him. "You give yourself to Fflir!"

She faced him, her eyes steady, seemingly without fear of the rage that choked him and urged him to strike her down. One thought, and he could destroy her.

"I have never opened my womb to him," she said.

"Nor to me!" he shouted.

"Yes." She frowned, and now anger that matched his stirred in her face. "Yes, Hihuan, always to you."

"Liar!" He gripped her arm and shook her. "Will you deny the rejection dealt a moment past?" She flinched at that, and he swung away, releasing her. "What gain is this meeting, Zaula? You vowed once never to willingly see me again, and because I am not as cruel as you think me I have permitted this defiance. Now you change!" He turned his head to glare at her. "You seek me out. You lie baldly. For what purpose? In an hour I shall be gone, and there was no need to stir up yet more hatred between us."

For a moment she seemed to struggle with herself, but instead of the angry retort he expected, she said, "Yes, soon you will be gone. To war, Hihuan. And if you do not return, who shall stand as heir to your throne?"

With a cry he whirled on her so fiercely that she drew back, lifting one arm protectively. His black eyes blazed. "*Lea'dl*, but you dare much, woman! I wonder you do not raise your force field as you say such things. Whose fault is it? Whose?" Then he collected himself and said bitterly, "You know who has the strongest rings after mine. He shall—"

She gestured scornfully. "Is that a true heir? An heir of your body, Hihuan? Forget the rings. This is what is real." She held out her hand. "Flesh against flesh." She seized his hand, and she pressed her palm against his sweating one. She drew nearer, and the perfume anointing her wafted up, clouding his senses, making his head spin. Her eyes held his. "My way, Hihuan. This once. Please," she pleaded softly, her husky voice making him shiver.

His anger fled, leaving his blood stirred in a different, more pleasing way. She was so beautiful, so alluring. . . . His hand tightened around hers, and he reached forth the ring of passion, only to have her draw back.

"No!" she said sharply, then at once softened her voice, pressing her pliant body against his armored one. "Please, Hihuan. Not the rings. They will bring pleasure but no child." Her face tilted to his, the ripe lips parting invitingly. "I know what happened to the ty-boy last night. And I have not the mental strength to meet you in the way you want, to keep myself from being crushed as he was."

Hihuan frowned, amused by this confided fear, and started to tell her the truth of that death. Then he did not. Perhaps at last she did fear him enough to surrender. He touched his lips to hers in a cautious kiss, not yet daring to believe her. One of his muscular arms encircled her, drawing her nearer and feeling her quiver responsively.

"Why does this please you so?" he whispered, kissing her again. "This pleasure in the way of lesser creatures than we?"

"Oh, Hihuan," she said when he finally allowed her a breath. "Please. Look upon me with truth and know I do not lie."

Startled, he stopped kissing her smooth cheek and gazed deeply down into her eyes, seeing there the fire of desire sharpened by fear. Sudden confidence swept him, and he laughed.

"No, I believe you," he said, certain that at last he did rule her. And what would it hurt, to grant her wishes this one time? His next kiss was harder and deeper, and she began to respond with increasing passion.

Her hand slid across his chest, unfastening his cloak, which fell to a shimmering heap of bronze at his heels. His blood flamed at the touch of her cool fingertips upon the back of his neck, and he began to kiss her eyes, her lips, her throat, with increasing urgency, his hand sliding inside the delicate bodice of her gown to curve around full warm flesh that trembled and responded to his touch. She was unbuckling the straps at his back that held the battle shielding in place, and with a low laugh at her eagerness he lowered his lips to the pulsing spot between her breasts, one finger gently parting her gown there as the fabric tore softly to her slim waist. The cloth fluttered down about the curves of her hips just as she succeeded in undoing the last buckle. The shielding encasing his back and torso slipped, and he pulled it off, tossing it to one side and laughing as it clattered on the floor. Her cool hands slipped inside his silk tunic, sliding across his flesh, which quivered at her touch.

"See?" she murmured, her voice so throaty it seemed to throb through his body. "Is this not pleasing, my Leiil?"

His kissed her for answer as he helped her remove his tunic. All thoughts of war and the treachery of his subjects faded from his mind, replaced by a rising exaltation. He had never, from the hour of their first battle, realized the extent of her naiveté. Her refusal to use her rings had seemed willful defiance; now he knew it was but ignorance on her part. His hands caressed her, making her moan softly as they slid downward to the hidden parts of her. In moments she would learn that it was not simply one way or the other, either mental or physical, but both if one intended a child. Passion throbbed through him as she pressed nearer, willing and pliant and his at last. For a moment he lost all sense of himself, his need for her overwhelming him entirely. Calling her name softly, he bent to pick her up, intending to carry her into the small adjoining room, where he was sure she had prepared everything for their pleasure. But even as his arms tightened about her, a shadow swift and deadly struck from behind.

The shock of the knife skidding across his left shoulder and plunging deep below it was like a hammer blow, stunning him for a frozen instant before the agony, white and blinding, began. He staggered, barely hearing a hoarse cry of challenge mingled with Zaula's scream. For a moment he could see nothing, do nothing but feel the pounding intrusion of metal in his back. Then it was yanked out, and his blood spurted with it. Moved by the instinct of self-preservation, he whirled on his attacker in fury, extending his rings into a force field of protection. His mind snapped out, crushing the other mercilessly. Screaming, Stregth clutched his temples, dropping the bloody knife. He sought desperately to recover and counter Hihuan's mental attack, but Hihuan was too strong. Stregth contorted under the pressure, his lips drawing back from his teeth as he fell to his knees. His face drained of color as his rings shattered, and his eyes started, bulging hideously. "Death," he gasped, writhing uncontrollably as Hihuan crushed him. "Death to the tyrant—" He fell, sightlessly staring at Hihuan's leg. Drawing in a ragged breath, Hihuan let his force field drop.

"Mercy of Lea!" cried Zaula, sinking to the floor by the dead man. The beauty in her face had drained away. She clutched herself, unconsciously trying to pull her ruined gown back up about her shivering flesh, but the cloth shredded in her fingers. "Who was he?"

"Stregth of the Soot'dla," said Hihuan coldly. He glared down at her, all belief and trust trickling away with the quickening drip of his blood upon the floor. "But surely you knew him, Dame Zaula."

The edge in his hard voice made her look up. She saw the blood and gasped. "No." Then her eyes widened, and she jumped to her feet. "No! You cannot accuse me—"

"Can I not?" Using his rings to temporarily seal the wound, he gripped her arm roughly, not allowing her to wrench free, although her struggles sent agony through him. "Who else insisted I flatten my rings so that I should have no warning? Who arranged the meeting here in this unguarded chamber? Who persuaded me out of my shielding at just the right moment?" Weakness dragged at him, blurring his vision. Hating her, he shoved her away with such violence that she fell sprawling. She began to weep, but he did not listen as he picked up his tunic and ripped it apart. She flinched at the tearing noise, shrinking away when he approached her and threw the cloth in her lap.

"Get up and bandage me," he commanded.

She gripped the cloth between her hands and sat there, shaking. "It was no conspiracy. I swear—"

"These lies insult both of us. Get up!" He hauled her to her feet. The pain made him reel, but with effort he subdued it. "Bandage me, or I vow that you'll share Stregth's death."

The threat turned her so pale that he thought she would collapse, but after a moment she knotted the cloth together and awkwardly began staunching the flow of blood.

"It is deep, my Leiil," she whispered, her voice so unsteady she was barely intelligible. "The healer must be summoned."

"I have not time to lie in bed for days," he snapped, barely keeping his rage against her in check. He hoped she knew how close to death she stood, for by the four moons he meant to see her pay for this morning's work.

She pulled the bandage tight enough to make him stiffen in pain and stepped away, hampered by the tatters of her gown still hanging from her waist. She stared at the floor, and her breathing was quick and shallow.

"You will die if you do not lie down and receive care," she said at last. She looked up at him, her eyes filling with tears. "I am not a part of this! I swear! Please—"

"Slut," he said, his voice a whipcrack of scorn. "You are no better than a Henan woman selling herself on the streets to Bban warriors. But you bear my rank and my name and my honor, and by Anthi's grace you shall bear my child also."

She stared at him for a moment in disbelief, then began backing away as he started toward her.

"No!" she screamed, her face a mask of fear and hate. "Stay away from me! I am cold, Hihuan." She dodged his hand, only to trip on her gown and fall. She began to weep, but as he gripped her arm and dragged her upright, her eyes still flashed defiance. "I am cold!" she screamed furiously.

"You shall find me ice. I will give you *nothing*!"

One hand still gripping her arm, he smoothed the other over her breast, watching dispassionately as she cringed.

"Your flesh is warm," he said, his voice hard as his black eyes burned into hers. Indeed, it was very warm. He pulled her nearer, ignoring his weakness from the wound as she again tried to wrench free. "You are on level five, Zaula. Do not deny it. And you are rising to six."

"No! I shall not! I hate you! I despise you! No!" But she moaned the last word, sobbing as she averted her face. "Oh, Anthi have mercy, no!" she cried, stiffening as he extended his senses, inflaming her despite her desperate struggles to hold her own rings flat and lifeless. Before, she had always managed to spurn him, but this time she failed. Her rings formed, extending under the brutal force of his guidance. Zaula shuddered under his touch, her flesh on fire as the strength of her defiance faded.

He gathered her unresisting body in his arms, his strength reaching beyond loss of blood and the agony still raging in his back, and carried her into the room where silken cushions waited beneath the heady fragrance of burning incense. She moaned, trying to escape, but she could not. Her mind was his, for now he controlled her nerve centers. Soon his mind would be hers. He laid her down on the cushions and pulled away the remainder of her gown to reveal the full perfection of her body. They would be one entity, their rings merged completely. Then she would feel his pain and beyond that his hatred of her, and if she survived true union, then she would bear the child she had asked for.

Her eyes, enormous dark pools of terror and passion, stared up at him through the scarlet and turquoise smoke of the incense. Her lips parted, and she whispered, "Please, Hihuan. *Please* let me live—"

But he narrowed his black eyes, unmoved by her pleas or her horror. His arrogant face twisted in a sneer. "The time for begging is past, my treacherous Zaula. Did Fflir ever raise you to the seventh level? Or Stregth?" She gasped, her lips forming a soundless, desperate denial. Hihuan smiled, not believeing her. He would never believe her again. "No, I think not. Know it now, my dear." And he put his hands upon her, laughing as her screams pierced his mind.

Chapter 9

Alone, Blaise drew a slow, unsteady breath. Glancing down at the waxen face of Picyt, he frowned. Nervousness rippled through his stomach, but at least if he failed now, it would be in private. That much, at least, he had won.

He might as well get it over with.

Sighing, Blaise knelt beside the twitching priest, bracing himself for what was to come as he cautiously placed his fingertips on Picyt's temples. The flesh was clammy and loose. He waited, and without delay the searing blue fire blasted through him like an explosion of power. Stiffling a cry, he shut his eyes and held on until the lash of energy calmed and began to surround him in a shimmering sea of blue light. The vision of Picyt formed in his mind as he looked on the inner structures of this particular point in the universe. There was the seal he had applied. With trepidation he reopened it, feeling Picyt jerk under his hands even as the order blurred with distortion. This time Blaise plunged into the vortex, going deep into Picyt, ignoring that part of him that cringed away. Cold, alien blackness sucked at Blaise. Then he suddenly felt the tremendous force of Picyt's mind and emotions, the pain, the delirious distortions of *yde* withdrawal, the terror, and the dark hate lingering at the bottom like some malevolent growing worm. It sprang at Blaise, seeking to wrap itself about him and crush him, but blue fire encased Blaise like a shimmering seal of safety. Nothing could pierce it.

"Picyt!"

And in answer the buffeting emotions cleared, permitting Blaise to enter the awful clarity of Picyt's very center.

They faced each other, formless and shrouded in blue fire.

"Enemy?" said Picyt, pulsing with dim energy against the vividness of Blaise. "Or friend?"

Was the priest afraid? "I have come to restore you," said Blaise. "Show me how."

For a moment he had no answer. Then with great weariness Picyt said, "I prefer release, *n'ka*. The service to Anthi has been too long. I am tired. I seek the long darkness of Merdarai."

"You must live!" said Blaise savagely, knowing that Tuult would not accept the information that Picyt wanted to die. "You have manipulated all of us to this point, and you cannot desert us now that the Tlar'jen are coming. The Bban'n want birth, whatever that means, and I—" He broke off, unable for a moment to master his own inner confusion.

"Perhaps Hihuan will not come," murmured Picyt, growing dimmer. "He is young and selfish. He may not care what we do."

Blaise snorted. "You could lie to Omari, but not to Asan. Hihuan knows, and he cares. He has already tried to assassinate me."

"False! He has not enough skill to reach this far!"

"You delude yourself," said Blaise with impatience. "If I do not restore you, Tuult will kill me—or try—and Uble will have to come here to save you."

"Uble is a fool. Unskilled—"

"Basai will push him into it. Show me what to do!"

Twisted, bitter amusement rippled forth from Picyt. "You have already crippled me. If you know enough to seal off my rings, you need no more instructions."

"Don't be a fool—"

"You are the fool!" shouted Picyt. "I gave you life! I gave you the power of Anthi, and in return you have destroyed my rings of completion. I will not go back, to stand with lesser men and face—"

"You mean you have lost your powers," said Blaise slowly. "You cannot—"

"I cannot give the Bban'n Anthi as promised. I cannot rule the order of life, maintain control of the serenity of Kkanthor, or guide the neophytes to understanding. If I am restored to life, I can no longer serve as First Honored. I cannot bring the Bban'n any further, and there will be no more steps taken toward the day of fulfillment. You did this to me, with your ignorance and your refusal to control the gift of Anthi within you! Do you think such power contains the freedom to wield it madly, thus endangering the rings of all around you? *N'ka*, you defile the form of Asan, and I regret upon my blood that I put you in him."

Anger stirred in Blaise. "You sought to trick me. You meant to destroy me. I was expendable in Asan's resurrection. And now that you've failed, you blame me for it. You *will* live, Picyt, power or not, rings or not. And you can explain your failure to the Bban tribes whom you've deceived! Live!" Fury guiding him, he swept forward, engulfing the struggling Picyt. For a horrible instant they mingled, entwining into one being, and only then did Blaise realize that Picyt's protests had been more deception, lengthening this mental contact in order for Picyt to draw upon Blaise's strength and trap him.

Again the blackness sucked at him. Blaise trembled and with all his might wrenched free and retreated, dodging Picyt's attempts to snatch him back into the connection.

With a shudder Blaise came out of it, his heart thundering at the narrowness of his escape. He jerked his hands away from the priest, who still lay unconscious. But his color was improving. Blaise's fingers curled, reaching for Picyt's throat.

"Is it done, Leiil?" asked a gruff, eager voice.

Startled, Blaise pulled back his hands and stood up, stumbling slightly as he stepped forward to meet Tuult.

"Yes," he said bleakly. For a moment he considered telling this loyal, forthright man exactly how his master had meant to betray all of them. But as Tuult pushed past him to stare down at Picyt, Blaise compressed his lips and held back. He would not be believed.

Weariness swept through him. "I will rest now, Pon Tuult," he said. "And I must eat."

Tuult straightened with new briskness. "All is prepared, my Leiil," he said. With a bow he turned and summoned others to come and attend to Picyt before personally leading Blaise away to a large, private chamber, worn with the centuries yet undimmed in grandeur.

Despite his preoccupations, Blaise caught his breath as he entered. It was as though he stepped into the heart of living flame. In the center of the room stood a brazier fashioned of a breathtaking piece of clear crystal, hollowed smooth inside and faceted outside so that it spun the light from blazing coals about the room in a dazzling burst of color. The chamber was round and thus had no corners save where a shadow-hung alcove extended off opposite the doorway. Heavy, magnificently detailed tapestries in rich hues covered the raw stone of the walls, and several tiny, obviously precious wood tables stood about supporting the light cubes that glowed out soft clear illumination. Thick carpet, woven with the blue symbol of Anthi, took the chill from his bare feet, and on the ceiling blazed a bold burnished coat-of-arms of plumed crossed swords over a triangular shield. A gilded ewer and goblets stood waiting for him beside a covered tray of food, and clothes were folded neatly on one of the chairs.

After an initial stunned second, Blaise walked nearer to the fire, unconsciously giving a nod. More opulent than any of the spartan surroundings of his past, the chamber pleased him and seemed even . . . fitting. With a sigh he sat down in a low-slung yet comfortable chair and stretched out his long, tapering hands to the fire's warmth. Sniffing the hot spices in the food, he had reached out to uncover it when Tuult became suddenly alert. Pausing, Blaise watched the Bban walk toward the alcove on swift, silent feet, one hand drawing his jen-knife. Tuult hesitated, then flung back the curtains to reveal a figure kneeling in the shadows. She sprang up with a cry, and Blaise got to his feet.

"Giaa!" he said in surprise. "What—"

"You were not chosen!" Tuult seized her arm and pulled her roughly from the alcove. "It is not permitted that you be here, Henan!"

"Release her," said Blaise sternly, stepping forward.

Reluctantly Tuult obeyed, and Giaa backed away from him, rubbing her arm, which had been marked by his grip. Her lips were trembling, but although her eyes betrayed fear, they also flashed with defiance at the Bban.

He stiffened and turned to Blaise. "Leiil Asan," he said with gruff vehemence, spreading his fingers. "It is not right that she be here. The law—"

"The old law of the Bban'n is not served now!" said Giaa, with a toss of her head. Then she shrank back as he growled at her.

"Enough!" Blaise stepped between them. "She may stay, Tuult."

"But she is Henan! Below caste! My Leiil is too quick to forgive this intrusion. There are other servants more fitting—"

"She will stay," said Blaise firmly. His eyes bored coldly into the Bban. "Dismissed."

Tuult's jaw clicked rapidly behind his mask, and the sound

made Giaa's cheeks darken. But with an abrupt salute Tuult came to attention.

"As my Leiil commands," he said, not bothering to keep the anger from his voice. "I shall guard thee to the blood this night. None shall pass thy door save by thy wish." With a swirl of his black cloak he left.

Blaise snorted, frowning after him, then gathered himself and smiled. "I am glad you are here."

She still stood by the wall, looking as if she desired to press herself against it and disappear. Despite the warmth of the room she shivered, holding her arms tight about herself.

"Here," he said gently, not liking to see her cold or unhappy. Pulling the cloak from his shoulders, he walked over to her and put it around her. She had changed into a belted tabard such as the slaves wore. His hands lingered for a moment on her shoulders as he settled the cloak there, and his gaze moved down over the curve of her breasts beneath the thin leather, and the bared lean muscle of her thigh. Her sweet, smoky scent rose up between them. He drew in a deep pleasureable breath of it. But his touch also made him aware of the misery within her and the unhappiness that stirred beneath her fear.

"Don't be afraid," he said.

Her silver eyes, luminous, opaque, and shining in the flash of light, lifted to his, then dropped away. She shifted beneath his hands, and her cheeks darkened again as she suddenly became more conscious of his nakedness.

"My . . . my Leiil," she said in a whisper. "Forgive me."

He moved away, uncertain why she was here or why she was so distraught, but determined not to frighten her further. After walking across the room, he picked up a tunic and pants made of thin, silken green cloth and put them on. Then he seated himself and lifted the cover off the tray of food. Glancing at her over his shoulder, he smiled. "Join me?"

Her eyes widened at the sight of such abundance. He saw the corner of her mouth quiver and knew she was hungry, but after a moment she put out her hand palm down.

"I am to serve thee, my Leiil," she said and averted her eyes. "To take thy food is wrong."

He frowned, but his own hunger was too great to be put off any longer. The eating implements were fashioned of polished animal horn and awkward to use, but he managed, gasping a bit from the fiery bite of the spices. After a while she came silently forward with an unaccustomed shyness and poured his wine for him. He drank, cooling the fire lingering on his tongue.

He met her eyes. "Thank you. Now take this." He pushed forward one of the bowls with the food he had saved for her. "I have enjoyed my fill. If you do not eat, this will be wasted."

She gasped. "Waste is not permitted."

"No." Gently, as though he were coaxing a wild animal, he pushed the bowl a little nearer to her. "Take it."

She reached for it, trembled, then took it. While she ate he sat motionless, watching the light glint off the golden wealth of her hair. Her loveliness drew at him more than ever, especially since he was no longer distracted by illness. He longed to reach out and touch her hair, to feel its satiny texture, but he did not dare startle her. When she was finished and had put down the polished bowl he captured her hand in his before she could move away.

"Don't fear me, Giaa," he said firmly, his eyes upon hers. "Why did you come here? Why is it wrong for you to be here?"

She looked nervously away as she trembled in his grasp. "I no longer fear thee," she said in a low, almost inaudible voice. It was a lie, and he was about to speak with more sharpness when she visibly steeled herself and looked up at him with a faint but practiced smile. She moved around the table, her scent again releasing with heady fragrance. "Please, my Leiil," she said, her voice stronger now. "I came here to serve thee. Let me . . ."

He felt as if something cold and repugnant had touched him. Annoyed by her falseness, he stood up and strode over to the brazier, warming his hands above the coals. He had Asan's abilities now; conscious of that fact, he glared at her until her smile drooped and faded. A flicker of certainty crossed his mind.

"Who told you to come here?" he asked sharply.

She flinched. "No one."

"Don't lie, Giaa! I know—"

Without warning she began to weep in silence, shaking, her hands pressed to her mouth. "I do not wish to! I do not! Oh, please, Leiil, mercy!" Bowing her head as he stood there frowning, she sank to her knees and huddled there on the floor, rocking herself back and forth in the noiseless grief of Bban'n.

His anger faded helplessly. Squatting down before her, he gripped her arms. "Giaa, don't." He gave her a light shake when she shut her eyes and did not respond. "Giaa! It's still me, Bla—" Caution made him drop that reassurance. "Am I the leiil, Giaa?"

Surprised, she blinked at him.

He resisted the urge to smooth back the hair from her face. "Am I?"

Slowly she turned her palm up.

"Then you must tell me the truth. Who sent you here? And why?"

She lowered her eyes, and for a moment he was certain she meant not to answer. Then she twisted a lock of hair in her fingers. "It is insult for Henan to approach one like thee. The elders wish revolt. They—"

When she did not go on, he nodded to himself and stood up. More enemies, he thought wearily. Would this maze never end?

"My Leiil?" she whispered, rising to her feet when he did nothing but stare thoughtfully into the fire. "Is it thy intention to spread my blood for this?"

"Why should I?" he asked, puzzled.

She spread out her hands, her silver eyes dull. "Because I am Henan, worthless . . ." Suddenly her lower lip began to tremble. "Oh, good Leiil, I have failed their will. I must die!"

"No!" He seized her by the arms. "No, Giaa, that's nonsense! No one can coerce you—"

"I failed the command of the elders—"

"Giaa, listen!" he said, frustrated as she looked away. "I command it!"

She stiffened, her eyes returning to his.

"That's better," he said sternly. "Now. Do you serve me, or your elders?"

She hesitated, then inclined her head. "Thee."

"Then you have not failed. I am not insulted by your presence. You please me, Giaa. You are beautiful and intelligent. I owe you a great deal for the care you took of—" He swallowed, averting his eyes. "Of the *n'ka*."

A tremor crossed her face. "I grieve for his loss, my Leiil. Forgive me. He gave himself unto thee and—"

"Giaa." He put caution aside, deeply distressed to see her so miserable.

She gestured quickly, turning away. "He did not know Anthi, or Lea and her sisters! He journeyed to Merdarai unprepared and shall spend eternity wrapped in torment!" She gasped. "I wish I might go there too. Oh, Anthi spare me this shame of being slave, of having no will—"

"Stop it." He made her turn around and face him. "You are no longer a slave. I free you."

For an instant something close to scorn shimmered in the depths of her eyes. "I am Henan and below caste. Slavery is not something man can give or take away."

"You can be anything you want to be, Giaa," he said, wishing he could make her understand. "When your will is free, when you decide to make it free, then no matter what others may do to you, you are not a slave. I learned that long ago."

She lifted her finger. "I am what Anthi wills, my Leiil. Only one man I have known was as thou hast said, and even he died for thee."

A queer shiver passed through Blaise. She pulled at him in a way he had never felt before, and it was becoming impossible to ignore the sensation. Involuntarily he reached out to touch her forehead.

"I am going to look upon you with my mind, Giaa," he said, unable to stop himself from invading her privacy. "Trust me."

Her docileness told him she was well accustomed to such treatment. He frowned, then gathered his senses and extended them hesitantly over her. For a moment he was buffeted by grief and confusion. He drew back, uncertain of how to reach through. He dropped his hand, unable to continue.

"My Leiil does not wish to look upon me with truth?" she asked in bewilderment.

He shrugged, trying to sort out his confusion. Something deep and warm stirred in his blood, but this time he held himself stiff, rejecting the desire to extend his senses about her. Until he understood exactly what he was doing, he did not dare give way to these strange emotions within.

"I am going to share a secret with you, Giaa," he said at last. "I . . . The *n'ka*—Blaise—did not die. He is here, Giaa." He touched his chest. "I am—"

"Truly?" Her eyes glowed with such joy that he was dazzled, then she gasped and drew back. "I do not understand."

"Nor do I. But it is true." He looked at her, wondering what had made him entrust her with a knowledge that could easily prove to be his undoing. "I may wear a new body, but I am still Blaise. And I wish to thank you for all the care you gave me these past days."

She drew in a breath. In the clear light her eyes were like deep silver pools of unfathomable water. "Oh, my Leiil, something inside bids me believe thee. And if it is true . . ." She sank down to kneel reverently at his feet, her face suddenly alive with emotion. "Oh, I *am* glad!"

Again his heart seemed to turn over as he smoothed the shining strands of her hair. "You told me once you were sworn to purity," he said, his voice a choked whisper.

Her cheeks darkened, and beneath the thin leather of her tabard her breasts rose and fell quickly. "I . . ." She swallowed and seemed to suddenly dismiss what she had been about to say. Her eyes dropped. "Surely thou hast knowledge of the curse born upon every Henan, that they are all of nature and cannot raise themselves into the mind as can the Tlar and the Bban'n. They are sterile. They are waste. It is against law—"

But he had stopped listening. "The Bban'n?" he echoed in disbelief. "Their powers are equal to—"

"Yes!" She stood up, facing him directly for the first time that evening. "The tribes live in the wastes of the Outerlands to avoid Tlar oppression, but because they live the way of barbarians does not mean they are less. They can follow the power of Anthi as easily as they obey the older circle of the four moons. When I fled the dara of he who sired me to serve in the courts of the Tlar, the revered noble offered me a better life. He looked upon me with truth and said it was the will of Anthi that I serve her sacred purpose." Suddenly her clear voice faltered. "If only thou couldst understand the shame to be as I am. Less than property, despised, without worth." She beseeched him with her eyes. "I could not please thee, my Leiil, who holds the *n'ka* safe. I have not the way of the rings to offer thee."

He longed to kiss away her tears, to chase away the fear clouding her beauty. What she said meant nothing to him. He could not accept rejection now, and instinct—or perhaps his heightened senses—told him her own blood had been stirred in response to the forces causing his to pound through his veins. If only he could find some way to reassure her, to free her from the shame that bound her. More than ever he realized the inadequacy of his understanding of this race and its cultures. Mere words could not clear away ingrained superstitions and training. Then to his surprise his mind stretched forth in response to the urgency within him, freely, with none of his earlier hesitation. The rings comprising his strength, power, and wholeness spread and extended around her, not to question her as he had tried before, but to cherish her. To worship her. He quivered. So the rings were a part of this too. He had not realized.

"Giaa," he whispered, drawing her into his arms.

She flinched as his rings encompassed her. But he was patient, holding them gently around her until she relaxed ever so slightly.

"My Leiil," she said softly, even as the stiffness of her body began to ease. "This is what the elders want. Is it thy—"

"It is what I want," he said, kissing her hair. "Is it what you want?"

She closed her eyes, her musky scent filling his nostrils as he began to infuse her thoughts with his own, caressing her mind as his lips sought hers.

"Yes . . . " she whispered.

In response he held her even more closely, her slim body pliant and willing. As his own mounting passion swept through the rings, inflaming her in return so that she cried out in pleasure, he took her up in his arms and turned toward the shadowed alcove.

"Asan . . . come."

The low call pierced the darkness, stirring him from slumber. At first he thought it was Giaa calling him, but she slept with her head pillowed on his shoulder, her breathing gentle and steady. He frowned, closing his eyes again.

"Asan . . ."

The call came once more from inside him. His frown deepening, he sat up, moving carefully so as not to disturb Giaa, and left the bed of deep cushions to stand tense and puzzled in the gloom. What was it? What did it want?

The call was repeated, touching a deep elemental chord of response so that he took a step forward before he realized it. Angrily he stopped himself. But by now his curiosity was pricked, so that impulsively he decided to obey the summons.

He padded across the carpet on silent, bare feet and found

his clothes, shivering slightly in the chilled air of the alcove. In the larger chamber the fire in the crystal brazier had died to a scattering of faint embers in the ashes. He brushed his hand over a light cube, bringing forth a dim glow of illumination, and pulled on thin leather slippers before taking a cloak of white borlorl fur from a chair to throw about his shoulders. Then he hesitated, wishing for a jen-knife or a fire-rod to thrust through his belt. Leiil Asan might possess supreme mental powers, but he was still Blaise enough to wish for a more tangible weapon comfortably close to hand. But there was nothing here to use.

With a shrug he gathered his cloak tightly and edged to the doorway, dropping a light cube into a pocket in the cloak as he did so. He paused, his senses spreading about him in an alert radius. Yes, Tuult still stood on guard, dozing, but with his senses fully activated. Blaise knew that if he lingered Tuult would become aware of his presence and awaken. Quickly he concentrated, compressed his rings tightly about himself until he possessed only a sliver of existence, then slipped out and past the Bban, not pausing until he was well around a bend in the dark passageway. There he loosened his rings back to normal and waited a moment without breathing. Tuult had not sensed him go by. Good.

Satisfied, he drew the light cube from his pocket and held his thumb upon it until it glowed just enough for him to see by. In silence he hastened on, following the internal call that still insistently summoned him. As he wound his way through the warren of caves and passageways, sometimes squeezing through low, narrow places that reminded him uncomfortably of past ambushes, always choosing the path that led down, he grew certain he was heading for the very heart of the mountain. But he did not fear a trap from Picyt. Whatever this was had nothing to do with the priest.

Though Giaa's mind was closed to him in many ways, he still had gained a wealth of information from her, which, coupled with his own constant self-discoveries, put him on much surer footing than he'd been just hours ago. And what Picyt had planned chilled him whenever he thought about it. Worst of all, he could not make Giaa understand that the priests and their gooddess were not to be blindly obeyed.

"*Asan* . . . come!"

He paused, startled by the intensity of the call. What was it? Deliberately he stayed where he was for a moment, alone in the black depths of the mountain. Somewhere in the distance water dripped with faint splashes. He shivered under his fur cloak, listening to his own rapid breathing. Then cautiously he went on. The passageway at this point had been bored and smoothed by engineers long ago; he slid his finger along a chisel groove in the wall. But not a footprint marred the white dust covering the ground before him.

He came to a dead end, stopped by a wall of metal that shone green in the light from his cube. Corybdium! How was he to get past this barrier?

He stared at it a moment, his keen eyes searching unsuccessfully for a seam or hinge. At last he set a hand upon the surface, only to snatch his fingers away from the warmth of the metal.

"Come . . . !"

The call reverberated through him, vibrating in his bones until he cried out. He fell against the wall, his hands clapped to his head, then struck at the barrier with a fist.

"I am Asan!" he shouted. "Let me pass!"

Something inside the wall clicked, but the barrier did not move. Impatiently he pressed both palms against it.

"By thc will of Asan," hc said, deciding his new name was a kind of magic passport, "open!"

A sequence of clicks sounded, and with a low rumble the door slid into the stone wall. Snatching up the light cube, Blaise stepped through quickly, and it slid shut behind him with a solid *thud*. He found himself in a funnel-shaped room, artificially lit and lined with sheets of corybdium. A steady hum vibrated through the place loudly enough to be an irritant. He frowned. Not only was corybdium rare, it also was one of the few peculiar metals found in the galaxy that was not a natural conductor. It had been used here to insulate the hum of machinery from the rest of the caverns. He wondered why.

Abruptly the lights cut off, plunging him into darkness. Startled, he whirled and dropped to a crouch.

"Arm of Anthi," said the voice within him, low, toneless, yet clear. "Come forth."

He straightened and turned about, unable to find its source. Even his exceptional night vision could not penetrate this darkness. He lifted the light cube and shook it. But it did not activate.

"I cannot see!" he said aloud. "How can I come to you?"

"To see is for the blind," replied the voice. "Come."

Sighing, Blaise extended his senses, hoping to use the rings as a sort of primitive sonar. To his surprise he found them a very effective means of guidance and groped his way to the opposite side of the room. There, at its narrowest point, he discovered a door, which slid soundlessly aside at his wary approach.

Light—blue, liquid, and almost tangible—rushed at him, dazzling his vision so that at first he stood frozen. But when his eyes recovered he realized that he was gazing at an enormous formation of crystal, perhaps three meters in height, cubed, spiked, and faceted in precise geometric shapes. Blue light flashed within it in a shifting pattern, now and then bursting forth in a piercing beam from the tip of a spike.

He stared at it in awe. Then his brain clicked over into cool, efficient gear, and he straightened.

"Anthi," said Blaise commandingly. "Identify self. Computer?"

"Asan," replied the thrumming voice within him, its vibration setting his teeth on edge. "I am the supporter. I am the guardian of life."

Of course! He put it together with a snap of excitement. Anthi wasn't a goddess from some myth. She wasn't even a megalomanic computer running out of control. Anthi was a life-support system, a maintenance unit for . . . what?

He narrowed his blue eyes. "Specify purpose."

The light flashed, mirroring the steady gleam in his eyes. "I maintain heat, atmosphere, and circulatory functions for all capsules. I am Anthi."

"Capsules?" His heart skipped a beat. "Explain."

"Life-support units, numbering eight thousand four hundred one, containing premier specimens of Tlartantla race—"

"Stop!" Demos, thought Blaise, turning away. He ran his hand rapidly along his jaw. It was the age-old horror story of the two galaxies. Someone was always claiming to turn up a sleeper ship from a long-lost race or find a dormant population waiting for some errant Prince Charming in a spacesuit to reactivate it. This just couldn't be happening. Maybe he was dreaming.

But, of course, he wasn't. Blaise sighed, grimly realizing that he was only the first in Picyt's plans. Hadn't Tuult mentioned it was time for the birth?

He turned back to Anthi, his lips compressed. "Identify Picyt."

"Original or present form?"

Jolted by the question, Blaise swallowed hard. "Both."

"Original form: Elder of Tlartantl. Keeper of the Seal of Libraries. Director of Education. Born in third year of Giamos, second index, to family of the House of Mura-an. Awarded seven honors during lifetime of service to crown. Responsible for selection of Ruantl as next birthsite—"

"Stop," said Blaise, clenching his fists. "Present form."

Anthi flashed for several seconds, then glowed a steady blue. "Present form: Regenerated through application of *yde* substance 7-R to maintain present form and capabilities. Responsible for directional education and civilization of native population preparatory for rebirth. Catalyst for initial restoration of Tlar leiil primary."

Not quite, thought Blaise savagely. Picyt had lacked the guts to go through with it himself. "Anthi," he said slowly. "Identify Asan, both forms."

"Original form: Leiil of race. Father of the creation. Master of the rings. Creator of the present purpose. Time of origin unknown. Regenerated nine times within race history. Victorious general in the Cataclysmic Wars and Duoden Conflict . . ."

Blaise glanced involuntarily at the scar on his inner forearm.

". . . eldest brother of Vauzier and Rim. Creator of Anthi. During ninth regeneration, conqueror of Ruantl and Bban race. Giver of—"

"Stop," said Blaise, breathless. "Present form."

Anthi blinked for several seconds. "Present form: Tlar leiil primary of tenth regeneration. Restored by instruction."

Blaise waited for a moment, and when Anthi said nothing more, he snapped: "Reason for my summons here."

"To comply with request of Anthi."

He frowned. "Specify request."

"Request permission to surrender guardianship by instruction."

"Request denied!"

Turning on his heel, he strode away from Anthi. Angrily he looked over the room but saw little of the complicated machinery banked along the corybdium-plated walls. Tall double doors slid aside at his approach, and impatiently he strode through, hardly caring where he went. But a cold, alien touch of air and a peculiar chemical scent plucked him from his anger. He stopped, staring with widening eyes at the enormous cavern stretching before him. It was as vast as a shuttle hangar on an Institute base, the pylon-ribbed walls of stone arching broad and high to a point overhead where a fissure bared the cave to the sky. It was sealed by a protective bubble, and through it Blaise could glimpse heavy purple clouds. His breath quickened; it must be past dawn.

But he forgot about time as he began to survey the contents of the room. Glass cases stretched out in endless rows, shrouded in a white mist that clogged his nostrils like cotton. Reminded of drone warehouses and worse, he wanted to turn away and leave, but curiosity drew him forward. Suddenly he wanted to see these people who would regenerate themselves at the expense of another race, for he knew the Bban'n would not survive transfer with their individual psyches intact as he had. His experience was a fluke, brought on perhaps by his own exceptional stubbornness of mind or the fact that Asan's essence was exhausted by nine previous regenerations. There had to be an eventual end to this attempt to thwart death. Surely there had to be!

Blaise shivered, drawing his fur cloak more tightly about him, although the chill could not be chased away. He had never been granted the luxury of many ethics, but still, this seemed grossly obscene. Did the Tlar travel from planet to planet, patiently preserving their bodies from death when time ran out, until the next race of expendables could have their mental capabilities developed into catalysts?

Not this time, he decided grimly, pushing away the thought that he, too, had chosen to cheat death by exchanging bodies. Guilt could be dealt with later. Right now he had to come up with a way to defeat Picyt. He did not like the Bban people, but they deserved their own destiny free of interference and free of the self-sacrifice of oblivion.

He strode forward, pushing through the thigh-deep mists, and stopped by the first capsule. He frowned, unable to see inside through the white gas swirling within it. Then, remembering Picyt's actions, he gathered himself to focus his rings and pressed one palm against the icy surface of the glass. A queer sensation—almost of physical loss—swept through him, robbing him of breath. The mists dissipated slowly within the container, revealing . . . nothing!

Stunned, he stared inside for a full minute. No one lay inside. Quickly he stepped to the next capsule and placed his palm upon it. Again, the case proved empty. Five cases later he was reeling with exhaustion from the expenditure of mental energy, and still he had not found a single golden body.

A muscle corded along his jaw, and he returned to Anthi's chamber, determined to know the meaning of this trick.

"Anthi!" His voice thundered over the hum of machinery.

Anthi flashed a sequence of light as he came to a halt before her.

"Explanation required! Why are the capsules empty? Where are the Tlartantla?"

Anthi winked to herself for several seconds while Blaise cursed the delay. "Request permission to surrender guardianship by instruction."

He swept out his fist in furious rejection, scarcely listening. "Request denied! Answer my question, Anthi, by the will of Asan."

"Subsequent space transports did not arrive. Reason unknown. Purpose is incomplete."

He eased out a shallow breath, stunned. So Picyt and a few others had come here to set up operations. The first Asan and those other three in the capsules in the central cavern had selected these mountains as their base, built a city on the plains near water and arable land, and made contact with the Bban tribes. How long, he wondered, had they waited? How long had it been before Asan gave up and put himself in preservation, king not of eight thousand elite Tlar men and women, but of nothing?

"Request permission to surrender guardianship by instruction," repeated Anthi.

With a start he frowned at Anthi's request. Was that the command to start the transferal process? He snorted wryly. "Permission denied, Anthi," he said and strode out, leaving the tomb and its guardian of nothing alone once again.

Chapter 10

Saunders crouched in the secure shadows of a stalagmite in the main cavern, keeping a late-night vigil she did not wholly understand or wish to examine. Hunger gnawed at her stomach, and almost absently she pulled a ration cube from her cloak pocket and bit into the crumbly, pungent stuff. As she chewed and swallowed, her eyes did not stray from the illuminated center of the cave where, amid the clutter of machinery, the remaining three Jewels of M'thra glowed.

She would have given five service commendations to be able to erase the day's galling disappointments from her mind, and she longed to be elsewhere, hidden from her own bitterness. But she could not drag herself away.

Only a few hours ago, Blaise Omari, her last hope of getting back to the Institute with her record intact, had died. To have turned the stubborn, devious renegade in to Security would have certainly gained her a promotion, and she need not have faced any investigation into her own loyalty. Now he was gone, dragged away by the emotionless Bban'jen to rot somewhere in the darkness of these dirty caves, his carcass unmourned and his absence unmarked. She had overheard one of the priests deny the Bban'n permission to eat what was left of him.

Shivering, she pulled her cloak tighter about her, hating the damp chill sinking into her bones. It had been horrible, standing there helplessly watching the very essence of life drain from Omari until he was nothing but a shriveled, sightless husk. She shut her eyes, striving to soften the memory by telling herself he deserved a far worse end. It did not help. She had not seen an execution since childhood; she could not forget the awful look of fear in Omari's eyes at the final moment. And as much as she had despised him, in an odd way she had respected him, too, and it seemed wrong that he should die afraid.

Don't be sentimental! she told herself sharply, and took another bite of food.

A squad of Bban'jen marched in to relieve the guards surrounding the Jewels. Saunders took advantage of the activity to move nearer. Now she could clearly see the sleeping face of Aural. She sighed with longing. How she wished she could exchange what she was for that perfect creature's body! Never in her life had she seen any woman so flawless in appearance. Instinct told her Aural was a woman who commanded respect without having to fight for it.

She had always scorned the beauty that nature had denied her, making up for it by applying herself to duty and training, strengthening her aptitude for mathematics, and making sure no one could say she wasn't a damned fine officer. But the admiration sparked within her at the initial sight of Aural had grown into a flame of longing so intense, she could not deny it even to herself.

She did not want to die as Omari had. Even seeing the magnificent Asan return to life could not quite move her to the point of wishing to be a sacrifice to Aural's resurrection. But with a pang she also wondered what sort of future lay before her now. How long would she last here, tolerated for her ability with machinery, the only one of her own kind, with no hope of return?

Her plan to bring an Institute patrol ship here via the distress beacons she had secretly set up both in Altian and here during unguarded moments, when the Bban'jen no longer paid her very much attention, had failed. No ship had come; probably the X ray interference from the black star blocked the signal entirely. The factors in favor of her rescue had run out. She was stranded, cut off from any chance of ever returning to the things that formed the nucleus of her life.

The pain of self-pity grew intense. Abruptly she stood up and walked out to wander aimlessly through the passageways, which lay empty and dark at this hour. Now and then she stumbled in the jen boots, which were too large for her, so weary each step dragged with exhaustion, yet unwilling to rest. *What am I to do*? she wondered. Once, when she'd been younger, the thought of dying in the service of the Institute had seemed unbearably thrilling. Now she looked harshly at herself and her values. To be a castaway was a sort of death for the Institute, and in it she found no glory and no reason for pride. *I am a fool*, she thought, her eyes stinging. Omari had told her so several times; she should have listened. The Institute cared for its own perpetuation, and individuals did not matter. With anger she pushed the thoughts away. He was vat scum. She would not pretend to respect him now just because he was dead. She would not adopt his opinions.

The sound of rapid striding footsteps coming toward her from around the bend ahead brought her up short. Her breath caught. She had heard the rumors of the attempt on Asan's life, and twice today she had seen overly excited Bban duel to the death. Without a weapon she did not dare brave an encounter with anyone save Picyt, Teecht, and a few others of the technicians whom she could trust not to attack her.

Swiftly she pressed herself into the shadows against the wall, holding her breath as light wavered and shifted upon the rock from the other's torch. Perhaps they were near an intersection of tunnels; perhaps he would not come this way; perhaps he would pass her by without a glance as someone of no caste. Still, she uncurled her tense hands into the fourth and eighth positions of kiamee fighting, tensing her muscles in readiness for whatever she might have to do.

The glimmer of illumination flashed around the bend, blinding her for a second even as she tried to guess who would dare carry about one of the precious light cubes instead of a torch. Her dazzled eyes could only glimpse someone immensely tall, cloaked in a pale sweep of white, before he spotted her and sprang with a hiss, his powerful hand closing unerringly on her throat.

Pinned against the wall with a violence that knocked the breath from her lungs, Saunders struggled vainly, unable to use her fighting skills at all. His height, strength, and length of arm put him simply past her reach.

"Release me, damn you!" she shouted, her voice a desperate croak as his grip tightened.

To her surprise, he did release her, and backed up a step. His other hand raised the cube, sending light spilling across her mask. Not daring to move, she dragged in several ragged breaths, then coughed, the translator that hung by a cord about her neck thumping against her chest.

"I am the *n'dl,*" she said warily when she had regained her breath. "I mean you no harm."

"Saunders," he said in a voice so deep and powerful it seemed to vibrate through her bones. He lowered the light cube, thus bringing his face out of shadow.

She gazed up at intense blue eyes, deep-set and whiteless, flecks of amber and jade glinting in them, with winged black eyebrows knitted over a haughty curve of nose. Sharp cheekbones flared on the sides of his face, and his mouth was thin-lipped and hard, with a hint of sensuality softening the corners. A rich cloak of white fur hung from his broad shoulders to his heels, and beneath it a green tunic cut of shimmering fabric hung partway open, exposing a glimpse of muscular, golden-skinned chest.

Her heart thudded painfully. She blinked, wishing she could look away from those eyes, but she did not dare.

"Asan," she said, finding her voice at last. Her throat was so dry, the word nearly stuck there. The Institute must learn of his race, she thought, trying to contain her awe.

He drew in a deep breath. "*Lea'dl*, Saunders! What are you doing skulking through here? I thought you were another assassin."

"I . . ." Her voice trailed off. She could not think of an answer. He seemed to fill the passageway, dwarfing her with more than size. How did he know her? Why had he not strode on as soon as he realized she was harmless?

He gestured. "Remove your mask. I must talk with you at once."

Puzzled, she obeyed, the chilly air striking her hot face as soon as the stuffy mask was pulled away. She pushed back her hood and tucked the mask under her left elbow, jen fashion.

He noticed, and a faint smile touched his mouth.

"I am not your enemy, Noble Asan," she blurted out. "What do you want with me?"

"Your help," he said. His blue eyes bored into her with a peculiar gleam. "I am Omari."

"What?"

She stared at him, as breathless as though he had struck her. Her fists clenched at her sides. "No!" she shouted, angry at the thought of being mocked. "You lie! Omari was vat born. He couldn't—"

"I have a soul and a mind that were not given me by the Institute," he said impatiently. "Look, Saunders, never mind about the hows and whys. And for once in your life do not argue. Just accept what you are told. I am in Asan's body. My psyche survived, not his."

Her brain spun, and she leaned against the jagged stone wall to steady herself. Could it be true? She began to believe him. But if so, then—

"Oh, damn you!" she burst out, no longer caring what she said. "And I had begun to wonder if Asan were a god. What a fool I am!" She put her fists on her hips, her cloak spreading over her arms. Scorn and hurt ground knives into her, and she stared at him in disgust, hating him and hating herself even more for having believed in his death. "So you don't lie when you say you always have a way out. Now you've even escaped death. How—"

"Enough!" He swept out his hand imperiously to silence her.

But she did not want to be silenced. "How did you do it, Omari? I suppose now you—"

She broke off with a gasp as invisible iron bands suddenly squeezed about her, clamping her arms to her sides, cutting off her lung power, and compressing her throat. She tried to move, to scream, to do anything that might shake off this paralysis, but she was utterly helpless. Raging inside, she glared up at him, only to blink—her fury dashed from her—at the sight of his blue eyes blazing incandescent light. *He* was doing this to her. Fright shook her as the bands tightened. She began to gasp for air, blinking against the spots blurring her vision. *Please, no*! she tried to scream, but her voice was throttled, and the words merely echoed around and around in her head.

Abruptly the pressure ceased. She dropped limply to her knees, lungs heaving, and brushed tears of pain from her eyes with the back of her hand. When she dared look up at him again, his eyes were normal, but hard in a face set in stern lines. Unease rekindled in her, chilling her despite the perspiration soaking the sides of her tunic. He was not just Blaise Omari behind a different face, she told herself dazedly.

She must be careful.

"Now," said the deep, commanding voice, and she flinched. "You have been much with Picyt. What are his exact plans?"

"Of all people, you should know!" she retorted, hating him for making her afraid.

"I have sources of information," he said bleakly, the initial warmth in his voice long since gone. "I know the summons to the Bban tribes has gone out, but by what means? Has he some sort of call beacon, or more direct communications?"

Her heart convulsed in fear. He must not discover her beacon! Useless as it had proved to be, she knew that were it found, she would die.

"Yes," she said in a low voice, not daring to meet his eyes, wondering if he could read her mind. "There is a general signal." *Think of something else*! she told herself, but the more she tried the more the thought of her beacon hammered through her brain.

"Well, then," he said. "Sabotage it."

Surprised, she rose to her feet and faced him with a frown. "Why? If the full contingent of tribes doesn't arrive soon, we won't have a prayer against Leiil Hihuan and his forces."

"If the Bban'jen are not here, there will be no battle," he said, sweeping out his hand. "I cannot permit Bban slaughter for something as worthless as—"

"I thought Blaise Omari would be the most eager to help liberate—"

"It is not freedom Picyt offers the Bban'n, Saunders, but death! He has taught these people to believe in a goddess that in reality is just a machine. He has deceived them into adopting a set of rituals they think is worship to Anthi, but all they have done is teach themselves mental surrender to whatever Picyt wants them to do." He gripped her arm with a hand like steel, his eyes so intense it was painful to meet them. "Deep in this mountain lie more life support containers like the one that held me. More than eight thousand, Saunders!"

She gasped, astonished by the number. "Eight—"

"I'm not exactly sure what type of species the Tlar are, but they regenerate themselves by selecting other species with mental abilities compatible with theirs, using them as catalysts to—"

"I understand," she said quickly, looking away with a queasy tremor at the all too vivid memory of the process. "I saw it happen to you."

"Yes." His voice softened, and his eyes grew thoughtful, darkening with memory. "You did see. By fluke, by strength . . . somehow I survived. But I wasn't meant to, Saunders," he continued, "Asan was not resurrected to lead the Bban'n to freedom. He was resurrected to lead them down to those eight thousand capsules and sacrifice them to the regeneration of his race. Picyt knows I intend to stop him. That's why I need your help."

"To sabotage the summoning so that the tribes won't come," she said slowly, attempting to comprehend his incredible story. She considered believing him, trusting him. But he is Omari, she told herself. Omari, even inside that magnificent body, could never be trusted. "But wouldn't it be faster to just pull the plug?"

"What?" He frowned.

"To pull the plug. Turn off the life-support computer maintaining the capsules." She thought of Aural crumbling to dust and shuddered.

A smile, wry and infinitely bitter, touched his lips. For a moment she saw centuries of age in those blue eyes. Then he said very quietly, "The cases are empty. Asan, Picyt, Hihuan, and the rest all came to this planet to make the preparations. But the Tlar never arrived. Saunders, Picyt has been waiting here for hundreds of years." He gripped her shoulders, and the strength in his hands frightened her. He could crush her if he wanted to. Before they had been well-matched; now he had the advantage.

"I think he has finally gone mad," continued Omari. "Too much *yde*, perhaps, or maybe he just can't face facts anymore. But he has blocked those empty cases from his mind. If we don't stop him, he'll transfer the Bban'n into *nothing*. Can you imagine a more horrible death?"

She could not imagine it at all. Something within her snapped, and she looked up at that imperious golden face, her decision made. If Picyt were stopped and the support machinery destroyed, her chance to become Aural would be gone forever. And if someone like Omari could survive the transfer, then why couldn't she? She lifted her chin. If she had to spend the rest of her life on this miserable, sand-blasted rock, crawling through caves like the miners she'd escaped long ago for the glory of the stars, then she'd do it as Aural and not as Saunders the *n'dl*, without caste or respect.

"Yes," she said swiftly, brushing aside second thoughts. "I'll help you."

"Good." His smile was warm and open, so unlike Omari's arrogant grin. But she barely noticed it as she nodded and hurried away, so intent upon reaching Picyt now with her request that she never saw the pair of scarlet eyes glowing from the shadows of a niche cut in the rock, or the cloaked, hooded figure that slipped behind her to follow Asan's striding figure with the furtiveness of a finger of smoke.

"So you seek the honor of raising Aural, Enchantress of the Winds and Keeper of the Blood," whispered Picyt hoarsely from his bed of deeply piled cushions.

Saunders still had not fully recovered from the shock of seeing the serene revered noble transformed into a living skeleton, his bones sticking out sharply beneath pallid, sagging flesh. His dark eyes, like holes cut in a death mask, were the only thing alive in his face. They glittered strangely at her as she inclined her head, and she felt as though something had crawled across her skin.

"Yes, Noble Picyt," she said, trying to hide her revulsion.

He grunted and lay back upon his pillows, half hidden in the shadows cast by the canopy over him. Two motionless, masked jen guards stood flanking the bed, their feet braced apart and their arms crossed over their black tunics. Flames of light glowed and flicked like orange tongues from the mouths of brass creatures hung upon the wall, and incense burned with belches of purple smoke from the small brazier standing behind her. She could not smell the stuff, but as she breathed in the smoke it stung and dried her throat. Resisting the need to cough, she stood motionless, waiting with the patience she had learned was necessary with the priest. His sunken eyes remained closed in thought. The suspense seemed endless, and she wondered if he had fallen asleep. But she did not relax.

Finally he opened his eyes and pierced her with an unwavering gaze. "What is your reason for this request?" His once deep, resonant voice now rattled and cracked with every strained word.

She kept her eyes averted. "I . . ." She paused and swallowed hard, trying to curb her rising unease. "I want to be beautiful," she blurted out finally, her face very hot. One of the guards clicked his jaw behind his mask, and she glared at him.

"And so beauty attracts you now, does it? We find this pleasing to hear." A ghost of mockery flitted through his voice, making her raise her head sharply. "Yes," he continued, his long supple fingers wandering over the coverlet of white and silver fur mitered in a rich pattern of texture and pale color. "Aural's spirit is legend. Her heart is flame, her soul fire. She shines from within." Picyt raised his sunken black eyes slowly to Saunders's. "Do you understand what Aural is, *n'dl*?"

Saunders stifled an involuntary burst of annoyance at being called by that term. She knew that quite simply it meant not a daughter of the planet, but the subtle inflections of insult still lashed across the raw wound of her pride. She looked at Picyt, who had always treated her with kindness but not with honesty, and raised her chin high.

"No," she said curtly, biting off the words. "I do not. Legends mean nothing to me."

"Yet you would be one," he said, steepling his fingers. "Why?"

She realized he meant to refuse her request and was merely toying with her now. Anger shot through her, and she nearly shouted the truth. Then at the last moment caution choked her. She knew then that she would not betray Omari and despised herself.

"Aural is by right the true Tsla leiis," said Picyt softly, his sunken eyes glittering in a way she distrusted. "She is the wife of the Tlar leiil, and the mother of the heirs."

"No." Breathing the word, Saunders drew back a step. Mate with Omari? *Never*! But Picyt must be lying. Aural was one of the four. She must be more than a royal brood mare. Saunders shut her eyes, beads of perspiration streaking her face from the heat, smoke, and tension. Picyt was twisting this, trying to manipulate her as he had done before, but she could not find his motive.

"Do you fear Asan?" asked Picyt.

Saunders answered shortly. "I know he is Omari." But was he? asked a sudden voice of doubt within her. Or was that another lie? Confused and trapped in a maze of lies and half truths, she stood there, exhausted. She'd be damned if she'd cower before Picyt or anyone else! "He is Omari," she repeated so firmly her voice rang out through the room. "Not some god or king you serve, noble, but Blaise Omari, murderer, thief, sel—"

"You do not truly fear these petty actions," said Picyt, his ravaged mouth curling in a small smile.

"They are serious crimes, and he must pay for them!" she said, even more vigorously.

"Then how shall you pay for your crime?" Picyt leaned forward suddenly from his cushions. He pointed his forefinger at her in an accusation that froze the blood in her veins and robbed her legs of strength. "Betrayer!"

He knows, she thought in despair, shrinking back from the dark eyes glaring at her so wildly. Everything inside her shriveled. Desperately she opened her mouth.

"Deny nothing!" he said, gesturing her to silence while the guards slapped ready hands to knife hilts. "We bargained, *n'dl*, but you have betrayed your word with this creation." He lifted his finger, and a slave hobbled forward from the shadows, bearing a small metal box in his gnarled hands.

Saunders stared at it. She tried to swallow and could not. "I gave you no word on this," she said in a strained whisper. Defiance surged back. "You betrayed me first, Noble Picyt. And upon that occasion you told me a second vow cannot bind the first." She spoke carefully and without sign of the fear hammering through her. "My first allegiance is to the Galactic Space Institute. Duty requires that I seek every means to obtain rescue from shipwreck, so the Institute does not lose any able-bodied—"

"Enough," he said impatiently. "Empty words, Saunders." He gazed at her for a long moment. Then the old wry expression of cynical knowledge and infinite compassion crossed his face. He smiled in the way that had half won her liking for him from the first. Troubled, she stared back at him. His smile faded. "This Institute you speak of so often, this that claims your blood loyalty, has shown you nothing in return. No ship of rescue has come."

Unwanted tears of chagrin stung her eyes. She blinked fiercely and shook her head.

"We have offered you life, Ryhi," he said softly, turning his palm up at her surprise. "Yes, I remember your private name. I know many things about you, and I have long admired your spirit and intelligence."

The gentle words tore at her in a way she did not believe possible.

"Ryhi," he continued, his dark eyes searching her face so intently that she wondered why he did not seek to read her mind. "Your place is here now. Old vows can no longer claim you. They have not answered your call. They do not care about you. But I care, Ryhi." He gestured, and the slave approached Saunders with a bow, his aged face averted carefully. He held out the beacon to her.

"Silence its call," said Picyt gently. "You have come asking to be Aural, to join us in the completeness of the rings of Anthi. And this we allow with gladness. It pleases us to grant your request to become her, for Aural has use in this time."

He is mad, Omari had said, and not to be trusted. The words echoed through her brain. She did not understand Picyt, who was first malevolent and mocking, then kind. He refused her, then gave permission. And what did it matter who silenced the beacon? Its signal had done no good. She stared at it with disgust. Slowly she reached out to take it, then abruptly drew back her hand.

"What use do you plan for Aural?" she asked, facing Picyt directly. "Besides . . . I won't be Omari's mate!"

"Asan's mate," said Picyt with a smile that chilled her. "But Omari's betrayer. You are clever at deception. And with my instructions to guide you . . . Yes, perhaps this *is* wise. There is time now while Hihuan's forces are held at bay in the wastes by the black devis." He extended a hand. "Silence the box, and let us prepare you."

Fear, nameless and unreasoning, struck at her. "No!" she said sharply. "No, I won't destroy Omari, not like that, not with a trick. I asked to be Aural for another reason, not this." She stepped back from the slave, who shuffled his misshapen feet and shivered.

Picyt narrowed his eyes. "Yes, you seek to be Aural in order to take your own vengeance upon him. That is not permitted. *Chi'ka!*" Swiftly the guards stepped to either side of her. Tensing, Saunders whirled, but at a gesture from Picyt the guards seized her arms and turned her back. *"Ny!"* snapped Picyt, and now in his eyes the black fire of purpose and determination blazed. "I am sworn to the raising of the blood. I am *sworn*. The Tlar will rule again." He sat forward, the incense curling thin fingers of colored smoke about his shoulders. "Not just this world, but all worlds of this new galaxy."

Saunders's eyes widened. "Impossible!" she said with scorn. "You have lost your technology. And the Institute as well as the Commonwealth of Planets would—"

"Defeat us?" he finished. "Fool! I and these few others are spent and feeble. The true blood flows in those such as Asan, mightier than any your race can throw against us."

She snorted. "Even eight thousand Asans are not enough to conquer—"

"*Merdarai!* You know the number in Anthi's heart?" He glared at her with terrible eyes. "*You?* Then he has spoken with you to poison your mind against me. And did he make you ask to raise Aural?"

"No," she whispered. *Run!* screamed her instincts, but the guard beside her had his knife drawn. Desperately she said, "Noble Picyt, I—"

"You were safe as long as you obeyed what was asked of you and stayed out of the move of events. But this meddling, *n'dl*, shall cost you dear!" He held out his thin, trembling hand. "We shall silence the box for you. But you shall serve me henceforth, and in the manner of my choosing. You shall bring Aural forth and make her serve me too."

Saunders whirled to make a dash for freedom, aiming a hard blow at the guard who blocked her way. But he was quicker and dodged, seizing her arm and wrenching it behind her so roughly that she nearly screamed with pain.

"And suppose I don't survive like Omari did," she said. "Suppose the real Aural comes forth. She'd be on Asan's side . . . against you."

Picyt's smile was evil and utterly merciless. "Which of you does not matter. For you, Ryhi Saunders, are mine to command, and *this* will make sure of Aural's cooperation." From his sleeve he drew forth a small vial of fine blue powder.

Saunders stared at it in horror. "No," she said, pleading and not caring that she did so. "For God's sake, Picyt, not *yde*! I don't want to die like that! Like y—" She stopped herself, but he knew what she had nearly said.

His eyes were as small and cold as black pebbles. "Anthi shall choose your life or your death," he intoned, raising fingertips to his brow in a gesture copied by the slave and guards. "But you shall always know how Anthi's fire shivers through your veins. You shall obey or suffer worse torture than the seven deaths of Merdar's shadow land. And Asan will know destruction by the hand of his beloved Aural before the next dawn. It is sworn." Drawing in a deep breath, he spread the fingers of his right hand. "Put it down her throat, Jutuu."

The slave took the vial and hobbled over to Saunders, who struggled to free herself. The guard's grip clamped down harder, making her cry out. Omari had not lied, she thought wildly, her heart pounding so rapidly that the rush of her blood made her dizzy. Oh, she had been a fool to come here. Her determination to get Omari had made her blind. Cursing her own stupidity, she tensed as both arms were pinioned behind her. The other guard took the vial from Jutuu and unstoppered it. She could not smell the drug, but its potency was evident by the way the guard swiftly drew back. He spoke curtly to his fellow, and Saunders cried out as the excruciating pressure on her shoulders increased.

There were measures to resist forced ingestion, and she tried all the Institute had taught her in self-defense, but the pain was relentless. Finally with a gasp she gave up her struggles. Powerful fingers gripped her jaw, forcing open her mouth despite her attempts to bite. The bitter, acrid taste of the powder filled her mouth, stinging her tongue like a thousand red-hot needles. She coughed and tried to spit it out, but the guard clamped his hand over her nose and mouth, choking off her air until in desperation she gulped and swallowed. His hand fell away and air rushed into her heaving lungs, but that no longer mattered. A queer blue haze smothered her. Then agonizing pain shot through her arms and legs as her veins seemed to burst. The last thing she heard before she slipped screaming into the black void of unconsciousness was the sound of Picyt's hoarse laughter.

Chapter 11

He was still being followed. Frowning, Blaise slackened his pace as he drew near his quarters. The shadow had joined him some distance from Anthi's chamber; he knew only that it was a Bban, one unknown to him personally. Blaise's frown deepened. Tuult would deal with him.

But Tuult no longer stood guard outside his quarters. Blaise stopped in the passageway. Warily he approached the door, wishing for a weapon as he eased himself inside the main chamber. A light cube burned brightly, revealing the overturned table and scattered chairs. The coals in the crystal brazier flickered like baleful red eyes.

"Giaa?" he called softly, but no answer came.

Fearing a trap, he moved silently toward the alcove, where he stopped again and listened, not daring to use his higher senses. Nothing.

"Giaa!" Suddenly he flung aside the curtains and burst into the alcove. The colored smoke of incense curled about torn, scattered bed cushions, and on the floor spread a dark puddle of wine spilled from an overturned ewer.

She was gone. She had been taken.

Loss wrenched through him. Quickly he returned to the main chamber as sudden fury raged through him, and he swept out his rings with a snap, seeking to capture the man who had followed him. But the creature was gone. He seemed to be alone in this sector of the caves.

"Demos!" he said aloud. *Fool*! echoed a sneering voice within him. To care for someone always meant to open a point of vulnerability to the enemy. He had learned that the hard way years ago.

Blaise's eyes grew cold as his anger burned itself into a hard core of fire. No matter what he might look like now, he was still the same Blaise who always survived because he moved quicker, thought more coldly, and held no attachments to anyone. Picyt meant to strike him through Giaa, but she was just a slave girl. He would not walk into a trap for her.

Blaise moved about the room in search of a weapon. It was time he left this place. He owed the Bban'n no allegiance or favors. He would not be drawn further into their problems.

On his way out he bent to pick up the overturned table, and as he did so he caught sight of a small object glittering on the floor. He picked it up and turned it over, his detachment shattering as he recognized Giaa's gold brooch. It was a favorite talisman with her; she always wore it. He closed his fist over it, and worry for her returned. Then, as clearly as though he actually saw her, she appeared in his mind's eye, her lovely face contorted with grief and pain as she stood bound to a narrow metal pillar.

Where?

He clutched the brooch, the metal cutting into his palm as he concentrated on focusing her image. He saw the glint of torchlight on her golden hair, and she turned her head. He glimpsed the sheen of tears on her face. His heart twisted as sharply as though a jen-knife had been thrust there. She was suffering because of him. He must go to her.

He pressed his fingertips together, cupping his hands around the brooch so as to not lose her image. He shut his eyes and concentrated, trying to reach her mind with his in hopes of finding her location. Instead, as he made the demand on himself, blue fire exploded through his veins with a force more intense than ever before, whirling him about so that to his annoyance he lost the image of Giaa. He tried to regain it, then realized with a pang of fear that he'd been struck blind and motionless. In the next instant the sensation passed, leaving him breathless, dizzy, and as cold as though he had lain in snow.

"My Leiil! Oh, my Leiil, you have come!"

Still dazed, he opened his eyes and blinked in astonishment. He no longer stood in his quarters, but in a rough-hewn chamber of rock. A smelly torch flickered out barely enough light to illuminate Giaa's incredulous tear-stained face.

"Merciful Lea, you have come!" she cried, her soft voice

breaking. For a moment she smiled at him, half incoherent with relief. Then her gladness faded. "It is a trap," she said with a gasp. "They—"

"Hush," he said, recovering from his amazement. How many other powers did Asan have? he wondered distractedly as he hurried over to her, checking to be sure that she was unharmed. He brushed away a tear from the curve of her cheek and smiled. When she smiled tremulously in return, he nodded and circled behind her to work on her bonds. They were fashioned of thin webbed fabric, incredibly tough and just elastic enough to prevent them from being snapped.

"Who took you?" he asked, keeping his voice low as he frowned and wished for the ability to produce a jen-knife out of thin air.

"Pon Tuult," she said, a catch still in her voice. "I had just awakened and found thee gone from me when the curtains of privacy stirred. I thought it thee returning, but instead it was that piece of dung." She turned her head in an effort to see Blaise's progress, long strands of her hair brushing over his forearm. "It is madness. Does he not serve thee, my Leiil?"

"He serves Picyt." Blaise redoubled his efforts to free her, using the sharp pin of her brooch to jab and tear at the straps. But progress came with agonizing slowness, for the soft gold metal tended to bend against the tough fabric. He swore under his breath, desperate to get her out of here before they were discovered. "I was a fool to trust Tuult," he said savagely. "I should have known Picyt would lose no time in acting against me."

"Against thee?" she echoed as the strap began finally to tear. "But why? Thou are the great leiil now. The revered noble is thy servant before Anthi—"

Blaise snorted, thinking of the emptiness Anthi guarded. The straps gave way, and he pulled them from her wrists, moving around the pillar to draw her into his arms and hold her close.

"I do not understand," she said as he rested his chin on top of her silken head, wondering how he could have even considered abandoning her. "All is not as has been proclaimed in the litanies. Nor as told by—"

"No," he said sternly, drawing away. He needed to concentrate on getting her out of here. She was no longer a tool of the

Bban elders, and he would not let Picyt have her either. But the door was certain to be guarded, and he did not know how to take her out by the way he'd got in. He sighed, keeping one arm about her. "The litanies are wrong, very wrong, but Picyt does not intend to acknowledge the mistake." He glanced about, measuring the room, then looked down at her. His eyes softened at the trusting bewilderment in hers. "Here, you're shivering." He threw his cloak of white fur about her and immediately felt the bite of chilly air through his thin tunic. Her feet were bare and mottled with cold, and she wore only the scant covering of her tabard.

"Now listen carefully," he said, still frowning as he considered the risks. "I am going to deceive the guards outside the door into not seeing us as we pass."

She seemed puzzled, but her large silver eyes remained trusting.

"You must make no sound," he told her, beginning to gather his inner forces. "How many guards are out there?"

"Four," she said and at his start of dismay, added, "But it is the usual number this near the Jewels of M'thra. They must be protected always."

Blaise moved warily to the door, listened for a moment, then motioned for her to come to his side. He pressed his fingertips together and extended his mind-touch cautiously, convincing the guards to unlock the door. There was less resistance than he expected; the bolts ground back, and the door swung open.

"Now," breathed Blaise, concentrating on narrowing the two of them to slivers of existence. He stepped slowly outside with Giaa at his heels, only to stop at the sight of Picyt standing there smiling with Uble and Basai beside him. Each of the three priests held a fire-rod aimed at Blaise. Behind him Giaa's breath came out in a muffled sob.

"So you have learned to seizert," said Picyt in a harsh whisper of a voice. "It pleases me to praise you. The skill is not easily learned."

"Or remembered?" retorted Blaise, meeting the mockery with some of his own.

Picyt narrowed his dark eyes, but his sinister smile did not fade. "You speak truly, Leiil," he said softly, his ruined voice whispering about the stone walls of the caves in echoes as light as the brush of batwings. "I shall not seizert again. But now perhaps you see I am not entirely without resources." As he spoke he lifted the fire-rod almost negligently while Uble and Basai stood like statues, their aim never wavering. Blaise thought to speak to the younger priest but held back, stopped by the anguished yet determined expression in those unblinking clear green eyes.

Weary of verbal fencing, Blaise drew erect. "Why did you have Giaa taken?"

Picyt raised his brows. "It was not by my order."

Blaise swept out a hand impatiently. "There is no need to lie. She was taken by Tuult, who is your right arm. Why? What do you want with her? To get to me? I have no intention of running from you." He frowned as he spoke, unable to believe he was spouting these words of bravado. Of course he meant to clear out. Anything else was stupid.

Then he realized such thoughts were pointless. The old Blaise was gone. And what had replaced him and Asan was somehow a combination of the two, king and thief. Giaa drew nearer to his side, and he felt a surge of protectiveness. It *was* his fight. His place was here. He must stop Picyt somehow. He *must*.

Picyt spread the fingers of his left hand, and a muscle suddenly twitched in his pallid cheek. "Tuult does not always act by my rule," he said with a sneer. "He is Bban first and a pon second. But perhaps I understand his reasons." As he spoke Picyt stared at Giaa, a queer expression in his eyes. "By the ancient rites—now forbidden—of Lea and the moons who are her sisters, any conqueror of the Bban tribes must lie with a Bban'dl of the highest honor, giving her a child as a gift in exchange for the loyalty of the tribes. You did this once long ago, Leiil Asan, and thus the first Henan was born." Giaa returned his gaze as though mesmerized. "It would appear custom has been served again, though incorrectly. I wonder why a Henan woman was substituted for a Bban'dl. No child can result. Perhaps I had better speak to Tuult concerning this matter."

"But, revered noble, I cannot be the one!" cried Giaa in fear, her fingers digging into Blaise's arm. "It is against the law of the rites. I was not purified. I have no caste to be defiled unto sacrifice—"

"Giaa," said Blaise in warning.

A gleam appeared in Picyt's eyes. "The supreme elders," he whispered, clenching his fist. "Do they dare rebel against the will of Anthi? I will have answers, girl!"

He reached out for her, but Blaise stepped between them. "Leave her alone, Picyt."

Picyt lifted his finger, and one of the guards, who had not stirred before, snatched Giaa from Blaise's grasp. She cried out, and with an oath Blaise swung at the guard, only to freeze as a blue bolt of fire crackled out, marking the stone floor scant inches from his feet. He wanted to ignore the warning of that shot and act, but he remained motionless, his heart thudding uncontrollably as he remembered the awful searing pain of his previous wound. The frustration of his own fear enraged him.

He glared at Picyt, who lifted his fire-rod in a small salute.

"The girl will not be harmed," said the priest, "unless you make another foolish move."

Blaise glanced at Giaa, who stood huddled in the gauntleted grip of the masked guard. Her face had drained of all color, and her silver eyes were dull with a resignation that infuriated him.

"What are you going to do with her?" He lifted his fist. "By Demos, if you hurt her—"

"It does not please me to see my Leiil so distressed," said Picyt sardonically. "She will not be harmed, provided you cooperate."

"Of course," said Blaise dryly, wondering why it had taken the priest so long to reach this expected point. "One intrigue after the other." He shrugged, conscious of Giaa's anxious, tear-filled eyes upon him. "So what is it you want me to do, Noble Picyt?" He stood there, wondering if he really would surrender the Bban race for Giaa's sake. Everyone would soon find out exactly what kind of grit Blaise Omari was made of, and how much of it belonged to Asan.

Picyt smiled, turning his head within the frame of his tall, fan-shaped collar, and extended his hand. "It pleases me to request thy help in raising Aural, Noble Asan."

It was so far from what he'd expected, at first Blaise could only stare at him. "What?" he asked at last, stupidly.

"Is it so difficult, this request?" demanded Picyt impatiently, misinterpreting Blaise's reaction. "It is the will of Anthi that she be brought forth."

By now Blaise had recovered his wits. "Is it? Or is it the will of Picyt?"

The other two priests gasped at this blasphemy, and even the guards clicked rapidly behind the anonymity of their masks.

Picyt turned over his palm, his eyes meeting Blaise's without any attempt to dissemble. "Does it matter?"

"No," said Blaise shortly, watching Uble and Basai exchange startled looks. "But who do you intend using in this procedure? Not Giaa!" he said more sharply than he intended.

"No." Picyt's smile was too smug to be reassuring. "By now you should be aware that Henen are of little use in any meaningful facet of life."

Blaise's temper flared, but he kept it under control. He did not dare loose the blue fire lest the guard at his back kill Giaa. Helplessness raged through him.

"Then let us be about it!" He stepped forward, gesturing for Picyt to lead the way.

"My . . . Leiil?"

Giaa's quavering voice stopped him. He looked back, desperately trying to keep his face expressionless, and met her strained silver eyes. She tried to smile, but began to weep instead.

"I'm sorry," she whispered. "May Anthi protect thee."

"An!" snapped Picyt impatiently, and Blaise had to turn away, leaving her uncomforted and alone with the guards.

Once again he passed through the narrow high-vaulted cave with the path that bordered the bottomless ribbon of water. But this time he was not carried helplessly along. This time he strode through, his muscles strong, his stride easy and sure, unlike Picyt's. The priest limped slowly, leaning on Uble's arm for support. His elegance and serenity, which had once been so marked, were gone, ripped from him as though in losing the life of his rings he had lost more than health and power. Only hatred pulsed strongly in his bent, drained body. Blaise shivered slightly in the dank gloomy air and wondered as they squeezed through the drapery formations if that hate was what now kept Picyt alive. A ripple of tension crossed Blaise's back. He must not let his guard down for an instant. And he must stay poised, ready to seize the first opportunity to defeat Picyt.

It *is* my fight now, he thought as he walked erectly along, ignoring the fire-rods aimed at him. He thought, *I really am a part of Asan, more than I originally suspected*. There was no going back to being the old Blaise, even if Giaa had meant nothing to him. He had acquired an altered set of values and a burden of responsibility along with a new body. And in facing himself squarely, he knew he did not really want to go back. Even his old personal war against the Institute no longer seemed to matter.

His keen hearing picked up the cadenced sound of chanting, low and clear priestly voices blending with the shrill, off-key ones of the Bban'n. An elemental part of Blaise stirred in response. It was a litany of worship, and despite himself his spine straightened, his shoulders came back, and a pleased glow swept his blood. Even his rings stirred and would have spread out in answer, but he held them in check. Picyt glanced back at him, and Blaise met his eyes levelly, betraying nothing. The priest would not catch him in this way.

A cheer broke out as he entered the cavern of M'thra, and even the priests could not keep to their order as perhaps a hundred worshipers rose from their knees to rush toward him. Picyt scowled and swept out his hand, but Blaise's own instinctive displeasure made him quicker. The adoration of slaves was hardly flattery.

"Ny! Chi'gra!" he snapped. "The time is not yet upon us." He spread his fingers in dismissal, and with chagrined bows the Bban'n covered their heads and hideous faces with folds of their coarse, tattered garments and drew back into the shadows, where stalagmites stood like silent sentinels.

Tuult stood with the guards ringing the three remaining cases. Recognizing the masked officer at once, for he now knew how to discern stance and build and body scent, Blaise stiffened and barely stifled a reprimand for Giaa's abduction. Instead he stopped and stood very still, his face as expressionless as any mask while he swept his cold eyes over Tuult from hooded mask to scuffed boot-toe. Involuntarily Tuult came to attention, but he did not salute, and Blaise did not speak to acknowledge his existence. Tension rippled between them, close to the level of actual blood challenge.

Picyt paused beside the case containing Aural and dismissed Uble and Basai with a low command.

"It is past daybreak, my Leiil," said Picyt in a breathless croak, his dark eyes glittering. "Nearly time for the service of blood oath to thee." He nodded at the murmuring group huddled in the shadows. "When the warriors of the Bban tribes come, they must swear to thee. Their fathers and fathers' fathers were sworn, but an oath of inheritance is not sufficient for what lies ahead."

Not certain if he referred to the raising of the nonexistent eight thousand or to Hihuan's army, Blaise shrugged. "The glory they come to worship is empty," he said and laughed inwardly at the angry gleam in Picyt's eyes. But for the sake of those listening he merely added, with no further attempts at double meanings, "Hihuan's army is not yet here."

"No," said Picyt with satisfaction, placing his hand atop Aural's capsule. "Teecht has been faithful in seeing that a black devi blocks the way Hihuan must come."

So they could control the weather! Or part of it. Trying to conceal his surprise, Blaise came closer, brushing by Tuult without a glance as the officer saluted and stepped aside. "And don't you likewise prevent the coming of the Bban tribes with your devi?" he asked.

"The Bban'n know the wastes best," said Picyt without concern. "Their ways of travel are efficient. Ah!" He looked across the vast cavern to where a group of priests had appeared. A figure, masked and robed in white, walked in their midst. Two youths in the banded robes of neophytes walked ahead, carrying long smoldering clubs that they swung in careful rhythm so that waves of purple and amber smoke curled forth in interwoven patterns.

"Impressive," murmured Blaise as they drew nearer. "Who is she?"

"Identity of the catalyst is unimportant," said Picyt. "It is Aural who concerns us. Look upon her, my Leiil, and recall her fairness." He moved aside as he spoke, giving Blaise clear view of the sleeping woman.

She *was* beautiful, coldly so, but as he gazed at her flawless figure and wealth of burnished hair, he felt no stir of interest and no memory of past associations. He kept seeing Giaa's dirty, tear-streaked face instead of Aural's, and the vision of those pleading silver eyes tore at him like the rake of fingernails over sore flesh. If only she were fully Tlar. But then, if it were so, she would not be his Giaa but instead a goddess with a purpose and a duty to something that had died long ago.

"What color are Aural's eyes?" he asked finally without great interest.

The priest glanced at him, not troubling to conceal the amusement in his eyes or the scorn in his face. "Oh, as I recall, my Leiil, a vastly interesting color. Have you forgotten?"

Fool, thought Blaise, impatient with his mockery. He returned his attention to the approaching catalyst. Now that the procession had nearly reached them, he could see the fine gold embroidery work on the white cloak and the delicate gold tracery on the white mask. But whoever she was, she walked strangely, almost like an automaton. Now and then she stumbled, but no hand reached out to steady her. Blaise frowned, noticing that the hem of her fine cloak dragged the ground by several inches and was soiled by the dust. An awful suspicion shot through him, and he extended his rings of perception slightly.

Picyt glared at him. "Disturb her not!"

But it had been enough. Furious, Blaise turned on him. "What in the name of Anthi are you up to?" he demanded so sternly that Picyt flinched. "Saunders is no catalyst for—"

"The *n'dl* made her choice freely," said Picyt. Though his hands were folded complacently inside his wide sleeves, his eyes were not serene. They glittered with the sheen of venom. "She came to me directly from your last talk with her."

The shock was like a blow. Blaise felt numb as he realized she had not sabotaged Picyt's beacon to the Bban tribes. Probably she had never intended to do so at all. Damn her for being such an idiot! Could she really think her alliance with Picyt served her in any way? Why, for once, just *once*, couldn't she have trusted him?

"Saunders!" he said sharply. "Are you insane? You can't do this!"

The procession had stopped and regrouped so that now the brown-robed priest stood behind her. The colored smoke of the incense curled over them all, stinging Blaise's nostrils as he glared at her.

"I desire it," she said tonelessly through the mask.

"Something is wrong," said Blaise. "Her morals would

never allow . . . What have you done to her?" He stepped forward, intending to rip off her mask, but just as swiftly Picyt lifted his finger, and Tuult sprang to stand between Blaise and Saunders, his hand on his knife hilt.

Blaise stopped, quivering with anger. He was close enough to her now to hear her slow, regular breathing and to smell an acrid chemical odor. "*Yde*," he said, spitting out the word with contempt. "You've filled her with it!" He turned on Picyt with his fists clenched. "This time you've gone too far, Picyt. I won't permit—"

"No," said Picyt softly in his broken husk of a voice. "I have not gone far enough. There is much yet to be done. By the will of Anthi, my Leiil, I swear the girl Giaa shall pay dearly for your refusal here." At Blaise's furious intake of breath, Picyt drew his shattered body erect until they were once again of equal height. "Indeed, Noble Leiil," he continued, squinting under Blaise's burning gaze, "you can slay me now with the power that flames within your heart. But do you truly value the *n'dl* over your Henan slave? Or are you false to both?"

Blaise hesitated. A few days ago he would not have been torn by compassion for either woman; now he knew only that he had made Giaa a part of himself and must forever bear that responsibility. But while he had always despised Saunders for her blind stubbornness and misguided loyalty, he could not willingly sacrifice her to this. What if she could not come through the process as he had? And worse, what if her psyche did survive, to be forever trapped raging and helpless in a soft pampered body that could never return her to her beloved Institute and the hard duty she thrived upon?

"It is against the will of Anthi that your blood be spread upon the sand," said Picyt in a snarl for Blaise's ears alone. "But, *Lea'dl*, I swear you can be made to wish to die while Giaa suffers the intricacies of slow Bban torture—"

"Enough." Blaise turned away from the priest to stare at Saunders's motionless figure once more. He gestured violently, hating her in that moment as he hated himself for not knowing how to save her or himself and Giaa. "Put her on the bier," he said roughly, and moved to Aural's capsule. Impatiently he waited while the priests led Saunders to the central bier and removed the fine cloak and mask before stretching out her unresisting form. Her gray eyes stared blankly, filmed with a dull blue haze that sickened Blaise. He did not dare look at Picyt, lest the fire building within him escape all control. He drew a ragged breath, closing his eyes against the sight of Saunders's broad, ugly face, slack and vacant and white. What he would not give at this moment to see her furious and red and bellowing. But even that thought twisted upon him viciously, for he would not give what was necessary. He could not.

"Now, my Leiil," said Picyt.

Without opening his eyes Blaise stretched forth his hands and flattened both palms against the container. Never in his life had he felt more wretched with guilt or more vulnerable as the priests stood ringed about him with bated breath and ready weapons. He drew in a deep lungful of air and called with his mind to Anthi, which answered at once in a loud thrumming vibration that shook through him.

"Anthi," he said, focusing inward. "The catalyst is prepared. Release Aural, by the will of Asan."

"By the will of Asan, guardianship of Aural is surrendered," replied Anthi.

The humming sound increased, deafening him. He felt a drain of power and knew with a flash of fear that any of the priests standing in the cave could at that moment spread their rings and crush him. But they were transfixed by the glory of Anthi, which they worshiped but no longer understood. Impatience replaced his fear. Why had they forgotten? What had made them want to forget? Was it fear, or laziness, or the insanity that drove Picyt?

Then Saunders's scream pierced his mind, banishing all questions. Helplessly he watched her soul drain away and vanish as the glass beneath his hands grew warm enough to blister his flesh. But he did not draw back, despite the pain, until a touch on his shoulder startled him.

Only then did he realize it was over. The spreading rings had closed; order had been reestablished. He dropped his hands away, stepping back with a slight stagger of fatigue while others hastened to open the case. Picyt himself placed the cloak about Aural, whose eyes slowly fluttered open. They were blue, intensely so, with flecks of silver and jade around the slitted pupils. Her delicate nostrils flared as though she smelled something unpleasant. Gently the priests raised her to a sitting position, and her burnished hair tumbled about her, spilling over her shoulders into her lap. She blinked several times before finally focusing on Blaise, who stood waiting, praying it was Saunders and desperately hoping it was not. Suddenly the dullness left her eyes, and they became as brilliant as sapphires in torchlight.

Recognition gleamed within their depths, and she drew a swift breath. "Asan," she whispered, and her voice was like the touch of smoldering embers.

"Aural," he replied, and stood there numbly while Picyt fitted the white mask over her face. The glory of her beauty was too precious to be seen by any save the most honored few. But it did not matter. Blaise bowed his head. Saunders was gone.

Chapter 12

Blaise stood apart from his escort cadre, his booted feet braced upon the rocky lip of a broad ledge overlooking the vast plains of Ddreui beyond. A light wind, sharp with cold, tossed his black cloak out from his shoulders, causing the bronze lining to flash and shimmer with light. Overhead the clouds raced in long tattered streamers, gilded along their undersides with gold and scarlet from the sun, while to the south a vast black-purple bank of clouds stood like a wall upon the horizon. Even at this distance flashes of lightning could be seen spearing vicious forks through it. Blaise shivered as the sun moved behind the immense mountain peak towering at his back, throwing him into shadow. A startled flock of furred nhulks flew up from a crevice in the rocks, bursting through the stunted growth of silver-needled bushes. He turned to face the masked, cloaked party climbing up the rock-strewn trail behind him. Mist, white and damp, swirled around their legs but did not stretch itself out onto the ledge where Blaise stood. The nhulks wheeled overhead, still crying out in their harsh twitter over the crunch of booted feet on patches of frozen snow.

Blaise's eyes narrowed behind his mask at the sight of the foremost figure, swathed in a cloak of thick frost-silvered borlorl fur. Her blue mask with its silver tracings of caste and rank stood out vividly against the spiked fur edging her hood. As she and her jen cadre appeared, the shadows deepened, and the torn clouds overhead merged, obscuring the sky.

She halted, and for a moment she and Blaise stared at each other silently in the buffeting whip of the wind. Then she turned to stare out at the plains below.

They have not yet come? she asked, her mind speaking to his as she spread out a ring to cloud the mental reception of the Bban'n surrounding them.

He frowned, well aware that she considered none of their conversations fit hearing for any of the Bban'n, especially their guard escort. *You should not be here, Aural.*

Nor is your presence intelligent, she retorted. *We are neither of us yet fully acceptanced by the Bban'n, although it could have been different for you, had they not been permitted to trick you with that Henan girl.* The contempt in her thoughts was open. *But what is your intention out here?* she continued. She stepped past him to stand on the edge. The wind stirred her furs into rippling life. *Is it your thought to make the Bban tribes come just by standing here and wishing*?

Blaise snorted in impatience. *You know I do not want them here.*

She laughed, and the sound swept mockery through his mind. He blocked it sharply, but she stepped closer, lifting her slender hands in their embroidered blue gloves gracefully.

I know *you are not eager to see the Tlar'jen come.* She cocked her head to one side, and he could imagine the scornful glint in her blue eyes. *Once Asan would not have feared his servant—*

"Hihuan is not my servant!" shouted Blaise, his voice ringing out through the crisp air, startling the crouched guards, who had gathered in a circle to roll carved pebbles in their beloved game of kri-gri. They swung masked faces toward Blaise and Aural for a moment. Then with rapid clicks and gestures they resumed play.

"You are reckless, Asan. Bban'n are too unstable to be trusted—"

"I trust no one," he retorted. "But neither am I afraid of revealing that the lives of the Bban'n mean no more to the Tlartantla than the sands of the wastes."

She breathed a curse at him, and even as his blood stirred in hot anger at that challenge, part of him cursed Saunders and the Institute that had molded her into an imbecile willing to die to bring this witch to life. Why had she done it? he wondered again. Why had she put herself back into Picyt's clutches?

"The Bban'n are willing!" said Aural. "They come willingly. We do not use force in this."

"Just deception and brainwashing." His blood ran cold again at the thought of those endless rows of empty capsules. "Aural, by the light of Lea, what purpose does this serve? The space transports never came. The capsules are empty—"

She sucked in her breath. "How do you know this? How did you come by such knowledge?"

He tensed. That had been a mistake! Damn his tongue! He shrugged, concealing his chagrin from his rings of communication.

"What has Picyt told you?" he asked, trying to evade her questions.

"All is in readiness. All is prepared, save for the willingness of your heart to serve Anthi. What has happened to you, Asan, to bring forth this cowardice? When last we walked together, your heart feared nothing."

Again Blaise curbed the fierce anger in his blood, fearing his powers might escape control. "The man who is never afraid is a fool," he said tightly. Then something made him add, "When last we walked, Aural, it *was* together, and you did not doubt me or give me opposition."

She turned on him, raising her fist. "Then you were worthy of service! You were—"

"What? What was I? One who regarded other lives with contempt . . . as you do now?" He swept out his hand. "The Bban'n deserve kinder masters than—"

"Maudlin fool." She turned away to walk near the edge, then stopped, gazing out across the desolate plains, the cold wind plucking at her furs. She sighed. "How barren is this world. Barren, harsh, and cold." She glanced over her shoulder at Blaise. "There is no appreciation of life here, no concept of the refinements of higher civilization."

"It will come," Blaise replied flatly.

She laughed. "Oh, yes, it *will*. And very soon now."

"No." He walked over to her as she stiffened. "You, and I, and the two others—"

"Your brothers!" she flashed. "By blood loyalty."

He lifted his finger in indifference. "They are the only two left on this planet under Anthi's guardianship. There are no others."

"That is a lie!" She swung up her hand to strike him.

He caught her by the wrist, stopping the blow, and held her hard when she would have twisted free. A tiny glass vial fell from a fold in her sleeve. As Blaise stared down at it glinting on the crusted snow, his eyes narrowed.

"*Yde*," he said, not concealing his loathing. In disgust he dropped her wrist. "So that is his hold over you. I should have guessed—"

"No, Asan!" she cried defensively. "*Yde* is useful. It spreads the mind—"

"It is a temporary enhancement that destroys the mind." He stared at her, wondering whether she was under coercion or really allied to Picyt of her own will. "You know that, Aural. Don't be a fool. Whatever Picyt has told you—"

"I believe!" She lifted her head. "He is a faithful servant. He has not lost sight of the purpose—"

"Noble Leiil."

The gruff, respectful voice of one of the Bban'jen interrupted. Turning, Asan saw him on his feet, pointing out at the plains.

"Look, Leiil!" His jaw clicked with excitement that communicated itself to the rest of the cadre. They all rose with sweeps of their black cloaks, and the stench of musk tainted the air.

His stomach churning, Blaise turned to face the plains of Ddreui, where the purple-black bank of clouds stretched across the horizon. He squinted, looking out over the short, leathery grass bent flat by the wind in ripples of silver and dull green. At first it seemed as though that distant storm had come closer. Then he began to make out movement and individual specks of black. He drew in a sharp breath.

"Which?" muttered Aural, shifting impatiently beside him.

But almost as she spoke, the guards leaped into the air, slapping each other on the chest and raising exaltant fists. "*By'he! By'he!*" they shouted in unison, their rough voices keening into notes painful to Blaise's hearing.

As he winced, Aural's fingers dug into his arm. "The Bban tribes!" she said excitedly. "They come, Asan! They come! Soon we shall have meaning again."

He turned on her, opening his mouth, but her contempt flicked against his inner rings.

"Crush the creature defiling your soul, Asan! Free yourself to be as you were in the past. Those less than we are to be used, for our purpose is well worth the price. Survival, Asan. Survival!"

She stepped back from him with assurance and regarded him for a moment before laughing and bending down to pick up the vial of *yde*. But his boot heel crunched down hard on the vial, splintering the glass. For an instant he caught the sharp, acrid smell of the drug as he removed his foot. Then the wind blew the powder away.

She clenched her gloved hands into fists. But she did not communicate further with him. It was not necessary. The battle lines had been drawn.

"Bban'jen!" she snapped aloud, curbing the excitement of the soldiers. "Attend me. *An!*" And turning on her heel, she left the ledge at a furious pace.

Excitement spread through the caverns like wildfire upon news of the tribes' approach. Unable to separate himself from his jen escort, which he had hoped would be swept away by the eager, babbling Bban women waiting within the entrance to the caverns, Blaise frowned and stripped off his mask as soon as the lead-shielded doors shut. At once the gloom and coldness of the cave rushed over him, making him shiver. Momentarily ignored by the exaltant Bban'n as they leaped and shouted with hoarse cries, Blaise was overwhelmed by a sense of dwindling time. He had no allies here and could make none. Giaa was still held a prisoner to hinder him. And now the tribes were coming. Somehow they had penetrated the desert storms in a way the Tlar'jen of Leiil Hihuan could not. Blaise pondered as the crowd jostled him. He must act now, and in a way that would not endanger Giaa.

But how?

The stench of Bban musk thickened. He coughed, and at once a hush fell as masks and glowing eyes were turned to him.

"It is a bad omen," whispered someone, and crossed fingers were raised in quick furtive signs of warding.

The crowd was small but intense. Blaise's breath shortened as he desperately sought some way of seizing this moment and turning it to his advantage. Hoping to play upon the Bban superstitions, he raised his hand swiftly to halt their murmuring.

"Hear me, Bban'n!" he said, his voice ringing with authority. "The tribes come—"

A cheer rose up, but with a savage gesture he cut it off.

"Hear me! They come to their deaths—"

"Approach the Noble Leiil!" shouted Tuult's voice.

Whirling, Blaise saw a full cadre of purposeful, swift-moving Bban'jen moving through the crowd toward him. At the mouth of a side passageway cut into the rock, Tuult stood with black cloak thrown back over his shoulders and his fire-rod drawn.

Blaise's heart thudded at the sight of that weapon. He tensed, looking for a way out, but it was too late to run. The ragged crowd was parting. The jen were nearly to him. He could see the gleam of torchlight off sleek black tunics and hear their intent breathing behind the masks. Their booted feet rang out on the dusty stone floor. The nearest one reached out a gauntleted hand for his arm.

Holding his breath, Blaise shut his eyes. "Forgive me, Giaa," he whispered and snapped his inner rings, letting the fire of Anthi explode through him. He felt the desperate clutch of strong fingers just as the force of seizert jerked him from existence.

He blinked, regaining consciousness an instant later in the corybdium-lined chamber where Anthi glowed and flashed in a pattern of blue light. Panting, still not quite able to believe he'd managed to elude the Bban'jen, Blaise lifted his hand unsteadily to dash away the perspiration from his forehead. He knew Picyt would direct Tuult to search for him here; he had not much time to open the doors leading to the rows of empty capsules. And he must collect himself and decide how to best explain Picyt's treachery. If the Bban'n could not be made to understand, then—

"Asan?" boomed the voiceless hum of Anthi into the center of his being. "Asan has come?"

"Yes," he answered, his hands on the double doors. He glanced over his shoulder at the large formation of crystal, its function masked by the beauty of geometry and color. "I have come." On impulse, he turned from the doors. "Anthi, help me. I am in great danger. The purpose is in danger."

"Asan," said Anthi with a rapid flashing of light at the pointed tips of her formations. "Come. My knowledge is thine. Come."

Was it the heightened awareness of his rings or his keen hearing that detected the faint clatter of running footsteps? His heart lurched. He had less time than he had thought. He stepped up to Anthi, his eyes squinting against the glare of blue light emanating from her center in steady radiance. The vibration intensified, lowering into a powerful throbbing that overwhelmed him completely. Numbly he drew yet closer and held out his hands.

"Asan," said Anthi, piercing him with the sound of his own name. "Permission requested to surrender guardianship."

"When I understand," he said tightly. The vibrations were growing harder to endure. His very bones seemed to be crumbling. Why must Anthi delay when time was running out? "I must have help!" he shouted. "By the will of Asan, Anthi, help me!"

A faint film of transparent energy dissolved from around the surface of the crystal. The light blazed forth with even more intensity, bathing him in its radiance. He shut his eyes, and still he could not escape its brilliance.

"My shields are lowered. By thy will, touch me," said Anthi.

He pressed his trembling hands flat against the surface of the crystal. To his surprise it felt warm to his touch, almost like living flesh. Anthi's blue light bathed him, merging with his rings, until her light became his fire. The warmth beneath his palms increased until his hands were seared with heat. He jerked, his entire body shaking, but he could not pull away. Something vast and terrible seemed to crush him.

"No!" he cried, falling to his knees. *"No!"*

"Fear may not lie between us," said Anthi into his whirling brain. "Release Asan. Nothing is lost."

The stubbornness at his core refused to give way to the immense, overwhelming weight. Despite the desperation of the moment, he could not bring himself to cross that final threshold of acceptance of what he was now and what he might yet become.

"I am . . . Blaise . . . BLZ-80-4163," he grated out, the muscles in his neck cording with the strain of resistance.

His rings nearly buckled. Then to his relief he sensed Anthi withdraw. The blue light within the crystal flickered and dimmed. From outside came the noise of scraped metal and the shriek of forced bolts. But Blaise was too exhausted to notice. He gasped for breath, defeated, and let his head rest on his forearm.

But his palms still remained in position on the sides of the crystal. And in that moment of dejection, he felt something deep within him stir as a longing and a need were reawakened.

"No," groaned Blaise as Anthi pulsed back into life in response.

But he could not fight forces both outside and within himself. His rings spread as that part of him that was truly Asan merged with Anthi to form a complete wholeness that buffeted Blaise, then swept him along into the depths of a fiery vortex. He thought he screamed from the blast of it, but even so he was conscious of the door being slowly, inexorably forced open behind him. The strength of Anthi poured into his ravaged soul before filling his mind with knowledge and visions that staggered him. For the first time he saw what the Tlar really were, and what he was, and the true nature of the purpose. He accepted it.

Only then did Anthi withdraw, to become muted light once again as at last the door gave way and the jen came running inside to surround him.

"Defiler!" shouted Picyt in a hoarse voice. "Seize him! Let his blasphemy be told by the spreading of his blood!"

Blaise was grasped roughly and his arms twisted behind him with force enough to make his shoulder joints grind painfully. He was jerked to his feet, and Tuult held aloft a jen-knife, the green blade gleaming in the light as it poised in the air, ready to flash down deep into Blaise's throat upon Picyt's command. Blaise stared at it, still reeling from the force and magnitude of what he had absorbed.

Anthi flashed. "Permission requested to surrender guardianship to Asan."

The jen-knife trembled, and Tuult hesitated, turning his masked face to Picyt, who stood leaning on Basai's arm, his ravaged face twisted with astonishment and shock.

"No!" he shouted. "No, Anthi! By thy will, I, Picyt, command no such—"

"By the will of Asan," said Blaise, regaining his wits. "Request granted."

A single focused beam of light shot from the pointed tip of one of the formations, aiming at the double doors leading to the chamber that held the capsules. As the doors slowly slid open, shocked exclamations burst from the Bban'jen. Some even sank to their knees, and Tuult stared transfixed, the jen-knife forgotten in his hand.

Blaise took advantage of their stupefaction to sweep out his reformed rings, snapping them hard at the mind-dampening force holding the Bban'jen enslaved by the priests.

"No!" cried Basai, staggering as Picyt flinched back against him. "Release them not!"

But Blaise swept on, seeking Teecht and his group of technicians, who were among their machinery directing the violence of the desert storm. He struck again, shattering the focus of their power, and withdrew, satisfied. Then he saw the light from Anthi stretch forth into the vast cavern beyond, shining into the nearest of the empty capsules. It faded, as did the center of radiance within Anthi. The formation of crystal stood dark and silent behind Blaise, and for an instant absolute silence held everyone there in a feeling of emptiness and loss as if Anthi's shutdown took something tangible away from them all.

"The purpose," said Blaise, drawing in a breath as he lifted his head high, "has failed."

With a wordless cry, Basai buried his face in his hands and turned away, staggering blindly to the wall to huddle there. Picyt stood frozen, staring at nothing.

"What have you done?" demanded Tuult, gripping Blaise by the arm and shaking him.

The confusion buffeting the Bban struck at Blaise through that touch. He deflected it, pulling free, and did not dare attempt to look on the Bban with truth at this moment.

"That which was purposed is ended, not to be completed," he said sternly. "Anthi has withdrawn herself from you, judging you unworthy of her presence. She is no longer the guardian of life." He gestured toward the chamber of capsules, his eyes steady and sympathetic as Tuult took an uncertain step in that direction. "Go and look upon the deception the House of Kkanthor has practiced upon you. It is over, Pon Tuult. There shall be no birth."

"Over?" The Bban raised his hand and slowly let it fall. He looked at the other guards, then at Picyt. "It had but come to the beginning. *By'hia!* Are we left, to drink no more comfort from the goddess? Revered noble, what has happened? How have we failed?"

Picyt shuddered, then looked up, his eyes blazing with hate. "Betrayal," he whispered. "Asan has destroyed Anthi and left all Bban'n at the mercy of the Tlar'jen. Death! Death to him!" Even as he screamed the final words, he seized a stone from the ground and hurled it.

Caught off guard, Blaise tried to duck, but the stone struck his temple. He was momentarily stunned. He felt as if he had been plunged below water and could move only with extreme slowness. Blood, warm and wet, began to trickle into his left eye. He shook his head and tried to speak.

"Tuult—"

"Kill him!" screamed Picyt.

A blow from behind drove Blaise to his knees. He skidded to the black edge of unconsciousness, hauled himself back, and clenched his fists in an effort to strike back. But the jen had surrounded him, and more brutal blows thudded into flesh and muscle. Furious, he gritted his teeth and rose, swinging out blindly as blood obscured his vision. His knuckles collided with something hard, and he heard a muffled grunt of pain. Then with howls the Bban'jen set upon him in earnest, their musk overpowering. He warded off a knife, was struck hard in the ribs, and fell heavily. For a moment he was blessedly far away from all feeling, then he dragged himself back toward consciousness one last time.

"I hold Anthi's power," he said in a croak. "If . . . I die, what hope . . . have you against . . . Hihuan?"

The beating stopped, and for a moment he heard only the sound of his own tortured breathing as he lay upon the rough stone floor with his fingers groping clumsily over his scraped and stinging cheek. It was such a small pain compared to the rest, odd that it should be felt more. . . .

"*Choi'hana*, Tlar-dung!" snarled Tuult, and a vicious kick sent Blaise spinning out into blackness with a last burst of agony.

Chapter 13

Slowly Blaise dragged himself to a sitting position and leaned his back against the wall to blow his breath forcefully in and out, before pushing himself to his feet. For an instant he swayed, fighting off dizziness, then crossed the room on unsteady feet, one hand pressed to his side. At the armored, bolted door, he paused, closing his eyes for a second to make the world stop tilting. With a grunt he bent to pick up the tray that had just been shoved through the bottom slot. The cell was a small niche cut into stone, and he bumped his head on rough ceiling as he straightened. But in his eagerness he paid no attention as he carried the tray back to the battered metal table and stool that were his only pieces of furniture. He snatched the cover from the small black pot, scorching his fingers and dropping the lid with a clatter. A heavenly aroma of stewed meat and pungent herbs rose along with the steam. His mouth watered, and his stomach growled in need. Wiping his grimy fingers perfunctorily on his torn tunic, he dipped them into the greasy mess and gingerly tasted it.

It was so hotly seasoned that he could not be sure if it had been laced with *yde*. Bitterly disappointed, he dropped the dripping chunks of meat back into the stew, swallowing hard as hunger rose like a wild beast within him, urging him to forget caution and eat. Shaking, he picked up the lid and slammed it back on the little stewpot, clutching the warm metal surface until the joints of his fingers whitened.

Demos, but this could not go on much longer! He was going mad with hunger, locked away in this filthy hole and forced time after time to shove back, untouched, the offering of food. He wondered how long it would be before his willpower broke and he let himself be poisoned. Soon his mind would go, even as his battered, dehydrated body was failing him now, and he would not be able to control himself further.

He coughed, his parched throat grating as he swallowed. He moved to grasp the goblet with trembling fingers. He picked it up, unsteadily enough to make the contents slosh out.

"*Merdarai*," he whispered, seized by a desire to lick up that precious escaping water. But despite his overwhelming thirst, he could smell the *yde* in it. They had made no attempt to disguise it as they did in the food, no doubt certain that thirst would undo him long before hunger.

He sighed raggedly and set the goblet down, licking his dry, cracked lips with a tongue nearly as rough. The left side of his face itched, and absently he scratched at it, his fingernails scraping away at the dried blood still encrusted there. Picyt would not get him, he vowed, anger welling up with fresh strength at the memory of his beating. He would not take *yde* and become Picyt's slave as Aural was, as all the deluded Bban'n were. Nor would he give up and die here.

With an oath he picked up the tray and stumbled back across the cell to shove it vehemently through the door slot. Then, panting, he sank down on his stool, winching at the catch in his side. He was too weak to seizert to freedom. And without food he could never regain the strength required. He shivered with cold, longing for his cloak, which they had stripped from him, and cupped his hands about the burning torch, willing to be scorched just to gain a little warmth.

From listening to his guards through the food slot he knew that Hihuan's army had come at last to the plains below the mountains. Suppose he reached out to Hihuan with a call for help? But no. That idea faded quickly as he recalled the sharp memory of Bban hands around his throat. Hihuan had reached out from Altian to cause that attack. He could not be trusted.

Blaise narrowed his eyes. And why could he not do the same thing in turn? It was Tlar nature to command and order all lesser things. He might have scruples against letting the Bban'n die for no purpose, but anything else was useless baggage.

He pressed his fingertips together, forcing hunger, pain, and thirst from his thoughts in order to concentrate. But it was like staring through darkness, and to form even one ring left him sweating and weak. He did not give up, however, and focused himself first on his guards outside the door. He had not lied when he told them he was their main hope against Hihuan. Obviously they had at least half believed him, or they would have killed him at the base of Anthi. But he must increase that belief in their need of him and amplify it until he meant more to them than Picyt did. Breathing deeply, he put all of himself into the effort and at last reached into the mind of one of the guards, forcing himself not to shrink from those rough alien patterns of imagery and concept. Exhaustion sapped him; for a terrifying instant he shook, certain he was going to be sucked into the guard's power. But what he had learned from Anthi steadied him, and instead he began to draw strength from the guard, using that in turn to shape the guard's thoughts. And from there he leaped to the next man and to the next and on until all four guards stirred and muttered uneasily around the tray of rejected food outside his door.

Bit by bit he wove images of himself as their leiil into their minds, a strong, just leader of courage rather than a priest of slyness and intrigue. He stirred the fiery centers of challenge and warlust in their blood and made them see afresh the threat of the Tlar'jen, with their weapons of mind and rings that Bban javelins and knives could not destroy. He made them see their need of him, and then he withdrew, leaving them with a touch of his own real exhaustion and suffering.

Blaise blinked, once more conscious of the grim, shadowy cell about him. He shivered, holding onto himself desperately as he waited with his rings of reception trembling and barely formed. Then, just as he lost hope, a glimmer of a questing thought touched him in return. It was alien, Bban, but possessed strong patterns of intelligence and ability. Triumph filled Blaise, but swiftly he suppressed it, projecting instead his true worth to the future of the Bban tribes. They did not establish a direct communication link, out of distrust and caution, but at least his message was given and received.

Suddenly Blaise's strength failed him, draining away as his rings broke apart, splintering one by one. He slumped from his stool, and distantly he felt the jolt as he hit the floor, reopening the wound at his temple. Warm blood gushed across his forehead. *"Please,"* he whispered, feeling the awful vortex of infinity sweep near him as the distortion of order from which he had once saved Picyt swirled for him. So this is death, he thought wearily, and in the far recesses of his soul he heard laughter. He stiffened, unable to quest for it. Was it Picyt? Or Aural? The vortex pulled him away, down and down into the void of its center.

And what did it matter anyway? It was not his fight, not his world, not his people. The laughter came again, mocking his death even as the distortion centering on him shook the room and caused a slight rain of dust and stone to patter down upon him. His anger stirred. By Demos, he would not go tamely!

With a shrieking grind of long bolts, the door burst open and his guards ran inside, shouting at one another as they knelt around him. Dimly Blaise felt a hand grip his arm for an instant.

"Dilgel m'a-anhr!" exclaimed one of the guards. "He burns with the fire of Anthi. Request the pon!"

"No!" said another, younger-sounding voice. "It is given us to serve the elders now. Do not seek Tuult."

"But—"

The cold blackness lapped over Blaise as the caverns shook again with low rumblings. Rock cracked nearby, terrifyingly loud, and he opened his eyes just as a strong hand slipped beneath his head and shoulders, lifting him.

"Drink this and live, my Leiil," said the young, unfamiliar voice.

Blaise stiffened. He would not trust a Bban ever again.

But a cup of warm, spiced wine touched his lips, and despite his fear he could resist no longer. He gulped eagerly until he nearly choked.

"Gently, Leiil. It is not the Bban way, to permit starvation. I ask thy forgiveness upon these who have mistreated thee."

Blaise frowned at the masked face over him. "Who—"

"I am Oliir. Now drink again."

The rest of the wine was tilted down his throat. And as he grew sure it was indeed wholesome and not drugged, he sagged with relief, lifting a trembling hand to rub at his face. "Why?" He clutched at the boy's wrist as his voice cracked on him, forcing him to swallow and try again. "You are . . . my enemy. Why . . . help me?"

Oliir was silent for a moment. Then he laid his finger gently on Blaise's cheek. "I am not thy enemy, Leiil. From birth I was pledged to the service of Anthi, and I have counted that service a great honor. But when thy hand destroyed Anthi and her will was lifted, I saw the falsehood and the emptiness of all of Kkanthor's promises. I have served a lie. I am deeply shamed unto the blood. And now that Anthi is no more, the power of the supreme elders has been freed. It is their wish that we bring thee out unto the keeping of the tribes. We will divide truth." He removed his hand from Blaise's tightened grasp. "Now take unto thee courage. Rest. The revered noble shall not harm thee again. He shall harm none of us again."

"It pleases us to see thee so well recovered," said the dark, erect Bban with the silver eyes. He stood far inside the tent that had been Blaise's prison these past few days, his leathery fingers stretched out over the coals glowing in the brazier. A broad sweep of cloak banded in black and scarlet hung from his bony shoulders, and beneath it he wore a white tunic and a long tabard of supple mail woven from metal threads into a heavy type of cloth. A wide metal belt circled his waist, and from it hung a gold-sheathed jen-knife. Gold armbands, nearly as wide as the length of his forearms, glittered in barbaric splendor from the firelight. Only a certain stiffness in the joints betrayed his age as he turned back to stare at Blaise, his skeletal face containing no expression that Blaise could read. "We understand this is not thy first walk in the land of Merdar, nor thine only return."

"No," said Blaise warily. "I suppose not." He stood at the entrance of the tent, one hand holding open the flap as he gazed out past the guards. Sunlight streamed down over the camp, golden and pure once again now that the dark clouds had lifted. It glinted off the polished tips of javelins as a group of laughing youths vied with each other in hurling their weapons at a stuffed leather bag set up as a man-size target.

The encampment of the J'agan-dar had been pitched in a sheltered niche off the wide, lake-bottomed valley below the mountains. Other tribes were camped all through these foothills; he had seen the lightning flashes of hand signals from the ridge-tops. Perhaps fifty broad, low tents stood on the uneven ground, sheltering several families each, as well as the thick-bodied chakas with their narrow heads and woolly black-and-gray striped coats. They were stupid, ill-tempered brutes, and at first he had thought them the only beasts of burden and transportation used by the Bban. But only that morning he had glimpsed the squat, black-metaled machines called porters, which carried one man on swift jets of air. Highly maneuverable and silent, they skimmed the rough terrain as effortlessly as the nhulks wheeled in the sky. And their riders were equally silent, equally efficient. Tall and desert-gaunt of body, they went about booted and mailed, wearing great curved swords in baldrics slung under their cloaks. Blaise rubbed his fingers over the tent material beside him, marveling again at the Bban skill in metallurgy that enabled them to spin lead into tiny threads and weave it into coarse but reasonably flexible fabric that served as an effective, transportable shielding from the deadly rays of the black star. These evidences of advanced technology jarred with the rest of what he had seen of Bban culture. Where had they learned these skills? Where had they got these machines? Not from the Tlar, certainly.

"What Tlar pride bids thee to this discourtesy?"

The sharpness of that question broke into Blaise's thoughts. He turned with a blink, letting the tent flap fall. "Forgive me," he said, spreading out his hands. "I failed to hear."

The glare in the old Bban's eyes softened a fraction. He raised his head. "Thy thoughts remain in the caverns. It is unwise, Noble Asan, to pay so little attention to thy present situation. We brought thee away from the hand of the Noble Picyt, but not to extend mercy unto thee."

Blaise frowned. "The footing will soon be too soft for effective battle," he said, deciding to see if he could find out what kind of military strategy the Bban'n would employ against the horde of Tlar'jen now camped on the plains of Ddreui to the eastern side of the mountains.

"Ah, battle." With an amused click of his long jaw, the elder gestured for Blaise to join him by the fire. As Blaise did so, lowering himself to the ground, which was covered by leather mats that squished softly beneath his weight, the elder said, "Thine age is far beyond our concept, Leiil Asan, and still thou has the impatient vigor of youth. The time is not yet arrived to worry about armies floundering in the mire of thaw." He struck a narrow tube hanging from the apex of tent poles, producing a thin chiming sound, and at once a veiled female ducked into the tent with a tray in her hands.

Blaise looked closely at her, then away in disappointment. It was not Giaa. He knew she was in the camp, but he had not seen her since he had been brought here.

The elder took a steaming cup from the proffered tray and

waited until Blaise did the same. As soon as the servant exited, he said, "We have bided the walk of time since the return of the Tlar. We have waited long for the downfall of Anthi and her accursed servants." Fitting the rim of the cup against the hinge of his jaw, he tipped back his head swiftly, swallowing the contents in one noisy gulp, then unfitted the cup and set it down.

Averting his eyes, Blaise sipped cautiously at the fiery liquid. "Anthi is no more," he said. "War is no longer necessary now that Picyt is—"

"All Tlar must be swept aside!"

Blaise stiffened. "No, Uxe Ggil," he said, using the formal Bban title. "We—"

"All." Ggil crooked his dark fingers. "Thou cannot comprehend the depth of Bban hatred for Tlar. We put away all things Tlar, even the name. We learned to accept what we became. We learned to take this wasteland into our hearts and make it ours, forgetting the lakes and meadows of home. Such things have been wiped from memory. Our youth are no longer told of them. But the elders remember." He raised his clenched fist as Blaise started to speak. "Was it not enough, to be on this world? Was it not enough to become Bban? Why did thy hordes descend upon us in the dark time? They took our freedom. They took our minds. They took our gods. And they meant to take our souls. Our souls! *Merdar*, if our past were known to the Tlar, Kkanthor would die rather than reach for us."

Staring at him in bewilderment, Blaise rose to his feet, wincing at the slight catch in his side. "I do not understand," he said, not quite certain he wanted to.

"No." The elder's gruff voice drooped, became less strident. "The Tlar do not understand us. How could they? But thou, Asan, thou should remember the prisoners taken in the Duoden Conflict, the prisoners convicted here on this barren planet. That was thousands of years ago, but we, too, have our legends of the mighty Asan and his consort."

Blaise's frown deepened. He did not speak.

Ggil paused for a moment, his silver eyes glowing. "Thy pride is great. Must I say it all? We were Tlar once! We stood smooth-skinned and proud. We were as thou are now."

Blaise stared at him, his mind spinning. "And you have mutated! The radiation—"

"Yes."

Ggil spoke in a growl. For an instant Blaise felt the pressure of Ggil's enmity rise against him, and his own blood stirred in reply. Controlling himself, he drew back a step. Of course! It answered many questions. It explained the disturbing similarities in Tlar and Bban mindset, in the way both races rose so fiercely to meet the same types of challenges, in the mental abilities. . . .

"Why did the Tlar return to Ruantl?" asked Ggil, lifting his hand. "Were there no more worlds to conquer, that thou must come back to feed upon thy victims?"

Blaise turned his palm down. "The Tlar have no place left to go. I—" He frowned. "I no longer have the reason. But no Tlar sleep in the caverns, waiting for souls to feed upon. The eight thousand did not arrive. The Bban are in no danger from that."

Ggil crooked a finger in disbelief. "Then why has Picyt pursued us through these centuries?" He turned away. "More Tlar lies."

"No! Picyt is insane. Why he hates you so intensely is something I don't know. But you must believe me." Blaise spread out his hands. "Why else would I have shut down Anthi?" As he spoke he drew in one ring of secrecy upon himself. He must let no one suspect that he had become Anthi's guardian, able to reactivate her once it was safe and assign her to new and different purposes.

"We give thanks for what thou hast done, even if we do not understand why," said Ggil, hooding his eyes. "My fellow elders find it difficult to trust these unexpected actions of the great Leiil Asan, held in all legends to be our most-feared enemy." He picked up a long metal rod and used it to stir the coals in the brazier. Fresh flames flared up, and he looked at Blaise through them. "For many years we have dreaded thy awakening, yet now that thou art here thou hast slain the goddess of enslavement and robbed Picyt of his powers. Why?" Ggil stepped forward, suddenly intent. *"Why?"*

Blaise hesitated, wondering how he could possibly explain the tangle of his reasons. Finally he tried the truth. "I don't really know."

Ggil growled. "It seems thy kind is born with guile in the mouth and trickery in the blood."

"No," retorted Blaise. "I happen to believe in freedom of

choice. And self-sacrifice to satisfy a madman's refusal to face facts is against anyone's morality."

"Better," said Ggil coldly. "When thou hast learned to look upon thyself with truth, then the truth of others will come to thee."

Blaise stiffened, his hand moving involuntarily for the weapon that was not at his belt.

Ggil clicked his jaw and flung out his arm, the gold band glinting. "*Pan'at cha*," he said with contempt, and moved past Blaise.

"Wait." Reining in his temper, Blaise dared block the old man's way. "Grant me one answer, Uxe Ggil. The girl Giaa—"

Whipping out his jen-knife, Ggil whirled on Blaise. "Thou speaks of her as thine. What gives thee this right?"

"She is mine," said Blaise. "If she desires to be. Release her from slavery, Ggil. You have the power as an elder. Let her—"

Ggil cut him off with a savage gesture. "Fool!" Without another word he strode out, leaving Blaise tight-lipped with fury.

His rings jerked in a desire to crush these arrogant savages. But he held himself in check, kicking a cushion out of his way as he strode around the tent. He was strong enough now to seizert to freedom, but he had no intention of doing so without Giaa, or without some means of adequate rations and protection from the X rays. He could not even send forth his senses to Giaa's mind, for he was close-watched in more ways than just the physical. His fists clenched. If they would just listen to him!

That night when a servant brought his food, he tried to delay her just for a moment. "Giaa. Do you know her? Will you tell her—"

With a snarl the female pulled a knife on him and waved it threateningly until he grimaced in frustration and stepped back. Then she fled, ducking out of the tent without a backward glance. Slowly Blaise walked back to the warmth of the fire, pulling his cloak more tightly about his body, and sat down to pick without interest through his food. He could not continue to sit here helplessly until Leiil Hihuan struck. But there seemed to be nothing else he could do without exhausting his captors' scant patience.

He was dozing fitfully in the darkness, rolled in his cloak and a fur robe in a not very successful attempt to ward off the cold, when a small sound from the rear of the tent awakened him. His senses snapped out, and he drew a surprised breath.

"Giaa!" he whispered, sitting up. "What—"

"Hush, my Leiil. I beg thee." She was no more than a slim shadow as she pulled back the section of tent wall she had cut and gropped her way to him. The smoky fragrance of her skin filled the tent. He grabbed her close and buried his face in her hair, letting his thoughts flow into hers, sharing what words could not. She breathed raggedly, and her heart thundered against his. Then she pulled back and thrust a roll of clothing into his hands. "These are the clothes of a warrior. Dress quickly," she said, her voice no more than a breath. "Council is held tonight. The warriors of five primary tribes are meeting with the supreme elders. We must move quickly and without sound."

Nodding in the darkness, he began to fumble with the clothes, scratching his hands on the mail and dropping the belt before at last he was dressed and booted. The fabric of his tunic was rough enough to chafe his skin beneath the weight of the tabard. Bban musk hung in the cloth, tainting it, but he made no complaint. When he was ready, she gave him a jen-knife to sheath at his belt and a baldric and scabbard.

He buckled the latter on awkwardly, unused to the weight of a sword. Despite the urgency of the moment he paused to draw the sword, hefting it and finding it needed two hands on the wire-wrapped hilt to balance the curved length. His fingers ran down the blade and felt the large square jewel set in the pommel. He wished he could see it.

"Where did you get such weapons?" he asked.

"I stole them as I did these clothes for us," she whispered impatiently. "Hurry. We cannot walk through camp at this hour unless it is believed we are warriors."

He slid the sword back into its scabbard. "We will seizert—"

"*No!*" Her hand clamped upon his arm hard with a strength he had not known she possessed. "No. My way. Hurry."

He did not argue, for he was unsure if he could really bring her through seizert. Following her through the darkness, he wriggled out through the cut in the tent and stood breathlessly in the shadows, glancing right and left along the row of tents glowing with firelight. The cold air stung his nostrils. Some distance away sentries stood on guard outside a large tent, from which the sound of heated argument could be heard. It was Blaise's intention to go in the opposite direction, but again Giaa touched his arm.

"This way," she whispered, handing him a strip of leaded cloth. "Put this on thus." As she spoke she fastened a similar strip across her face, covering everything save her glowing eyes, and pulled the hood of her cloak low over her forehead. And when he had done the same, she squinted at him. "Make thine eyes glow as when thou art angry."

He frowned, but obediently concentrated on lifting an inner ring of deception. His eyes grew dry and began to burn.

"Good. Come." Again she touched his arm and stepped away from the shadow of the tent, carrying herself erect, even managing a swagger as her heavy boots crunched quietly over the frozen mud.

Blaise followed, matching his pace to her unhurried one. As they drew near the sentries he spread his ring of deception to reform the surface pattern of his thoughts to Bban. The sentries did not stir, and he could not help cast a glance into the open tent as they passed by. Bban warriors crowded inside, jostling each other with rough elbows and growling as the speaker in their midst raised his voice. Blaise stiffened. Tuult! What was he doing here?

He slowed, gazing inside with open curiosity despite Giaa's impatient look back. He looked over the assembly, seeing one cloaked, mailed figure after another. Gold belts and armbands glinted in the flaming torchlight; green corybdium swordblades gleamed in naked splendor, held in the impassioned grasps of their owners. Shouts, angry and fierce, rose up in hoarse chorus, and Tuult snapped back undaunted replies. Blaise glimpsed him at last as a burly warrior turned to harangue someone at his side. The pon stood erect in his black jen uniform and mask, his scarlet eyes glowing intensely as he swept out his gauntleted hand. Blaise took a step toward the tent entrance.

At once the guards crossed their javelins to block his way, and one growled. A few inside the tent noticed and turned their heads. Realizing his foolishness, Blaise ducked his head with a gesture of apology and backed away, hastening to catch up with Giaa, whose back was ramrod stiff as she walked on. When he joined her once again, she glanced at him without a word, but he read the accusation in her silver eyes.

By this time they had reached the edge of the camp. The odors of smoke and chaka-droppings mingled in the dense, cold air. Blaise could see his breath as they walked along. He relaxed a fraction, only to stiffen as he felt a peculiar prickling sensation across his skin. He stopped abruptly not moving even when Giaa tugged at his arm. He lifted his hand to quell her as he frowned and faced north, where the mountains loomed over them. Out in the rocks on the ridge, a sentinel shifted position, stamping his feet against the cold and scraping the barbed tip of his javelin against stone. Only two of the small moons shone this night, pale glimmers that did nothing to illuminate the countryside. Still Blaise stood motionless, questing with his senses as much as he dared so near the camp. He felt the prickling again, more sharply this time, and instinct told him to run.

"Quickly!" he said, shoving Giaa ahead of him. "Run for the rocks."

She started to obey without question, only to stop with a gasp. Blaise stumbled into her. A column of blue light flashed ahead of them, stampeding the chaka herd into bawling panic. Shouts rang out as warriors erupted from the tents.

"Merdarai!" swore Blaise in a fury, and seized Giaa's arm. "Circle it!" He started to run, dragging Giaa with him, but the light spread, crossing their path a second time, making them plain targets for the Bban'n. He skidded to a halt and threw himself down in a crouch behind the inadequate cover of a thornbush.

"What is it?" Giaa gasped for breath, her free hand clamped upon the hilt of her jen-knife. "Merciful Anthi, what is it?"

"We've got to find a way out." Blaise sprang up again, intending to head for the better cover of a group of boulders to his right. But the blue light narrowed into a column, and a figure began to shimmer into existence in its center. Blaise glanced over his shoulder. The Bban'n had stopped and were staring, the light glinting off their weapons, throwing needle-thin shadows across the ground.

When he looked back, he felt a stab of anger mingled with fear. Aural stood before them, robed in white luminous cloth, without cloak or mask, her burnished hair tumbling down about her like a garment.

"I come," she said in a voice that rang like a bugle. "I am Aural. I seek the Leiil Asan."

Giaa drew in her breath audibly and shrank closer to Blaise. He put an arm around her in reassurance, but inside he was suddenly hollow and cold.

"You see?" shouted Tuult over the hush. "I have not betrayed the tribes as is claimed. It is the leiil you have brought into your midst. He is the betrayer of the tribes."

"Give unto me Asan," said Aural, lifting her hand, which glowed with blue phosphorous. "And you shall no longer be troubled by Tlar."

"Dung!" shouted someone in shrill defiance, and a javelin was hurtled at her, only to shatter on the shimmering blue force field surrounding her.

"Fools!" She flung out her hand, and a bolt of energy struck down two Bban'n. They fell, screaming, and the stench of burning flesh filled the air.

"*N'a en wulrad*," said Tuult in awe, stepping forward to kneel before her. "We are thine, Dame Aural—"

"Ny!" snapped Blaise, too furious to permit this to continue. He ran forward out of the shadows, warding off Giaa's snatch at his arm, and kicked Tuult sprawling. "Worship her not! She—"

"It is a trick!" shouted someone from the crowd. "A Tlar trick! He came here to betray us. *Chi'zan ahl! Choi'hana!*"

His rings warned Blaise. He whirled, his heart pounding, and raised his hand. Deflected at the last moment, the javelin splintered against the force he flung at it and fell short at his feet.

"He is Tlar! He has heard our strategies. Death to the slayer!"

They surged forward with howls. Ignoring his instinct to flee, Blaise held his ground, lifting a shimmer of blue force field.

"We must talk, Asan," said Aural. "Come, let us be gone from these heathens."

"I have nothing to say to you. If Hihuan's army alarms you and Noble Picyt—"

"And is it your thought that the Bban tribes are safe?" she retorted with a hint of desperation. "When your hand destroyed Anthi—"

"Go!" he shouted, unwilling to listen further. He glared at the warriors circling him with drawn swords. "I won't put myself back into Picyt's hands."

"Do I ask that?" Her eyes flashed. "We must talk, you and I. Now. Before I am missed."

He gritted his teeth. "Then talk."

"Fool! This is not for Bban ears."

Bban musk, hot and nauseating, tainted the night air.

"Asan!" shouted Giaa in warning.

Blaise spun, ignoring the sword that slashed vainly at his force field, and flung out a hand even as a javelin hurtled death at her. His rings snapped between her and the weapon barely in time, and she stared, dumbfounded, at the broken javelin lying at her feet before catching her breath with a sob.

"Oh, my Leiil," she cried, falling to her knees. "Is there nothing beyond thy powers?"

He deepened his concentration to maintain the effort of protecting both himself and her, and his reply was lost as more Bban'n attacked. His rings shivered; he braced his feet and lifted one hand unconsciously to his temple as the strain increased.

"Henan-dung!" They swarmed toward her, barking savagely like a horde of wild animals.

Desperately Blaise dissolved his own protection to cast the full strength of his rings around her. But even as he did so, Aural's rings sliced across his, jolting him to his knees. A stone struck him in the shoulder, then another, then a wall of blue energy formed around him. Aural's energy. He lifted his head, panting and furious, then sprang to his feet as he saw a howling warrior lift Giaa's unconscious body. Her golden hair spilled over the warrior's arm, and blood dripped through the shining strands.

"No!" cried Blaise, pounding at the force field with all the strength of his mind.

But Aural held him a moment longer. "Are you Tlar or beast?" she asked with contempt. "On my vow of your life, I swear this is no attempt to bring you into Picyt's presence." She swept out her hand as he reluctantly turned to her. "You see what the Bban'n think of you. Come. Let us talk. Let us parley, you and I, apart from all other Tlar . . . or Bban."

Was Giaa dead? His mind reached out, only to be blocked by the chaos of the Bban'n rings overlapping uncontrollably. A youth, clad in mail tabard and mask, ran past him with a shrill yell and severed Tuult's head just as the pon gathered himself to run toward the rocks. The head rolled like a gruesome ball, its mask falling away with a clatter upon the stony ground.

"Thus we deal with Tlar and Tlar-lovers!" he shouted, dancing defiance at Blaise as he swung his bloodied sword through the air.

A terrible fury burst within Blaise. He wanted to destroy them all. The dancing, taunting warrior wavered in his sight as blue fire consumed him. He drew his sword and gripped it with both hands.

"Release me, Aural," he grated, conscious of nothing save the fire in his blood. "Release me!"

"Fool—" she began furiously, her rings wavering about him as he gathered himself to crush her from his way.

"Chi'ka!" shouted a sudden, stern voice.

Turning with a glare, Blaise saw the elder Ggil flanked by two other aged Bban'n coming forward. Silence fell over the battleground.

Ggil gestured, coming to a halt some distance from Blaise and Aural. "Take Giaa to my tent," he said, his voice gruff with anger. His glowing silver eyes bored into Blaise, who lifted his sword.

"I shall revenge the spreading of her blood upon the sand," he said, his voice tight with grief.

Ggil lifted his head. "Revenge is not thy right, Tlar leiil. Go from us and say this unto the jen of Hihuan: We spit upon them. Our coming is soon."

"I'm not your messenger boy," snapped Blaise. "And I shall take revenge how I please." He spoke directly to Aural. "Release me. We shall meet on the wastes."

She obeyed without a word, dropping the force field that held him.

Gathering his rings tightly about himself, Blaise looked once more upon the elder. "I shall not return in friendship, Bban."

"We do not seek it, Tlar," retorted the old man. "Begone

from us, you and your female. We swear on the blood that no Bban shall rest until all Tlar are cleared from our land."

"So vow the Tlar!" said Aural proudly.

"Damn you both." Desperately Blaise threw himself into seizert before he could give way to his sorrow and rage and become as brutal a savage as they all were. *Oh, Giaa*, he thought, his heart tearing as he swept through the cold void of nonexistence. *Giaa!*

Chapter 14

In the barren expanse of the desert, the night sky loomed overhead, stars sprinkled sparingly over the blackness. Blaise stood alone upon the crest of a dune, his booted feet planted wide apart in the loose, shifting sand. Before him the wind swept out in cold loneliness, tumbling a tall dune down on a smaller one before eddying in a circle and whipping away. Nor was the desert empty. Beneath the sigh of the wind and the faint rustling of the sand he could hear the smaller sounds of creatures prowling and slithering among the stones on the ridges.

It should not have taken Aural this long to sense his location. Increasingly suspicious, he was on the point of leaving when his skin prickled in warning. Blue fire flashed through the night, dazzling his eyes. Then Aural stood before him, a scant ten feet distant. She now wore a cloak of shimmering blue and silver and a thin gold circlet upon her brow. She was alone.

He stared at her in silence, in control of himself once again. But it was a tenuous, brittle grip. He had sealed his heart in ice that might shatter if his resentment against her grew much stronger.

She held out her hand, cupping the palm, and after a moment a tiny flame of cold blue light flared there, shining between her fingers. She tossed it down onto the black sand between them, and the flame curled and glowed more brightly, illuminating her face and, he supposed, his.

He kept his fingers curled tightly about the hilt of his sword. "We are here," he said coldly. "Speak."

She inclined her head, possibly as a sign of obedience, but the movement also prevented him from reading her expression. "Your attitude makes it difficult."

He snorted. "And your treachery compounds itself."

"No!" She raised her head at that and started to extend a hand in appeal, only to drop it once again to her side. "Why must you be so blind?" She bit her lip, glancing away. "How am I to explain?"

He said nothing.

"Please." She stepped forward, but stopped as he half drew his sword. Something of her usual scorn flickered in her face. "Bban weapons between us, Asan? Do you not now hate the Bban'n for what they have done? Forswear their cause—"

"I am not Tlar," he snapped, no longer bothering to curb his impatience. "And what I swore against the tribes is my personal battle. Now tell me why you wish to speak with me! If it is to persuade me to rejoin Picyt's forces, you may save your breath. I am not his tool. There is nothing you can say now that will convince me to trust him, especially after his attempt to addict me to *yde*." He sneered, hating her. "Was that your idea? I wonder."

Her face tightened. "Your accusations are true," she whispered. "I am here at Picyt's bidding. But, oh, Asan, wait!" she cried, throwing up her hands as Blaise drew his sword with an oath. "Please, please hear me! I had to; you know how he commands me with this torment in my veins."

Reluctantly Blaise lowered the sword and glared at her. "I know. And what would you do now, Aural, persuade me to ally myself with you against him?" He laughed with a scorn that darkened her cheeks.

"Can no appeal pierce this harshness?" Her breathing was ragged. "*Lea'dl* are you all Asan, or does Blaise Omari still exist somewhere within you?"

He frowned. "Why?"

"Because . . ." She pressed her hand to her trembling lips and shut her eyes for a moment. "Because I am Saunders."

For an instant it was as though reality had been suspended. He stood there staring at her while the wind whipped between them in a sudden gust. Then he strode to her, still gripping his sword, and seized her arm with his left hand.

"What lie is this?" he demanded with a snarl.

"N-no lie!" She gasped, trying to wrench free without success. "You are crushing my arm."

"I care not." He stared with fury into that proud, flawless

face. "You are *not* Saunders! I am not such a fool as to believe that."

"But I tell the truth!" Tears sprang to her eyes as his fingers gripped harder. "I—"

"Saunders could not have acted the part," he broke in, tired of her lies, tired of everything. "If you wanted me to believe this, Aural, you should have appeared a little more stupid and a great deal less mocking."

"But Picyt has told me what to say and how to act. He commands my powers." Again she tried to twist free. "Please, you must believe me. There has been no chance for escape. Please—"

"*Merdarai*," he said in disgust and pushed her away. Her tale had the ring of truth, but he refused to consider it.

She stumbled, falling to her knees in the sand and cutting herself as it ripped through cloth and flesh. Tears spilled down her cheeks as she looked up at him imploringly. "Why will you not believe me?" she asked, her voice breaking. Unsteadily she got to her feet, trying to shake the vicious sand from her clothes without touching it. "Look upon me with truth, if you must."

Suspicion stabbed through him as he stepped back to sheath the sword with a vicious *snick*. "Oh, yes, how very clever," he said, mocking her. "What better way to entrap me than to have me enter your mind. You think like a snake, my dear."

Genuine anger flared in her eyes. "And at what time has the strength and power of Aural ever surpassed that of Asan? Have you become such a coward then, to fear the truth?"

He narrowed his eyes. "Very well. Permit my sight. But I warn you of this." He clasped the sword hilt once more. "This can kill just as well as the fire of Anthi."

She compressed her lips. "I am aware of that."

Cautiously he extended his senses over her, even more wary and distrustful than he had admitted. But on the surface of her mind lay all the confusion and anger and dislike of him he had known in Saunders. He recognized the mental pattern of Saunders, blurred now by tendrils of *yde*. Jolted unpleasantly by the cold contact with her, he withdrew, not choosing to go deeper.

"Well?" she demanded.

He gestured, dropping his hand away from the hilt. "You look better than you used to."

She frowned, then sighed with relief. "So—"

"I may believe you, but I don't trust you any more than before," he said curtly. "Less, in fact."

"But why close yourself to me?" she asked, sweeping out her hands in exasperation. "I understand now what Picyt is. He forced me to take Aural's form. And now he wants me to bring you back to him so that he can take your powers for his own."

A chill coursed through Blaise. "How? No, never mind," he added quickly, preferring not to know the grisly details.

"He has not much time," she said. "Hihuan toys with him in this waiting game. But by now his spies have surely learned that the Bban'jen have left Picyt's side. Hihuan will attack soon, and Picyt is mad with fear. He needs you to restore Anthi's power, and he means to have you."

Blaise spoke sharply. "Yes, and for someone claiming to be good old Saunders now willing to take up my side, you needn't have betrayed me to the Bban'n."

She gestured scornfully. "What else could I do? I have told you, I am under Picyt's will. It is my life if I do not bring you back."

Something of his suspicions returned. "Can he reach you even out here?"

"No," she said, pulling back the strand of hair the wind had blown into her face. "But how long can one survive in the wastes?"

He sighed, nodding with comprehension, and walked several feet away to stand frowning out across the barren dunes. She made no attempt to speak or approach him, and perhaps it was that which made him brush aside his doubts and turn back to her.

"Well, Saunders," he said grimly. "I suppose he must be stopped before he tries something more insidious." He met her strained, serious eyes, and when she did not answer, continued: "What chance have we of Hihuan's assistance?"

She shivered and ran her hands briskly up and down her arms beneath her cloak. "Little. Remember that he does not choose to relinquish his position as Tlar leiil to you."

"Demos, what does it matter!" exclaimed Blaise impatiently.

"It matters to him. He has force-marched an army here to preserve what he has. He will not trust you."

"But is Picyt not more his enemy?" insisted Blaise, unable to understand why they should not at least try to form an alliance.

She eyed him steadily. "You would have to fight him first, to the death, to gain his jen for your own. It is the way of the Tlar, whether we understand it or not."

And he knew in his heart that she was right. He sighed, uneasy and restless. "What, then, do *you* suggest?"

She gestured, looking as reluctant as he. "I think you know the only thing that can be done."

"We must go into Picyt's lair," Blaise responded.

She turned up her palm. "Together. To betray him this last, final time." Her eyes sought his. "Will you go, Blaise Omari?"

"Yes," he said after a long pause, while she grew tense beside him. "There is nothing else I can do if he is to be stopped."

She smiled in relief. "Then let us go quickly and finish it."

The dank, cold interior of the caverns of M'thra made him shiver with a coldness that cut to the soul. He glanced swiftly up and down the narrow stone corridor, catching his balance after the brief vertigo of seizert, and took two strides forward only to stop and press himself against the jagged stone wall as he heard footsteps. But it was only Aural who approached him.

"*Merdarai*," he breathed, releasing his sword hilt.

"Come," she whispered nervously. "We are not far from his private quarters."

He smiled grimly and gestured to indicate that she go first. "After you, Saunders."

"Very well." Sneering, she swept her blue and silver cloak tightly about herself and moved down the passageway at a rapid pace.

Blaise followed more cautiously, one hand on his weapon. *Lea'dl!* Try as he might he could not curb his mounting sense of unease. Pausing for a moment near a bend in the passageway, he spread out his rings warily, well aware that to do so could lead to discovery.

"Come!" Aural whispered, looking back at him. "Hurry!"

His senses told him nothing. No one was near save the

guards outside Picyt's quarters. Blaise frowned, not yet certain how to get past them.

When they reached the end of the passageway, she stopped. "Let me go first and distract them," she said, her voice scarcely audible. "They know my task."

For a moment he wondered why she did not use mind-touch, since the need for silence was very great this near the guards, and then he cursed his own stupid suspicion. Of course, if they communicated mentally, Picyt would pick it up at once. Silently Blaise nodded to show he understood, then, seeing her strained expression and the intensity in her eyes, gave her a brief encouraging smile. She looked at him but did not smile back. With a deep breath she straightened and put on her mask before walking out into view of the guards with the serene grace of Aural.

Not daring to watch, Blaise held his breath and listened to her murmur something to the guards. She even laughed. He raised his brows in reluctant admiration. Saunders had come a long way in the art of deception and duplicity. And, to his surprise, she succeeded in leading the guards down another passageway branching off from the widened intersection of tunnels. As soon as the sound of their footsteps faded, Blaise drew his jen-knife, wishing for a fire-rod instead, and eased out with silent catlike steps across the open space lit by flaring torches to where the door of Picyt's quarters stood slightly ajar. If Saunders kept the guards away long enough, it would take only seconds to kill the defenseless priest. Blaise swallowed, frowning as he prepared to kill in cold blood. It had to be done.

He listened for a moment at the door, and heard nothing but the harsh, regular rasp of breathing. He extended his senses imperceptibly, seeking a trap, but detected none. Tensely he pushed the door wider and eased his way inside the darkened room. There he paused, waiting for his eyes to adjust to the gloom, before creeping forward to the figure lying among silken cushions beneath a canopy. The thin draperies rippled softly in the drafts. Blaise readied the knife and reached out to draw the draperies back.

He stiffened, staring through the dim illumination from the incense burner at Uble's smooth, unconscious face. He could smell the faint bitter scent of *yde*. He turned to flee, only to stop at the sight of two figures standing in the darkness between him and the door.

"Does my Leiil now believe?" asked Picyt's hoarse, ruined voice.

Defiantly Blaise started to answer, but the second figure swaggered forward, activating the light cube in his hand.

"We do indeed believe," he said, his youthful voice deep with arrogance as he raked his black, purple-flecked eyes over Blaise. He curled his sensual lips in a contemptuous smile. "The true Asan would have swept down upon us with fifty cohorts of jen warriors rather than creep through the shadows to strike down his enemies in the coward's way."

Blaise felt sickened at his own stupidity. Why had he trusted Aural? Why? "I am no coward, Hihuan," he said, masking his despair with a level voice. Without warning he flicked his jen-knife across the room at Hihuan, remembering that day of trickery and pain, but by casually lifting his hand Hihuan deflected the blade with a flash of blue fire. The knife clattered harmlessly on the stone floor.

"That was foolish," said Hihuan, his black eyes narrowing. "Take his sword, noble."

Picyt, even more decrepit and ravaged than before, stood bent and shrunken in his vast white robes, glaring resentfully at Hihuan. "I am not thy lackey, Noble Leiil. Let the guards return and deal with him."

Hihuan frowned, but he summoned the guards, who reappeared almost at once with an unmasked Aural. She looked sullen but unharmed.

Raising his personal force field, Blaise glanced at her, but she did not respond.

"I have done thy bidding, Leiil Hihuan," she said, stepping away from the masked guards who flanked her. Tlar'jen, Blaise saw at once, reading the marks of caste and family rank upon their masks. There were four of them. Jen-knives with jeweled hilts that glittered in the light hung at their belts, but unlike the Bban'n, they carried their fire-rods in the cuff of their gauntlets and wore plated breast shielding beneath their cloaks instead of mail. Aural gestured, her blue eyes the color of smoke. "Permit me to retire."

"Oh, not yet, Dame Aural," said the Tlar leiil, leering at her. "You are a sight that pleases us."

She compressed her lips in anger, and she started to speak.

"Well, Saunders," said Blaise before she could do so. "I hope you are to be generously rewarded for this night's work. Do you still expect the Institute to come orbiting some day and rescue you?"

"Oh, silence your imbecilic tongue!" she snapped, tossing a strand of hair back from her face. "I am not Saunders, you fool, and had you not been so besotted with that accursed Henan girl, your senses would have told you so." She swung away from Blaise as the blood rushed furiously to his face. "Revered noble," she said proudly to Picyt, "you desired that he be brought. He is here." She extended her hand impatiently.

"Ah, yes, my promise." Picyt twisted the pallid, dead flesh of his face into something resembling a smile and drew a vial of *yde* from his wide sleeve. He placed it into her hand.

Her fingers closed tightly around it, and Blaise saw hunger quiver through her face. Sickened, he swung his eyes away from her as Hihuan stepped forward to put his hand upon hers. She flinched back, and with a low laugh he let her go.

"Is it possible to find an eighth level?" he murmured, his black eyes glittering at her with undisguised appetite.

A bitter, malicious smile curved her lips. "Take care, mortal Leiil, lest I put you there and leave you untouched." She raised her brows at his frown. "That is your favored game, is it not?"

Scowling, Hihuan moved away from her and flicked his hand at his guards. "Seize Asan! This affair wearies us."

Swallowing his boiling rage, Blaise refrained from his desire to issue challenge as he glared fiercely at Hihuan. "I think you will find it grows even more tiresome. Good-bye." He gathered his senses together, but although fire seared his veins he did not seizert. He blinked, stunned by this failure, and tried again with no success.

"No, Asan," said Hihuan with a deep laugh. "How much the years have permitted you to forget. We are Tlar here, not simple-minded Bban." He nodded toward the guards with their drawn fire-rods, and only now did Blaise realize they were not firing on him. Instead, they had reversed polarization in their weapons to draw the energy from his force field. That was why he could not seizert, not as long as they continued to drain his power.

Swiftly Blaise drew his rings tightly in, dropping the force field abruptly. One fire-rod began to glow and its owner dropped it with a curse. Blaise seized that split second of distraction to draw his sword. Moving onto the balls of his feet, he hefted the curved blade of green corybdium with its thin inset of gold, swinging it lightly to make it sing in a soft taunt.

"Fool!" shouted Hihuan, and gestured at his guards. "Fire! Cut him down!"

"No!" cried Picyt with horror. "The key to Anthi must not be destroyed—"

A bolt of energy crackled from a fire-rod, moving straight at Blaise. But the full force of his mental concentration was locked on that attack. He compressed his rings into a spearhead and shot them the full length of the blade, which hummed in answer, the metal glowing with heat that seared his hands. Yet he felt nothing as he swung up the blade and deflected the bolt back at his attackers. A guard fell, screaming, and two more fired. He deflected these also, the power shining through his blade as energy shot recklessly about the room, one bolt slamming into the wall beside Aural, who ducked with a cry.

"Madness!" shouted Picyt, cringing behind a chair. "Fools!"

But the battle went on, and even Hihuan drew a fire-rod, dropping to one knee to fire it low. Blaise knew it was coming, and the memory of his former wound drove him to dodge too soon. Thrown off-balance, he cursed himself as he ducked again and barely deflected a second bolt from Hihuan with the tip of his blade. The shock of absorbing and deflecting so much energy was tiring him. A shudder ran through the sword, and he gripped it more tightly, seeking desperately now for his chance to seizert.

One more deflection . . . *now*. Scarcely had he knocked the bolt aside when he withdrew his rings from the sword and reformed them. But just as he achieved seizert a wall seemed to appear from nowhere, slamming him back into the physical plane with such force that he sagged, stunned, to his knees, the sword slipping from his loosened grasp.

"Hold fire!" shouted Hihuan, rising to his feet. He smiled at Aural in surprise. "Well done, Dame Aural! Well done! But we would have had him in another moment. These ancient methods of doing battle exhibit great flamboyance but are not very effective."

"You would have had his death," she snapped. "And Anthi would be lost to us all. Would you have the revered noble die through your bloodthirst?"

Hihuan's fleshy, handsome face darkened. "Perhaps that would not be such a dreadful thing."

Picyt responded bitterly to that. "Arguments serve no purpose save that of our enemies. Let the task be done."

"Agreed." Hihuan smiled. There was a grim ugliness in his eyes that boded no good for anyone. He nodded at the three remaining guards, who seized the still groggy Blaise as soon as Aural withdrew her force field. Their rough hands dragged him to his feet, stripping him of cloak and baldric. Something dim within Blaise urged him to fight his way free, but he could not get past his sense of disorientation. The ringing in his ears made him grimace, and he muttered a sharp oath as his arms were twisted painfully behind him and shackled.

"Why is Anthi's return so important?" he asked woodenly, snatching at anything to gain time for his wits to return. He focused his eyes upon Hihuan's unsmiling face. "Surely your army does not need a life-maintenance computer in order to defeat the Bban'jen."

Hihuan sneered, but it was plain the question had struck a nerve. "You know the many functions of Anthi. She supports the protection shields over Altian and blocks Bban mental vibrations, among other things. You know this, Asan. Seek not to make us think you more a fool than you are."

Blaise smiled without amusement. "In other words, Anthi is the primary unit that supports secondaries in your capital. Small wonder you fear the Bban, if it is to be a fair fight."

"Silence!" Hihuan's black eyes blazed. "You—no," he said with abrupt softness, as he regarded Blaise's sword, which one of the guards held. "Bring that to me."

The guard obeyed with visible puzzlement, and Hihuan snatched the sword from his hand, turning it over so that light flashed along the blade. "This is no common Bban weapon. It . . ." He tapped the large jewel set in the hilt and with an oath pried loose the stone with the point of his jen-knife. The jewel bounced off the stone floor, and with a savage stamp Hihuan crushed it beneath his heel. "So much for Bban trickery," he said, snarling, kicking at the powder beneath his foot. He flung the sword across the room, where it landed with a loud clatter.

Blaise winced, his blood flaming at the insult even as another part of him cringed. No, he would *not* believe Giaa had given him the weapon as a deliberate trick. "And what makes you think Anthi can be restored?"

Hihuan scowled, holding his left arm as though it had begun to pain him. "Bring him," he snapped at the guards, and strode from the room with a sweep of his bronze cloak.

The great armored cave with its green walls of corybdium plates stood shrouded in cold darkness. Flames shot up from the torches in the drafts, lighting the blackened crystal mass of Anthi with a ruddy glow. The tall metal doors leading beyond into the cavern where the empty capsules stretched in long silent rows still stood open. As Blaise was dragged in and forced to his knees before Anthi, his determination hardened to a final bedrock core. He would not give in, not to anyone.

"Unchain his hands," said Picyt, scuttling off into the shadows to light more torches until the room blazed with illumination. One of the crystal capsules lay several feet from Blaise. It was occupied. His blood froze as he stared at it.

"No!" he said.

"Yes!" rasped the priest, clenching his clawlike hands. "I shall take Rim's form. Mine will not last much longer. Now hurry. Hurry!"

"Patience, revered noble," murmured Hihuan, smiling sleekly at the priest's trembling hands. "Make yourself serene and await Anthi's return."

"The computer is off-line," said Blaise curtly, trying to ignore the cold knot in his stomach. He knew of no way out, and yet something within him still refused to consider the only option remaining. Sensible as it might be in terms of his own survival, he would not reactivate the computer. "It shut itself off. Why do you keep insisting that I can somehow restore power?" He shrugged. "Let me go, Hihuan. Surely this world is large enough for both you and the Bban tribes. Go and leave me to my own method of survival."

For answer Hihuan lifted his finger, and one of the masked guards pressed the tip of his jen-knife to the base of Blaise's skull, pricking the flesh slightly, chilling him. He tensed, and Hihuan laughed softly.

"Consider this, mewling coward," said the Tlar leiil with a

sneer. "One thrust of the hand and Merdar shall welcome you into the shadow land with swift arms."

"You—"

"We are not fools, Asan! Nor are we superstitious Bban'n whom you may deceive. We know Anthi's functions. The key to her reactivation lies within you. Release it, or die now."

Blaise grinned without mirth. "Why don't you place Aural's hand upon Anthi? She is my equal."

Somewhere behind him Aural breathed a vicious curse, and Hihuan said savagely, "You know Anthi is coded to follow only the bidding of Asan."

Blaise twisted his head to look straight up into Hihuan's angry gaze. "Then kill me," he said calmly, though he was shivering inside. "I will not give her to you."

One of the guards swore, and Hihuan scowled at Blaise as if he were tempted to give the order. But he hesitated, and Blaise's self-confidence rose.

"Now see what thy arrogance has brought us, Noble Leiil!" shouted Picyt, his voice breaking with anger. "Nothing but delay. Nothing but impasse. Must thy way be always to crush rather than to bargain? What choice has thou given him but proud refusal?"

"Enough!" Hihuan's face darkened with fury as he flung out his hand. "Beware lest your wretched blood go to the sands, priest."

They glared hotly at each other while Blaise shifted slightly, trying to draw away from the point of the knife. The guard's hand clamped down hard upon his shoulder in warning, and Blaise dared not move again. He grimaced as his knees grated on the stone floor.

"Perhaps, now that you've come around to my way of thinking—" he began, but stopped as Hihuan lifted his hand at Aural.

"Dame Aural," he said with a casualness that alerted Blaise. "Prepare a goblet for our guest."

She frowned, hesitating as Picyt gasped and said, "It is a great risk, noble."

"Do it!" snapped Hihuan, and with a bow of her head she left the cave.

"No!" cried Picyt, his withered mouth stretching in protest. "Not *yde*! His mind will be destroyed. And there shall be nothing left. Nothing! Not Anthi, nor my future—"

"Silence." Hihuan shoved the priest away so roughly that Picyt stumbled and fell. "Now let us hear no more from you," he said, kicking him aside. Picyt dragged his trembling, furious body across the floor to the case of Rim, where he huddled, mouthing curses beneath his breath.

Blaise attempted to seizert. But in his desperation he had forgotten the guard's hand on his shoulder, had forgotten that the guard was Tlar and could sense his intentions from that touch. His spirit flung itself wide, but even as blue fire flashed through the air, reflecting off the darkened sides of Anthi, the guard struck his skull hard with the knife hilt. Blaise snapped back into his sagging body with a jolt severe enough to make him retch with nausea. The room seemed to dance around him, and when he finally regained a hold on reality, he was lying on the ground, a dull ache hammering steadily through his head. Dimly he heard footsteps around him.

"You took long enough," said Hihuan petulantly.

The silken hem of Aural's robes swayed to a halt inches from Blaise's blurred eyes. "Creating a mixture of full potency takes time, my Leiil," she said, her words low and slightly slurred. Blaise wondered if she had sampled the stuff while she was gone.

Hihuan snorted. "Lift him."

"No," muttered Blaise, but the world still spun and his voice sounded very far away.

Rough hands jerked him off the ground, scraping his cheek across the stone and flipping him onto his back. He was half lifted, and strong fingers entwined themselves in his long black hair, yanking back his head hard enough to make him gasp in pain. That, and the sting of his bleeding cheek, roused him from his grogginess. He heaved himself up, managing to get his feet under him, but his struggles were in vain against the three guards holding him.

What would the real Asan do? he wondered in frantic despair, clamping his jaw shut with such force that the muscles bulged.

Hihuan bent over him and placed the goblet against his closed lips. Blaise was desperate. His heart pounded, and his blood seemed to thicken in his veins. There was no return from *yde*!

Hihuan glanced at the guard holding Blaise's head, and that

ruthless grip on his hair tightened until it seemed half of his scalp was being torn off by the roots. He resisted as long as he could, until with an oath Hihuan punched a fist hard into his unprotected stomach. Blaise jerked, trying to choke off a cry, but Hihuan's thumb dug into the corner of his mouth, forcing his jaw open. Blaise tried to bite him, but Hihuan tilted the entire contents of the goblet down his throat so rapidly that Blaise had no chance to spit it out. He coughed and wheezed, feeling as though he were drowning, and the guards released him, letting him fall to the ground.

The *yde* was acidic, bitterly so, with a sickeningly sweet aftertaste. His aching stomach burned from it, and he hoped he might throw it up. But already lassitude spread over him, dulling the fire in his veins and flattening his rings. He tried to fight it with all the strength left in the last lucid corner of his mind, but it was like hitting water. He could do nothing but lie there, helpless and frantic, as his long body shook uncontrollably with the progress of the drug through his limbs.

"His hands," said Hihuan's voice from far away. "Place them upon Anthi. It will not be long now."

Blaise tried to scream at him, but he could not speak. Words, disjointed and meaningless, floated through his brain in a swirling babble. He . . . must . . . stop them . . . must . . .

To his surprise, the lethargy began slowly to clear away, freeing his mind once again. For a moment relief raced through him as his rings snapped out full and sharp and whole, only to die as he realized it was just the enhancement of the drug. That effect would not last long, and then he would fall back into the vague shadows of dependency, needing more *yde* simply to remain lucid.

But his anger did not keep his mind from extending freely in all directions, sweeping through the caverns of M'thra before crossing the valley where the Bban tribes massed for battle. A new banner unfurled above the rest there. He paused, puzzled by the sight of it, and curiosity drove him into the large tent where a tiny, masked, shrunken figure sat regally in a chair, guarded by her Tlar warriors, discussing battle plans with a hostile council of Bban'n. A flicker of hope kindled within Blaise. Had the Soot'dla, those few Tlar rebels against Hihuan, come at last to join the Bban tribes? If only they would advance now, while Hihuan was still unprepared! But before he could attempt to warn them he was swept on, driven by the drug to reach out farther across the wastes, to Altian itself, lying in uneasy slumber beneath its dome with the silent slums sprawling around it. The Tsla leiils slept there, life in her womb. And intrigues in other shapes crawled through the city. But now he must return; the vision was fading.

His body jerked spastically, and once more he plunged into confusion and disorder, losing grasp of his mind bit by agonizing bit. No! He must . . . he must have more *yde*.

But his inner core of stubbornness refused to surrender to the mounting torment of his craving. He groaned and twitched, his body writhing in contortions, but still he would not cry out for more.

"He dies!"

"No," said Hihuan grimly. "Not yet. Put his hands again upon Anthi. Keep them there."

Blaise felt nothing but his own torture as his brain seemed to unravel, strand by strand, into a vortex of stripped nerves and horrifying nightmares. Beneath lay the compartment that guarded Anthi. He must not release that! Loss of that final bit of control was what Hihuan had gambled on, but Blaise did not mean to give it to him. His back arched, and he thought he screamed as white-hot pain burst through him. *Yde!* No, he must not have more!

Then, to his horror, Anthi stirred within him, disturbed by the chaos tearing him apart. Blue fire, cool against the greater heat of pain, flickered along his veins, strengthening him for an instant. He opened his eyes and saw a faint glimmer of life spark deep within the crystal. *No*! With all his might he held it back, and the light dimmed away.

"Almost! Almost!" cried Hihuan in triumph.

That was when Blaise saw the answer. A way out did exist. But, oh, Demos, it meant giving up his very soul, his psyche, everything that was *him*. Such total surrender of identity was something he had always fought, first in his dangerous childhood, against the regulations of conformity dictated by the Institute; then in his reckless life of blackmarketeering; even during the transference into Asan's body. But now Anthi held his escape from Hihuan, from betrayal of those damned Bban'n, and from the addiction to *yde*, provided he gave himself up to whatever Anthi chose to create of him.

Fear burned through him, for a moment more overpowering than the pain from the drug. There had to be another way!

But the only other alternative was death, and he was still unwilling to die.

Grimacing as once again Anthi flicked through his body, causing the crystal to flame more brightly this time, Blaise made his choice. With the last dregs of his strength he threw himself inward to Anthi, submerging himself in her power, which flamed up in blinding force to devour him. And beyond Anthi waited the other, who had lain quietly all these days, biding its time. Awesome, dark, *cold*, it engulfed Blaise, who even now could not help but struggle. But it was too late to make a different choice. He fell, spinning helplessly into a terrifying void, and as he vanished beyond the point of no return his last coherent thought was of Giaa and what could have been. . . .

Chapter 15

Asan returned to consciousness slowly, his mind clearing almost at once, although the weakness from the drug still sapped his body. He frowned at this, swiftly regulating heart-beat and respiration to a better rate, and warily permitted one eye to flicker open.

He was lying sprawled like an abandoned plaything against the wall of Anthi's cave, still garbed in his Bban mail and tunic. Anthi blazed with life, humming with purpose. Hihuan and his henchmen were gone. Picyt lay on the floor beside Rim's capsule, gripping a transference rod in his clawlike hands as Aural called on the will of Anthi and bent to place her palms upon the dome of the capsule.

"Blasphemous fools!" shouted Asan, anger flaming his blood to the fifth intensity. Even as Aural gasped and whirled, her face draining of color, Asan rose to his feet. Anthi flashed blue light over them all as he raised his hand in command. "Stand away from the crime that you would dare, Aural."

"B-but how?" she whispered, still staring at him, stunned. "Even were you not really dead, the drug would—"

He smiled faintly. "Aural, Aural," he said gently, "you are not yourself. Do you not know your true Leiil when he stands before you?"

She gasped, her eyes widening as recognition dawned. "Asan!" she breathed, shame flickering across her face. "The *n'ka* is gone!"

"No, not gone. He has stepped aside for me." Asan lifted his head high. "You may no longer deal with me in the manner you used with him."

She flinched at his sternness and started to speak, but a ragged moan from Picyt brought her attention back to the priest. "He has not much time left!" she said. "I must be quick—"

"No." Asan stepped forward, frowning now. He pulled her away from the capsule, glancing only once at the priest, who was now in the final stages of deterioration.

"But he is Tlar!" she protested, stiffening in Asan's grip. "He is Picyt, your faithful servant. If he dies—"

"He died long ago, Aural," said Asan, staring at her, recalling a happier time when they had walked together and he had refused no wish of hers. Brushing aside old memories, he did not relent. "Picyt died on the day he permitted himself to forget the true intent of our purpose."

She jerked free, her blue eyes flashing angrily. "The purpose is to preserve our kind!"

"We are all that is left to preserve!" he said heatedly. "You, I, Rim, and Vauzier. We are the last. Picyt and Hihuan know that. All Tlar know it. Picyt kept us imprisoned here in these caverns for centuries, driven to madness by his own quest for immortality and his fear of achieving it. Had he and Hihuan not fallen into a power struggle, we would sleep still."

"Then give him gratitude for raising you," she said urgently. "Let him enter Rim."

"He is not worthy to join my brother's soul—"

"And were the ones who raised us worthy?" she shot back furiously. "If he dies, that is one less to fight the Bban'n—"

"We do not fight our own children!" said Asan firmly, his look quelling her when she started to protest. "Yes, Aural, ours! They were Tlar once, until we put them here. And now we have come to this world as beggars. There shall be no war here. You are too wearied to think clearly. But soon, I promise you, it shall be over."

Angry tears welled in her eyes as Picyt fought for breath, his withered body shuddering at their feet. "And who shall give me *yde* if he dies? He commands the growing—" At last she believed the refusal in Asan's eyes. With a snarl she broke off and whirled, throwing herself at the capsule with outstretched palms.

He threw his rings before her, stopping her just short of the capsule. She sank to the ground, racked with weeping.

"Fiend of Merdar!" she cried with hatred enough to make him flinch.

Hardening his expression, he pointed at the door. "It is not

Rim's time. The question is finished. Now go. I intend to seal this chamber from all who would abuse it."

Even as Asan spoke, Picyt loosed a long rattling sigh, and his hands slid limply from the transference bar. The scent of death lifted into the air.

"I shall go," said Aural with a break in her voice. She dragged herself up to face him with eyes that were cold with hatred. "But I swear upon the blood that once bound us, Asan, I shall not forgive." Stumbling slightly, she left on unsteady feet.

He shut his eyes for a moment, the weight of responsibility crushing down on his shoulders as heavily as the counting of the centuries. Then he shook his mind clear and opened his eyes, gazing down at Picyt's body for a long while.

"Anthi," he said at last. "By the will of Asan, preserve the Noble Picyt n'Kkanthor dl'Mura-an with the honor due his house."

Anthi pulsed in acknowledgment. Blue light glowed forth over the priest, bathing him in its radiance. As Asan watched, Picyt's ravaged face smoothed and filled out, the flesh growing once again firm and peaceful, as though he slept. The lingering resentment within Asan was put away. If this small act counted as a sign of forgiveness toward the man who had robbed him of years, manipulated his subjects, alienated his leiis, and sought the destruction of an innocent race of beings, then so be it. He could not give more.

Grimly Asan spoke once again to the crystal. "Anthi," he said, "preserve Rim and Vauzier until their time. And seal yourself against all who would enter without my right. You must serve no other purpose."

"Anthi shall obey," replied the computer.

Inclining his head, he gathered his strength and strode from the chamber, closing the great doors behind him with a hollow boom that echoed down the passageway.

Instinctively he turned left, moving rapidly along the narrow tunnel without need of artificial light, for he walked by the sight of his senses through the complete darkness. Finally he reached Picyt's quarters, having encountered no one. It was as though the entire maze of caverns lay deserted. But Hihuan and some of his men might still be here. They must be found.

Without hesitation he pushed his way into Picyt's chambers, where Uble still lay in a drugged trance. Asan walked over to him and lightly placed his fingertips on the youth's forehead, releasing him from that bondage. Uble stirred and fell into an uneasy sleep, and Asan turned away with a grim expression. The sword that had been Giaa's gift still lay on the floor where Hihuan had tossed it, the hole where the transmitter had been gaping black in the hilt. Asan picked it up, running a finger along the blade, which hummed responsively. He half smiled and sheathed it before gathering up his cloak and mask and donning them.

"My . . . my Leiil?"

Startled, Asan turned sharply to find Uble awake and propped up on one elbow, frowning at him through the dim light from the coals in the brazier.

"Fear not," said Asan gently as Uble's eyes widened. He raised his force field and, through the blue shimmer of light, smiled sadly. "You are free of the service of Anthi. Picyt is dead, and the House of Kkanthor stands dissolved upon my order. Do you understand? Your life is yours now."

"I . . ." Uble rubbed his hand over his eyes in a dazed fashion. "But what is to be done? Where are we to go? Art thou our—"

Asan inclined his head, pitying this young man who had been led all his life. "Farewell."

Gathering himself, he seizerted, rematerializing in the midst of the Tlar camp on the plains of Ddreui. Dawn had just broken like a banner of bronze and scarlet, and the wind blew coldly over the frost-covered ground. Asan stood where he was, feet braced and force field shimmering between the dying light of two sentry fires. One of the sentinels jerked awake from his shivering doze and cried out sharply in alarm. At once men sprang from tents, stumbling, half asleep, and shaking with cold as they pulled on pieces of battle gear and clothing.

"It is Asan the Mighty!" cried someone, and perhaps half the men faltered and dropped to their knees, only to be prodded angrily back to their feet by their fellows.

"It is the impostor!" jeered another. "Let us test his—"

"Silence!" roared an arrogant voice, and an officer appeared, masked, cloaked, and armed over his sleeping robe. "What means this disturbance? Are you fools, to bring the

Bban'n down upon us before the day is begun?"

As the men reluctantly fell back, muttering among themselves, Asan looked briefly toward the towering mountains. A faint glimmer of light glowed at the foot of the slope. He frowned. So the Bban horde had moved, and swiftly, too, to be in position by the light of dawn. His nostrils quivered over the crossing of scents in the frosty air. Battle was not long off. It must be stopped. He had brought the purpose here to this planet. But the purpose was over. He would not carry the weight of these fools' deaths too.

His gaze returned to the officer who stood, fists upon hips, boldly regarding him.

"You do not know me," said Asan flatly.

The officer flipped over his hand. "Should I? If you are an emissary from that treacherous hag, Agate, I warn you—"

"What is your name?" asked Asan with sudden impatience.

The officer stood stiffly erect. "Pon Fflir. And yours, bold one? You dare much entering this camp—"

"I am Leiil Asan. I come to lay challenge to Hihuan."

"Asan!" A mixture of emotions betrayed themselves in Fflir's voice. "But that is myth—"

"I come to lay challenge!" snapped Asan, grasping his sword hilt. He had no time to depend on the reactions of these soldiers. Like Picyt, Hihuan was a troublemaker, unworthy of the position he held. "Summon your master."

With a jerky bow Fflir turned and gestured savagely at a gawking sentry. "Inform the Noble Leiil. Challenge is laid!"

"And accepted," said a deep, petulant vice from the shadows. Fflir moved aside hastily as Hihuan came swaggering into sight. The Tlar leiil eyed Asan without expression, although his breath seemed to come a bit shortly. "I left you dead."

The sun was rising rapidly, a brazen ball over the horizon. Wind whipped in noisy gusts across the plains, sweeping the wiry grass flat.

Asan smiled grimly behind his mask, building his rings one by one in preparation for this battle of blood. "A mistake, Hihuan," he said lightly, and unsheathed his sword. Some chance trick of the sunlight caught the blade and reflected blindingly off its length, as though the sword had suddenly taken life of its own. The jen drew back in awe, but with an oath Hihuan dragged off his cloak and called for his weapons.

"My Leiil!" A sentry came running, his fire-rod drawn. "The Bban'jen! They come!"

"Form ranks!" shouted Fflir, and the men ran obediently to seize weapons and battle shielding. "By the grace of Anthi," swore the pon in disgust, pulling on his gauntlets. "Can they not even allow us food to fight on?"

"Bban have no honor," said Hihuan with a sneer, before returning his gaze to Asan, whose eyes had narrowed. "Well, challenger? Will it be your pleasure to wait until this matter is finished?"

"Blood does not wait," snapped Asan. *"An!"*

He seizerted to a point midway on the plains between the Tlar camp and the approaching Bban horde, taking a stance on a rising knoll, the tip of his sword in the earth, both hands resting on the hilt. Every muscle was coiled in readiness. Doubtless Hihuan would use all means of treachery available. Asan's lips tightened, drawing on the hate within the other for additional strength. For blood challenge he was not above trickery himself.

Blue fire flashed through the air. Hihuan appeared, his force field in place, a long straight sword, almost slender in appearance beside Asan's, in his fist. He glanced about, the sun glinting off his bronze mask, and gestured in displeasure.

"Will you have us run down by their attack?" Faint yells of the approaching horde could be heard now. Soon the porters would come skimming down upon them.

"They will not interrupt blood challenge," said Asan with assurance, his heartbeat quickening as he watched for the slightest move from his opponent.

"You planned this, did you not?" asked Hihuan with anger. "Just when victory is assured us, and the Bban threat about to be ended for all time, you—"

"Two leiils cannot rule the Tlar," broke in Asan grimly, his blood rising to the sixth intensity as the fire in his veins blotted away all other considerations. "The place was given you for a time, but rightfully it is mine. Do you surrender now?"

For answer Hihuan hurled a mental attack, seeking to break Asan's rings of concentration, but Asan was prepared for that and held firmly. He swung up his curved sword with both hands, sunlight flashing along the blade. Already the first ranks of the Bban'n were upon them. They came to an astonished halt with howls of rage as the porters wheeled just short of the knoll, bucking like living things on sputtering jets of air. A javelin hurtled down at them to shatter harmlessly off force fields as Hihuan and Asan sprang at one another. The clash of sword blades rang out loudly through the air, silencing the enraged howling of the Bban'jen.

Hihuan was stronger than Asan had expected. Gasping for breath, he strained against Hihuan's weight as their blades slid with a screech of metal to lock hilts. His heels dug deeply into the soft earth for purchase, for already the ground was thawing beneath the heat of the morning sun. Soon it would be a morass of mud, and the ranks of infantry would be unable to maneuver against each other. Asan smiled grimly to himself, hoping his battle would be done long before then.

Hihuan slipped, and they broke apart, circling warily, testing both mental and physical guards.

"Choi'hana!" shouted the Bban warriors suddenly in encouragement. "It is a death-duel of the Tlar leiils. *Choi'hana!* Death! Death!" And the reek of their musk rose up over the air.

Asan feinted with a swing of his sword, then sprang in close, seeking to knock Hihuan's sword from his hand. Their force fields collided with a furious crackling of incompatible energy, and Hihuan wrenched free with an oath, throwing himself forward almost at once in a fierce attack. Bracing his feet, Asan met it, although the shock of their clashing blades vibrated up his arms. He saw an opening and lunged for it, channeling his mental power to the tip of his blade. But just as he pierced Hihuan's force field, Hihuan dodged by seizerting. Grimly Asan spun about, seeking to be ready for Hihuan's reappearance from any direction. In that moment he had time to look out and see the Tlar'jen massed and ready, farther away than the Bban'n, the sunlight shining down upon their black, disciplined ranks. He regarded them scornfully. Did they think Anthi would still mute the Bban'n powers to give Tlar an advantage? If so, they had a rude awakening due. Look at them, two thousand against a dozen times that many!

"Hah!" With a roar Hihuan reappeared, almost within Asan's own space.

Alarmed by that recklessness, Asan spun away, stumbling

as his boots sank deep into the moist earth, and Hihuan's sword thrust through his force field, shattering the barrier with a crackle of sparks. He missed Asan's ribs by a hair-breadth. Grunting, Asan dropped his force field altogether, rather than bother to reform it, and shot pure mental fire at Hihuan with a flash of his eyes. Hihuan reeled back, shaken, and Asan had time to scramble upright.

The cold air whipped about him, making him shiver without the protection of his force field, but still he did not raise it again. Instead he held himself ready for Hihuan's next move. When it came, it was an unexpected one. Hihuan snarled something and dropped his force field, startling Asan. Then he drew a fire-rod from his belt and fired it in rapid short blasts at Asan, who threw himself flat, rolling off the knoll in a desperate attempt to dodge the blue bolts. Catching his breath at the bottom, he flung up part of his force field barely in time to deflect another blast and hurled his jen-knife in retaliation. It was an impossible throw at that angle, but grimly he guided its flight with his rings and had the satisfaction of seeing it rip into Hihuan's side where the heavy battle shielding was weakest. Hihuan staggered and fell to one knee. Asan frowned as he sensed Hihuan close the wound with a mental command. That was a dangerous game.

Asan seizerted himself back to the crest of the hill, only to gasp as he found Hihuan's blade waiting wickedly to impale him as he rematerialized. How had Hihuan known? he wondered, twisting desperately to one side. Was Aural watching this with her senses, guiding Hihuan? The very thought of such evil treachery took his breath. Despite his dodge, the knife still found its mark. Blood, warm and vital, spurted down his side, staining his battle mail, taking some of his mental force with it. Only then did he realize how much his triumph over *yde* had drained him.

"*Choi'heirat! Za! Za!*" howled the Bban warriors, rattling their javelins in a deafening din.

"Finished!" gasped Hihuan in triumph, but Asan was not.

Not stopping to consider the consequences, he closed his own wound, warding off the pain and shock, and swung his sword at Hihuan's head with all his strength. The blow came agonizingly near, but somehow Hihuan deflected the blade, grunting at the shock of impact. Both swords went spinning, and Asan leaped at Hihuan, driving him to the sticky earth. Hihuan rolled under him, one hand ripping away Asan's mask as he grasped Asan's throat in a throttling grip, the other bringing forth his jen-knife.

Gasping as his vision spun, Asan seized Hihuan's wrist, striving to hold the knife as far away as possible while his rings hammered viciously at Hihuan. They strained at each other for a seemingly interminable time. Then Hihuan's ring of defense gave slightly. With a grunt Asan pressed his mental attack harder. Hihuan writhed, abruptly dropping the knife. Asan tried to seize it, but Hihuan got him by the throat with both hands, swearing hoarsely.

Asan's lungs heaved, and the world spun into frightening grayness. He was being shaken like a rag. His control over his wound slipped, and blood gushed forth again. He groaned, bringing up leaden hands to flail vainly at Hihuan's mask.

"Merdarai!" swore Hihuan, his voice a hoarse croak of determination. "Why will you not die?"

His rings were shattering when his desperate fingers suddenly clasped the knife. But he was too weak to lift it, too weak to plunge it through the heavy battle shielding protecting Hihuan's chest.

Anthi give me grace, he thought in a blur. But even as he resigned himself to defeat, the other lying deep within him stirred fiercely to urge him on. His air was gone; he thought it impossible to move; any moment would see the exploding of his heaving lungs . . . yet somehow he must bring up the knife.

He struggled, his powerful will hurling itself vainly against exhaustion and agony. There was nothing left; all resources of strength had been tapped. And then, suddenly, almost incredibly, he sensed the presence of another, dimmer ring beside him the ring of a single individual . . . Fflir. He made no further move, for to enter the challenge of blood unbidden was not permitted. For a moment pride blocked Asan. But he felt his lungs shake, and in desperation he flung his rings wide, permitting Fflir to focus through him. Their strength combined. He gripped the knife and plunged it straight through one of the meshed eye guards of Hihuan's mask.

Hihuan's scream rang out as Fflir withdrew. Asan felt the splintered disorder of Tlar death and swayed toward it, then drew back, opening his eyes and dragging in a painful, but delicious lungful of air. Profound silence hung over the plain. After a moment he grew aware of it and grinned feebly. He managed to push Hihuan's heavy body off and roll onto his stomach, resting there another moment before getting on his hands and knees, then rising to his feet. Hihuan's blood glistened across the front of his mail, and his side still oozed. Pressing a hand against the wound, he stood erect and wiped his face with a trembling hand.

The two armies stood on either side of him, silent, waiting. He fought off a wave of dizziness and lifted his head, regaining a bit of strength as he recovered his breath.

"I am Asan of the Tlar. Hear me!" he shouted, his deep voice ringing out. "Blood challenge has been fought and won. Hihuan is no more."

No one spoke or made a sound. With difficulty Asan picked up his sword from the mud and staggered down from the knoll. He held it out. "The blood of a Tlar leiil has been spread upon this ground. No lesser battle can be fought here."

Pon Fflir came forward stiffly to take the blade reverently in his gloved hands. "We claim thee as our leiil, Noble Asan," he said in a clear voice, falling to one knee. "Permit us to carry the battle to another place and fight the Bban horde under thy banner."

But for answer Asan turned to the Bban warriors. "Is battle still your desire? It is not my wish to rule over Bban'n or to make quarrel with the tribes," he said, to the obvious shock of the Tlar'jen.

"My Leiil!" cried Fflir in protest, anger in his voice, but Asan ignored him.

"Let us part in peace," said Asan. He lifted his head with pride as they stirred restlessly. "I have kept my word to you. Anthi is no more. Tlar tyranny is no more. Battle is not required."

The Bban'jen growled among themselves. Asan had closed his eyes for a moment, certain they meant to argue the matter until he collapsed. But when he opened them, it was to find that one elder warrior had stepped forward, his scarlet and black cloak whipping in the wind.

Fierce silver eyes studied Asan's face, and at last Ggil said, "Thou art not the man I know. What manner of guile hast thou brought unto us now? And why talk of peace today, when last night thine heart swore revenge upon our blood?"

Asan's lips drew back in a smile that was more a grimace of pain. He pressed his hand to his wound. "As you have said. I am not the one known to you. No man can ever know the Tlar leiil. Let us make an agreement of peace."

Ggil's silver eyes shifted past him to the Tlar'jen massed in tense silence. Reluctantly he raised a fist in salute. "There shall be no battle this day," he said gruffly. "But we are not settled, and let the Tlar'n not seek to deceive us again." He drew himself proudly erect. "The Soot'dla we trust to a measure. They shall come to see if there be truth in thy heart."

"They shall be received," said Asan. As he spoke he lifted his eyes to the sky, measuring the endless sweep of it. How good it was to know the scent of the wind in his nostrils once again! He breathed deeply, then glanced down at his side as blood bubbled through his fingers.

"Come, my Leiil, and let us tend thy hurts," said Fflir, stepping forward after giving the sword into the keeping of a Tlar subaltern. The Bban'jen, with mutters and much rattling of their javelins, were turning away to go back the way they had come. "Good Leiil, lean upon my support," said Fflir, putting an arm around Asan.

"No," said Asan, listening to his own thoughts. Grief welled up suddenly as he faced the end of the purpose. The Tlar ships would never come, bringing true men to stride the earth of this harsh world. Tlar civilization would never raise Ruantl to the greatness comparable to the rest of the known galaxies. The black star would never be tamed as he had planned it to be. Those who lived here must forget the old ways, must learn to adapt and start again from the very bottom of existence, as the Bban had done. They must eventually become as the Bban were.

He sighed, aching beneath the bitterness of disappointment from what could have been and was never to be. And *yde*, although conquered, had robbed him of a measure of strength, never to be replaced. The challenges Ruantl presented no longer stirred him. He knew only a great fatigue. Besides, how could he go on without Aural? She hated him now. Never again would she walk willingly at his side. Never could he ask her to soothe away the homesickness for their old world of lakes and long meadows of sweet cighi flower. No, it was far better to lay the challenge in another's hand, someone who would never miss the fiery passion of Aural's rings linked with his own, who would never know the past that was lost or the future that was not to be.

"My Leiil! Please! Let us tend thee!" urged Fflir's voice, but Asan scarcely listened, though he knew he owed Fflir much.

As a father gazes tenderly down upon his young sleeping son, Asan smiled and ordered himself to calmness as he spread his rings one by one, until they could be spread no more. "Blaise . . ." he called gently within, feeling the other stir as he let himself float beyond the stretched circumference of the rings. For an instant he knew fear. Then he faced the final void and permitted the rings to snap together again behind him. There was a brief agonizing rip of separation, and then all pain and sensation ceased. . . .

Blaise swam forth from the darkness, frowning at the unwelcome assault of noise, pain, and noxious smells. So the *yde* had not killed him after all, he thought bleakly as his eyes flickered open. To his bewilderment he realized he was sitting propped up against a stranger's knees while another figure in mask and cloak smeared a stinking salve on his side before binding a length of cloth far too tightly around him. He winced in protest, unable to understand how he came to be outside in the middle of nowhere, sitting in the mud, surrounded by an army.

"Careful," muttered the man supporting him, and the physician paused for a moment before knotting the bandage and standing up.

"I can do no more here," he said. "With quiet and rest the wound shall heal cleanly. But he should return to Altian at once for proper care."

Wound? Blaise looked down, blinking at the quantity of blood drying to a black stain across his mail. What had happened? How had he got out here? What had the *yde* done to him?

He raised his grimy hand to his forehead and rubbed it. "I . . . do not understand," he said, and the weakness of his voice puzzled him. Irritated for not snapping back more quickly he glared at the physician. "How do I come to be here?" he asked sharply. "Where is Hihuan?"

Several of the onlooking men glanced at each other. "Thou

spread the blood of Hihuan upon the sands," said the man supporting Blaise. "Gently . . ." He helped Blaise get to his feet, keeping a steady hand on his elbow. "My Leiil fought a noble fight."

Blaise turned to glance back at the small rise of ground where Hihuan's body lay, now covered by someone's cloak, which had been pinned to the earth at all four corners by spears. Striped banners of bronze and black fluttered from the shafts. He drew in a deep breath, wincing at the pull in his side.

"Tell me exactly what happened."

As the officer complied somewhat anxiously, Blaise frowned. An unclear tangle of memory seemed to unravel in his mind as he followed the hesitant words describing his appearance in the camp at dawn, his challenge, and the battle. And the memories unfurled back yet further, into the caverns, toward other deeds. But they had not been his deeds. He had known nothing once the *yde* smothered him. Determined to reach to the bottom of this, Blaise lifted his hand to silence the officer and looked on himself with truth, tightening his rings into a shaft of concentration. And then, suddenly he knew. The other . . . the real Asan was gone. It was *he* who had done those things, and now he was gone.

A surge of relief swept through Blaise, and he could not hold back a smile. Freedom! At long last . . . complete freedom!

"It is time to go to thy tent, my Leiil," said the officer, tugging gently at him. "Let us place thee upon this litter."

Blaise looked at him, blinking, and accepted the mask he proferred. "What is your name?" he asked.

The officer saluted. "I am the Pon Fflir. Now, please, let us retire to thy tent. We must not meet the Soot'dla unprepared, for they are harsh bargainers."

Fitting on the mask, Blaise signaled assent even as the first qualms shook him. Diplomacy on any scale was not in his past list of occupations. Furthermore, while these Tlar were honor-bound to serve him, they were too proud to welcome that service readily. They would have to be won. With that thought he finally realized that this planet was indeed his, to rule and mold as he chose. But it was not as he had envisioned in all his days of cursing authority. He suddenly saw responsibilities looming up, decisions to be made and implemented, hard work. Yet even as he frowned, he knew he would not wish to go back.

Tlar leiil . . . First Honored of Ruantl. He stood erect, hiding his wince behind the mask, and lifted his head high as he turned to face the waiting men.

"We have much to discuss, my Tlar, of the changes that will come," he said as a hastily fashioned litter was brought forward. He swept out his hand palm down. "Pon Fflir, give me the support of your arm. I shall *walk* to my tent."